a Ribbon
a Rock
and a
Garrotte

Part One

Alan Gooding

Michael Terence
Publishing

First published in paperback by
Michael Terence Publishing in 2019
www.mtp.agency

ISBN 9781912639717

Cover image
Christos Georghiou

a Ribbon a Rock and a Garrotte

Part One

Alan Gooding

To the special neighbourhoods of Kentish Town, Camden Town and Somers Town.

Mannerly people with a staunch community spirit.

Sunday mornings in fine company at splendid Alehouses.

Scruffy, noisy, happy kids playing everywhere.

If only we could have it again as it was then.

CONTENTS

LIST OF CHARACTERS

Twyford, George (44)
Amiable Chancer, Principal Character

Twyford, Mary (35)
Estranged wife of George

Their Children:
Twyford, Kevin (16)
Twyford, Niamh (13)
Twyford, Maread (11)
Twyford, Alan (7)

Twyford, Amelia (aka Min) (69)
Mother of George

Members of G.Twyford's Inner Circle:

Bass, John (45)
Plumber of St. Pancras. Wife Megan, of the Valleys with unusual Welsh rectitude

Butler, Michael (44)
Impoverished Piano tuner. Wife Teresa (Irish), valetudinarian

Curry, Dan (44)
Impecunious carpenter. Batchelor

Esterbrook, Owen (44)
Impecunious Costermonger. Wife Elsie

Hogg, Lestor (45)
Out of work electrician, illegal bookmaker. Wife Doreen, bored

McMahon, Fintan (36)
Brother-in law to G. Twyford. Ex Lightweight Boxer, Minder to Ruben Benson. Wife Bridget (Irish)

Nash, Frank (44)
British Rail foreman. Wife Naomi

Nolan, Gerry (46)
Underachieved plumber's mate. Wife Ivy. Estranged. Nurse, prostitute, lover of Dr. Howard Wadsworth

Quill, Mornington (44)
Struggling Military tailor. Wife Violet. Volcanic

Swindells, Stan (44)
Lighterman, London Docks. Wife Olive, no nonsense

Thorp, Kitchener (45)
Impecunious Butcher. Batchelor

Tinker (44)
Horse and Cart drayman. Wife Ginger. Horse Ginger

The Others:

Benson, Ruben (56)
Housing Baron, Ex Moneylender. Dangerous, nasty. Fieldsmen, Laurie Newman, Maxy Kendall, Nobby

Blair, Rodney (50)
Ex- Oxford Prof. of Economics, now Government Officer for the Security and Protection of Sterling

Bones (30)
Corporal, American Airbase, Bury St. Edmunds

Brown (48)
Untitled advisor to nameless body of Senior Ministers personally appointed by Churchill

Chesney (45)
Security Director of the Bank of England

Connaughty, Teddy (60)
American-Irish Industrialist. No fan of G.B.

Donna Laura (38)
Wealthy Spanish Heiress

Gay, Joey (13)
Budding young spiv. Brother of Kathy

Gay, Kathy (29)
Comely lady of Kentish Town. Friend of Mary

Gowan, Timmy (44)
Admiralty Adviser, Kentish Town background

Grogan, Donald (48)
Ex-Srgnt.Major, Blackwatch and G. Twyford's superior in the Great War. (Highly trained, vicious). Now well-connected Speculator henchmen, Tam, Alex

Higby, Nell (46)
Carefree divorcee, Friend of Mary

Hughes, Jim (66)
Dealer, black market

Hunt, Barry (58)
Superintendent, Kentish Town Police Force

Jacobs, Irving (44)
East end Solicitor. School chum of George

Jacobs, Benjamin (46)
Felonious Accountant. Brother of Irving

Jacobs, Roy (42)
Nefarious Entrepreneur. Cousin

Kirby, Cyril (45)
Senior Investigator, H.M.Revenue. Liverpool

Krudineer, Marius (40)
Sth. African Police Inspector. Murder squad

Lenny (39)
Head Bouncer, Café Luxor

Le Roux (50)
Well-to-do political refugee, French

Lucky (65)
Colourful character of St. Pancras. West Indian.

Mullins (38)
Ex Marine. Personal bodyguard to Chesney at Bank of England

'Nero' Richard Falco (40)
Leader of Specialist undercover Police team of 4, suitor of Mary

O'Brien (41)
Irish Builder

Pat Passmore (46)
Acrimonious Widow. Friend of Mary

Priest (38)
Senior Investigator, H.M.Revenue, London

Radna (28)
Icelandic Nightclub Singer. Paramour to George

Rita (36)
Provocative ladyfriend of Kitchener's

Roper, Steve (35)
Costermonger, Roman Rd, market. Roper the groper

Rowe, Willy (64)
Coal merchant, Kentish Town

Sally (Miss Poole) (32)
Alluring School Ma'am. Ladyfriend of George

Saverisi, Pasquale (60)
Head of Italian family that ruled Soho in the '40s

Seymour-Heyden (58)
High level Group Leader at MI6

Shaw, Archie (55)
Merciless Thieftaker, Station Sergeant, Kentish Town Police.
Father of Mary

Spider (54)
O'Brien's batman

Small, Howard (34)
Hospital Doctor. Wanted for Manslaughter

White, Chalkie (42)
Fellow member of Specialist undercover Police team of 4.
Adulterous lover of Doreen Hogg

Kentish Town (West)

Kentish Town (East)

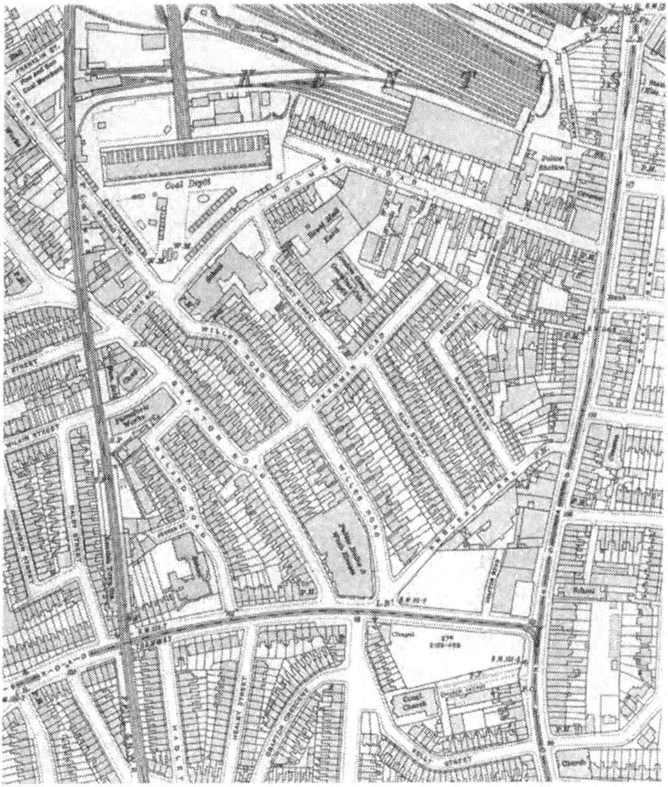

CHAPTER 1: NEVER ONE TO BE DISCREET

King George V1: It is the love of peace that has stirred our peoples and given them a unity unknown in any previous war. We are fighting against wickedness and this conviction will give us the strength to persevere until victory is assured!

The corpse was known to the Birmingham Police, a crook of some notoriety and no great loss. What had caused a stir was the manner of his death. It looked as if a type of cheese-wire had been used to strangle the man, leaving his partly severed head with a suggestion of contemplation -tilting, as it did, to one side; shiny, baked blood showed the remaining join on an otherwise pallid, puffy countenance. Even more perverse, something had been half swallowed then set alight in his mouth. When the orifice was emptied, amongst the ashes, a small, curled corner of paper was discovered with two numbers still legible. The officer in charge thought it might be a fragment from a five pound note.

And as one chancer exits life's strife... -Another makes his entrance...

"You flash bastard!"

Most verbal descriptions of him ended with 'bastard', 'cocky…', 'funny…' but today it was *flash* bastard. This first impression was instant and crystallised by a customs officer observing a 'possible' ambling along the dock of Southampton towards the customs building. A 'possible' looked too nondescript or too loud, and this one deafened. Incognito was not an option for no amount of camouflage could help this man blend with the others alighting from the SS Swedish Prince, safely arrived from the Cape on that foggy November morning in 1943. The confidence paraded in front of him, an irritating grin beamed from an altogether annoying face and he gave off the suggestion of stepping out onto the stage of the London Palladium. Six foot and loping with the agility of a lame wolf; probably early forties and clothed in a beige suit, a strong blue shirt and an incandescent tie of gleaming gold. His fair hair was slightly longer than the usual short back and sides with a little grease that induced shine. The customs officer allowed himself a pleasant moment, "Perhaps he wanted Rio but boarded the wrong boat?" and longed for a cloud-burst to stair-rod down before he reached shelter.

Queuing to enter customs hall, the face stopped outside the window. It might have been quite attractive had it not been for a few digs around the chin and a thin two-inch scar below the left eye.

"How can you have a suntan in wartime? I really don't like you." adjudged Officer Bates, his coffee steaming up the window. He rubbed a circle on it to get a clearer view of his prey and mentally measured himself against him. "Yes, you're right up my street, you. I'll wipe that mock off your block! "

With a perceptible drag of the right leg, beige suit shuffled in with his fellow passengers as they studied the floor tiles in silent prayer. Bates was positioned halfway along the hall and had joyously forgone the rest of his coffee-break for this one special visitor. He scanned the area, professionally skipping over 'Flash', and savoured the eschewal of eye contact. Beige Suit was four yards past and almost at the door. This was the apogee. Three yards...two… 'Just a moment, Sir.'

Flash stopped, the crowd shuffled on. He turned and surveyed the customs officer whose crook'd finger, half raised, beckoned him back. 'Yes?' the man answered, not moving.

'If you could step over here, Sir.' Bates had to shout and lost a little warrant in doing so.

'Certainly.' Flash carried a brace of large, brown, hide suitcases, well used but good quality, across to the line of flat tables separating the two of them and swung one up for inspection.

'The other, if you don't mind,' said Bates, eyeball to eyeball and glowing as his authority returned; this was bullying in its finest form.

'A pleasure!' Even the curt reply managed a hint of insolence. Swinging one off and the other on, he placed the first case between his legs and produced a bunch of keys. Selecting a small one, he leisurely handed it across. 'Nice morning,' he remarked pleasantly in a distinct London accent but, by now, any utterance was goading.

Bates moved mechanically through the suitcase, lifting out the crisp shirts, two suits, more trousers and a pair of brogues then feeling down the lining and corners of the case, replacing the shirts at the other end. He felt the trousers and suits, squeezing the underwear for hidden treasure and, lastly, studying the contents of a leather toilet bag; nothing. "Bollocks!" He glanced up from his toils, only to be met by the upturned lips. "He's taking the piss out of me!", 'Passport, please?'

Flash handed it across, the officer's eyes traversed the pages in seconds:

Name: George Twyford, Born: Euston, London 1899. Two South African stamps, entrance 1939, exit 1943. "Why come back now? Too late and too old to join up, too far away for spying." Moroccan stamp, Casablanca, four days ago. 'I see you entered Morocco?'

'Yeh, a day's sight-seeing while they took on supplies. Don't half hum!' Bates looked towards the second case and nodded for it to be put next to its twin. Twyford nodded back but didn't move.

'The case! I want that, here!' he said, pointing.

'Oh, you only had to say..'

The officer would not normally have bothered but any inconvenience to this bastard suited him. A key was selected and the case was opened. Loose collars rested on woollens and beneath those, spread from end to end, a pair of corduroys greeted them and when lifted uncovered a beaten-up briefcase. Mortified but giving away nothing, George Twyford looked on. The briefcase had a combination lock either side of the handle.

Triumph twinkled in the piggy eyes, 'Could you open this?' The 'Sir' being dropped loudly.

'No.' George replied, casually.

'NO!' repeated Bates, unsure of whether to be annoyed or pleased.

'Not here,'

'In that case, you'd better come with me,' then, resisting the temptation to prod him along, he took the suspect firmly by the elbow and marched him, regardless of his limp, through a door marked 'No Entry' and down a long corridor to a room identified as No. 5 -Examination.

Bates entered and a thickset man wearing an identical uniform but, definitely for effect, just too tight and stretched around the biceps, stood up with military precision. He was the sole occupant.

'Hallo, Andy.'

Bates ignored him and strutted to the only table in the room, sat down and pointed to the chair opposite. George had carried the briefcase in, leaving the rest of his luggage out in the hall and open to the world for inspection. The guard stood between Twyford and the exit, legs braced wide, hands behind his back. No expression and yet menacing.

'Right, open it, now.'

'Must we, Andy? It's only papers.' sweetly said but, by now, the face was severely grating.

'Open it, and its Mr.Bates to you.' His voice was raised somewhat and deciding to bond with Officer Dempsey in case of any hiccups, added glibly, 'I only allow friends to call me Andy.'

'Shouldn't think there's too many of them with your attitude.'

remarked George, flicking the combinations as he spoke.

Bates snarled through gritted teeth and began, 'You saucy...' But before he could continue the briefcase had been laid flat, sprung open and spun round so that it flashed up like a box of chocolates. Mr.Andrew Bates inhaled sharply. There, neatly packed side by side, were stacks of brown ten shilling notes, green pound notes and big white fivers; longways, along the bottom, a line of smaller, green dollar bills. Officer Dempsey, who may have appeared oafish but far surpassed Bates in mental arithmetic, attempted to make an educated guess at how long it would take him to save that much. He lost count at twenty lifetimes. Quickly, back in control except for the slight tic on his left eyelid, Bates stood up and leaned his face closer to George. 'Now then, cocky, I think you'd better tell me where all this money came from, don't you?' As he spat the words out, George was transfixed by his fanglike, nicotine-stained teeth which locked together in a snarl while the fat lips contorted into elasticated shapes. 'Oi, I'm talking to you!' But the nearing, leering mouth mesmerised and momentarily stole any reply. Taking the silence to signal victory and delighting in such intimidating power, Bates marched on shouting, 'Are you stupid? Answer me!' The beration was accompanied by an unpleasant belch of stale tobacco and last night's rum.

Twyford came to life and observed, 'Your breath don't half smell, Andy. You ought to do something about that or you'll have even less friends.'

Clenching his fists dangerously, Bates craved to lash out and hurt the deriding face in front of him; Twyford's arrogance had stoked the boiler and the taunts were pressing him to blow.

'I warned you, its Mr. Bates, now say it!'

Obediently George repeated, 'Mister Bates,' then leaned back in the chair and aired a reflection, 'So at school I suppose you were Master Bates.'

The piggy eyes widened, the tic accelerated and, seething, he rounded the table until his chin almost touched Twyford's forehead.

Tilted at a precarious angle, George looked directly upwards and voiced quizzically, 'You must have had a nickname?'

The unexpected change of direction caused a drawn out, 'Wha-aat!'

'I know,' laughed George, 'I bet it was "And Shandy, get it!?'

Grunts and growls covered for words lost in a fury that took Andy Bates over the top. With surprising speed his left hand grabbed a mop of Twyford's hair while his right knee smashed George solidly on the ear. The chair skidded away and hit the skirting with a crash, the same time as Twyford hit the floor. Moving even faster Bates dropped down, crunching strong knees onto his ribcage. Depleted of all wind, Twyford's jawline caught several hefty right-handers in swift succession; his only defence was to curl up tightly, arms automatically trying to cover his head which was jerked by the hair each time a blow rained down. Bates waved an arm for Dempsey to join in, who immediately sent a powerful kick to the small of Twyford's back; a halting hand was then raised. Artfully, Dempsey was now implicated, two corroborating statements if needed and now Bates could relish dishing out the rest of this beating himself. The raised hand theatrically closed to a fist that smashed down onto Twyford's cheekbone, the following blow equally punishing; and as the pain reverberated through his head, the faith in his plan seemed to lose what little foundation it may have had. With his consciousness numbing, from his horizontal position on the floor he thought he glimpsed a pair of grey, pinstripe trousers and well-polished, black shoes enter the room unheard. Shiny toe caps stepped behind Dempsey, who stood poised ready to rejoin with Andy in his bombardment.

'You vicious brute, I demand to see your superior!' croaked George, suddenly re-energised.

'You'll see me!' screamed Bates, punching straight down at the jaw again but finding a protective arm muscle. 'I'm the governor here!'

'Aaah, no Andrew, that's me.' A voice filled with such authority that on the 'Aaah' the two officers snapped smartly to attention. With one arm still raised for protection, Twyford warily sat up and took in his saviour. The new arrival was Mr Charles Pendlar, Director of Operations, Customs & Excise South Coast. He'd been passing the room and heard the commotion. His lads were nearly all ex-military police and thought themselves bouncers at the front door of England and, as such, could easily get too heavy-handed. Pendlar usually had a knack of appearing just in time to defuse these situations; this one, however, had gone too far and would need very delicate handling. Short, dapper and balding, the overall picture of Pendlar was diminished even more by an enormous pair of thick-lensed spectacles that gave him an owl like appearance. He stepped sprightly into the centre of the room and the two officers immediately moved back a pace.

'Thank you, Andrew. My office, now!' The voice brooked no argument. Bates coloured to a deep purple, held his breath and left the room; the other officer remained by the door. 'Dempsey, help this gentleman to a seat.' He continued, 'My apologies if he seemed somewhat..over-zealous.'

'Over-zealous! I thought the Gestapo had already landed!' retorted George, shaking. Dempsey hoisted him up to sit against the wall and, as they were eye to eye, Twyford winked. Comprehending his exoneration, Dempsey briefly brushed his jacket before moving back to man the entrance. Twyford, exaggerating dizziness, tried to focus on Charles Pendlar.

'Can I offer you coffee or brandy?'

'Brandy,' answered George. With a nod from Pendlar, Dempsey left the room. 'I demand you have that madman dismissed, he should be arrested! I feared for my life! I've come here with the power to invest big money in Britain, and there's not too many doing that at the moment, then this barbarous, homicidal maniac sets about me as if I'm the criminal! Insane, the man's insane and should definitely be locked away from respectable people! I ask you, how can that lethal lunatic be allowed to operate in such a position of authority? I suggested privacy, didn't want all and sundry made aware of what I was carrying, instead the whole of bloody Southampton knows now! So, what do you intend to do about it?!'

The passport had fallen to the floor. Pendlar picked it up and flipped it open.

'Now, Mr… Twyford,' George tried a nod. 'I am sincerely sorry for the treatment you received from a member of my staff. There can be no excuses for thuggery but this is wartime and hard men are needed for a difficult job: ever vigilant, tough with no nonsense -but fair. Occasionally, the proverbial bad apple pops up, abusing its authority. I repeat, no excuses, I abhor bullying in any form and I assure you that the punishment will be commensurate. But before we continue with that let's talk about your quest, confidentially of course. You mentioned investors, obviously very

wealthy men.'

'Yes,' agreed George.

'Speculating a little further, the reason the money's in cash is because they wish to remain anonymous?'

'Correct again. You see, if it got out that certain well-placed people were taking profit from our misfortunes their businesses could suffer, and worse, the taint might bring ruin to some.'

'Yes, I fully understand how difficult it must be. Anyone who is successful could be accused of profiteering, even though this country will need all the outside support and investment it can get. How much is in the briefcase, approximately?'

'Fifteen thousand Sterling and five thousand American, and that's just the beginning, the deposit as it were.'

'My Word! What a handsome sum.' Adding with the faintest hint of sarcasm, 'They must be very trusting.' Just then, Dempsey returned with an extremely, large brandy in a bowl glass.

'So that's what happens to the confiscated contraband.' In the circumstances the riposte was silly and Twyford cautioned himself not to be too acerbic, the play had yet to end. Being careful to under act, he lifted the glass hand and allowed it a slight tremble.

'Dempsey, wait outside.' That voice again; incredible.

Pendlar found it difficult to accept that men of power would have this 'spiv' in charge of such sums of money, but then fast profits make for the most unlikely bedfellows. The idea becomes more plausible with the mere fact that anyone of breeding could easily deny all knowledge of one such as George Twyford. That aside the job in hand was to win him over and make absolutely sure no official complaint was made.

'I understand why, on arrival, you said nothing about the money but may I offer you this advice as I assume you'll be passing to and fro with more of the old filthy lucre. I suggest when entering any customs area you ask to see the senior officer privately. When you have his ear, mention my name.' He handed Twyford a business card. 'Let him ring me and then you can be escorted through safely and discreetly.'

'Cheers, that would be more than handy,' replied George, momentarily slipping from character.

'Back to our friend Bates.'

'That wouldn't be my first description,' mumbled George.

'You surprise me!' tried Pendlar, amiably. 'But, in all seriousness, please allow me to deal with this matter. I have the power to suspend him from duty without question and, after a short period of time, he will be dismissed from service. This way he is punished to the full extent and you can leave with the minimum of delay, no awkward questions to answer or forms to sign. Are we on the same wavelength?'

'I'll leave it entirely to you,' said Twyford, shaking hands at once. 'Just one point, Charles,' he added, closing the briefcase and patting it with care, 'would it be possible to get a lift to the station, I'm running a little late?'

Pendlar thought, "You cheeky bastard!" but achieved a thin grin. 'I'm sure I can arrange something. Finish your brandy and I'll be back in two ticks.' With that, he marched from the interview room, along the hall and up the stairs to his office. Bates sat there glowering. 'Did I tell you to sit?' quizzed Pendlar, daring an answer. Rising immediately, eyes forward, Bates waited for the barrage. 'It always has to be you, does it not, Andrew? But regimental association or not, this is it. I shall never cover for you again, do you understand?' This was stated slowly and calmly, causing the officer to visibly wilt.

'I promise you on my eyesight...' he began, but Pendlar lifted a hand, abruptly cutting him dead.

'Ring the Yard. Check this bastard out with them,' he ordered and handed over the passport. Bates smirked and moved to speak but the Excise director flashed a glare of disgust and dismissed him with, 'Just get on with it!'

Scotland Yard were much too busy but they had taken down the passport name and number and would look at him, hard.

The suitcases were collected and put in the squad car that was to be George's taxi. A few minutes later Pendlar returned the passport and guided him to the awaiting Police escort, patting his shoulder in a fatherly fashion. The two men shook hands like old friends and the car sped Twyford off to Southampton station.

Charles Pendlar returned to his office and lifted the phone. The switchboard answered almost immediately.

'Get me Inland Revenue, Special Investigations. Ask for Mr Kirby.'

CHAPTER 2: WHAT'S LIFE WITHOUT A PLAN?

1943, Guildhall, London. Churchill: We bear the Sword of Justice and we resolve to use that sword with the utmost severity…to the end!

The London train had already departed brim full with passengers travelling up to see the exciting side of life.

"No tragedy." George thought and wandered into the station buffet bar, ordered a drink and contemplated a dalliance with the rather beddable barmaid. He felt she took a shine to him by the way she leaned her breasts forward onto the bar for his appraisal and smiled right into his eyes but then when he checked his money realised that she'd taken his pound and tried to slip him change of a ten shilling note. Whilst supping on his first pint of Bass for a long time, he reflected on the ironies and luck of life, the circumstances that had returned him to England a very wealthy man; temporarily perhaps, for Twyford knew only too well that the whore they call Lady Luck teases, flirts, but seldom stays the night. His hard-practised hero's limp had failed to draw the sympathy that might have avoided Customs examination and, once selected, he had no choice but to take an enormous risk and instigate the discovery of the money he carried. He planned it in as much detail as could be guessed then provoked a seemingly unwarranted attack on his person by an Excise officer. The turmoil such actions caused for those in overall authority erased any thought of further searches. A hoard of that much cash left little point in concealing a Swiss watch or a bottle of perfume,

except that taped behind his testicles was the largest, purest diamond he had ever come across; the King of Kings. Its probable value must frighten the most formidable and to view it makes one its prisoner for life! Poetically, he considered if this gem's energy met direct sunlight the sky would crack open! *And* unbelievably greater still - IT WAS NOW HIS!

Three months ago in South Africa, through *(for once)* no fault of his own, he became embroiled in certain very, grave circumstances and made a reckless decision to help someone knowing the last four years of his life, working as an overseer in the diamond mines, would be washed down the Swanny. But for every action there is always a reaction and, completely by chance, he had fallen into a deal that won the pools AND found King Solomon's mines! This was just the start of monumental worry, aggravation, studying, scheming, gambling and chancing his arm yet again. Doing it right or losing it all: another adventure, life was wonderful! With the second pint, all the nervous energy burned away and had the train not arrived so soon, George might well have persevered a little longer with the barmaid. He left the lounge with the wench's beguiling pout of what treats he *may* have been rewarded with.

Waterloo was shut. An unexploded bomb had been discovered on the approach tracks and the train was re-routed to Victoria. No one seemed to mind, in fact it was almost to be expected these days. He alighted and to remain inconspicuous a little longer caught a taxi. As Twyford's arse hit the seat the cabby went straight into his spiel. He proudly pimped for a Soho hideaway that specialised in ladies who could fulfil *any* urge George might have. Twyford feigned astonishment, stating he was a man of the cloth and had never been so shocked! Hardly slowing for oxygen the cabby, who obviously excelled as a practised liar, impressed him immensely by replying that though he loathed the work the small remuneration it earned went towards finding shelter for homeless orphans, (any kind donations go to helping the poor mites.); the man swore he worked every hour cabbying and barely earned enough to cover his fuel. As they passed through Camden Town, George switched off from the driver's lamentations and took in the devastation; the huge rubble gaps where family shops and pubs used to be. The distressing ride continued along Chalk Farm, turning right towards the Mother Shipton public house. The Witches' mural looked down on him. 'You're back then,' she seemed to say.

Luckily, the gas lights were all out in St Leonard's Square and by arriving at 6pm it was as black as Newgate's Knocker. He paid the cabby handsomely but still the greedy swine tried to shortchange him, -and never showed the least embarrassment when George pulled him up on it.

Using a stern scowl to smother his amusement, Twyford suddenly cried, 'Mountebank, due to your dishonesty those poor mites will have to suffer yet another night under the arches!' And took back the change and the tip, leaving the cabby with an empty palm and an open mouth still trying to fathom what a mountebank was. From the first four people in England he had spoken to -one had bashed him up, the barmaid and the cab driver had tried to diddle him and God only knows what trouble Pendlar would stir up! With a sad shake of the head, Twyford got out, collar raised just in case then slipped up the path to number sixteen. A finger through the letter box produced a key on a long string. Tiptoeing the passage, he could hear 'Let yourself go!' being swung by Ginger Rogers and dismembered by his mother. Amelia Twyford, better known as Min, was in the kitchen inharmoniously droning the wrong lyrics and dancing with her shoulders, as usual. Creeping closer he saw that, instead of sizing the old newspaper cuttings for the nail in the outside loo, she was actually opening a proper toilet roll.

'Expecting company are we, Mrs. Twyford?' he remarked in a swanky tone. Being deaf in one ear for a second she thought it came from the wireless then, turning, her eyes lit up and she whooped and jigged towards him at such a rate of knots that she trod on the cat's tail before it could get out of the way. Twyford stepped in, scooped her up in his arms and spun her around, both of them laughing, tears streaming down her face.

'Oh, Georgie!' she said, out of breath, 'you've come home for my birthday, you good boy!' pinching his cheek until it hurt. 'I bet my makeup's all messed up, now. Have you been round to your house yet? Seen the kids, have you?'

George would normally have remembered his Mother's 69th and, at the very least, sent a letter, but such had been the escalation of hazardous events which compelled his flight from South Africa that his overtaxed brain had missed it completely.

'Not yet Mum, it's your birthday so I've come to you first, thought I'd surprise them tomorrow. Throw my hat in and see if it comes back with a meat skewer through it.'

'Well, I hope you know what you're doing,' she replied sombrely then turned and began the tea ceremony.

George sat in the armchair next to the range and closed his eyes, the two of them using the silence to think about what went before. She put the cup on the arm of his chair and studied her only son. He looked very well, thank God.

'I'm out with Cissy and Lou tonight, we're shall be imbibing at the Malden,' she announced regally, and added, 'so I hope you're gonna come and treat us!'

'Course I am, but don't tell a soul I'm back.' he said. 'Are most of the boys still about? It's Friday night, they should be there.'

'All of them except Mickey Butler. I heard he lost his work and she can't walk at all now, poor love.' Mick's wife had been diagnosed with Multiple Sclerosis two years before George fled the country.

"That's my first job in the morning." he thought.

While his mother went upstairs to prepare his room, Twyford nestled in the kitchen getting quite excited about seeing his close friends again. Their crowd had been pals since primary school and still lived around an area in Kentish Town called the Mother Shipton. In and out of jobs and trouble most of their lives they had always stuck together, an unspoken bond cherished above all else. So when two of them were forced to enlist the rest had volunteered for the same regiment, which was strange seeing as it was a Scottish regiment full of

Glasgow's biggest scallywags, who carried on as if Culloden had occurred the week before! But like all things you get on with it and occasionally come across individuals that loom large in the memory; a few become real mates and then there's always the odd rabid barbarian you could be forgiven for running over. His mind considered each of his friends and what their attitude to his return would be. Most would revert right back to how they were before he left while one or two, like Kit and Mornie, might be a dash more reserved until a few pints had been downed. That was why he decided not to get there until a quarter to ten. They'd just be approaching 'a touch tasty' and an entrance had to be made, a short, sharp shock to let everyone know the wizard had returned; his high opinion of himself never faltered. Another good thing was that tongue-wagging wives seldom ventured out on a Friday night but, most assuredly, the war drums would beat the news first thing in the morning -then sparks would fly. He yearned to hug the kids and see how grown up they were but facing their wild bitch of a mother was not to be done without a lot of preparation, after all, her father literally ran him out of the country. Yes, his friends with their memorable chance opinions and remarks over the years had unknowingly assisted him, whilst abroad, to balance the bigger decisions. There was nothing he wouldn't do to bring them good fortune and now he may never be in a better position.

Wings of skate from the fish shop, chips and shuddersome pickled onions were the footings to build the beer on. The old tin bath was brought in and boiling kettles went on overtime to spoil him with plenty of hot water for a soak good enough to ensure wrinkles.

'Min' was ready early and once she had departed, George moved like lightning. He first rooted around for a torch then went to the brick shed at the bottom of the garden where a lifetime of old tut had been stored. He pulled half of it out and, after inspecting everything, decided on a tennis ball that had seen better days. He took it inside and sawed a carving knife into it. The cut, which went two thirds of the way around could only be noticed when the ball was squeezed. Inside this, wrapped in a wad of cotton wool, was placed the diamond, for various reasons George had named it 'Bounty'. He glued it together very delicately and put it by the range to dry. The next move was to take a hundred pounds from the briefcase, re-lock it, then conceal the case under the loose floorboards in the scullery. George stamped the lino' back into place, picked up the tennis ball and returned outside.

At the bottom of the garden was a break in the old wall and George proceeded to sneak through it. The house and garden which backed on to 16 St Leonard's, was number 21 Marsden Street. It was his house by rights; his wife and four children lived there on the ground and first floors, while his Uncle Bert had the top floor and attic. Twyford crept through the darkness, down the well-trodden path towards the outside wash-house. The door had never closed properly so he slipped inside and flashed on the torch. It was full up with boxes, dolls and memories. There was the old ball-bearing scooter that he had knocked up for Kevin and, next to it, the trolley with a wheel still missing. He wedged the tennis ball between these two and stacked more toys on top until it was completely hidden then began to reconsider. He didn't like to be parted from it and couldn't find sound judgement but eventually decided the gem should be stashed with the jumble. Debatably satisfied, he moved silently back outside. All of a sudden, George had a strong urge to take a gander, to see if she had changed; a whim, nothing more, but still he had to. He crept nearer the high kitchen window; the blackout curtains were drawn tight, except at the top, and the only way to peek in was to climb the drainpipe.

"This is silly," he mused, "I despise the disloyal bitch anyway." But still he shinned quietly up the pipe. He could hear her talking but could not get the words. What was he doing? Then a man's voice, "Who the fuck's that?" he thought, and with illogical anger jumped to, "Sleeping in my bed!my bleedin' bed! Just swerve," he told himself, "before anyone comes out. The prat! What do I care anyway?"

Twyford melted into the darkness, back through the gardens and indoors, shoving her from his mind with a snort. 'The state of me!' he said to no one in particular, rinsed his dirty hands in the old bath water then went in search of a mirror to make sure he really did look as dashing as he imagined. 'I'm back! No point in hiding,' the good people of St. Pancras were about due a reminder.

Short of a best trilby but dressed in a midnight blue drape suit, white shirt with a thin red stripe and a crisp, white, starched collar; a navy, red and gold tie set the finishing touch. Twyford stepped out, closing the street door behind him quietly, shivered and sniffed the raw night. A little patchy fog clung around the gas lamps, which were now alight. At the top of the Square he turned right towards the Malden Arms, which was about half a mile further along and had not gone more than twenty yards when someone called his name.

'Georgie-boy, anything I can do for you?' as if he'd only seen him yesterday. Jimmy Hughes was sitting on the steps to his front door, shrouded in darkness as always. He had been a good friend of George's father, and could 'acquire' anything from nylon stockings to tickets for the Royal Garden Party.

'Hallo, Jimmy mate. What's on offer?'

'No one's had a sniff of any scotch,' advised the portly entrepreneur, and his persuasive patter soon convinced Twyford to purchase two bottles.

Whilst Jimmy wrapped them in newspaper, he gave George a brief idea of what was in short supply and just how much some people were prepared to pay for those treats. More than a little interested in acquiring such up-to-date information, George walked down the steps, held up his purchases and suggested a late drink. 'Keep them covered up!' warned Jimmy sternly. 'Your father-in-law is cuffing too many these days, there's a snout about!'

Another of Twyford's misjudgements was never taking life too seriously, he bounced off chanting, 'The Peelers got a squealer, there's a snout a-bout. The Peelers…'

"Waste of bleedin' breath." Was Jimmy's concluding deliberation on the subject.

The Malden Arms was a big, old, noisy pub but there was something special and welcoming about it. Standing proud on a prominent corner, it offered three entrances, a side door from Grafton terrace and two doors on the main road which brought you in either side of a three foot high stage for the resident three-piece band. The counter was on the left as you entered and served the length of the original Saloon. Opposite, on the far wall, half a dozen cosy snug areas were raised a step and each seated eight people then, in front of the stage, were a thicket of round tables set higgledy-piggledy; these seats were always taken first. Behind them, and one step higher, used to be the public bar before it was all knocked into one and, apart from two more snugs at the back, the rest was standing room only; this was where his pals would be. Unlike a lot of other watering holes it had been well thought out; wherever you stood it was comfortable, with easy access to the bar and very little shoving. It was grand, a *proper* pub, the best in Kentish Town and packed to the gunnels that Friday night. A mixed age group used the Malden because the band could play all the favourites and everyone had a song that they could be called upon to perform at the drop of a hat. It crossed his mind to wonder what his song might now be. The music was audible before he actually turned the bend and looked upon the place so much of his life had revolved around. As a nipper, Saturday night would find him sitting on the step with a lemonade, while Mum and Dad enjoyed a drink; or the Sunday morning 'beanos', hanging about the charabanc for the kids' scramble when the men flung out ha'pennies and farthings; and there he was, back again. Young Joey Gay was loitering outside, with some of his scruffs. George reckoned he must be about thirteen now and called him over. Stick thin, Joey always looked like he needed a good meal -but sound as a pound. Flipping him a 'tanner' he instructed the lad to fetch the scotch bottles in the side entrance when the next song finished, whatever it was. The music restarted and he recalled the voice straight away. A local girl, Lily Hall, began a belting, "Heart of my Heart".

"That suits me." thought Twyford. A comb whipped through his hair, the tie was straightened for the umpteenth time and he bowled in through the door on the corner. He stepped up onto the stage behind Lily, slipped an arm around her waist and joined in at, '0h how we could harmonise...' If she was surprised she didn't show it and professionally held the mike between them. One or two at the front looked up at hearing a duet then people from the snugs began turning round, others at the back, half recognising the tones, livened up and still Lily and George carried on with 'When friends were dearer then, too bad we had to part'. Some in the far corners pushing to see, shouts of, 'Look who it ain't' and 'Thought I scraped that off'; cat-calls and laughter getting louder from all sides. He could see his mates had moved to the front of the left-hand corner, pointing and making rude gestures. Finishing the song together, 'If once more I could listen to the gang that sang…' and everybody joined in with 'heart of my heart, he-art of my he-art'. As Lily handed him the mike a familiar anticipation of coming entertainment brought forth an encouraging uproar. Horace the Landlord was livid, hollering at everybody to keep quiet, but he just blended with the general cacophony.

A pregnant pause..., then, 'Lift your glasses!' shouted George.

'NO!' screamed Horrie. But this was Twyford's party piece. He stepped onto the balustrade and hopped from one table to another, towards the back. Old and young grabbed up their drinks and pushed back in their chairs, as one foot landed on their table and leapt off to the next, gaining momentum as he went. The Chaps loudly willed him on towards them then realised, too late, that he wasn't going to stop. George used the last table as a springboard and dived right into their midst. Three of them took the main brunt and cushioned him as they sprawled to the floor; the unfortunate three cursing, the other six wetting themselves with laughter. Horace was round the bar, roaring threats of barring the ruddy lot of them, they'd never been any good and he certainly wouldn't starve without their couple of bob.

As they picked Twyford up, he said, 'I haven't 'alf missed you, Horrie!' and with that little Joey Gay squeezed through and gave him the bottles. 'For you, dearest Horace,' said George sweetly.

Grudgingly, with a suppressed retort, he accepted the gift but forewarned, 'Behave yourselves, you lot.' then looking at Twyford's grin, remarked, 'Cunning bastard, you are. This better be the proper gear!'

George suggested helpfully, 'Open one of them; give us all a nip and we'll find out.'

Horrie's mouth shaped up but before any protest could emerge Twyford had placed two fivers in the jug which held their 'whip', saying, 'Keep them coming please, Rose darling.'

Rose was Horrie's wife, a fine, big-chested woman and the opposite of him. She was a saucy madam, full of innuendo and always had a soft spot for cheeky sods. The lads gathered round George, some shoving him about in a show of affection, others a tad more reserved, but he could see that they were as excited as he was. Once Horace had gone back behind the bar the pub returned to its normal hustle and bustle. There was a lot more to talk about now, now he was back. The band was accompanying Kitchener Thorp through, "Happy Days and Lonely Nights". The old girls loved that one and every so often one of them would stand, open their arms, and belt out a line like 'Your kisses linger yet...' and then sit back down again. His Aunt Lou, Cissy and Mum waved over, raising their glasses in thanks for the drinks he'd sent across and, gripping a pint, he gestured a toast in return then went back in a huddle with the boys. It seemed the main problem was not just the Germans; it was paying the rent and the moneylenders, holding down a day's work and generally keeping afloat.

'T'was ever thus,' he said to them, 'there's them that's got it and they ain't giving none of it to us.' Before any could disagree, he continued, 'Are those in Westminster short of anything? Course not, and that mob down the city are earning more than ever. Anyone with money now is having it bang off; a concession here, a tip there. They pass information about like a half zipped bag of boiled sweets, strictly between themselves. The chosen few invest and get richer while you lot sweat buckets of blood just to put some bread on the table.' The whole crowd moaned in agreement at this.

Owen Esterbrook interrupted Twyford's flow with an unclear point. He'd been the one earlier whose opening line as they hugged each other was, 'You been surviving on pickled onions?'

Esterbrook's interjection was, 'Hold up a minute, you said, "you lot" why not "us lot?" '

'Good point, Owen, 'cos I've got a plan!' His reply was immediately accompanied by a chorus of loud groans.

'Course he has!' laughed one, and 'What's life without a plan?' mimicked another. Twyford gave them a moment to chide him for all the schemes that had, so often, landed them in the mire.

'Here, what's this I hear about Mickey?' He was always good at shrewdly swerving his audience, especially this lot, away from sticky points, usually returning from another direction as soon as their concentration faltered.

'Not good,' announced Gerry Nolan, the oldest member. He was forty six, and being two years their senior, still received the respect of older wisdom. 'His wife's getting worse,' he said, 'he used to bring her out in the wheelchair of an evening but since he's lost his job...' By trade, Mickey was a piano tuner in the family business until the shop was bombed. Due to the war they could not afford the insurance, so the lot was lost. 'I think Ruben Benson's been giving them a bad time over the rent.'

'Does my brother in law still work for that robbing bandit?' asked George.

Gerry continued as spokesman, 'Yeah, I think he drives him around but Ruben's got himself a team of seriously mean heavyweights squeezing any tenants that can't pay. One big lump called Maxy Kendall's been threatening Theresa and Mickey, comes from Notting Hill, nasty piece of work, I hear.'

Twyford listened; with so much to do, he'd need to contact some old school chums and call in a few favours. 'Right well, we'll sort that out on Monday.'

A couple of the lads looked at him quizzically though all they got back was that old grin, and God knows why, but they seemed to draw confidence from it. Then a raised arm, a call to Rosie and it was full pints all round again.

The conversation was then further interrupted by a surprise to the evening's entertainment. A plumber's wife had left the kids at home and turned up at the pub unannounced and unexpected to catch the plumber partaking of a quiet drink and a chat at the counter. It seems that the plumber had been plumbing one of the barmaids on the side and now the wife timed her moment to scream graphic accusations and a trenchant volley at the two of them. Trying to keep what little was private in her life from becoming engrossing gossip for all of St. Pancras, the spirited and hale barmaid immediately leapt the counter to eject her. They came together like two stags locking horns. Heads down they pulled, tugged and twisted each other's hair in a mad dance that zigzagged the floor until some good sport, to give them more room, opened the corner doors and the interdigitated pair traversed out onto the pavement, swinging each other around by the locks, while huge clumps of brown and blond hair flew about. Most of the pub had turned out to watch and cheer, especially when one of the barmaid's breasts made an appearance. The only person trying to stop the fight was the plumber but each time he managed to restrain one, the other would spring in with flying fists. He caught more than a few whacks himself before eventually succeeding in separating the 'candidates to be plumber's mate', and the audience gave a splintered applause then returned back inside.

Keenest to know, Danny Curry couldn't hold any longer,

'Come on then, tell us about this plan.'

"Gotcha!" thought George, 'No, you'll have to wait and ask me nicely.' Shouts, as they entreated with him. 'Now, let me tell you all about the tribal maidens.' Back to the huddle.

At first soft voices, then more excited with hoots of 'NO!' 'Streuth!' and 'Leave off!' The laughter abounded as the stories unfolded. Most of the men watching them wished they could be party to the conference, whilst the women tutted at the disturbance but kept looking over all the same.

There were now only seven barmaids working the bar and Horace was out collecting glasses, he had sacked the eighth wench for the earlier altercation. Without his knowledge or approval, Rose had already rehired her for the Saturday night session; pert bar staff were too hard to come by. George stepped behind the ramp and took the already opened bottle of 'White Horse' and a soda siphon and carried them over to the snug. A bevy of fetching females sat in one of the booths with near empty glasses. They were good friends of Mary's and probably could not wait to carry her the news.

'Hallo girls! How've you been?' he asked and began pouring scotch into each glass. No one refused, it seemed whisky was a luxury therefore it was fashionable. Had it been plentiful, he doubted whether any of them would have drunk it. Twyford easily impressed by casually squirting just the right amount of soda in each drink, one-handed from a distance.

'Seen Mary yet?' challenged Pat Passmore, going right for the throat.

'No, but if this good fortune holds out I'm a certainty to win the pools Saturday!' he answered, looking at the five faces to see what they knew. All he found was genuine concern and a little hostility.

'You're horrible to her.' stated Kathy Gay, who was the prettiest by far.

'I know.' he replied. 'Come over and have a drink with the lads, we're on afters.'

The ladies looked at each other and Kathy decided, 'Oh, alright then, but you'll have to see us home afterwards. There might be another blackout.'

'I'll see you home alright,' said George with such undertones that the gaggle giggled and, with the ice melting nicely, they rose and followed single file through the tables to join the fellows.

Cissy Dibble looked at George's mother and remarked, 'Oh, there's a surprise!' Aunt Lou and Min just nodded and sipped their Guiness.

CHAPTER 3: ONE KNOCK AND WELCOME

Today Hitler visited Munich for his annual beer-cellar speech and promised the German people victory over their enemies, saying, "Even If, for the present, we cannot reach America, thank God that at least one country (Britain) is near enough for us to tackle, and on that country we will concentrate with all our might!"

Earlier that same evening, as Twyford's cab passed through Mornington Crescent bringing him home, Ruben Benson looked out of his window and watched the factory workers opposite stream out of the Craven A building, collars up against the bitter wind that blew along Hampstead Road towards Camden Town. His new suite of spacious offices was in a good position above Mornington Crescent tube station, very close to the West End. The accommodation below was more cramped and housed ledger clerks, a rest room for his fieldsmen and two private interview rooms for enquiries or problems. He had started working-life as a money lender, taking over the business from his father before him, then at the outbreak of war the property market in and around London crashed. He bought blocks of houses for next to nothing at the start of the bombing. Companies, who knew but didn't care much for the problems war would bring their tenants, rushed to sell him rented property cheaply in fear of the Luftwaffe. A lot of it was seriously dilapidated, probably came with a health risk and, although tenants still had some rights, it was wartime so what could they expect? If they couldn't do the necessary repairs, tough; verbal complaints were ignored and written ones filed in the bin. Anyone who didn't pay was made to pay, or evicted; simple really. The bombs had almost stopped now but there was always another desperate tenant and a lot more minor civil servants needing to be housed nearer to the centre. Business was good but what he really desired was an enormous building, just like the one opposite, that could be rented out to the war effort for a couple of years then converted into smaller units and he would never have to worry again. The problem was a huge lump of liquid cash. At the moment, it came in in dribs and drabs, and he had big expenses; backhanders oiled the right people at the council, sweeteners paid for making noticeable waves disappear -and intimidation handled the ripples, but it all cost money. Admittedly the return was excellent, not to say fabulous, but the average house in St Pancras rented between ten and fifteen shillings a week and you always had to chase payment. So it was a fine line between going too easy or too strong; his collectors (he preferred the term 'fieldsmen') had to be kept in line as much as his tenants. Ruben was fine with the menace shown to certain bad payers; given the chance most of St.Pancras would take liberties and withhold the rent. Therefore putting the frighteners on some was necessary but recently one of his collectors had pulled out a shiv and, as a penalty for interest on 5 weeks back rent, demanded an ear or a little finger then wanted them to choose which one he cut off! Mad bastard; another one with too much ferocity and not enough common sense. Why hospitalise someone and stop them earning wages to pay their bills? All he required was fixed weekly income not regular interviews at the local constabulary! A knock at the door interrupted his train of thought and Fintan McMahon entered a second later. Ruben had originally employed him as a 'fieldsman' but he was never pushy enough. Sometimes, instead of collecting, he'd actually believed the hard luck stories and paid it himself, thus, he became Ruben's chauffeur and minder. He dealt with any aggression towards Ruben quickly and effectively, yet never with malice: Fintan was an enigma, he had to force himself to be nasty. Had it not been for ball joint problems he could have been a very successful lightweight, small, wiry and devastating, but his left arm had come out of its socket too often to retain a manager's interest. He had married one of Mary's younger sisters ten years earlier and she seemed to be constantly pregnant ever since. The girl worshipped him and he doted on her, they moved away to Kilburn but brought the kids back to see her mother every Saturday without fail; it was a marriage meant to be.

'The motor's warmed and ready when you are, boss.' said Fintan.

Ruben lived in a large house at Frogmore, so private that they seldom knew the next door neighbours. The firm's car was a smart Humber Super Snipe and, once the boss had been delivered home, Fintan could usually keep it for the weekend.

Well wrapped against the cold, the chap sat upstairs at the front of a number 24 bus, in utter darkness, and waited. Across the street from the bus garage another patient man, similarly dressed and concealed in a doorway, watched the gaping entrance. Always deserted for the small hours, it was a tested safe-haven for meetings of a clandestine nature. The two operatives were from a unique team of four that worked covertly in the more lawless districts of London and this night, in Chalk Farm, their rendezvous was with an informer of extraordinary aptitude.

It was six o'clock, Saturday morning. George had only been in bed a short time and a dreadful pounding headache had slaughtered the last precious thirty minutes of it. There was no solution except to get up and have a run; he found that usually cleared a thick head. It was a habit he picked up, whilst numb with boredom, in South Africa. As their only mode of transport, most people there ran good distances every day, whereas in England exercise training was considered to be a sort of army punishment and stopped once the men returned to Civvy street. So it was for the want of something to do after work that he took up distance running and now fitness was almost an addiction; albeit he had never felt or looked better in his life and was sure it stimulated his best ideas when jogging alone. Hence, Saturday morning, in the dark, finds George flying up the street and narrowly missing the milkman coming out of number two, trying to close the gate with empty bottles on all fingers. He turned right at the top of the Square and along Malden Road towards Parliament Hill fields. Twyford passed the brewery horse and cart waiting outside the Malden whilst the drayman tried to wake Horace and Rosie with a delivery. George shouted across to the trouncer 'Drop it down and I'll put it away in a minute.' Profanities commenced and concluded the terse response, nevertheless it was always worth a try, you never knew when fate might offer up a mug. He continued past the Priory and on towards Hampstead Village; the sun was threatening to come up and he was feeling better already. Hampstead Heath was beautiful any time of the year but breathtaking that frosty morning. The pace was held steady as he passed the all night fishermen on the ponds and wondered what enjoyment there was in freezing your equipment for a tiddler. George slowed over a leafy rise and down a gentle gradient, building up speed where it flattened out for fifty yards, then hit the hill with everything he had. He sprinted to the top, heart striving to come through his chest and collapsed at the summit of Parliament Hill. Twyford lay on the damp grass, gasping for air, superbly happy and thought about another optimistic dreamer who had once stood on the same spot, years before: Guy Fawkes had hoped to see Westminster blown to pieces from there and George wondered whether it would have made that much difference. "Would the millions still have died in the last war, did we learn anything at all from that terrible slaughter? Evidently not, or we wouldn't be at it again. We'll win eventually," of that he had no doubt, "because countries, like armies, tire and weaken. When the energy of these islands looks to have run its race and almost expired, only then can we British achieve that second wind. We alone can call on something deeper inside ourselves to wake an ancient and terrible power that slumbers beneath the tilled fields of Great Britain. Then Drake's drum will beat time and the ghosts of every valorous, fighting Briton that did battle at Balaclava, Waterloo, Agincourt and Trafalgar will rise up and march with us. When it happens, and it will, nothing will withstand our onslaught. All enemies will be trampled underfoot, our skies will be free again and England shall rejoice." He often enjoyed inventing these fancies but managed to flatten this one with, "The rich will return from America, patting each other on the back, and it won't make a blind bit of difference to the hardship of the people round here!" With that, he jumped up and raced down the hill. He had a lot to do and was in a hurry again to get on with it.

Twyford arrived back at the Square around nine and ran all the way to the door. Had he walked through Queens Crescent market he would have had to stop and chat every few yards, but most people he passed offered a smile. George poured the boiling water into the teapot and refilled the kettle in readiness for a scrub, he hated washing in cold water and doubted that Churchill or Attlee suffered these problems. As his vest came off the back door opened and in strolled a young lad with fair hair mowed very short and spiky. George knew him straight away and could not believe the size of him. The youngster eyed his bare chest suspiciously.

'Are you a burglar?' he asked with caution, 'This is my nan's house.'

'Your Nan's my Mum,' came the reply.

'Yeah? If you know her then who am I?'

'Your name's Alan Twyford, you're seven years old and never at school, so I hear.' The youngster smiled for the first time, liking the casual banter.

'So how'd you know me then? Where's my Nan anyway? Here, are you my Uncle?' He talked man to man, George liked that.

'I've known you, your brother and your two sisters since you were born. Your Nan's making the beds and I ain't your Uncle. Anymore questions before I have a splash?' The boy couldn't answer, his brain and his heart were arguing. 'Right, I'll tell you what. Go up and ask your Nan who I am.' He said it ever so gently.

The lad went into the passage, giving Twyford a wide birth, stopped at the foot of the stairs to look back and then belted to the top shouting, 'Nan? Nan?'

'I'm in here, Alan.' The door slammed.

George washed swiftly and as he pulled his vest on, Alan came back down, with Min a few steps behind him, and stopped again at the bottom. The father was as nervous as his son. He bobbed down to a crouch and put his arms out. Alan hesitated for a second and then ran at him, jumping that last yard into his arms. Neither of them could speak for a few seconds then Alan blurted out, 'I knew you'd come home, I knew you would.' inferring that someone had been telling him otherwise.

'Your Dad's home to stay, Algie, and anybody don't like it just send them round to me.'

'Oh yeah!' shouted Alan, loving this kind of talk. 'Oh yeah!'

George carried him over to the armchair then plonked himself down with his son still attached; they cuddled in front of the range. Alan asked all manner of questions about boats and lions, his eyes widened more with every answer. This was better than his birthday for George was an excellent raconteur.

"They are so alike," thought Min, hating to interrupt. 'Alan, there's a gang of boys outside, are you supposed to be somewhere?'

'Oh, Gawd, I'm late!' he cried. He came to Min early every weekend for pocket money and then off to the Saturday morning pictures.

'Go on son and take this for some comics.' said George, digging deep in his pockets and passing over a handful of change. 'Give us a kiss, and I'll see you tonight, right?'

'Right,' said Alan, looking down at what he held in both hands, there must have been more than five bob. It was his birthday! 'Ah, Dad, thanks!' He flung his arms round George's neck and, without dropping one coin, gave the biggest squeeze he could muster, kissing him hard on the cheek then dashed up the passage towards the street door.

'Here, Alan,' Twyford called out, 'don't anyone round home know I'm here?'

'Dunno, no one was up when I come out. See ya!'

'See ya,' said George, as the door slammed.

"One down and four to go," thought Min. 'Any tea left, son?'

'Yes Mum, but its stone cold now.'

'Then get off and see your family!' she ordered.

He had thought about little else since he'd got up; how to begin, what to say to the kids. Fuck her; she was the least of his worries. "Yeah, I'll go round and see if Romeo's still there," he thought. "Rather him than me, I'd sooner suck a stinging nettle. She won't be ready and she'll hate being seen like that." These pleasing thoughts speeded him along. He dressed smartly without over doing it and, instead of crossing the gardens, walked around to the front of her house, letting everyone in Marsden Street know he was back. George lifted the knocker and rapped out two loud thumps immediately sowing confusion, as it was one knock for downstairs and three for his Uncle Bert. Plenty of movement was audible but still nothing happened, so he knocked even louder.

Mary's voice called out to the inhabitants, 'Will one of yees open the frigging door?'

The accent was as strong as ever even though she had lived here all her life. It was not surprising for she was part of an enormous Irish family with aunties and cousins dwelling in every other street in the area. The only member George could not abide was her father -and he was the only Englishman among them. His lawful wife, Mary, was giving out to the girls for not answering the door fast enough and having to come down and do it herself. She wasn't happy, but when was she ever? Saying, 'Get some clothes on and tidy your...' the stiff front door jerked open, '...room.' she tailed off. Mary looked at him in utter shock for several seconds and then ran to the back door, a hand over her mouth, trying to hold down breakfast. This was not quite the reception he had expected. Thinking to catch her off balance, his plan was to breeze in as if he had never been away then, while she was still speechless, duck out before the shock had time to turn to venom. The door was open so George stepped inside and moved towards the kitchen. His two daughters, still in dressing gowns, were each draped across an armchair, their noses in comics. He could have been a whirling dervish for all the notice they took of him. Niamh was thirteen and the elder, tall, shapely and growing up fast. Mairead was eleven and more like her mother, she was probably as tall as Mary already. Both were beautiful, and not just because they were his.

'Not much of a welcome for a wounded soldier.' he said, smiling that old smile. Two heads popped up in unison, stunned for a fraction of a second, then rising together to hug him.

'Daddy, Daddy!' closely followed by, 'Have you brought us anything? Oh, what have you brought?'

'Not yet. Make out you love me a bit more first.'

'Oh, we do, we do!'

So he teased them for a little longer expecting Mary to come back any moment and explode. Perhaps she was taking this long to compose herself.

He asked the girls, 'What's the best thing I could have brought you?'

They fired back answers, jumping over one another, until they had exhausted everything they could think of. George pulled a serious face and began with, 'I couldn't bring you anything because I didn't know your sizes now and, you're so grown up, you might not have liked any of it.'

Niamh believed him and tried to hide her disappointment but Mairead said brightly,

'It doesn't matter, Dad, Mummy will buy you a present instead.'

"I know how much," he thought. 'I only had the fare money,'

he carried on, 'and a bit extra, so I thought you could buy yourselves something with this.' and he gave them a white fiver. For various reasons this was the first money he had been able to treat them with for four years and, when you consider the average man's wage was between one pound, ten shillings and two pounds a week, -that was an awful lot of money. The girls had never been given so much in one go and were frightened.

Niamh said, 'Mum would never let us have all this!'

'Listen, I haven't been able to spoil you in a long time.' Then smiling added, 'So, if you don't tell her...' he left the sentence unfinished. 'Buy yourselves whatever you want, it's alright, I swear to you it's alright.' Wanting to be convinced, yet still a little concerned, they looked at one another.

'Go and hide it somewhere while I pop up to see Uncle Bert.' and the three of them marched upstairs. The girls went in their room first and Twyford quickly opened Mary's bedroom door, saw it was empty and stepped inside for a fast inspection then out and up to his Uncle's, where there was no reply. George was not surprised; Bert worked all hours on the railway. He came downstairs and his daughters were already in the kitchen, whispering excitedly about what they were going to do with the money. Still no Mary. It was time to withdraw from the field, he made an excuse to go, kissed them goodbye and asked them to tell their mother that he would pop in tomorrow and if they wanted him, to leave a message at Nanny's. Twyford left via the front door relieved that there had not been a scene.

Mary sat on the outside toilet biting holes in her hanky. She was disgusted with herself, how could she let that bastard witness what he could do to her? Just seeing him today made her throw up, followed shortly by a bad dose of the runs. How was it possible? It couldn't be him, unless it

was the effect four years of loathing can have by poisoning the system. The cheek of the bastard turning up like visiting dignitary, bold as brass. She should have slammed the door in his face.

"I'll wait here for a while, he won't stay long, far too important," she thought, getting angrier. "The next time he comes around, I'll rip the face off him!" The anger made her shake. "Who the hell does he think he is, just wait till my Daddy finds out he's back." It was then she started to sob.

CHAPTER 4: 'AND IT'LL ONLY GET BETTER!'

English Channel: German torpedo boats sink the British cruiser 'Charybdis' and destroyer 'Limbourne'.

London: Vice Admiral Sir John Cunningham becomes C-in –C Mediterranean fleet.

Birmingham had failed and the murder had almost caused the ruination of plans of immense importance. Originally, she had been taken with his arrogant competence and easy approach to skullduggery so, with such a limited time frame, she set him enterprises. At first, the Scotsman was purely motivated by the substantial monies offered but he handled her dubious assignments well and had proven to their group that he gave outstanding value. Still on trial, she had tested him further with additional employment of an altogether heavier, unlawful nature. He went about their business with professionalism, never querying an instruction and using any means to ensure he succeeded at her tasks. With such an attitude he had made himself the ideal candidate for the special work to come. And so she bent him to her will. Using her own highly individual techniques of deviant, sexual enticement she disarmed him and left him open for education, then effortlessly gifted him the pleasures of masochism - and his obedience was secured. Birmingham was originally his undertaking but not *his* failure yet he would now willingly volunteer to be punished for it, - and she would unequivocally accept!

The Butler residence was under the arches in Leybourne Road and each time a train came by, the house shook. The row of houses once faced their twins but a line of bombs had demolished the odd numbers in the street and flattened the three other corners on the quite busy cross-roads. Now, you came out of Mickey's front door and faced four bomb debris;

eyesores, but wonderland for the kids. Twyford hammered the knocker twice and then wished he had tapped more gently, it must have sounded like the bailiffs. Mickey came to the door in his vest, probably could not risk ruining a good shirt. Two of his elder kids stood behind him, frightened but nonetheless ready and armed with empty milk bottles. Stunned, Butler shouted abuse at him and the air was blue in no time as George and Mickey strutted up and down, laughing and slapping their thighs. Doors opened along the street, people peered out then, reassured, returned inside. His boys beckoned them both into the house; Theresa was calling, wanting to know if the War had ended. 'No, even better,' cried Mickey, 'look who's come home!' Twyford stepped inside the kitchen and though his face never changed from a beaming grin, his heart broke. Theresa was lying on a bed in the corner; she could only move her head. Her covered arms were out of the sheets and clamped up tight to her chest. The wrists were skeletal and the hands and fingers were clenched at awkward angles. A blanket covered her knees which were locked on to her stomach, one higher than the other. She looked at George and smiled kindly. He came to the bed and knelt on the floor taking her hand in his, feeling its fragile rigidity.

'Hallo, gorgeous,' he said, tenderly.

'Not so gorgeous now.' she answered in a frail wheeze.

'Course you are, look at them flashing eyes, I'd be your slave only I'd do the work and he'd get the kisses.'

'Give us a kiss then,' she said, and as he moved his head closer she whispered, 'You ain't gonna take him away are you?' Tears already forming.

'Leave off!' echoed George and Mickey almost together. 'Theresa,' continued Mickey kneeling down and taking the same hand as his friend, ' Don't talk daft, you're stuck with me for all eternity.'

'I've just got back and heard a bit about your problems, I only bring good news. I know someone who's got a job for Mick, a proper job.'

'Oh George, you ain't just saying it are you?' begged Theresa.

Mickey was looking at him in astonishment too, wondering if he really meant it. 'Straight up?' he gasped.

'I swear to God,' answered Twyford and the three of them pressed heads together, not wanting to move until they were ready.

'Go on, you two,' said Theresa, breaking the spell. 'You're busting to talk and I'm getting a mite tired.' Looking at George she said, 'Michael will tell me all about it later.' Twyford kissed her on the forehead and rose.

Mickey pulled the sheets up, kissed her tenderly then motioned him out into the hall, shutting the door quietly. 'I'll get my jacket.'

'Put a shirt on for Christ sake! Scruffy bastard.'

The two strolled to the corner and into the public bar of the pub opposite. It was eleven thirty, Saturday morning, and yet they were the only trade. George called two pints of Worthington and asked why?

Imparting things he perhaps should not, the barman answered, 'We got raided last night. The Governor acquired a van load of Army boots and half-hour later he's nicked. As if it 'aint hard enough, now we got a grass on the Manor!'

George remembered his chant and repeated quietly,'The Peelers got a squealer..?'

The barman looked over his shoulder, leaned forward and confided, 'That's the word, alright.'

'You mind somebody don't trip over your tongue.' advised Mickey, and purposely moved to the furthest table from the bar.

They raised foaming jugs to each other and drank deeply. Never before had George seen him looking so gaunt. 'What do you want to hear about first; the girls or the job?'

'The job,' Mickey said anxiously.

'Right. Well it's working for one of the finest people I've ever come across,'

'Not you?'

'Of course me: who else would put up with you!'

'Don't muck about, Georgie, the mire is up to my bottom lip, you don't know the half.'

'So tell me,' said Twyford, 'how much rent do you owe Mr.Benson?'

'Fourteen weeks at fifteen bob plus interest. I know it's bad but I couldn't help it, I kept skipping the odd couple of weeks 'cos of the things that Theresa needed and we couldn't afford to do the two. I thought he'd give me a bit more time but it's gone on and on and now it's caught up with me. What with the piano site getting bombed, I've been so low 'me chin keeps hitting the floor, and the mob what's working for him, they're naughty people. Benson charges interest after two weeks and then if you still can't pay, interest on the interest. They've threatened us that if nothing happens this week...' he left the sentence unfinished. 'That's why I'm frightened to leave Theresa and the kids.'

'I make that ten guineas and fuck the interest,' said Twyford, putting his hand into his pocket and producing two white fivers and a ten bob note, then leant across and shoved them at him. 'Cop hold. Now that ain't for the rent.' Mickey took the money, not understanding anything, just hoping that it was really happening. 'That's for food and whatever Theresa and the kids are short of. You might not be paying the rent after all.' said Twyford, thinking out loud. 'Anyway, leave that to me. You are now employed in an advisory capacity to study the wants and needs of the community with special dispensations to our friends and acquaintances, specifically in the designated areas of Camden Town, Kentish Town and Somers Town. Your wages will be three quid a week plus remunerations and bonuses at the discretion of the Management, paid out one week in advance.' handing him another three pounds.

'You're serious!' said Mick, not moving. 'What are you talking about? Where's all this money come from?' He began to lose some of his earlier fears, yet still in shock.

'It'd take ages and this ain't the place,' said Twyford, 'listen, you've got to go back to Theresa and I want to look up a few people so I'll see you Monday morning.' The rest of his pint was downed in one and George stood up, waiting for his old mucker to do the same.

'Have one more,' coaxed Mickey. 'My treat, believe it or not I'm loaded!'

'One, if you're sure it's alright, and I'll get it.' Twyford walked to the bar and looked in the mirror behind the shelves. He could see Butler's reflection, the head had emerged out from between the shoulders and he looked more like his old self already. "And it'll only get better," promised George.

That afternoon he caught a sixty-eight bus from Chalk Farm to Somers Town and walked through the alleyways to where his mother-in-law lived. She was a smashing woman, which was a lot more than could be said for her husband. They dwelled in an old, grey block of flats built by the Peabody Trust. Each block of flats was square in shape with the balconies facing inwards overlooking a very pretty railed garden, which was permanently locked so the residents couldn't use it. George glanced up and down the street casually until he was convinced it was clear then climbed the four flights of stairs to the top floor. His in-laws lived in the corner flat. Twyford was sure his father-in-law was at work because the evil swine lived for his work. He would have preferred not to take this risk, but needs must. Fintan should be there with his family doing his Saturday penance. He, too, avoided the father-in-law and as the Humber was parked downstairs it was feasible that, unless things had changed dramatically, it was safe. Had Archie Shaw been in the vicinity, Fintan McMahon would have left Bridgid and gone for a drive. George actually enjoyed his mother-in-law's company and, as a bonus, his visit would certainly annoy Mary, but the main reason for coming to this dangerous spot was to have ten minutes with Fintan. He flapped the letterbox and waited. Bridgid answered the door a few seconds later; she gave him a hug and let him in. Fintan was sitting on the sofa, eyes everywhere watching that the kids didn't break anything while mother-in-law, Josie, made tea in the scullery. Fintan jumped up and pumped his hand then moved along the sofa, making room for him to sit down. Josie popped her head out to see who it was. 'Well now, it's yourself, it is!' She had such a lovely way of stating the obvious.

'It is, is it not, to be sure!' he said, playfully.

The usual hugs continued, followed by the usual 'Now, its tea, is it?'

'It is,' he replied. Returning to the kitchen, Josie busied herself with cutting chunks of home-made soda bread and loading the tray with butter and gooseberry jam, while George, Bridgid and Fintan discussed the latest conflict news.

'Forget that old War,' said Josie, coming in and putting down an array of goodies. 'The prodigal has returned, I won't ask if you've seen your wife yet.' and expected an answer.

George grinned like a mischievous school boy and slipped that one with 'And I won't tell you what she said! I've come to see you. We'll sort your daughter out later.' That was enough to dispel any disharmony there might have been and gave Josie the opportunity to begin. She chatted non-stop for fifteen minutes, with the occasional prompting from her audience to change direction every so often. She expounded astutely, her opinions were exceptionally well measured, never passing judgement nor coming down on either side of any disagreement, seeing everyone's point of view. George had always found her to be a remarkable woman and, again, was mystified by her romantic affiliation; still, it takes all kinds. Twyford stayed just long enough not to be rude. Josie knew well the friction between her husband and her son-in-law and, allowing for this, she admired him all the more for coming to see her. Fintan offered a lift and George readily accepted. The ladies saw them to the door and no mention was made of the problems that had ripped them apart as a family; that was an unutterable short-fuse to a minefield!

The Humber drove through Camden Town and they chatted lightly about what it could do then the subject moved on to its owner; was Fintan still with Ruben and was everything going well? The answers were in the affirmative but George felt a negativity in the response. He pressed a little harder, Fintan was always an easy person to talk to and normally his heart decorated his sleeve so in no time he was voicing doubts about the future. He admitted no dislike for Mr.Benson, in fact he was a good governor, but in business the man was totally ruthless and getting worse. Ruben Benson employed more and more heavies and, although it had very little to do with him, Fintan disliked the brutish company policy of violence for any non-payment. Common sense told him to turn a blind eye and continue taking the wages, how else could he keep up their standard of living?

'There might be an altogether better way,' said George and took him into his confidence. Fintan was stunned by what George was proposing but listened without interrupting. Twyford's schemes were always daunting but this one would surpass them all. It was so bold that Fintan wanted to be convinced. They pulled up at the top of St. Leonard's square and watched the street kids hitting 6s everywhere. Well out of cricket ball range, the discussion continued for a further twenty minutes and finally an agreement was struck Rules and guidelines were confirmed because like all good men, Fintan lived by a code of ethics, a code for life. He was to remain employed with Ruben for three months and be their inside man. If, by the end of that period, George had established the planned graft then with great pleasure, Fintan would join him.

Never off work, the duplicitous informer, imputed locally as the "Nark", waited at a bus stop and observed the Super Snipe until it discharged it's passenger then speculated why George Twyford should be having discussions in Ruben

Bensons prize Humber in a back street of Kentish Town. There was probable work afoot, remunerative work to be researched, and pondered on which acquaintances to be lightly probed...

Arriving home, young Alan was waiting for him in the kitchen and George would hold the picture in his mind forever: hand-me-down short trousers far too big, filthy knees, muddy football socks down around his ankles and the grubbiest finger inserted deeply up his right nostril -whilst completely riveted in a 'dreadful'. A warming glow of fatherhood struck him soundly for the first time in 4 years; this wonderful little 'oick was his. The lad had received permission to have tea with his Dad and was to be home directly afterwards. George marched him to the sink and scrubbed his hands then lifted him up and sat back in the armchair to carry on where they left off. Blaming rationing, Min dished them each a slice of meat that had a remarkable similarity to crusty, old boot leather with mash potatoes and baked beans. The boys rambled merrily all through tea, equally exaggerating every recollection. "He was his father's son right enough," thought Min and after allowing two portions of 'Just five minutes more, please Nan,' she sent him across the garden to his Mum and bedtime.

CHAPTER 5: 'WHAT COMES WITH RATIONING?'

Italy: Autumn rains help Germany slow Allied advance. General Montgomery paused to regroup hard pressed 8th Army and 4 German divisions moved up to oppose him.

George washed, shaved and chose a good, old, tailored suit from his limited winter wardrobe and improved it immensely with a fresh shirt, starched collar and another lairy tie, of which he had in abundance, and was ready at ten to nine when Mornie called. Well passed parsimonious but admitting only to thrift, Mornington Quill lived close by in Belmont Street, two doors from Gerry Nolan. A fit lad, he still played football to a decent standard every Sunday morning and as the pubs closed at 2pm on Sundays he earned himself the dubious title of "10 to 2 Mornie" for he would always pace his presence to avoid the bigger rounds and thought no one realised. His friends politely described him as "careful" and would regularly counteract his timely disappearances by telling him the whip was a florin more than it actually was thus balancing the pot without a harsh word needing to be uttered. Bordering six foot, he was a military tailor by trade. Potless, of course, but belied the fact by restyling his old clothes and therefore always appeared well turned out. They collected Johnny Bass from thirty four St Leonard's and walked to the Malden. As they approached, Nolan's warbling chords reached out to meet them, straining through "Those Little White Lies". When the pianist played a few notes of your special number, up you got. Very occasionally, someone sang another's song, but not often, it wasn't good form. If Mary turned up with her chap, George would make a point of singing something detrimental that would drill a nerve and counteract any attempt she might make to besmirch him, the bitch. Earlier, Twyford had again tried to get a glimpse from the garden but the blackout curtains were pulled in exactly the same way, and the last thing he wanted was for anyone to think that he cared. It was just simple curiosity to see what mug could actually enjoy suffering that miserable mare for a tedious couple of hours.

All the lads arrived within the next twenty minutes. Most of them were married with just a few exceptions, one of them being Gerry Nolan. He had left wife Ivy years ago and was back living in two rooms with his Mum but held on to her street-door key and would occasionally pop in, intoxicated, uninvited and amorous. Slight of frame yet acid of humour, his overtures began with teasing then, helpless to stop himself, rapidly increased to tormenting her and any company she may have been getting comfy with. She, on the other hand was taller, quite athletic and very fiery and would eventually erupt, duff him up and kick him out. He found the process endearing and though regularly damaged was never disheartened. The rest of the boys were allowed out with special dispensation because George was back home, 'safely'; a pitiful excuse but seemed to do the trick. The jug was loaded with the whip and the jokes and debates roared into top gear. Kathy Gay and a few of the girls were on the town and acting in their ambassadorial capacities with overseas gentlemen, who seemed to bastardise the English language with phrases such as 'Hey buddy, this beer's too warm. You got any ice?'

To which our genial host Horace would reply, 'No. So, if you don't like it... Fuck off!' Horrie wasn't, what might be described as, 'fond' of our colonial cousins. It cheered him to see their money freely thrown towards his till but didn't appreciate how they would cluster around Rose, magnetised by her more than ample breasts. So 'fuck off!' was one of his wittier replies, he was a Grand Master of repartee after all. Taking everything into consideration it was a splendid Saturday night's entertainment and, with a little persuading, Twyford could con a few of the lads into venturing up the West End to the Café de Paris or the Savoy, where the motto was "Live now, for tomorrow, who knows?" The conversation turned to rationing and how much they hated it; being deprived of petrol, meat, clothes and luxuries that had once been every day items.

'I love it!' said George, to provoke argumentative amusement.

'What are you on about now? You've been on holiday for four years -with one thumb in your mouth, the other up your arse! You haven't been here.' declared Owen Esterbrook derisively, to jeers of agreement.

'Graphic and possibly true, therefore allowing me the time to ruminate upon the plight of you, my dearest friends. And, what's more, I've arrived at your solution! All we've got to do is be a bit active.'

'And how do we do that?' asked Tinker, who always enjoyed George's reasoning. He had their attention.

'We form a trading company.' Groans. 'Using all our contacts to chase everything that's short, distribute it at a profit, earning bundles whilst serving the community; easy. Trust me; have I ever put you wrong?' Everybody tried to answer at the same time. 'And you've got to admit, didn't we have a laugh? See, no one's forgotten those special times and on the strength of that, I shall treat the lot of you to the Café Luxor.'

'I don't think we'd be let in,' said John Bass, 'Kingy plays piano down there for Toot Robertson's dance band, -he's coining it, but he told me that only the titled are entitled to get passed the front door.'

To use his full name, Greatorex Alexander King went to Holy Trinity School when they were small and even then he was different. His Mum made him learn the piano and he was never allowed to play out with the other kids. Rex tinkled the ivories in all the school plays and the carol singing. He was a very talented lad.

'Who, Kingy? He's one of my best mates!' George coaxed, 'Come on, let's give it a try. Look at us, has anyone ever dressed this sharp? Course not, and if I'm paying, what have we got to lose?' Not convinced, but game, they left the pub and caught the tube from Chalk Farm to Leicester Square and twenty minutes later they surfaced in Soho. The streets were busy with people, mainly in uniform, wandering about quite happily with no real destination. It had been much too long since they frequented the West End clubs so the lads had become quite thrilled about their night out. They approached the Café Luxor and could see well-dressed people being refused by four very large silverbacks in black Crombies. Whatever happened, George had to get in. It was not only a question of face but he needed to give the boys confidence in what he was planning. Nine was an unacceptable number to stand the slimmest of chances therefore George decided on a full frontal. Palming a white five pound note, he walked straight towards the four with a wide grin, each of them thinking he knows one of the others; the lads followed gingerly. He reached the first two and increased his pace between them towards the widest one on the door, guessing it was his decision who entered and who did not. George's hand stretched out in greeting and speaking before he reached him, asked, 'Is Rex King here yet?' They shook hands and the fiver passed across; the bouncer's expression changed not one iota.

'Yeah, the bands on now, he said to look out for you boys. In you go.'

Twyford stepped to one side and the lads trooped by, nodding to their new friend as they passed. Before tagging on the column's tail George interceded the welcoming customary warning and assured the head doorman, 'Sweet, I promise you, they're good as gold.' The bouncer's eye predicted what would happen if they were not.

The foyer led into the ballroom with the bar on the left as you entered and the others had congregated at one corner of it, making themselves comfortable. The stage was half way down the hall on the right and the dance floor, like a moat, separated the band from the huge half-moon shaped seating arrangement. In a splendid setting, before an array of Brass and Strings, Rex worked his grand piano while an attractive redhead passionately embraced a refrain made for late night liaisons. Seeing that tables were filling fast, George peeled a pound note and claimed the nearest waiter. The man's eyes lit up for most of the clientele, by their mere presence, expected to be looked after without needing to tip. He found them a round table for ten in an excellent position immediately opposite the stage. Once seated, the lads loudly voiced their disbelief at the bar prices, for one round of drinks had assassinated the whip. A couple of bottles of gin and two dozen tonics arrived and they settled down to enjoy mentally undressing the singing vision opposite whose voice quavered with an effected, husky French accent. As the only all male party present, most neighbouring tables showed interested in them and, even more pleasing, a nearby brunette caught Twyford's eye, held his glance and challenged. The singers had changed and a swarthy fellow began a tango. She gave a slight tilt of the head towards the dance floor. George loved forward women. Standing, he buttoned his jacket and moved across to her table working a smile that took in the other ladies seated with her. The women appeared hopeful that others might follow his example; the men in their company huffed a little and ignored him. He moved her chair and she pushed out her chest as she rose then, taking his hand, led onto the dance floor. Nudging each other, the lads willed him on for they were all good dancers and the Tango was their forte.

Many years before, Old Mother Hart had run a ballroom evening once a week in St Silas church hall. The only way to be successful with girls was by dancing, therefore it was compulsory for all the youngsters. A right old tyrant perhaps, but she was a perfectionist and no one left her charge without a certificate. For most it was the only diploma ever earned.

The lady wore her hair in a tight, wavy perm, an evening dress hugged her figure and a long slit up the side showed a shapely calf and ankle. They danced well together, she followed easily his every move. Swarthy's next song was slower and they nestled closer, moulded figures moving as one. He flirted for a third twirl and then returned her to the table with an open invitation to join up for a drink later. George sat down with the boys and was plied with questions about the lady and her friends. He reminded them, 'Believe me, the more we are seen to be having a good time, the more people will hanker to join our company.'

Enthused and showing a bravado he had not displayed for years, Kit jumped up and strolled across to the band as they were finishing "A nightingale sang"; a bad choice. The tune was well played but they were losing the crowd. Kit spoke to Rex King, who knew how well he could sing, Rex in turn murmured to the band leader. Accepting the suggestion, Toot Robertson tapped his baton, and as Kit snapped his fingers creating a faster tempo to, "Lover, come back to me.", separate sections of the band swung in at intervals to perfectly boost his rhythm. Kit's voice rang with a fine quality making the whole effect jazzy and instantly popular. The pulsating beat compelled everyone to flood the floor and liven up their usual steps. George's new friend Geraldine and her girls left the company they were with and brazenly asked some of the boys to dance. Twyford beamed and aimed Geraldine at Danny Curry who locked her on his arm and whipped her away. Everything seemed to be moving along nicely for the lads were hungry and in need of some madness. The remainder of them left the table, hunted down partners and joined the throng. Kit was singing his own version of "Perfidia" and to support him they would suddenly stop dancing, sing a backing line and then carry on. Soon, as everybody knew the words, they too were stopping dead, giving vent to a line of the chorus then breaking in to dance steps straight after. The singers changed and Kit returned victorious, he had created a mood that put New Year's Eve in the shade.

The band took their break half an hour later than normal and the lads assembled around the table with their new friends. To seat them all, another table was added. Needing no further prompting, George left them to intertwine and meandered to the bar. Rex King was there on a stool with the curvy singer *avec l'accent.* George sent drinks to their table and Rex waved him across. They shook hands warmly and Twyford was introduced as the boy Rex was never allowed to play out with. The luscious lady's name was Radna and she was pleasantly surprised when George guessed it was Icelandic. She hailed from Paris, once gay, and had only been in England since the German occupation. To complement perfect skin, naturally thick red hair and high cheek bones, she was gifted with unusually grey eyes flecked with red and gold – and they smouldered! Until then George hadn't believed eyes could behave in that fashion. He felt a compelling desire to have this woman. She looked in to him, passed his show at casual indifference then traced her fingernail lightly down the scar on his cheek. The action started one of those special moments that little can impede. He caught her hand as it dropped from his face and walked her to the dance floor; Rex watched their sashay, politely abandoned. George held her close and they swayed slowly, feet hardly moving. Tingling fingers brushed his neck and nerves stood on end. The spell broke when the lady was called back to prepare for a duet with Swarthy. George returned to the table to find that everyone had paired off and he was the gooseberry. A chair thumped beside him and Rex squatted the wrong way round.

'I can't believe that just happened!'

'What are we talking about?' asked George.

'The way she changed, looking at you, touching you. Men bore her, they pursue her all the time and never a flicker of interest. She's made from ice.'

'There are, I hear, hot springs in her country -perhaps she fell in one?' debated George, then mused, 'Or is there a special someone?'

'Maybe. I have seen her leaving with a beefy looking character several times but I don't think he's been around lately.'

'Now she's beheld me, there can be no other,' George said with a grin. 'I affect women like a fever.'

'More like gastro-enteritis!'

'Funny you should say that.'

'Are you going to…you know, play games? As I remember you were the only kid to get carpet burn from Postman's Knock.'

'I'm gonna play alright; Attila and the Nubian slave, desperate to be abused.'

Rex asked, 'On behalf of the band, may we watch?'

'If it's for instruction there will be a charge.'

'You don't think she's doing it to make me jealous, do you?' he queried hopefully.

'Yeah, an artful manoeuvre; the wily minx!' laughed George.

A trumpet played two notes off key, recalling the main band. His parting shot was, 'Oh well, this could all be for the best; to appreciate champagne one must first try cider!'

At two thirty Sunday morning, and with half an hour to go, the dance floor was vibrating. The boys were in excellent fettle and their crescendo was the last dance. Nolan directed all the carousers for the siege of Ennis. This is an Irish eurhythmy where two armies face each other. It should be boy, girl, boy, girl, but this often gets mixed up, making for chaos and far more fun. The lines skip forward and when they meet, the first couples link arms and swing around in circles as fast as possible, then back into formation moving between the other's ranks until all lines are spinning. The movement is dangerous, especially when intoxicated, but nevertheless exciting and finally ends when they have completely changed places. During the twirling people often fly off in all directions, and three or four did finish up on their arses, but not, thank God, hospitalised as it's a fact that in the Camden Town clubs the Irish attack the dance with such gusto that ambulances are parked outside in readiness.

The party eventually came to an end and other revellers drifted to their table and thanked them for an entertaining evening: handshakes of introductions and farewells. Some lads had 'one in tow' and were seeing them home to God knows where. Nolan's new friend lived in Leigh-on-sea, a district famous for 'a pint and a plate', which made for some new and lewd suggestions of ingesting such delicacies. Oaths were taken to be on parade, twelve noon sharp then everyone left, the band disappeared and apart from Twyford, who waited for Radna, the only ones still milling about were waiters cleaning tables. The bouncer, he had spoken to earlier, sauntered across and George hoped that they hadn't gone too strong, for obvious reasons he wasn't an individual one would wish to fall out with. The strapping fellow asked Twyford's name, introduced himself as Lenny, then affirmed that everything was sweet and, if he cared to, the manager would be pleased to make his acquaintance. Intrigued, George followed through not so well-kept corridors until Lenny stopped at an unmarked door, knocked loudly and waited.

A voice, 'Come', and lounging behind a huge, teak desk in a chamber bursting with gaud was another 'Swarthy', rather odorously overdone with brilliantine but dressed impeccably in a black evening suit and bow tie. He greeted them with a charmingly, professional smile.

Lenny did the introductions, 'Mr Mavropolous, I would like you to meet a very good pal of mine, George Twyford. George, this is Tony Mavropolous.' He pronounced the name with the respect reserved for Royalty. The two men shook hands, George taking to him straight away.

'Thanks for popping in. I would like to say, the marvellous night. You and your gang as a breath of spring, blew. That was my club in days bygone.'

Accents interested Twyford and Tony enunciated to perfection with that Greek way of stressing the last letter of every word, while rearranging the sentence.

'Well,' said George, 'we were down this way and had to say hallo to Lenny.'.

'Please, all of you have the invitation open.'

'Tony, that's very nice of you. We've been made welcome tonight and I look forward to coming back soon.' George felt it was time to go and moved to the door.

Tony went with him and shook hands, 'Rex tells me you're a

rascal. We must together go out.'

'I'd like that,' said George, 'good night, now'.

At the main exit Radna was waiting with two of the doormen. As they approached, but well out of range, Lenny warned, 'Watch her boyfriend, big jock with a nasty look about him. I'll never understand what such a lady could see in a lump like that. Still, funny buggers, women.'

'Thanks for the tip, Len. Be seein' ya'.' He walked past her, raised an elbow for Radna to hook on and they stepped into the night. Her apartment was in Regents Park and she preferred to walk, pulling up the collar of her fur coat. "That must have cost a nice few bob, a present from one of her admirers, no doubt." he mused, trying to imagine this refugee homeless and helpless; what utter nonsense. She was poised, polished and elegant, with an exquisite beauty that demanded adoration. Regardless of that, Twyford was at ease with her from the first minute, holding hands as they strolled, talking and laughing, so interested in each other, the world's troubles merely background. That night would always be one of life's treasured memories when there was no one he would rather be with. Tomorrow he may feel differently. Fuck tomorrow. Too soon, they were outside her apartment in Canterbury Mansions. What now? But cheek marched him up the steps and a concierge, in brown and gold, opened the glass doors and wished them, 'Good evening'. Across the foyer, up another flight, more swing doors and a thick carpeted passageway brought them to number thirteen. She let him in but left the light off and instead lit a candle on the hall stand. Unusually, George felt a little awkward and so drew her to him, slipping his arms beneath her coat and around her waist. The body came willingly but she held her head back just a few inches making him lean forward then brushed his lips with her own and, with a flash of smoulder, slipped away. He followed on to a luxurious sitting room furnished to be cosy where she lit more candles and took his jacket. In the warmth of the apartment, George perched on the settee regretting his choice of braces. She came and knelt before him, taking his shoes off. He took her head in his hands and leant to kiss her again. Instead she grasped his wrists and firmly pulled him forward on to his knees, until they faced each other. Holding his arms down by his sides she kissed his ear, his cheek then his eyes and her tongue swept faintly across his closed eyelids. George showed masterful control, though his passion was building. His mouth strove to find hers but each time she stopped the attempt by moving just out of reach until he was still, then returning to kiss his neck lightly, again and again, getting closer to his lips. It was strange to kiss and touch without using hands but still she restrained him. George was getting hotter now, impatient to be a part of this lovemaking. She opened his shirt and sucked warmth from his shoulders as her fingers brushed his chest and flicked his nipples, over and back. Newly discovered nerves waited for each return sweep and were bringing him to the most wonderful climax ever savoured. Madness. Knowing she could sense his approaching premature arrival, he tried to resist…still Radna took him further, tantalising, teasing lower. George strained, eyes squeezed shut, hold on, toes curled, hold on…. Too late. He erupted like Vesuvius. She held him tighter against her as waves of pleasure released him from the furnace. Relaxed, spent and feeling slightly silly, Twyford rose and performed a kiss of hunger that endeavoured to belie his sated appetite and only when his grip lessened did she take his hand and lead him through to a curtained four poster. It was the bed of his fantasies and resided in a pink boudoir heady with perfume that filled his nostrils and drugged him deliciously. He lay down while she undressed him, gently and easily, before disappearing to return naked with a hot, moist towel. She bathed his parts, dried him and then covered both of them under heavy blankets and crisp, white sheets, her arm wove around his shoulder and once his head found the soft pillow of her breast, George floated into sleep.

She woke him with a peck and a cup of tea. Twyford responded at once, he wanted more than a peck. No. Here we go again. Radna was dressed in a hugging, black, one piece trouser outfit made to look outstanding by a wide, golden leather belt at the waist. She opened the curtains and a bright day blinded the room. He called her back to the bed, knowing it wasn't on but good form required one to try. She came close, looking into his face intently and again running her fingernail down along his scar then changing to, 'Arise Oh Master, your breakfast awaits.' He was shocked to find it was past ten. She served him a treat of bacon, eggs, sausage, mushrooms and tomatoes with brown toast and butter but said little through the fine repast and ate even less. Had he blown it? Being faultless the possibility of that seemed very remote so maybe she needed to be quiet in the mornings; some women are strange like that. He saw no value in dwelling on it so tucked into more toast and a huge helping of marmalade then it was off to the bathroom to indulge in a wash down with hot water. This lady had everything, more proof for the debate later. He disliked goodbyes but had that urge men get to be gone. What to say? Some weak promise of making contact; best he left quickly, he was good at that. Radna saw him out and bestowed an embrace not easily forgotten, then whispered, 'You know where I am. Come to me.' Even though he was pleased to have departed, her few words lifted him for the frosty march across Primrose Hill to Chalk Farm, over Maitland Park and swiftly to the Malden. Only ten minutes late. He meant to see the kids first but had he called in wearing last night's suit or made no visit at all, Mary would still know he had been out all night. He sighed and bowled into the pub.

Danny Curry was the keenest. 'Come on George, tell us this plan.' The twelve huddled together in the snug, ten squeezed in and two standing.

Twyford sat in the corner against the wall and waited until they were all listening, then began,

'Right, the side effects of this war are putting everyone out of the game. What comes with rationing?' He answered his own question, 'No work and no money,' silence as he continued, 'but you went out last night. Did you see any shortage of booze or food or cars? No, 'cos if you're producing plenty of cash it all comes to you. That redhead who bedded me had all the clobber and food you could think of. She even had running hot water and I know that takes some believing but I swear it's God's truth.' They were astonished.

'There was plenty in the Café Luxor toilet.' observed John Bass.

'None of us knew that, you must have a thing about washing?' challenged Owen, hoping Bassy would enlighten them as to what he keeps washing and why. But he just tapped his nose with his finger.

'What d'you wash your nose for?' asked Owen and scraped a laugh.

John snapped out, 'Jackanapes!' and sewed bewilderment through the ranks as a few thought he was name-calling while most guessed it to be a posh word for "Bollocks!"

'Can I carry on?' begged George, feigning hurt dignity.

'Please, Mr Speaker, my guest,' said Owen.

'Listen, now the main two things are work and housing. Summing up work, what we got? John Bass, plumber, Gerry Nolan, his mate, equally good but no City & Guilds, both talented and overqualified for work on the Borough Council; skint. Lestor Hogg was an electrician but not enough work, now grafts illegally taking bets and selling bent gear. Mornie Quill's an excellent tailor but can't get enough material to stitch a button: again skint. Stan there is the best paid of you all, a lighterman down the docks, where everyone's fiddling and imagine what he could buy at the right price if he had plenty of cash. Owen's fruit stall's half empty through lack of funds. It's the same thing with Kit's butcher shop; poxy rationing again. Now you two tell me, is there plenty of gear down Spitalfields and Smithfield?'

'Bundles.' said Kit.

'Anything you want if you can shell-out the shekels.'added Owen.

'See what I mean,' said George, 'so, that leaves Tinker with his horse and cart delivering out of Kings Cross potato market, stacks of potential there and at the moment our only form of transport. Frank Nash is handy too, on the railway with good information, and lastly, you, Dan, a carpenter with no timber.'

'Alright then, but what about Mickey there? He's out of work and the worst off of us all.'

'No, he's the first employee of our company on three pounds a week.'

'That's the same wages as me!' said Stanley Swindells, sort of annoyed.

'Everybody who works for the company full time will be on that wage, and the others who'll keep working elsewhere, as long as it suits, will still get their divvy at the end of the year.' George was talking serious now so they let him carry on, with just a question here and there. 'Not a very thrilling collection but put the lot of us together and you've a real force.' They still couldn't see how or what he was getting at. He had to dangle a bigger carrot so asked, 'Don't you want to own your own houses?' That whetted appetites. 'Lestor,' George continued, 'how much a year is fifteen bob a week?'

'Thirty nine pounds.'

'And how much is your house worth?'

'About two hundred pounds.'

'That's nearly twenty percent.'

'Near enough.' agreed Lestor.

'You'd like that coming in all day long, wouldn't you?'

'That's why they say money goes to money.' he replied.

'Yeah, well now some of it's gonna come to us. The first house we're gonna buy is Mickey's.' Shocked looks all round. 'This week will be an exercise. After work Monday, let's gather down at the Butler residence. I want a price for all plumbing works including new sinks, new toilet. In other words, the dearest evaluation you can justify. We can always smash it up a bit.' Mickey was as baffled as any of them. 'The same with the electrics, the gas, all internal and external decorations, again we go right over the top.'

'It might be interesting to see what Ruben'ud do with this estimate?' Said Owen, ' cos I heard he only uses tissue paper in the outside loo!' They spoke of Ruben like an old friend.

'That's my job and my pleasure.' replied George.

'There's a geezer that grafts with us on the council,' said John Bass, 'he's a roofer, likes a bit of private work. I'll get him down to look at the slates.'

"That's better," thought Twyford, silently thanking Bassy for losing the negativity. 'Right Stan, next point, any material down the docks?'

Stanley took a moment. 'Loads of parachute cloth, been there for months. They produced too much of it.'

'I could make cracking shirts out of that.' said Mornie eagerly.

'See what it'll cost, Stan.' said George. More questions received favourable answers. 'Can you lose a load of 'tatoes, Tinker?'.

'I can get 'em. But where do you hide ten ton of spuds?'

'You get them and I'll tell you where to deliver them.' Things were moving beautifully now. 'Owen, see what fruit you can buy black market. Kit, you look at the meat options down Smithfields. If everyone finds out what's about by Monday, I'll get some trading capital and bearing in mind the phantom informer, let's keep all this between ourselves. Enough for now, refills all round, I think.' The pub turned out by two thirty and they walked down together with plenty to think about. The chaps were happy he was back; a touch of vim to disperse the despondency.

CHAPTER 6: WITH ARMS THAT CRUSHED TREES

Poland: 5 SS factories in the Lublin area are closed and over 17000 Jewish workers are machine-gunned into preparatory graves. This 'Bloody Wednesday' marks the end of Operation Harvest Festival in which 50000 Jews have died.

Sitting alone in the kitchen, Mary remembered that terrible time. It had been four weeks before Christmas and George had said he would be away for a few days. Some work had been offered, 'hard collar', though it should pay well. He got back on the Sunday night and came in singing and laughing, picked her up and spun her off the ground. She had been shrewish all that day, unreasonably waiting to carp at him, but when his ebullience flowed like that he could transform her mood in seconds. George gave her a month's money just to get the presents with and a bit more to buy herself something. He said they had been chopping down Christmas trees in Scotland and had sold load after load for really good money. She smiled when she thought of the celebration that night at the pub when he had sung to her "You'll never know just how much I love you". Three days later, while they were having tea, her father came in and went out the back yard with George. When they came inside George sat down but looked really worried and Archie left without saying 'goodbye'. Her father returned around nine the next morning. She had just seen the kids off to school and was going back to bed with George; Mary would do that sometimes, if he'd been good. He got dressed and left with her Daddy and she had not seen him since until Saturday last. Archie called in at about four o'clock the following afternoon and told her to quickly pack some things for George; he had to go away for a while and not to worry. Finally, a couple of days later, she found out, through the family, that her husband had really done it this time and if Archie hadn't got him on a boat out of the country, they would have locked him up and thrown the key away. Mary wondered how she had ever loved someone as empty of feelings as he obviously was. How could he have left them? A little money would come regularly: conscience money, but never once had he tried to get in touch. He was nothing more than a sewer rat; her Daddy had been right all along.

8am Monday morning. Twyford's father in law sat in the front passenger seat of the police car that collected him every morning and brought him to work. The driver looked straight ahead not daring to pass any comment, he had made the mistake of friendly banter and been silenced by the low, animal growl. The Sergeant was not happy, therefore you kept well away. Archie Shaw was six foot four inches tall and built like a gorilla, an enormous chest, big broad shoulders, arms that crushed trees and large, scarred hands with muscled fingers that could choke the life out of you. His disposition, never pleasant, might change in an instant to downright barbaric. On the rare occasion that he lost his temper, he showed uncontrollable savagery. Never get on the wrong side of Archie Shaw. He was station Sergeant at Holmes Road police station and the law in Kentish Town. There were turnings in the area, such as the notorious "Litcham Street", where policemen would seldom venture down in threes; when he walked the beat, every street was safe for good people. He dished out his own brand of penalties for law breakers. Drunks would be bounced off the walls, bashed and left on a tip to sober up. Aggression or violence was not allowed under any circumstances. If he came across trouble, it was put down with force, perpetrators were mostly hospitalised. Thieves and robbers were busted and broken; they always confessed their crimes and were tried and imprisoned. Villainy was not the wisest of occupations on Archie Shaw's manor.

His mood this day was dark for an obvious reason - that bastard was back. He had forced him to leave England four years earlier: had escorted him on to the boat for South Africa personally with the grim instruction of never to return. "Now, not only is he back," he thought, "he's been in my front room! The nerve of the bastard." The huge hands opened and clamped shut as he contemplated what would happen to Twyford when he found him. The squad car pulled in to the yard and Sergeant Shaw walked through to his little cubbyhole beyond the main office; as usually occurred, other officers busied themselves elsewhere. Awaiting him was a desk heaped with paperwork and top of the stack was a telegram from Scotland Yard. He began to read; 'Need urgent information on one George Twyford of Marsden Street. STOP. Arrived Southampton Friday 1st November from South Africa. STOP. Customs report Twyford carrying very, stress, very, large sum of money. STOP. Investigate with caution and revert. STOP. Chief Inspector Colan.' Bordering on apoplectic, Archie forced himself to calm down and read it again. There was no mention of stolen money, the directive was to find out whom it belonged to and where it had come from. They were to make discreet enquiries and report their findings. No further action. Anyone else but him, the mongrel had been home five minutes and already Scotland Yard wanted to know about it. 'We'll see about discreet.' he said out loud. 'PC Harris, get my car out the front now!' The police car pulled away and the other officers grouped together to discuss the latest bit of excitement; they almost felt sorry for George Twyford.

The Special Inquiry Office for His Majesty's Revenue was based in Liverpool. After his informative telephone call from the Southampton Customs, Senior Investigator Cyril Kirby had decided to travel to London first thing Monday morning. He caught the train from Lime Street station and was met at Euston by two Revenue bailiffs who were to provide whatever support was necessary. Such purported sums of money came under scrutiny from his department which considered any large amounts, with possibly disputed ownership, must become the property of His Majesty's

Revenue. He was driven to the house in Marsden Street, Kentish Town, recorded as being the residence of Mr George Twyford. The bailiffs were given their orders; they would remain in the car unless the subject proved difficult and needed to be physically restrained. No more conversation, he was used to being obeyed. Kirby rapped the knocker hard. As Mary opened the door, he moved forward and put a foot on the doorstep. She saw the manner and become nervous. Now what?

'Yes?' she asked.

'Inland Revenue. I'm here to see George Twyford.' he stated it as a matter of fact and briefly showing a warrant card to her chin, pushed past her.

'He's not here!' exclaimed Mary, leaving the door open and pursuing him down the passage. He reached the kitchen and looked in, it was cluttered with dirty plates and heaps of clothes to be washed, but no one else was there.

'I'll wait.' A statement.

'Not in my house!' she shouted at him. What had that bastard brought down on them now?

Ignoring her, Kirby looked around for a seat, shushed a tabby cat from one of the armchairs and sat down. Mary had been caught off balance again, only this time she responded quicker. 'He doesn't live here! He's gone, four years!' she shouted. 'This is my house and I'll not have a little gobshite like you pushing me about! Get the hell out of it!' Her raving had not moved him at all. He looked at her with what might have been disgust and when he spoke his voice had a extremely cold edge to it.

'If you don't want to lose this house and all you stand up in…get him down here, now!'

The door opened and a policeman came in -fast, filling the room. He gripped both of Kirby's lapels with one hand then yanked him out of the chair and up to his face. The Revenue man had never been so frightened. Between the huge helmet and a bristly, fire-red beard, two eyes, with a hatred that paralysed, bore in to him and he was propelled backwards along the passage. Kirby's hands hung onto the wrist for balance, his feet hardly touching the floor, as Archie Shaw bounced him off one wall and slammed him hard up against the other. Mary was close behind them. 'He nearly pushed me over, Daddy! Barging in here, he wouldn't listen to me, even swore at me, he did, Daddy!' she finished tearfully. Anyone attempting to mistreat the family would behold a fury beyond imagination. Mary knew this well and her crocodile tears fuelled this anger. Little upstart deserved it anyway.

'Never come here again. Never bother my daughter again.' He punctuated every third word by banging Kirby's head against the wall. 'Have I made myself clear?' Kirby nodded like mad. 'Or do you want me to rip your rotten little head off?' Kirby was now shaking his head like mad. The Sergeant opened the street door and marched him faster towards the car. One of the bailiffs, foolhardy man, set one foot on the pavement and tried to get out. Archie's free hand squashed his twisted leg with the car door then released the pressure and snapped his toecap at the chap's shin. The fellow's face contorted in soundless agony and gracefully he sank to the pavement. Kirby's head was still nodding about like a blithering idiot, Archie Shaw yanked open the rear door and threw him in. The driver got out and came sheepishly around to the near-side, helping his colleague back into the car. They drove off at speed, not looking back. Archie took his Princess inside and, as always in times of anguish, made a cup of tea. Mary sat at the kitchen table and looked out into the back yard, towards her mother-in-law's house. He remained standing, leaning on the sink. 'When did he get back anyway?'

It was said in passing and, without looking at her father, she answered in the same flat tone, 'Saturday morning, I think, just turned up here with the usual sauce. I couldn't even look at him, Daddy. All I could do was to run out the back, I was useless. When I think of all that you've done for him, Daddy. Ungrateful swine! I didn't want the money he'd sent; just a note to let the children know he was safe but not one word!'

'He was never any good, girl. He's carrying a lot of money for somebody -and it won't be for anything legal, we both know that. Scotland Yard have asked me, of all people, for information about him.' Mary looked up suddenly. 'It's alright,' he said, 'it's only for information,' then paused and added, 'for the moment anyway.'

'What did he do that was so terrible? You can tell me now; I'm a big girl, Daddy.'

'Don't ask me, Mary. You know I can't say anything. If anybody found out, I'd still be in deep trouble. They had enough evidence to lock him up for years and you and the kids would have had to live with the shame of that. I hate the chancer but I still did what I reckoned was best for the family.' Mary stood up and put her arms around his waist and her head on his chest.

'What would we do without you, Daddy? Will that old tax revenue man cause any more trouble?'

'No, course not! They should ask our permission before they go ferreting around here. We don't co-operate with each other at all. Mind you, I wouldn't want to be in his shoes once they get their choppers in to him, that crowd won't stop until they've devoured his liver and had his kidneys for afters! George came down Saturday to see your mother.'

'The cheek of the bold-faced bastard!' she said, then 'Sorry, Daddy,' as he frowned at her, 'but he'd make a Saint swear, he would.' Archie kissed her on the forehead and said he had work to do but that he would find George and have a little chat with him.

'He won't be bothering you, I promise you that,' he said. 'Bye bye, my darling.'

'See you, Daddy, take care now.'

The car carrying the three revenue men arrived back at Euston Station ten minutes after parting company with the charming Sergeant and apart from groans of pain, no one had spoken during the journey. The driver asked delicately if Kirby would return or did he have any other instructions for them. He was white-faced and got out still shaking but his resolve was as strong as ever.

'Find out what you can and I'll be back next week. Twyford belongs to us.' The passengers flinched as the car door crashed shut.

George had left the square around 8am. Earlier, he had taken a jog up Primrose Hill and was now wearing a dark suit and tie and on a tram to Aldgate. He carried a briefcase containing a lot of papers about nothing in particular -and a thousand pounds in cash. His first stop was Spitalfields Market. This was a wholesale fruit market, similar in size to Covent Garden. George had worked there before and after 'doing his national service' and still had many friends in the trade. These people were gifted with razor sharp brains and a wit to match, so being in their company was to study at the greatest school of life and Twyford could not have wished for a better education for his eldest son. To get into the markets you had to have family already working there and because George had earned a fair reputation as a salesman, Kevin was readily accepted. His job was empties boy, the starting position on the firm from where, given a keen intellect, you can work the stocks for a discreet, little earner.

Twyford passed along aisles full of fruits and vegetables, giving off all manner of pungent aromas. Porters and salesmen called out to him, never too busy for a joke or a quick chat. He'd missed Kevin twice when he called at Mary's, both times the lad had been with his girlfriend, Jackie, but had popped in Sunday evening and they had had quite a reunion. He was nearly a man, with a good head on his shoulders, so George thought it a sound idea to drop in to see his old governor, and it wouldn't do Kevin any harm. He stayed for a cup of tea and a salt beef sandwich with the boss; Kevin wasn't junior enough for such luxuries yet and was sent off to the cafe for them. It was his first visit to Dino's which usually seemed packed with unshorn, noisy roughnecks. He stepped inside the door and jumped to one side as a big, black rat ran out from the kitchens, closely followed by a hefty, sweating and shirtless man in a greasy vest, who he took to be Dino, in hot pursuit with a broom handle. The rat escaped and Dino returned shouting at the breakfasting customers, 'Alright, which one of you bastards brought that rat in here?'

Kevin was so naïve that when the proprietor looked at him, he said, 'I didn't, honest!' Back at the firm he recited the incident and it took him a while to work out why everyone found it funny. Soon George was off, through the back doubles, up Brick Lane, across Bethnal Green Road and into Club Row. He knew the side streets pretty well, yet the deeper he went the more the changing mood of the place got to him and the more he stood out as an intruder, a foreigner. He could sense the hostility. The area was completely Jewish and they had good reason not to trust strangers. It had always been called the Jago, which stands for 'no go' to the inhabitants, and outsiders, especially police, do not venture there. Books had been written about this place. There were two streets leading in, or rather several dark passageways set across with posts but, once inside, the area was bursting full of busy people. He went along Edge Lane to the Boundary estate, this again only had two entrances and no exit if you were not welcome. The estate was made up of many blocks of flats with balconies all facing the main courtyards. Slight men pushed handcarts, trolleys and prams, full of bags and boxes, stout women carried baskets on their hips and children were everywhere, climbing railings or chasing each other in and out of overloaded washing lines; a tough place, where hard working people struggled but survived. Pickpockets, thieves and swindlers never plied their trade in the Jago and were safe there. George admired these folk for their community spirit, no one was ever going to give them something for nothing and they knew it and looked out for one another.

He strolled past several blocks in no hurry and came to Mandalay House where an old school friend lived on the third floor. Climbing the stairs, he suddenly found his path blocked by three surly, young men - then from nowhere three more were behind him. Trapped on a dark stairwell and instantly alarmed, George backed into the corner, took the stance and prepared to defend himself. The silence made the unexpected confrontation all the more menacing. From his circumspect position, he inhaled deeply then watched sharply for the first one to launch the attack. Loud footsteps from above broke the tension and a warm voice rang out with 'Hail, Georgimus.' Six shadows melted away as a short, stocky chap came down and bearhugged him.

'I see security's still not up to much 'round here, Irv.' said George, breathing easier and attempting imperturbability whilst returning the embrace with equal vigour.

Irving Jacobs lived in flat39 and used 38 as his office. A good solicitor by any standard, he once had a city practice, now word of mouth got him more than enough business and he was happier working from home. His brother, Benny, another old Cowperian, shared the office flat. Of a similar height but half the width, he was an accountant and sensibly they passed contacts on to each other; apparently they were a good double act.

George and Irving started in the same class at Central Foundation school, in Cowper Street, and had remained the greatest friends since that first day. Old times immediately came to mind then hyperbole and badinage consumed another pleasurable fifteen minutes until the conversation touched on the property market giving George the opening to outline his plans. The Jacobs were already thinking along similar lines and Irving filled in a lot of gaps for him; property could and should be purchased now. Their idea was to borrow as much as possible and buy to rent out then wait for the house market to rise; there could never be a better time to invest. George explained what he wanted to do for Mickey's house. As an old tenant, the only way he could be evicted legally was for non-payment of rent. This was their weakness and where a case of risk to health must be made. No rent had been paid because the landlord hadn't kept the property to an acceptable standard. George spoke of the repairs that were needed, vermin control and anything that could hit Ruben in the pocket. Irving suggested first bringing a court order against him for not complying with his obligations as a landlord then produce estimates that would prove the house was in need of extensive repair. In these cases, the courts usually came down in favour of the tenant, and spending money on repairs would be totally unacceptable to Ruben, so he would be forced into selling the house cheaply. George needed several safe bank accounts that would stand up to any scrutiny, where large amounts of cash could be deposited and no questions asked. Ben clarified that, to do this legally, the ownership must be in the names of nominees of non-UK residents and this could be arranged. With these opened and the power of authority to run them, the company would have all the finance necessary. Another separate bank account was needed from which George wanted money transferred monthly to South Africa. This was for one of the backers who must receive regular dividends.

'No problem at all,' said Ben, 'the banks roll out the red carpet for anybody with chunks of dough to deposit.'

Irving, in the meantime, would form the company and immediately act against Ruben. It shouldn't take more than a week for a writ to be issued. George went over the final details then much to their surprise handed them a thousand pounds cash to open four accounts with separate banks. Anyone who didn't know them would not believe he could just pass over so much money, but it never crossed his mind; he trusted them implicitly.

CHAPTER 7: UNLUCKY BASTARD, THAT FRENCHMAN!

Kos; After a week of living on locust beans, British survivors of the ill-fated Kos invasion are trying to make their way to the Turkish coast. German infantry forced men of the 1st Battalion Durham light infantry to disperse and doggedly continue to hunt them down!

Following up information on the recent murder in Birmingham, police are interested in talking to a well dressed couple seen wandering into the area where the garrotting took place; among the undisclosed evidence the man was described as conspicuously camp. A police spokesman said, 'We need to eliminate them from our inquiries but, hopefully, this couple may have unknowingly noticed someone or something that may help us further our investigation.'

Twyford arrived at the house in Leybourne Road around four o'clock and most of the others had been there all afternoon. The estimates were already arranged and now it had matured into a street party. A fire was roaring on the bomb debris opposite and the boys were sitting around swapping the old adventures. A milk crate with potatoes wedged all through it was roasting in the middle of the flames and quarts of cider were being passed around; buckets of water were on hand in case the fire warden came calling. Theresa was wrapped up warm and brought out in her wheelchair. Some of the locals sat with her, on boxes and blocks, and listened to the lads recount tales from their past. The stories got better and better. It was great to remember and laugh all over again at some of the mad escapades from scrumping and run outs as kids to impersonating police officers as forty year old kids. The perfect setting, a bruised but undefeated neighbourhood spirit enjoying a get together on a bomb debris, a Spartan banquet of feasting and merriment; a magic night.

After the bonfire, George and Johnny Bass strolled back home, the others had dropped off one by one until just the two of them walked down the Square and sat on the wall outside no. 34. The talk was of how they joined the army. John, George and Mickey had gone rustling near Glasgow. The first World War was on and there was no meat so John dreamed up a plan; drive to Scotland, kill a cow and bring it back - simple. Frank Nash had borrowed a lorry for them out of the Fish yard in Castle Road. With Uncle Bert's old army rifle, four rounds of ammunition and enough diesel money to get there and back, the trio set off for the highlands. An area was selected for it's remoteness where hopefully the gunshots wouldn't be heard. They parked in the dark and entered a field that Mickey had reconnoitred earlier and shot a whopper. They shot it twice, making sure it didn't suffer, nor chase them; but their problems had only just begun. John would not drive the lorry in to the field in case it sunk, so they had to get the carcass to the lorry which was a good 100 yards away. But no matter how hard the three of them struggled, they couldn't lift the beast. After plenty of swearing and cursing, all to no avail, they took the ground sheet from the lorry, laid it flat and managed to roll the slaughtered carcass on to it, then began to drag the sheet towards the lorry. As they neared the fence a flash light came on, followed swiftly by several others. The three sprinted away before the beams could search them out. In their haste George's shin connected with the water trough and he fell, headlong, into deep, smelly mud. Almost submerged, he lay dead still while the other two kept running but the clunk had attracted the torch beams. Scrambling through hedges and over barbed wire fences, they were eventually caught a couple of miles away by the army. It had been their mascot the boys had killed, and a bull to boot.

George had hidden under the trough until the sky began to lighten then crawled to the road to find that the lorry was still there. The squaddies had not bothered to move it, thinking there were only two of them. Climbing in, George drove back the way they came and returned safely to London stinking to high heaven.

John and Mickey were brought up in front of the local beak and been given the option; prison or the army. They'd mistakenly gone for the latter and were allowed just enough time to write a note home before being escorted to the Black Watch Barracks at Perth and signed on straight away.

George found out three days later. The gang were all waiting for their call-up papers anyway so Lestor Hogg, Mornie Quill, Tinker, Kit and George decided one regiment was probably much the same as another and, that very day, bunked on the train from Kings Cross and made their way to Perth. The Jocks were a little mystified as to why five more cockneys came all the way to Scotland to join them but, as the British and French armies had recently lost six hundred and fifteen thousand men, killed, wounded or taken prisoner at the Battle of the Somme, all regiments needed fattening; therefore anyone volunteering was signed up double quick.

The boys were instructed in hand-to-hand combat by some of the most vicious bastards God ever put breath in to. Weapons training included pencils, nails and newspapers. You were never to break a bottle except over your opponent's head, saving the jagged edge for his jugular. After four months they were dispatched to the Western Front and arrived at the Chemin Des Dames to join the armies commanded by General Sir Douglas Hague. That first night General Hague made his one and only speech of the War.

He said, 'With our backs to the wall and believing in the justice of our cause, each one must fight on to the end. The safety of our homes and the freedom of mankind alike depend upon the conduct of each one of us at this critical moment.'

John remembered George's words at the time and reminded him of them.

He had said, 'What, my old mate Justice? Funny, I ain't seen too much of him lately. I wonder, would mankind mind if, at this critical moment, I fucked off while the rest of you fight it out to the end?' It was spouted for bravado but none of them expected to come back. They were classified as A4 boys, which was to do with being under nineteen and therefore technically under age for an active theatre of war. Thousands of eighteen year olds, their basic training scarcely completed, were marched off 'to fight the foreign foe'. The new formations were inducted into the mysteries of trench warfare by spending periods at the front line under the tuition of experienced NCOs.

As the harrowing memories seeped back it recreated the lack of faith, he experienced, in what he was about and, for the life of him, George couldn't work it out. His neighbourhood was St. Pancras, his neighbours St. Pancras poor; what was he doing there, decked out with weapons of death and preparing to kill people he didn't hate on the say-so of someone he didn't know? Only God understands how but he actually won the military medal in that terrible place.

One night they were to go on a furrow raid. These were mounted to snatch prisoners from German trenches on the other side of no-mans land, which was about 250 yards away. This night in particular his unit had been up at the barbed wire waiting to go into the darkness. The officer always led, pistol in hand; George and two jocks made up the patrol. Sergeant Grogan, co-ordinating the snatch, stayed at the front line, sending each man over after a gap of fifteen seconds or so. The Shipton boys had had a bad run in with him when he was a corporal at Perth. Captain Troy who led them came from a military family, but was too gentle for this type of operation and the unit's confidence ebbed somewhat. He was keen to do well though and went over the top on the instant. George was next and terrified but ready. Grogan sent him up too quickly, five seconds or so behind the Captain. He thought it was wrong but the Brass were supposed to know what they were doing. The two of them moved forward, quietly and quickly, almost together. No one else came out of the trench. A minute had passed when suddenly a flare went up, seemingly from the British side: two silhouettes for all to see. They sprinted towards a bomb-crater in the middle of no-man's-land. George could see the dead lying all around the cavity. Captain Troy leapt in first and two gun shots rung out simultaneously. A wounded German had propped himself up against the wall of the crater and fired a second faster. George landed in to see the German's right shoulder explode open and his rifle drop to the floor. There was already a gory stump where a left arm had once been. Spread-eagled in the mud, Twyford peered around and saw the Captain as the ghostly light from the flare began to fail. He was squatting with his knees pulled up and his arms around them, rocking slowly, forward and back. George crawled across and noted the blood leaking out beneath him. He tried gently to shift his knees and find the wound but the Captain's arms were rigid. Twyford wanted to stay and hide but he knew that if he didn't move the Officer straight away, the molecule of courage he had in reserve would desert and fear would root him to the spot. The German was adding to his dread by wailing into the night, pleading for someone to help him. George spoke schoolboy French and German rather well but couldn't think of anything to say then, jerking himself back to the urgency, fiercely pulled the Captain's arms away from his knees.

Troy screamed and Twyford ordered him to listen. 'You're not gonna get me killed so keep your trap shut and hang on 'round my neck. One sound and we're both dead.' Troy's face was screwed up with pain but he did as he was told. George looked back at the German and nodded then slithered out of the crater with the dead weight on his back. After a few yards, a body blocked his way, he crawled over it and it grunted. "How many bits of people are still breathing in this wicked hole," he thought, inching across the land the troops had nicknamed "Death's waiting room". The British line seemed to be hopelessly beyond reach and he was forced to stop each time the Captain's grip loosened. Then Twyford would sink his teeth into Troy's hands to keep him awake, any moment expecting a flare and a bullet.

After an interminable time he neared the wire and friendly

whispers egged him on, 'Come on, son, you can make it!' Arms reached out and pulled Troy from his shoulders and he went back for the German. 'Don't be a mug, son, you've been lucky. Leave it!' And that was when they presumed he was going back for one of their own.

George ran, crouching low, another flare, although in the distance. He dived to the floor and two shots zinged over his head, much too close. Snipers everywhere, waiting for the chance to kill on the third light. Silence, followed by darkness, and more silence, a burst of fire from raw nerves. Bodies were scattered all across the wasteland. Odd shouts and cries piercing the stillness; the Angel of Death had not gone hungry. This must truly be what hell is, yet George crept forward cautiously; the darkness like a blindfold. Feeling his way with each step, long seconds passed until his foot connected with a body and it grunted again. Instantly he knew where he was. Twyford sprinted six yards, jumped and landed in the centre of the crater. The German was still alive, looking at him, now amused and half-smiling, accepting death and waiting for it.

George spoke to him gently, 'Never fear. We go to doctor. Everything good. Trust me.' He loosened the heavy belt around the German's uniform, then threaded his own through it and strapped it back over his head and right shoulder. Surprisingly calm, the fear and panic had left him, yet his senses were heightened. He knew exactly what he was doing and his mind, eyes and ears were sharp, all with the same purpose; it was as if he controlled the night. Twyford rose to his feet, the German felt light, hitched up piggy-back fashion. He peered in the direction of safety. 'Grunt' stood out clearly in the moonlight and he took his bearings from there. Even the clouds were in time with him and obediently covered the moon. George climbed out and walked briskly towards the British line. As he passed 'Grunt' he stooped and gripped his jacket collar dragging him along with them, the man's boots scraping loudly on the rocks. Twyford's progress was made much slower but still no bullets came to snatch his life away. The clouds were remaining faithful.

A challenge. 'Halt, who goes there?'

'A friend.'

'Approach friend and be recognised.' He had reached 'our' barbed wire. He loosened his strap and the German slipped from his back; willing arms whisked him off to the MO. 'Grunt', it appeared, was a Frenchman and all George had to do was drag him a yard or so, across the barbed wire, and it would be over. Then a wave of exhaustion came upon him, the moon suddenly appeared, shots broke the silence and Twyford dived head first in to the trench. Two bullets thudded into 'Grunt' as he was dragged in, one struck the sole of his foot and the other up his arse - unlucky bastard, that Frenchman.

It begins like a joke, but the Englishman, the Frenchman and the German all survived that night. Captain Troy still carries the bullet with him; it lodged itself in his lumber region and was too dangerous to remove. His guts were pushed back in, sewn up and apart from having to use a walking stick, he suffers very little. The German was on the danger list for four weeks through losing so much blood. The shoulder was patched up and mended well. Most of his arm was left somewhere in no-man's-land but the army surgeon cut off a bit more to save it from gangrene.

The Frenchman had a total of three operations and was left with only one lung, but his arse and his foot had the bullets removed and healed well. Two months later Twyford was told to report to his platoon commander who informed him that he was to be awarded the military medal for gallantry. George posed a question, "Would he still be receiving this had it been a private he rescued and not an officer?" but the words stuck in his throat. Still, he did it, he had earned it and he was bloody proud of it; thinking about that he must ask Mum if she's still kept it safe.

'I have nightmares about the Great War, you know?' said John, in an unusually pensive mood. 'We were lucky to all come out of that.'

'Yeah,' said George, 'so much death, it makes you want to savour every minute, fill every second.'

'And we will!' said John, lighter.

'Yeah. See you tomorrow,' then for some strange reason they shook hands.

Just before he fell asleep, George thought about his two youngest. They'd have enjoyed it around the bonfire, the socialising only lasted for a couple of hours but it had been fun. He would have to talk to Mary civilly, persuade her to let the children spend more time with him. Prepare carefully for it and not let their animosity for each other rub off on the kids.

CHAPTER 8: A MOMENT OF VICTORY, A FLATTENED TRILBY.

Kos: The SS have shot 90 Italian Officers for collaboration.

Tuesday morning, George woke early but could not face a run; it was miserably drizzly and gusty. He tidied his paperwork, put the estimates in a folder ready for Irving then washed, shaved, applied a dab of Brylcream and combed his hair; it took time to get it just right. He meticulously 'threw on' a blue shirt, undone at the neck, brown corduroys and brogues, protected by a long, navy raincoat coordinated with a new Trilby; he especially didn't want to get his hair wet. George meant to look good and rub her nose in it. He went the long way round and at a quarter to eight tapped once on the door. Mary should just be dishing up the children's breakfast and was bound to be looking a right state. This way she'd be embarrassed and would probably agree to anything to get rid of him; a good plan.

She opened the door and again Twyford's smile saved him, it covered any trace of his horror; she was beautiful. Mary had been about to go out and wore a pigeon-grey fitted coat tied with a shiny black leather belt, heels to match adding four inches to her height and an elegant black, deer stalker hat, tilted at just the right angle. Her eyes shone, her teeth flashed white and her lips were so full and red, he wanted to kiss them.

'Sorry,' he said, 'if you're going out I can come back. I hoped we could talk for a few minutes.'

'No, come in.' she said, like a cobra tempting a rabbit.

He went through to the kitchen. No girls but thank heavens Alan was sitting there reading an old comic. As George came in he threw it across the room and ran to his Dad. Twyford, forgetting himself, tossed off his hat and grabbed him up. There can be no better feeling on this earth than loving a son who loves you equally as much. Four long years he had missed this. Never, never again, he swore to himself.

Mary watched George's broad back and Alan's beaming face over his shoulder, squeezing his Dad's neck as hard as he could, and waited patiently for them to remember she was there.

When Twyford put him down, she told Alan to get his coat and pop over to Nanna's in case there were some errands to run before he went to school. 'There's a good boy.' Alan, happy as ever, grabbed his coat, kissed them both and ran out the back door.

George felt deserted, trapped. What could he say? She was going to eat him alive.

'I only wanted a minute to talk about the kids.'

'Four years go by and not a word and now you're prepared to give them a minute.'

He was right; she was going to devour him.

'No, I meant longer but...'

'Oh so kind!' she spat. Wrong tack.

'I was hoping to spend a bit more time with them, take them out and…'

'You came back a day and they went mad. They expected you Sunday morning but you did another vanishing act. They looked for you at their Nanny's but you weren't there, either.' Her voice was slowly rising. 'How could you do it to them again? You're rubbish!'

'Yeah? Well, that's just your opinion. Been drumming it in to them have you? Putting the poison in? Well I'm their father and I've got my rights!' he shouted back, plunging in to a row he knew he should not be having.

'There's more to being a father than sending conscience money.'

'I didn't see you sending any of it back, you money-grabbing old cow!'

'You bastard! You never once wrote to them.'

'What? So you could sling my letters on the fire? Remember, I know what a nasty mare you are!'

She was starting to look dangerous. 'Don't call me names!' she yelled, then grabbed a half-eaten bowl of porridge and threw it at his head. He tried to duck but the cunning prat had thrown it fast and low. It ricocheted off his temple and smashed into the wall. She grabbed the bread knife and he bolted for the back door. She lunged, but he moved quicker and was out into the garden and gone. Knowing she could not chase after him in those heels, he slowed down before reaching his mother's house and walked in casually. His Mum was in the outside loo hanging the old newspapers again, (perhaps the toilet roll *was* only for visitors), so he slipped into the scullery to inspect his head. The china bowl had broken the skin and a purple lump was already beginning to protrude from his forehead.

"I should have read the signs," he thought, "stupid of me." He had only made matters a thousand times worse.

Taking her coat off, Mary delighted in her moment of victory. She had actually won a battle. Mary could never forgive him for what he'd done and he had a lot more coming. She would make him suffer only for as long as her body breathed. She too had risen early that morning and had prepared herself to have a few things out with him. Mary had actually been on her way around to see George when he'd knocked. "What good fortune," she thought, and stamped on his hat.

Twyford caught the trolleybus to Old Street, another along Great Eastern Street and walked back towards the Jago. On arrival it was no surprise to find Ben pouring him out a cup of 'cha. He pulled up a chair and said, 'You'll have to tell me one day, how you know I'm coming.'

'One day.' said Ben, looking at Twyford's head.

'What do you keep smirking at?' asked George. Ben answered with another question.

'Why've you got bits of porridge in your hair?'

'Oh God don't! I thought it was my bruise people were staring at.' he said, and checked himself in the mirror. A comb whipped through his hair and after flicking bits of stodge from its teeth, he enquired, 'Anyway, how we doing?'

'It's all prepared.' announced Irving, entering the room with a pile of papers, 'We apply for the court order today on health grounds then someone must serve it into his hands, preferably in front of witnesses.'

'I can't wait,' said George, 'this'll make him sit up. No one's ever had the money or the pluck to try this before.'

Irving cautioned, 'Benson's no fool, if he puts you in hospital no one's gonna try again so do watch yourself!'

'This'll teach him that he can't shit all over people. He's only knows the heavy treatment, he's a landlord who still thinks like a debt collector.' then added, 'Oh, with any luck, there'll be some more deserving cases come Friday. I'm seeing Mr Benson on Thursday, I'll be sure to make an appointment and then let you know his reaction.'

'Go steady,' said Irving, shaking hands, 'this ain't a game.'

George replied, ' Most people have had a shocking war, but not him; now its his shock, like a bolt of lightning right up his nostrils till the sparks blow out of his arse!

Wednesday morning was still drizzling but it was imperative to run. It had become an addiction and Twyford knew he'd have been annoyed with himself had he not gone. Hampstead seemed more inviting and he found that having stepped out and greeted the day, once the street door shut behind him, he was happy. George ran easily up St Leonard's, went past Mickey's Mum's house in three paces and again an hour and a half later when he returned. There was a police car down the bottom. Twyford checked his speed and doubled back up Ada Butler's path. Mick's Mum kept an open house for everyone and welcomed him kindly.

'Smell the brew did you, or don't you want to see your in-laws?' she said, laughing.

'It's him, is it?' asked George, making himself comfy.

'Yeah. I saw them drive down. Handsome man you know.'

'Who, him? He's a caveman!'

'If I was ten years younger, I'd show him the time of his life!'

'Leave off, Ada!' laughed George, 'I'll tell the old man.'

Ada reckoned up, 'He must be about fifty four 'cos how old's Mary now?'

'Thirty four.'

'That's right; she would have been eighteen when she had Kevin.'

'Yeah, the little cow told me she was twenty three. She got me in so much trouble.'

'George, this is me you're talking to. That was one thing you and Michael didn't need any help with! God knows where the two of you would have finished up if you hadn't married good women.'

Twyford sipped his tea and pondered on Mary. She was so pretty when she was younger. "Mind you, she didn't look too bad yesterday," he reasoned, grudgingly. "She hates me, ME! The cheeky bastard! But it couldn't be anywhere near as much as my loathing for her!" No one knew why he left or that Mary had given her father a photograph of himself and Mickey which Archie showed to the eye-witnesses. That was all the evidence the police needed. She betrayed him; he could never forgive her for that.

'Mick's alright,' he said, making a joke of it, 'he never married a witch!'

'Mickey told us he'd seen you,' George nodded, sipping more tea, 'said how you're helping him. Thanks, Georgie. If ever we can…'

'Shut up, Ada! I'm embarrassed now, you're making me blush. It ain't just me. We'll sort it out together, all of us.' With that he stood up and swallowed the last mouthful of tea grouts, making her pull a face. 'Let's see what joyous tidings await!' he said and, planting a peck on her cheek, bowled out affecting more confidence than he felt. With fortuitous timing the police car had gone and he jogged down to his Mum's house.

'Archie's been round,' said Min, 'handsome brute.'

'Oh don't you start, Mum!'

'He said he's sorry he missed you and could you pop round for a chat. Here, maybe he's got some work for you.'

'Mum, the only position he'd have for me would be in a landfill site, starting at the bottom.

Twyford had time to kill so he readied himself and dropped in on the Butlers, just to run over everything. On Thursday morning Mickey was to take Theresa off to a relation's house in Hertfordshire. George would be there to meet the rent collector and would appear to be painting the kitchen, in case it went wrong. That finalised and having no other plans, for the writ was not available to collect from Irving until after four o'clock, he wandered towards Primrose Hill.

A robbery was planned on certain, fully ladened, Post Office goods lorries regularly parked overnight at the Royal Mail Parcel depot in KentishTown. The unique Asset had yet to be amiss with his information so the Police committed time and effort in setting up an observation post in one of the big houses close by to view the entrance gates, which were locked securely each night between 10pm and 4am. High perimeter fences and a night watchman provided further security and, with only one way in and out, the Police now had little to do but wait. Several nights passed without incident then, at 1am on the fourth night, a cyclist peddled slowly along the road and put those watching on alert by peering around, a fraction too much, as he neared the gates. A short while later a van pulled outside, a one-note whistle was barely heard, the gates opened and the vehicle passed inside. It remained quiet for another twenty minutes then the gates reopened and the van leisurely drove out. Two black Mariahs screeched across their path and uniformed officers swarmed out of the fenced gardens opposite. All the van's doors flew open at once as two men jumped from the front with three more bursting out of the back; and these men were not going quietly! Largely outnumbered but panic-stricken to escape, they sprang at the officers and engaged them in a frenzied affray; madly swinging spanners and kicking out with intensity. The battle was barbarous, brutal and brief. Truncheons matched their anger and smashed them to their knees where hobnailed boots finished the job.

Even after the beatings, one thief struggled still; he was stripped of shoes and socks then dragged separately to the second Mariah. In an outside toilet, the Police discovered an old night watchman who was bound and gagged and bleeding excessively from a head wound. He was untied and also taken into custody as a possible accomplice. Sergeant Shaw would interrogate each one personally and his methods seldom failed to uncover the truth.

Once again the Asset had produced a fine coup and now it was Archie Shaw's turn to go to work. The prisoners were lawbreakers of the most abhorrent kind; they had used violence AND used it without thought or regret. Even worse, they had struck Officers of the Law and now they would learn. The gang members were isolated to the basement and secured in barely lit cells for individual attention and the miscreant, previously without footwear, was in the middle one. The inmate had had 12 hours to consider his plight and the more sensible ones usually understood what was required of them very quickly. But, after being torpedoed and rescued twice in twelve hours in the mid Atlantic, this Ordinary Royal Naval seaman had eventually been safely returned to Portsmouth and changed his life's course by deserting the moment he was given leave. He had been on the run for five months and had led a band of successful thieves for most of that time. With the rope as his probable sentence, escape at any risk was his only option

Archie Shaw would have a full confession and the names of everyone involved; how long it took was up to the detainees. With no particular malice, Sergeant Shaw entered the middle cell and left the door open; the prisoner was leaning against the wall with his head down and didn't look up. Archie began to state what was to happen when the man leapt at him and snapped out a trained kick at the Sergeant's testicles. Possibly faster than the eye could see, Archie's hands came from behind his back and caught the instep, inches from it's target, then in one movement, squeezed and twisted upwards spinning him over onto his front. Baring his teeth in a hideous snarl, Archie stood on the man's left foot while firmly gripping the right, chest high, then in a wishbone effect twisted the ankle sharply to an unsettling crack. With further twisting the grating chords of intense pain that pierced the silence spurred those in the proximity to the path of cooperation. Presumably, the sergeant's wish came true!

CHAPTER 9: INTERLUDE

Rangoon, Burma: Japan has laid a railway line from Bankok to Burma. The single track, which crosses mountains and jungle along the river Kwai Noi valley, was built by 200,000 Asians and 69,000 Allied P.O.Ws. 100,000 Asians and 16,000 P.O.Ws died in the process!

Radna's apartment overlooked Regents Park and he decided to call on the off chance. "What do night-club singers do in the afternoon?" His mind conjured up fantasies, spurring him on, "What fools we are for a sniff and a promise." Before he knew it he found himself scaling the front steps and asking at reception if she was in. The desk porter shrugged and suggested George went up and knocked. What the fuck was his job anyway? He gave the porter a pitiful look and went to see. The lady opened the door and flung her arms around his neck, kissing him long and sweet; his response lasted to lockjaw. George was still in the corridor and she dragged him in, peeled off his jacket, threw him in the armchair then laced herself across his lap. She seemed rather pleased to see him. Now that was how men should be greeted.

Normally sharp on the uptake, he attempted to indulge further straight away; nothing like rushing to show real finesse. She bit his ear hard to stop the wandering hands and made him tell her what he had been doing. The maid had pined for her gentleman and bet he had not missed her at all. She hadn't crossed his mind until today, he lied. He was passing and looked in on the off chance then, feigning a parched throat, informed her of her failings as a hostess and hung his tongue out for a scotch and soda. Radna poured one very large measure and sat on his lap, feeding him sips, describing how boring life was and what a good girl she'd been. They talked all afternoon. George shared his hopes and schemes and she listened intently. More than Mary would have done, he thought at the time, only then remembering his meeting with Irving. Twyford explained his imperative departure and, on the spur of the moment, asked if she might like to go with him. George described it as dangerous and she jumped at it. Sadly, the excursion was a failure. She met the Jacobs briefly but Radna had not liked the Jago and wanted to leave quickly. He thought to show off a little with his rough connections but she was understandably frightened. Coming back on the tube, Radna was ceaseless with her apologies and suggested having the night in to create something special. George didn't think she meant food and readily accepted, but he needed an hour to alter some arrangements and would return at eight o'clock.

What was he doing? He had promised to take Alan to the pictures with Owen and his son. A cowboy film was showing at the Forum and the youngsters were looking forward to it. He swore to Alan that he would make it up to him and left him at the Esterbrook's house. Downright envious, Owen volunteered to take both boys and would see Alan home safely. George dashed indoors, washed, changed and didn't get back to Radna until eight thirty; she never said a word. It was so refreshing to find a woman who did not moan and sulk if you were late, just accepted that was how you were. Over dinner they spoke more of his plans for the future. Radna wholeheartedly agreed with his intentions, saying that what was right and wrong differed with circumstances. She had contacts, certain business people who might be in a position to put a lot of work his way. She could not expand on what they did exactly but felt it could be very useful to him. George topped up the wine glasses and they moved to the sofa. Some romantic band music and the outside world was forgotten. Radna began easing her clothes off very slowly, 'Concentrate on me,' she ordered in a whisper. He obeyed her with eyes and mind that became captives to her anatomy as she revealed parts of her flesh he had yet to see. By candlelight, she posed before him in a flimsy see-through slip and eased first one strap then the other from her shoulders, allowing the garment to fall to the floor. Spellbound by the bra, panties, dark stockings and suspenders, George tugged at his shirt buttons. The suspenders stepped further away. Two yards apart and his shirt was off. She focused hungrily on his chest and wet her lips, the look and the tongue did their work. Radna spoke endearments in French, urging him to watch what she did. Closing her eyes, her hands moved up her body to her breasts. She shuddered as one slid inside the bra and caressed herself. Her fingers explored lower, down past her navel and inside the panties, while her face revealed the gratification.

'Come pleasure me.' He came closer and they brushed lips. 'On your knees.'

He obeyed and knelt in front of her, kissing her body as he watched on. She stood above him, magnificent. 'Tell me what to do. Order me.' he said in French.

She took him beyond by restraint, instructing, 'Kiss me where I touch.' His mouth followed her fingers. 'Wait. Here. Stop. Now here. Wait.' She was sending George mad. Their coupling began soft and gradual on the deep carpet, 'Be gentle. Slowly! Pause!' The suspense from each 'hold' sent shock waves through him. Seconds stretched to lifetimes then to boost his tension even more, little by little, she disengaged and gracefully rolled onto her front to change position by lifting her hind quarters and permitting him re-entry. With admirable control he eased his penis into place then, indulging himself in the performance, waited for further instruction. She backed onto him forcing him deeper, 'Be still, just feel my rhythm.' He thrilled to the role she played and his own subjugation so much so that the madness became all engulfing then lastly, in the bedroom, he was made to strive for the release. Finally on the brink, her appetite was primed and she cried out lasciviously for him to punish her. They fucked with a momentum that increased with every moan, accelerated with every sigh. Using steaming words, she whispered her carnal desires, fantasies that drew such lust and took him to paramount power until, like a cannonade, all his seed was ridden out and they collapsed, gloriously exhausted.

Twyford awoke around two a.m., her body snuggled warmly against him. He was so relaxed and comfortable, rising from that bed and going out into the freezing night was one of the hardest things he had ever done. George got home before three and managed a few hours sleep; there was a very busy day in front of him.

CHAPTER 10: CONVERSATIONS WITH A CAT

Penicillin becomes a wonder drug for casualties of war. Discovered in 1928 by accident by Scottish scientist, Alexander Fleming, its crucial healing ingredient was only isolated in 1940 and is now being given to 1000s of war casualties to control blood poisoning from infected wounds.

The Birmingham police had their work cut out. In life, the murder victim was known to have been a tricky piece of work and, at one time or another, had cheated many of the local footpads and thieves so the list of suspects was a very long one. Added to that, two plainclothes officers from a 'never before heard of' department arrived one morning and withdrew the evidence box. Then, for no apparent reason, the daily newspapers were forbidden to print any further details of the story.

The next morning George arrived at Irving's for 8am, collected what he needed and was back to the Butler residence by nine o'clock. Mickey left with Theresa shortly afterwards; the kids were all at school. George donned white overalls, white peak cap and waited. The collectors usually arrived around ten. He would get out of the car at one end of the street and stop at each house for the rent, pushing his way into any of them that were behind as a warning. The car crawled along near him, but the driver seldom got out, just loitered for a few minutes here, a couple there; he was for show. They never had a problem, people were too frightened. The 'fieldsman' came to Mickey's and, instead of knocking, kicked the door with his heel. Sipping a piping hot cup of tea, George cheerily opened the door and saw the man was bigger and wider than he had anticipated. Discounting any defiance from Twyford, Max Kendall stormed straight past. 'Where are they?' he demanded.

'Gone out; I'm their decorator, can I help?'

'Where's my money?' He bellowed aggressively, and swept ornaments from the mantelpiece in his search.

'Is this what you're after?' Maxy turned to receive a faceful of scalding tea, blinding him momentarily then a knee, with terrific force, found his balls. The collector doubled over, eyes bulging in an effort to focus, hands automatically protecting his testicles. Witless now, his ears were gripped and a knee smashed into his face, crunching the nose bone. Either blow would fell a normal man but Maxy possessed immense strength and though George tried to force his head down the brute locked his arms around Twyford's right leg and began to rise. Maxy Kendall's bulk lifted George like a babe-in-arms. In shock and going more off balance each second, Twyford yanked and twisted Max's ears to howling pitch then pirouetted to transfer the weight, stamping his right leg down whilst bringing his left knee up into the same target and following through. Kendall's head shot up, his nose exploded with blood and gore reaching opposing walls and he went over backwards. Maxy's crown smashed against the kitchen table and the body slumped to the floor. George was not a vicious man but this was an animal and, unless dealt with there and now, could prowl back another day and hurt Theresa or the family. The "behemoth" was out cold and a thorough body search revealed a knuckle-duster in one pocket, a bulging wallet in another and tucked down the rear of his trousers was a spring-loaded cosh. Twyford slipped the duster on, claimed the cash and hid the cosh in his waistband. Looking through the front window, the Austin was parked two doors away. George stepped out, walked around the back of the car and along the off-side. The driver was looking to the front and hadn't noticed him. Twyford threw open the door and punched him on the side of the head then, before the man could respond, grabbed his hair, jerked him out of the car and struck him twice with the cosh. The swift beating had slaughtered any gameness he may have had. George left him laying in the road and went back inside to where the other was still unconscious. Twyford wedged an arm between the floor and the wall and stamped down; it snapped in a loud pop. Maxy came to life with a scream and passed out completely. Believing in symmetry, George considered doing the same to the other then deciding against, with difficulty, heaved him up in a fireman's lift and tottered out to the car. He opened the boot and, with very little grace, tossed him in. A crowd of locals soon gathered, some on the other side of the street and the nosier ones, (mainly the old dears) who had had a bellyful of Maxy's behaviour, came right up close. George took no notice, even obliged them with the occasional smile while he carried on with his work. Methodically, he went through the driver's pockets as he lay groaning. The man looked to have no weapons but a white handkerchief flowing with elan from the top pocket of his jacket advised of an open razor; nasty. George spoke to the nearest woman, 'What's this one like then, alright?'

'Yeah, comes over as a bit sly but not too bad,' said one neighbour.

'He ain't never been that good, neither!' said another. 'He sat there and watched him,' pointing to Maxy Kendall in the boot, 'knock my Ron right over. He's sixty nine Ron is, and that one never lifted a finger!' It was turning in to a debate. George needed him to deliver a message so, instead of wedging him with Kendall, flung him across the back seat.

'Do me a favour girls, fetch us your rubbish. The dustman's come early!'

Half a dozen neighbours enjoyed the audience participation and were back in no time with boxes and shovels full of garbage. One of them dragged out her dustbin which George lifted on to his shoulder and also tipped in to join Maxy. It reeked. Twyford shut the boot and took the car to collect Mickey's sisters, then went to keep his appointment with Ruben.

The injured driver had raised himself to a half-sitting position and, after bleating about the pain he was in, asked George why. 'I can understand that Maxy got it, he was a bully, but what have I done?'

Twyford was amazed that he actually didn't know. 'Because you were there, many times, when he threatened a woman in a wheelchair, and you, gutless turd that you are, did nothing about it; that makes you as guilty as he is. I ain't hurt you, not really. I've left you with the powers of movement and speech cos I want you to circulate and enunciate.' The driver, known as Nobby (reputedly to do with the amplitude of his penis), looking puzzled. George suggested nicely, 'Shall I elucidate further? Okay then.' And with that his tone changed, 'Tell all your pals that anyone who attempts to take reprisals against my people will regret it for the rest of their natural. Benson might pay well but there ain't enough money in the Bank of England to compensate you for what'll occur! Have you got that?!' Nobby felt the menace and submissively muttered his clear understanding.

Doris and Margot were Mickey's older sisters and came to deliver written complaints on their own homes, also to witness Ruben receiving the writ. Always in good humour the girls jumped in the car, front and back. With a glance at the driver's face, Doris said, 'One lump or two?' and they both burst out laughing. This pair did not care a tittle –or a whit!

The appointment had been made in the name of St Pancras Properties. Twyford parked the Austin outside Ruben's offices and ordered the driver, who the girls had renamed 'Knobbly', to remain in the car and not move. The timing of their arrival should be perfect for through Fintan he knew that none of the fieldsmen returned until after 2pm on a Thursday. Fintan himself would be at the bank collecting the payroll so, apart from four clerks and a typist, Ruben would be alone. Before he left Mickey's, George had lost his bloody overalls and changed in to a dark suit. Now the epitome of a smart estate agent, he presented himself at the outer office and waited patiently in reception. A ledger clerk, who was too senior to involve himself in such trivial matters, grudgingly came across to enquire of Twyford's business. George mentioned his appointment and he and the ladies were shown upstairs and into the private office. Ruben Benson was sitting at a highly polished desk full of papers and importance and gushed forward with professional warmth, to shake hands, not yet recognising George. Twyford slapped the folded summons into his outstretched palm and stepped back. The clerk guessed what it was and cowered. Realisation dawned quickly and Ruben thundered out, 'Who the fuck are you?' and tried to shove the paper back at him.

'That's a writ, you're in the shit!' said Doris in sheer delight.

'Let me introduce myself'.' said George, taking the initiative. 'My company represents some of your unhappy tenants and that's a writ. Until now you have put needy people into dilapidated properties and forced them to pay exorbitant rents.' Everything was spoken simply and with a smile. 'Anyone who complained was intimidated and anyone who refused to pay was assaulted.'

Ruben yelled for his staff, 'Get some fucking boys up here, now!'

The clerk informed him, 'Maxy and Nobby are parked along the road.'

'Ha!' said Ruben. 'We'll see about this,' and ran from the office, down the stairs and outside the main doors. He waved his arms hurriedly, calling them over. George had followed him down and gripping Ruben's elbow firmly, escorted him to the car. Benson looked in the back and saw Nobby who peered out at him, raised his arms hopelessly then shook his head. Twyford opened the boot and there embedded and reposed among the cabbage and tin cans was Maxy , his nose mashed to a pulp and his face a complete bloody mess. Ruben was suddenly afraid, nothing like this had ever happened before. "Be calm," he told himself. "Money can sort this out, it's not worth getting hurt for," then became annoyed with himself for thinking that way; evidently the good life was having a bad effect.

George accompanied Benson, who now was faintly out of kilter, to his office where the girls had made themselves comfortable. They had discovered Ruben's cigar box, extracted two large Havanas and were in the process of using his desk lighter.

He sat Ruben down and towered over him, a threatening finger floated just in front of his eyes. 'You sent that filth to frighten two friends of mine at 11 Leybourne Road.' Ruben didn't answer. 'Do you know the Butlers?' George began calmly.

'Yes, but business…'

'Did you know that Mr Butler has lost his business?' The voice louder.

'Yeah, well…'

'And did you know Mrs Butler has chronic Multiple Sclerosis and is now completely handicapped and bed-ridden?' Ruben's eyes widened but passed no comment. 'Did you?' Screamed George. If ever there was a time to say nothing, this was it. Benson's silence brought a calmness to George. 'You, Ruben, are a dog! That girl's so ill and yet you instructed this filth that if they didn't get all the money, Mr Butler was to be hurt badly, to take anything of value and then throw the family out on the street. Now I ask you, is that nice? Are we being neighbourly? It's obvious you've seen the error of your ways and feel the need to pay all that money back to your deserving tenants, and we're the boys to help you do it. We're stronger than you can ever begin to believe and we'll drag you into court for every case where it can be proven that you're guilty of neglect. I'll have them backed up with surveyors' reports and builders' estimates; we'll also have witness statements of harassment and intimidation. You, Ruben are snookered, fucked, its checkmate. Now, you think long and hard, pay for all the advice you can buy and when you want to talk further, I'll be at the Spaniard's Inn, Tuesday night at eight o'clock. Don't be late. Ladies, we should be off, we've taken up enough of Mr Benson's valuable time as it is.' George and the girls got to the door, Ruben, in the meantime, may have been prudent with his courage but his brain was doing somersaults trying to land his grey cells sure-footed as to where he knew George from; in desperation he made a stab at it.

'I remember you, now. You're with that crowd of ponces from the Elephant.' hoping for some feedback and sure now that Twyford meant him no bodily harm.

'Ten out of ten,' said George, 'and it's their concern for your well being that makes them want to come over this side and share so much with you. Oh another point, if any of your pets come looking for me, or anyone remotely connected with me, we'll pay a visit to 101 Frogmore and you won't want us coming on your knocker.' Benson was aghast at the mention of his address; that was a very, closely guarded secret. Twyford salaamed and left Ruben with his best smile.

Fintan McMahon arrived back shortly after all the excitement. The clerks were full of it and Fintan showed great interest as they embellished the story. He went to find Ruben, who was pacing up and down his office, stopping every few yards and talking to the Craven A building across the road, 'I hate dealing with the public, ungrateful bastards!' Then off he went again, wearing out the shag pile. Fintan stood and waited. 'Why ain't I got you and a nice government contract?'

'You talking to me, boss?'

'No! To them fucking cats!' There, outside the building opposite, sat two enormous statues of black cats and Ruben had actually moved in to these offices so he would be the first to see the 'For Sale' sign, if ever the property went up for auction. 'We've had fucking murders here! I've been threatened and not one pair of arms to help me. Where were you all? He slapped me a writ!'

'Have you been hurt, boss?' asked Fintan, concerned.

'No, but I could have been!'

Fintan visibly relaxed. He had given all the times and movements needed for George to be in and out and was quite impressed with the way Twyford had dealt with the fieldsmen; Nobby was no mug and Maxy had been a bare knuckle fighter. The worry now was to ensure no one put George and himself together.

'Right. I want everyone in this office the minute they're back. I've rung Sonny Green and told him you'd pick him up in the next half hour; that fucking solicitor can start earning his retainer! I'll see you back here in an hour.' Ruben was a perspicacious and powerful man; he would react like lightning against anyone who dared attack his business. The next few weeks would be interesting.

Twyford and the girls disappeared down Mornington Crescent station and departed in different directions. Pleased with himself, George's route took him to Irving's where he relayed everything that had happened and brother Ben made notes. Step one had been to catch Ruben completely unaware and to weaken his 'neck lock' of intimidation. It had been successful, but how would Benson respond? Probably with violence, if he knew exactly who to direct it at. He had no scruples about hurting women, therefore the girls might get a visit, but that would leave Frognal open to repercussions so they agreed Ruben would act with caution unless he could secure Twyford.

'It's best I keep out of the way until Tuesday night.' remarked George. 'If you need me urgently, some of the lads will be taking up residence at Mickey's house all weekend.

The Butlers were staying out past Barnet with Theresa's mother. In the meantime, Gerry Nolan, Dan Curry, Johnny Bass and Lestor Hogg were going to strip the family residence down to the bare bones. Photos would be taken in its dilapidated state and then, hopefully, one of Ruben's men would visit and report back to him. There was also the worry that he could send in the heavy squad.

Friday passed soberly and, still nervous of impending aggravation, the four boys rose early that Saturday morning. They had already stripped the walls the day before and were in the process of ripping up the old floorboards and some of the beams in the attic. The house was as bad as it was ever going to look when there came a knock. The builders armed themselves and Gerry opened the door. Ruben stood there with Fintan, nice as pie, and asked politely if he might come in. He explained that such was the nature of the complaint he had received from the Butlers that he thought it better to come himself. Ruben seldom ventured into any of the houses he owned, they were commercial propositions and were bought on the advice of accountants. He was dressed smartly casual and moved with care, past Nolan, through the passage, hopping from beam to beam into the kitchen. Fintan waited at the door and slipped a note across which Gerry pocketed then followed Ruben through, explaining the deplorable conditions. Benson listened, sympathetically nodding his head in agreement. It was a two storey house and from a point in the kitchen you could see through the rotting floorboards and missing roof tiles to the sky. Even he hadn't imagined it would be this bad and, needing no further inspection, he thanked the workmen for their time and left. The boys didn't know what to make of that, until they read Fintan's note. Ruben didn't speak all the way home, just sat in the back wondering how much of his property was that neglected. The Craven A building was moving further out of reach.

CHAPTER 11: A STRUMPET AND A CLOD.

Aegean: The destroyer, HMS Eclipse, is sunk by a mine and a German glider bomb sinks the British destroyer, Dulverton, off Kos.

That afternoon George had called at Mary's and collected his sons. They came straight out. He was taking the boys to see the local derby between Arsenal and Spurs, and both proudly wore their red and white scarves. They walked to the top of the street and didn't notice the car parked on the other side of the road. It drove passed them slowly while they meandered to the Mother Shipton pub and boarded a charabanc outside. The revenue men had taken some good photos of the man they took to be George Twyford. It was a reasonable assumption that the coach would return with the same passengers around six o'clock, when they could pursue their quarry to his lair.

The Twyford menfolk arrived back and partook of fish and chips, then walked home demolishing it. George saw them to the house. Mary let the boys in and, as he tried to speak, shut the door in his face. He threw the screwed up remains of his vinegar-soaked newspaper at the knocker and stormed off.

Jimmy Hughes stood in his doorway in Malden Road and watched George fume by and then noticed two men walking together. Uncertain what to do next, Twyford dallied on the corner of St Leonard's. The strangers stopped. They separated and one crossed the road. Deciding on a piece of rock salmon for his mother, George walked beyond the square and aimed at the fish shop. The men were following on either side of the road; Jimmy slipped on an overcoat and went in the same direction. On a Saturday night there was always a good queue at Gowan's and Twyford was on the tail when he got there.

'Hallo, Georgie-boy,'

'Hallo, Jim.' said George, brightening. 'How've you been?'

They talked about Oswald Mosley's surprising release from Holloway prison and when Twyford said farewell, Jimmy whispered, 'You've got company, son; two geezers, one on either side of the road.' George said nothing and stepped out in to the cold, dark night. Leading them away from home, he turned left down Prince of Wales Road and ambled along for ten minutes then darted right into the mews leading to Castle Road. Unless you knew your way through the railway arches, it appeared to be a blocked turning. He came out quickly, crossed Castle Road and hid in the wood yard opposite. Within minutes the men had regrouped and were conferring hurriedly, not five yards from where George had concealed himself.

One was cursing and warned, 'If he's clocked us, Kirby'll have our balls.' Then with one last look the strangers returned the way they'd come and this time it was Twyford's turn to follow. Their car had been left in Marsden Street and George took the number when the lights came on, then watched them drive off. He understood they must know Mary's address but who were they and who the fuck was Kirby? Another admirer perhaps, his fan club was expanding.

The street lights were mostly out and while ensuring his homeward wend was next to invisible, Twyford considered acquiring an apartment like Radna's with a nice view over the park. He had the money to do it and his relocation would safeguard his mother if a 'stroke' backfired.

It was Saturday night, all the chaps would be out in the company of their good ladies and it may be the only time the Butler residence would be empty. The bits of decent furniture were lodging with close neighbours and the grand old Duke of York with all his men could not have made it any worse than at that moment.

George left 16 St Leonards about an hour later; he was feeling the cold more and more. The better suits he owned were the height of South African fashion and, though light and bright, were very thin; Cape Town was twenty degrees warmer than London in November. Nevertheless, he still refused to wear a vest …just in case. Pushing both doors open he bowled into the Malden to find Mornie holding their usual corner of the bar with Gerry Nolan. Genial host, Horace, was nowhere to be seen and the barmaids were straightening chairs or polishing glasses, preparing for the rush. The bar flap was open and Rose was bending over, bottling up the shelves. George slipped behind her, his cold hands gripped her thrupennies and his mid-section began a repetitive motion on her rear end.

Rose shrieked, she had the dirtiest laugh, and pushed her bum backwards into him, yelling out, 'He's only being serious! Either that or there's a bottle of stout in his pocket!?'

'That's enough,' said George, stepping away to applause from the barmaids. 'I feel a headache coming on.' And being the only one flush with money took a jug from under the bar and loaded two fivers in it to stretch the whip until he disappeared a little later. The pub began to fill and the three piece band was warming up the punters with, "It's a long way to Tipperary." On cue, Fintan and Bridgid made a surprise entrance.

'See?' said George, pleased to greet them. 'See what happens, one fiddle plays and these bleedin' Micks spring up out the roadworks!'

Rose took the tops of three Guinness's and mentioned, "Ere Georgie, where were you last night? Seeing Bridgid just reminded me, Archie was in asking after you.'

Unanswered retorts hung in the air and Bridgid laughed, 'Come on you two, you know you love my Daddy!'

'Life wouldn't be the same without Father-in-law,' mused Fintan, 'if he was to emigrate everyone would want to go with him.'

'Yeah, to make sure he leaves!' added George, teasing. 'No, no, you know we don't mean it.'

The gang arrived in a great crowd and the men gathered at the bar while the women found tables close by to catch up on the gossip. George and Fintan collected their drinks and returned to Bridgid to find her holding her big sister's hand and deep in conversation. Mary had come in with Kathy Gay, four more of the girls and three fellows that George had never seen before. She stopped chatting to greet Fintan who kissed her on the cheek.

God knows why but George felt silly and finding nothing better to say, ventured, 'Hallo.'

She glanced and, with a curt nod, returned to her conversation with Bridgid and Fintan. Her body turned just enough to blank and leave him hovering alone. Mornie had witnessed her classic move from the bar and stepped in to cover his old pal by catching a passing barmaid, with an arm full of empties, then saying loudly, 'This is the one you wanted to meet, Angie. George, this is Angela.'

Mary's head moved slightly but enough for Mornie to know she had bitten. George needed no further prompting and smiling, put an arm around her waist and sighed a suggestion in her ear. She laughed and nodded, and went back behind the bar. George squeezed through the crowd to Mornie, 'Thanks mate! I nearly looked a right pillock there. Do you reckon Mary heard?'

'Oh yeah. While your tongue probed the workings of Angie's ear'ole I saw her watching you in the mirror.'

'Lovely! Hey, who'd you reckon them three geezers are?'

'Never seen them before, you don't give a carrot anyway, do you?'

'No, course not! I just wondered what's in those cases they've got there.'

'Perhaps its tackle for a dirty weekend,' chuckled Mornie, nudging him in the ribs.

'Yes,' answered George, forcing a grin too wide by half.

They moved back to the boys and got in the middle of the debate. Fintan joined them and soon after, unnoticed, the two slipped out to the gents and were back a short while later; so far so good, on to step three.

In the meantime, the men in Mary's company took to the stage: one brandished a violin, the next opened a bigger case and withdrew an accordion. He started the band off and the third broke in to 'Serenade in the night'. It was well done but the song was posh and old fashioned and George half-hoped that someone would pass a derisory remark to slaughter him but instead, when they finished, the applause was long; to make it worse, Mary clapped louder than anyone. So this was her chap. George studied the three as they re-grouped round the table. Smartly dressed in tailored suits but they looked useful enough, and the singer was probably the best looking. He was tall with hair parted in the middle and slicked down, a long, thin face with prominent cheek bones, a strong chin and a Roman nose. George decided to name him Nero. Perhaps he played the fiddle too, perhaps they were wandering musicians; perhaps not. "She's got a new man, good luck to her," then mused, "as long as he doesn't lay a finger on my kids." His next thought was embarrassment at the last one. With stupidity like that the best thing he could do was swerve or he was only going to make a complete buffoon of himself. Twyford heard the first strains of, 'Once in a while' and knew he'd have to watch. Mary and Bridgid must have rehearsed the piece, it was that good. Next, Frank Nash was pushed up and to change the mood, he sung the rousing, 'Goodbye, Dolly Gray'. At once the men brightened and marched about dragging one leg and saluting each other. Someone followed on with, 'The Boers have got my Daddy' and pretty soon the pub was one big party. The only thing that almost spoilt the atmosphere was when George, full of too much Dutch courage, interrupted Mary chatting with friends by prodding her, perhaps too forcefully, on the shoulder.

She contemptuously turned to him and responded with, 'Yes?' She could even make that sound like an insult. He had meant to ask if he could take their younger ones to the Vale of Health on Sunday morning but instead the booze urged him into flippancy.

'The tongue is the deadliest of all blunt instruments.' He knew what he meant.

As she spoke she gave the impression he was constantly bothering her by retorting, 'Just piss off and leave me alone, can't you?'

George may have been a might 'beery', but he was not beaten that easily. 'My point exactly: a strumpet like you inferring that I could be interested in a return match. I'd sooner suck venom from the lips of a viper! All I ask is a little time with my children and you refuse to let me see them.' If she wanted to wash her dirty linen in public then cop hold of that! Mary held a glass and was quite capable of throwing it at him. He side-stepped, putting her friends between them, and continued, 'You're wicked. Evil.'

With that, up popped her chap, 'Is this clod annoying you?'

Mary smirked at the description. George's vocabulary dropped several notes and he said, 'Listen Nero, keep that fucking trunk out of my business!' And, with peacock pose, stuck his chest out and moved aggressively forward. Nero, unabashed at the slur on his good looks and game to win the lady's favour, did the same. It was broken up before they reached each other but not before George had added, 'Stoke the rusty old boiler by all means and give me more grounds for a divorce. I'm already using exceptional ugliness and acute mental derangement!'

Nero coloured, whatever it was he thought, the expression on his face showed the impact; he was completely out of order and knew it. Mary took him to one side and explained briefly what was what. Meanwhile, Dan Curry and Lestor Hogg, who had moved quickly to separate the 'cockerels', had returned George with them to the corner of the bar. Kit handed him a fresh pint and it was all forgotten. But a few minutes later, Nero came over and asked politely if he might have a word.

George answered, just as nicely, 'By all means, shall we take the air? After you,'

Nero went to the side door and as Twyford followed, for insurance, he slipped an empty bottle into his deep trouser pocket. Unspoken rules forbid the use of weaponry in a straightener, but one never knew what to expect from strangers.

Twyford's fingers circled the bottle's neck and let Nero begin, 'I must say I'm most awfully sorry. I had no idea that you and Mary were...'

'Married?' George helped him along.

'Well, yes. I didn't mean to um...' George nodded, helping him further. 'Well, it's none of my.., you're entirely right. I would very much like to apologise. In my defence, I'm rather fond of Mary...'

'Mary don't come in to it. Listen pal, you don't come round here throwing your weight about.'

'Absolutely not,' Nero agreed.

'This is my manor and you're a guest here; a visitor. Have the good manners to act like one.'

'You're one hundred percent correct. I'm utterly in the wrong.' How can you argue with someone who agrees with everything you say? Wherever possible George always preferred to be friendly so suggested a drink; they shook hands and went back inside. One of the lads called for an extra pint and Twyford made the introductions. Nero was quite taken with his new nickname and seemed to be enjoying himself in their company until Mary sent Kathy Gay to prise him away.

George saw her coming and whispered in his ear, 'None of my business but this is the one you should be getting hold of.'

Nero looked across and, too polite to disagree, replied, 'How nice to be so spoiled for choice.'

Kathy was around thirty, taller than Mary with blue eyes and a fair complexion, blond hair to her shoulders, a figure like a film star, not over bright with a great personality. Perfect really.

'George,' she said, 'I'm on orders to save this man from contamination.'

'Only if you kiss me,' said George offering her his cheek. She puckered and leaned forward but he turned his face quickly and she kissed his lips.

'That's it! Get me in trouble now. You're terrible, you are!' And laughing, pulled Nero away. Mary scowled, George smiled back, radiantly.

It had finished up a good night and ended too soon. The bells rang for 'Time, Gentleman, please,' and the doors were thrown open to whisk in the night frost and drive out the night larks. Everyone loitered outside the pub, loathe to go home and in the mood for a party. A taxi passed with the 'for hire' indicator up and George hailed it, instructing the driver to the Café Luxor, then hopped on the running board, blew everyone a kiss and was gone; making an exit was of equal importance as making an entrance. As it pulled away he noticed Mary and Nero, both far too wrapped up in each other to have seen him go; sweet.

Lenny and his footmen were at their usual post and he chatted to them for ten minutes then made his way inside. Radna had finished her break so he had to find company until she was ready to go. Luckily, Tony Mavropolous was at the bar with a couple of chaps who apparently oozed money. George joined them and Tony did the introductions. He was a master at putting people together and the conversation flowed well. Twyford listened mostly; the other two were in politics and passed opinions on how powerful America had made itself at our expense. They were about to eat and were waiting on one more guest, George was invited to join them. "Why not," he thought, they seemed well informed in all aspects of how the War was moving and he was hungry for any real up to date news. The guest arrived from behind George and, as he turned to make his acquaintance, the name and face registered instantly.

'Donald, this is George Twyford. George, meet Donald Grogan.'

It had been twenty two years since their last encounter.

Sergeant Major Grogan. Recognition had been quicker with the Scotsman.

'Oh, George and I are old friends. Nice to see you, George.' Then to everyone, 'Gentlemen, I must apologise for being late. Shall we eat?'

Twyford smiled and went along cursing himself for drinking too much earlier; he needed a clear head. What was Grogan doing to be in such company? This man was the Corporal who had turned their first days in the army into a terrible nightmare -and dragged them through hell! He had picked on Mickey Butler more than anyone else and was singularly responsible for Mickey being hospitalised, his leg broken in two places. The lads had taken strong measures against him to protect themselves. When they were dispatched to the War in France, Grogan had followed soon afterwards. Battles create death on the one hand and fast promotion to fill the gaps on the other. He rapidly rose to Sergeant Major.

The meal was more a steak and salad snack and Twyford was relieved when, after the cheese and ports, Tony suggested that he and George take their leave. They returned to his office and had coffee.

'I felt you were not at ease there, my George. Did I solution the correct motion?'

'Tony, you were spot on,' and he gave Mavropolous a brief outline of their connection, hinting that they had had some differences, but left out the finer points.

The shrewd Greek digested it all and discreetly confided, 'I understand him to be rather well connected and exceedingly rich, I also feel he could be a man dangerous if pushed the wrong way. Radna knows him better than I. Ah, she is here and looking for you, lucky man that you are. Come in, come in. See, she has impatience for you.'

Radna was swathed in yet another fur coat and looked delicious. Tony organised a taxi and waved them off.

'Lovely man, Tony,' he said as he sat back. 'That reminds me, I met another lovely man tonight; Donald Grogan.'

‘I have known Donald for some time and I wouldn’t describe him quite like that though he could be very useful to you, believe me. But let’s leave that for another day, I am very tired and want you to hold me and kiss me and take me to bed .’

Unusually preferring to come second, George indulged himself in first pleasuring Radna, several times, before discharging his own euphoric reward.

Not so frolicsome the following morning, he decided on a low profile so no pub and schlepped home in a penetrating pea-souper that was in for the day. There would be much to recount when he saw the others, especially the emergence of their favourite Sar’nt Major.

CHAPTER 12: LIKE PUSHING MARSHMALLOW INTO A SLOT MACHINE

Sweden: Germany blocks the Skaggerak.

North Sea: British blockade runner to Sweden, Master Standfast, is captured by the Germans.

Twyford hated writing letters, but there was one he had to pen. So, with a couple of hours to spare before collecting Alan for an outing to the pictures, he prepared himself and pencilled his first attempt heading it with Irving Jacob's address in thc Jago.

'Dear Colm,' it began, 'Greetings from the bomb debris once known as England. I am wary of putting things on paper so I'll be brief. I arrived back safely with the proceeds from the sale of our little friends. In Casablanca's medina I seriously thought my throat would be cut. What a place! But your contact was very professional and after weighing everything produced the cash within the hour. I am happy with the deal so whatever he earns, good luck to him, more importantly, I still have 'Bounty'. Good friends are helping me establish investments and, once they are in place, the interest will come out every month. The first two hundred pounds is being prepared for transfer to your account in Karinna as this letter is being written.

How is Malla? Once the baby is born it won't take a genius to work out who the father is. Tell her I touch her and sing to her every night.

I am keen to know what happened with the Police. That Africaan Inspector delves too deeply. He questioned me again the night before I slipped away and is very persistent about that dreadful incident but I am here now and I don't think the authorities could collar me this far away.

Write soon to the above address and, for safety, destroy all my correspondence.

Best regards,

Your friend.

He left it unsigned and read it through. It seemed to say enough, Twyford quickly copied it out properly and addressed it to 'Father Colm Kavanagh, The Mission of St. Bundoras, Allega Township, Near Karinna, Rand Plateau, South Africa.' George sealed the envelope, locked it in his briefcase and looked outside; the fog had not moved. He walked down Marsden Street on the opposite side to Mary's with his torch on, passing the car and its two occupants. Being there confirmed they had no clue where he was staying. He crossed to the house and tapped the knocker gently. Before Mairead answered it, he could hear her singing at the top of her voice along the passage. She opened the door and George enthused, 'That was lovely.' He caught her as she jumped at him and lifted her up in to his arms. She was still a baby really, enjoying the bliss of childhood, whilst Niamh was eighteen months older and a young woman, conscious of everyone. "Such a shame they have to grow up." he thought. George made no move to go in but Alan hadn't even got his shoes on yet so he gingerly stepped into the passage to waited there. Mairead couldn't understand why he hadn't carried her through and so took his hand as he lowered her down then hauled him along into the kitchen. It was crowded; Kevin was listening to the wireless with his girlfriend and stood up, all manly, and held his hand out. George grabbed it, pulling him forward in a bear hug and gave him a big kiss on the cheek, embarrassing the life out of him in front of 'what's-her-name'. Niamh wiggled across in a skirt that was tight enough to stop her bloodstream and, on tiptoes, pecked him dutifully. Alan was struggling with his bumpers trying to get a foot in without untying the laces and the dog was going mad. Mary didn't look up from her book.

'Won't be a minute, Dad!' said Alan, now trying to stamp his way into them.

'Don't worry son, plenty of time. It's an Alan Ladd film, you might have been named after him.'

Still no response from Mary. They left five minutes later. Because of Alan, George was more than a little worried when both bailiffs got out of their car and followed. They never tried to catch up, just stayed forty yards behind them in the fog.

The two Twyfords had to pass the police station in Holmes Road on the way to the pictures. George had his collar up as he approached but luck was not with him. Standing outside on the pavement was his father in law talking to another policeman.

All 'Bobbies' had to be above six foot but Archie made two of this one.

"Sod it," thought George, there was nothing for it but to front him. Twyford called out from yards away before Archie had time to recognise the next generations of his family tree.

'Just a moment, Father-in-law,' he hated being even remotely related to George. 'I want a word with you.' Challenged firmly, if Archie was surprised the other 'Bluebottle' had palpitations; no one *ever* spoke in that tone to Sergeant Shaw. A deep growling rumble warned of the impending earthquake but, unimpressed, Twyford carried on, 'I've got some matters to discuss with you in private but first you can tell those two heavies of yours to piss off!' and pointed behind him. Archie's eyes went to the men who were emerging from the fog.

'I don't want them lurking around in the shadows frightening Mary and the kids.'

The men had stopped dead still and stared. Archie tensed and leaned forward, arms out slowly like the gunslinger preparing to draw. 'Come here, you monkeys!' he snarled.

First one broke the invisible bonds that rooted him to the spot then a second later the other, evaporating back into the fog. Archie was after them in a flash, the constable in close support. George swung Alan up onto his back and ran in the opposite direction and didn't stop until they were outside the pictures.

'Your Grandfather can't half run! Do you reckon he caught them?'

Alan was chuckling away, 'As long as he don't catch you, Dad, eh?' Then both of them were laughing, everything was good fun when they were together.

George vowed, 'Do you know, you're my best mate in the world?'

'And you're mine,' declared Alan.

The film ended after Alan Ladd killed a complete warparty *and* won the leading lady. Twyford took his son across to the Tally Ho for lemonade and an arrowroot biscuit . Strict laws permitted no one under eighteen in pubs but with pitiful takings that night the governor agreed it was too cold and foggy to leave him outside. In those days everyone knew everyone and there wasn't a pub in the area where George couldn't find a drinking partner. Sitting at the bar was a black man called 'Lucky'. Probably the only black man most of the inhabitants of St Pancras had ever known. He was so called because when George was small, the braver boys would run up and touch him for luck. They shook hands and George insisted on buying the round, he called two dark rums and two pints of Stout.

Lucky spoke with a West Indian accent, 'Someone's died, I know, and left you a fortune.'

'Something like that, old friend, you look exceptionally well. Still getting plenty?'

Lucky took his meaning correctly and replied, 'No, no, at my age it's like trying to push marshmallow into a slot machine!' They guffawed loudly at the comparison. George had always enjoyed Lucky's company, he was a wonderful conversationalist and no matter what the subject could comment intelligently, usually with first-hand knowledge. He had been everywhere, sailed the seven seas *and* met people who made history and though it was often hard to believe, you could never catch him out.

First checking Alan was out of earshot, George began, 'I must tell you, I've been in South Africa for the last four years.'

His companion looked surprised, 'Not the friendliest place in the world.'

'No, but when I travelled to the Townships all the kids used to touch me for luck!'

'I bet the girls tried to cut your hair, perhaps one in particular?'

'How d'you know that?'

Lucky grinned shrewdly and encouraged him to confide more of an obviously interesting tale which, in turn, gave George a chance to air a few worries. As the story unfolded Lucky was shaken slightly but gave some overdue, sound advice. Delighted to have shared parts of his weighty secret and pleased with the evaluation, Twyford called a final round of warming rums.

As a treat, George took Alan back through the Coal Wharf, which meant they had to walk along the railway lines in the dark but it was the only way to avoid the Police Station. George had a torch so it wasn't too bad and Alan loved the adventure. It was a great short cut and also one of the places the youngster was not allowed to go. They came to Marsden Street to find the car was still there, locked and empty, so Twyford let the tyres down.

'If ever you do this, stick a matchstick in the valve, see, and walk away quick; that way you're gone while it keeps going down.' He was such a shining example to his boy.

George knocked and Mary opened the door, done up to the nines. He was tempted to taunt her but for once sought the right path. 'Anytime you want a baby-sitter..?' he tried.

'Thank you, but Niamh's old enough and quite capable of looking after them.'

'Yeah, just a thought.' Alan kissed him and went off inside.

George made to go and then mentioned, 'By the way, I noticed a couple of fellows in a black Ford opposite, hanging around like bad luck. They haven't bothered you, have they?'

'I'll say they've been bothering me. They're from the Inland Revenue and their boss came here, pushing me about and asking after you. Daddy sent him away with a flea in his ear. Daddy said the Yard is checking up on you as well. You've been back five minutes and you're bringing all kinds of trouble to the door!'

'Yeah, well I've been round to see your Daddy and told him I want a word with him.'

'You liar, you wouldn't dare!'

'Am I? Ask Alan. Go on, he's in there.' He looked at her like she was mentally retarded, shook his head in pity and walked off. Of course he didn't show it but her words had put the wind right up him. The Revenue and the Yard, what did it all mean? "Was the adventure over?" he wondered. 'Not yet!' he said out loud, now more set than ever to get things on a firm footing then it wouldn't matter quite so much if he had to disappear. One had to admit it was hotting up and he had only been back nine days.

The two Revenue bailiffs were chased through the fog for what seemed an awfully long way. By splitting up they had eventually lost their pursuers and themselves, having arranged to meet back at the Shipton if they became separated: which, after roughly an hour, they did do. It was far too risky to collect the car so the men decided to return the following morning and keep this night's fiasco to themselves.

Sergeant Archie Shaw had returned empty-handed to the station, knowing the chancer would be gone but, as Alan was with him, it would have been too difficult to carry out what he had in mind. Anyway, he was very proud of his Grandson and always took time to try and teach him right from wrong; he could never have the boy thinking badly of Pop. Archie entered the station and called together all members of the force who were working that Sunday night. He had wanted to handle this personally and now he would set his staff the task of information-gathering on one George Twyford. Just information.

CHAPTER 13: ALL ST.PANCRAS AS FAR AS THE CROSS AND NORTH TO HAMPSTEAD VILLAGE

Germany: The German navy's new submarine goes into service at Kiel, it has a snorkel to provide the diesel engines with oxygen while it is submerged!

Berlin: Himmler orders all gypsies to be sent to concentration camps.

Dressed in an impeccable business suit, knocked up by Maestro Quill, and armed with a briefcase containing his letter to South Africa and eight thousand pounds, Twyford joined the Monday morning throng descending into Chalk Farm Underground. The Northern line dropped him at Moorgate and, conspicuous by repeatedly looking over his shoulder, he made his way through the narrow city streets, across Shoreditch and into the Jago. People of the alleyways and those outside the small shops said 'Good morning' to him now. He felt he was actually being accepted, until he got to Irving's. Benny was pouring the tea out as he entered.

'I know. That kettle's always boiling. That's how you do it.'

'No. The message this morning was, 'A briefcase is on its way up, bringing a shady Yok with.'

'What do you mean?' said George, 'It suits me, I blend with these city people'

'Are you kidding?' asked Ben. 'You look about as out of place as a rabbi touting bacon joints.'

'I had my eye on a Bowler an'all; you've really hurt my feelings now!' said George. Irving came in carrying the usual stack of paperwork. 'I reckon those papers are just for effect and you cart them about everywhere so you can look *terribly* important.'

'That's because I am *terribly* important -unlike you who has ceased to exist, you'll be glad to know. You were boringly easy to find now you're complicated and almost interesting,' said Irving, and continued, 'I've got papers allowing other papers the authority to cover documents authorising payment to other documents and you've been lost somewhere between here and the Cape.'

'Excellent, and here's one more document,' said George, passing him the letter, 'to go with these papers.' handing him the eight thousand. They spent an hour going through everything and then another on the plans for Tuesday night, if Ruben actually saw sense and turned up at 'The Spaniards' for their meeting. When George left it was with a sense of relief, knowing that at least half of the money he had arrived in England with, was safe and secure within the banking system, legally operating, earning interest and soon, hopefully, to be producing dividends. He had made funds available to his traders as well, not on the same scale but he was keen to see how they were getting on and was now on his way for a meeting with a coal-man.

Perhaps lifting and carrying coal for most of his life had caused Old Willy Rowe to have a hunched back and consequently an awkward gait but he was still strong as an ox, canny as a fox and he had a yard just inside one of the smaller entrances to the Coal Wharf. With an acre of open land and five big railway arches for storage, it was well out of the way, protected by a very high perimeter wall and two bloody great Alsatians. Mr Will, as the boys still called him, (to his face-and Quasi to his back,) had employed many of them when they were lads. The business was always a good earner and he loved a pound note. When George arrived at the yard an articulated lorry of coal and coke was being unloaded. Willy and two big fellows were each shouldering hundredweight bags, tottering into one of the arches and stacking them inside.

'Hello, George!' smiled Willy, glad to relinquish the graft to others. They clasped hands firmly and clapped coal dust.

'You timed that just right,' he said, quietly, and shouted to the workforce, 'I've got a meeting, don't interrupt me unless it's important.' He led George in to the on-sight office. It was a proper traveller's caravan with gypsy writing all over it.

'What a smashing piece!' said George.

'Yes, ain't it just. I swapped a load of nutty slack for it. A work of art, that's what it is.'

Inside was all wood, but ornately carved and shaped. Willy poured two glasses of scotch. 'Now, what have you got in mind?' he asked, handing Twyford the smaller measure.

'I think we can do a lot of business,' replied George. 'How many wagons do you operate now?'

'One big lorry and two smaller run-arounds, three horses and carts.'

'And what area do you cover?'

'All St Pancras, as far as the Cross and north to Hampstead Village.'

'How do you feel about selling food, maybe booze, anything that's hard to get? I've got a deal going with the Yanks.' The Americans were supposed to have anything that was in short supply and to mention their name conjured up images of good living.

Often compared to an eel, Willy feigned uninterest, 'I'd love to do it, son, but all my money's tied up in stock. I couldn't pay them until it was sold and I doubt they'd be too keen on credit.'

George smiled, 'Aah, but they don't know you like I do.' The deal, briefly, was that George and co. would supply everything and Willy, who served coal on a regular basis to most people in the borough, could offer them all manner of black market goods, too. The old coalman expressed the correct reservations though, by the tone, Twyford knew he would give it a try. Also, with fuel being on ration, the yard was never used to capacity so George could have a makeshift office in one of the arches.

The meeting ended and Willy walked him to the gate saying, 'You know me, boy, I'll be straight down the line with you and who I don't know ain't worth knowing! That's it, you do the planning and I'll do the selling.'

George ducked the sooty, circling arm of the farewell hug but shook a palm of spit and grit to seal the deal then was off to see Tinker to arrange the first lost load of potatoes.

Monday night was Loan Club night at the Queens Arms in Queens Crescent and a good reason to see the troops. Everyone else traded on credit so, with actual readies, Owen, Kit and Stanley had never been so popular. Cash was the key to every locked warehouse and they were offered everything from eggs to petrol. Kit stated that trading legends, who before had only ever been whispered about had suddenly found *him*, knew his first name and invited him to breakfast. Keith added that now, when he strolled onto a pitch, instead of drawing half a blank his "new mates" offered him a cigarette, walked him out of earshot and took his diabolical bids with a smile!

'The pound spoke all languages,' mused George, as he listened intently. The parachute white had been acquired for next to nothing and was arriving Tuesday together with two hundred yards of Worcestered flannel, Scottish tweeds and navy serge. It would all be stored at the coal wharf and taken as it was needed. Everyone on the firm was being treated to a new outfit and Mornie was busy booking the fittings for suits and shirts. Lestor Hogg was the perfect candidate to do the books and be responsible for stock control. Tinker was on call for collections, anywhere, anytime. Hundredweight bags of potatoes and other bulk items were to be delivered out inside clean coal sacks. Apart from the sales created by the coal wagons the two places for taking orders would be the market butcher's shop and the fruit stall, owned by Kit and Owen respectively; that way only people known and vetted would be served. Any visitor coming to the Wharf should be refused entry and, from that night on, the business would only ever be discussed at the office. Due to the fabled extent of the Informer's knowledge (he was now spoken of with hushed reverence), it was agreed that wives, girlfriends, family and friends, in fact anyone outside the firm, could never be party to any information.

'The problem with living here and now is not so much a shortage of money but families need coupons from ration cards to purchase most of their basic essentials. The service we provide should help everyone and include a handsome profit.' The glass was raised to a quiet pledge, 'Success!' A toast held great significance and all Partners echoed the sentiment then a game of darts led to an early night.

The coat was one size too big as was the pulled-down trilby, a scarf masked the lower half of his face. This outfit was only ever worn after midnight and disguised his shape perfectly. A gloved hand flipped open the battered old fob-watch and sharp ears might just have detected tiny bells that beat eight times and guessed it played "All through the night." It was time. He came silently around the corner and stopped; nothing stirred. Still he paused, blending well with the shadowed nooks of the bus garage walls, and studied both ends of the street then smoothly sidled inside the entrance. Information was at premiums and he had plenty to cash up.

CHAPTER 14: SPANIARD'S WOOD IS AN EERIE PLACE

Quoting the words of Longfellow, in his own hand to Churchill, President Roosevelt wrote of Great Britain:

"Sail on, oh Ship of State, sail on, oh Union strong and great,

Humanity with all it's fears, with all the hopes of future years,

Is hanging breathless on thy fate..."

Tuesday morning came and George hopped a bus from the Shipton. He was now training himself to notice faces around him, to get lost on the tube and constantly check for shadows. Passing Camden Town Station on the Northern line going south, he returned ten minutes later and walked through the streets to Mickey's house. The four workmen were having breakfast, the building had been reduced to a skeleton in preparation and George reckoned that if Theresa saw it now she'd kill him stone dead! The improvements could not be started until the deal was struck. Would Ruben come tonight? Might there be trouble or would he see sense? Some feared a battle Royal may be inevitable. Twyford left them after an hour and spotted the bonnet of a black Austin nosing around the corner. He was walking away from it and it passed him at speed. As it whipped by George thought the driver could have been 'Knobbly'. There was a passenger who studied Twyford through the back window until it was gone from sight. Conceivably, it was a warning, maybe Ruben trying to put the wind up him? George walked over the canal bridge and along busy Chalk Farm Road then, hoping to confuse anyone tracking him, disappeared down a side crescent. The turning had been badly bombed and showed no signs of life; a mistake perhaps? He decided to run through it, had he not his life could well have ended that morning. He heard the screech of tyres and, without turning, sprinted at an enormous pile of rubble to the side of the road thirty yards away. The black

Austin accelerated around the bend expecting Twyford to be closer and so be crushed beneath the wheels. The car was in third and screamed as it raced towards him. George felt the engine's heat on his back as he leapt at the rubble. Holding its course to the final split second the car veered away, missing him and the heap of bricks by a "rizla".* It was gone and he stood there alone, filling his lungs, a school boy playing king of the castle. Twyford moved into the skeletal cover of a bombed house and got his breath back then, cautiously, returned to Chalk Farm Road and boarded a bus. He sat upstairs at the front, examining the traffic for more lethal adversaries, while he brushed himself down and polished his shoes with a handkerchief. Soon deposited safely in the West End, he rang Irving to ensure all documentation was completed for the purchase of 11 Leybourne Road. George was fuming but gave no indication of it. 'I'm changing the plans slightly,' he said, 'Copy those documents for six more.' and called over half a dozen new addresses.

'That's all fine with me,' agreed Irving, 'but am I permitted to ask what prompted this?'

'He just tried to kill me and that's gonna cost him.'

'Oh good. Okay then,' said Irving, bemused, 'I'll get Ben to bring them over, which funeral parlour shall I direct him to?' George arranged the meet for six o'clock and rang off. His next call was to Ruben and giving his company name was put through immediately.

'Can I help you?' was the first thing Ruben could think to say, already aware of his failure.

'Now that was a silly thing to do, wasn't it?'

'Yes. It was done against my orders and the people concerned are at this moment being dismissed.' lied Ruben. 'My instructions were to frighten you, I apologise sincerely.'

'Well, I'm so frightened that my people are on their way to Frognal now.'

'NO!' yelled Ruben, panicking momentarily. 'No, let's meet tonight as arranged.' And controlling his alarm as best he could, carried on swiftly, 'If you ask you'll find I've been to see the property personally and I'm sure we can come to an agreement.'

'Mmm, I'm not so sure,' said George.

'Listen, there's no need for this!' said Ruben, pushing the point. 'Trust me; we can sort it out like civilised people over a quick drink.'

'Trust? Did you say "trust you?" What do you take me for? You attempted to assassinate me today! Now, my governor says an example's got to be made, somebody at Frognal; you can choose who gets it.'

'Please, please, not my family!'

'I warned you. There won't be another chance, do you understand?'

'Yes, I understand.'

'Your stupidity is gonna cost you. Make sure your solicitor and accountant are with you tonight and no one else.'

'What about my driver?'

'He stays with the motor and waits in the car park.' That way Fintan could report back on everything mentioned during the return journey.

'Agreed.'

The Spaniards is a famous old Inn and landmark on a road that passes through Hampstead Heath. It is surrounded by thick woodland and prostitutes often ply their trade along both sides of the tenebrous road. A bagwash van pulled up outside the Inn an hour early and Danny Curry bounded from the passenger side to let five others out of the back; they went swiftly into the pub. George drove the van into the unlit car park and reversed it into the darkest space facing the road, for a quick exit if necessary. While locking the doors he was accosted by two ladies; one had all the patter and suggested some delights that the three of them might partake of. George thanked her for the offer but declined. The quiet one knew his voice and turned away too quickly. She had recognised him and as they walked off George scrutinised her shadow then realised who the woman was. He caught up and spun her round.

'What the fuck do you think you're doing here?'

'Earning a living!' replied Ivy Nolan.

'Does Gerry know?'

'It's got nothing to do with him how I get my wages.' she said brazenly. 'He's never given me anything but debts and sleepless nights!'

George grabbed her by the arm and propelled her towards the pub. 'I think you'd better tell him that! He's in there waiting for me.'

'Oh, my God!' she said, resisting against the momentum and trying to pull away. 'Don't tell him please!' She was begging, the cockiness all gone.

'Go home now! I'm coming to see you tomorrow. Be in!'

'I ain't got no money, George! I can't pay the rent.'

'Take this,' he said, giving her a five pound note, 'and don't you ever do that again!'

She snatched it and walked quickly away, leaving him to lament, 'What a bleedin' good night this is turning out to be.'

The old alehouse had low ceilings that were all higgledy-piggledy, the other lads had separated in to three pairs and spread throughout the saloon, which was quite busy. The only occupants of the public bar were four scruffs who were drinking noisily. Doris and Margot sat at a window table, near the garden exit, with empty glasses. George stuck his tongue out at them then ordered a jug of bitter and two gin and tonics. Ruben arrived five minutes late with two well-dressed gentlemen. He looked George in the eyes and shook hands firmly then introduced his associates. One was tall, greying, and immaculately smart, the other was of equal height, but considerably younger, probably early thirties. They looked big enough but were both rather limp-wristed, like shaking hands with a soggy lettuce leaf. One certainty; any fisticuffs would not be instigated by these two. The girls shook hands with the younger one last of all.

Doris first, who said, 'Here, Margie, feel how smooth and soft his palms are.'

Margot took one hand and Doris held the other. 'Oh yes!' she agreed, 'With such lovely long fingers!' and led him to sit between them. George, Ruben and Sonny the solicitor took their seats and no notice of the girls. The young accountant sat as naturally as he could, in the circumstances, and tried to join the discussion. After a minute or so he began to redden. The girls carried on their own conversation about the softness of his touch and had put his hands high up between their thighs and locked them in. George was trying to come over as a hard negotiator but couldn't help laughing; they didn't give a monkey's toss, these two. Their banter actually lightened the moment, which should have been thorny in the least, for business to be coolly thrashed out with someone who a few hours earlier had tried to organise the other's demise. Before any of the finer points came up Ruben asked George for a private word and the two stepped into the Garden bar. The rowdy crowd had left and George looked around for a quiet corner but Ruben carried on into the garden.

'You're not thinking of doing anything silly?' sighed George, in a weary voice, following him out.

'That's not me,' answered Ruben. 'Let's have it crystal clear. Are you moving in on me? Is it business or is it personal?'

George did not answer immediately, just pulled his collar up against the damp fog.

'Let's just say you've gone too far and upset people who, if you knew them, it would be the last thing you'd want to do. Let me give you some honest advice. The incident earlier…'

'Which I had nothing to do with!' interrupted Ruben.

'No matter. You're responsible, they can hide; you can't. Now please, for your own good, listen to me. You've made it personal. Threatened violence against people like the Butlers can't occur without serious repercussions. You probably have no idea who they're related to.'

Ruben looked bewildered, 'No?'

'Well, I'm mentioning no names,' said George, groaning inwardly, thinking of Doris and Margot, 'and today's attempt on me made it worse. You're going the right way for acute harm; legally and physically.'

They had reached the end of the garden and carried on along the path that led into Spaniards Wood. George took an envelope from inside his jacket and handed it to Ruben. 'Here's a list of six more houses that you own. They're in the same state as 11 Leybourne Road. The deal is three hundred and fifty quid for the seven and no more problems.'

'They're worth two hundred pounds each!' spluttered Ruben.

'I told you that mistake would cost you.'

'You can fuck right off!' declared Ruben, rooted to the spot and at a loss for a more eloquent reply. Ignoring his protests, George walked on and the trees grew thicker. Spaniards Wood was always a wild and remote part of Hampstead Heath where few ventured after dark but Ruben, with dander up and a lot more to say, came after Twyford, who had moved out of sight. He rushed along the winding path and saw George just ahead, stationary and looking down the slope. Ruben's eyes followed his gaze and there, eight yards away across a narrow gulley, stood the four noisy louts from the pub, only now they were statues in the fog, standing silently around a shallow ditch, leaning on shovels or holding them across their chests. George had planned it and the sight of them even scared him. Ruben's eyes bulged from his head, full credit to him, he bellowed, 'This is ridiculous! You'd do this to me for a few poxy houses! You bastards!' and, stepping guardedly towards the ditch, dared, 'What have I ever done to you?' Common sense stopped him there. 'I don't deserve this,' he muttered, as four pairs of eyes stared icily back at him. He looked around at George, 'You can have your fucking deal, just don't do this.' Still said with a certain amount of backbone and, no matter what, Twyford couldn't help but admire him. Plainly enough was enough.

George took Ruben's arm and eased him away saying, 'Let's go back now, it's getting colder.' Neither of them looked back. They were in the pub in seconds and had only been a short distance from it...but Spaniards Wood is an eerie place.

Benson spoke briefly to his advisers, 'I've agreed to sell seven houses to this man's company for three hundred and fifty pounds.' Noticing how Ruben's pallor had changed, the solicitor wisely said nothing but the young accountant, glad for a chance to stand up and extricate himself from the girls' legs, began to voice his objections. He was quelled, gruffly, 'Don't argue. Just book them out as sold, in need of extensive repair.'

The accountant said no more, he had his instructions and no wish to know what had happened outside. Addresses were exchanged; the deal would be completed by 4pm Friday evening. They left without shaking hands. George should have been elated, and he was for Mickey and Theresa, but in his heart he felt rotten. He had taken no pride in the action; a hollow victory.

Violence was redundant, the plan had worked to a complete success and a celebratory mood settled on the conspirators. Gerry, Owen, Lestor, Tinker, Danny Curry and John Bass joked with the girls and after waiting a while outside, in case Ruben's fieldsmen had made an appearance, the gravediggers joined them. Each with a slightly different view of Ruben's plight, Stanley, Kit, Frank and Mornie aired their stories but George found none of it funny, he hadn't enjoyed playing the heavy and challenging a man's courage. Still, thank God, that was taken care of.

The other six to be purchased by the company were Margot's home in Albany Street, the Quill and Nolan residences in Belmont Street, Stanley Swindells's and Frank Nash's houses in Prince of Wales Road and a cottage in Healey street that Tinker had been renting since his own was bombed. These were the only properties, in their crowd, owned by Ruben Benson. Everyone else paid rent to the council or, in Owen's case, the church and a slightly different approach might be called for with those landlords. Tinker had borrowed the small coal lorry from the yard and had the four gravediggers on the back and the Butler girls in the cab. The rest piled in the van with George and sang all the way home.

CHAPTER 15: HOW MUCH *CAN* A STREETWALKER EARN?

Insterburg, East Prussia: Hitler sees a demonstration of the prototype Me262 jet fighter, and orders it to be mass produced – as a bomber!

George Twyford awoke sweating. It was still dark and he'd had a lousy night's sleep, spiked with dreams that had repeatedly turned in to nightmares. He arose and went downstairs, turned the lights on and opened his briefcase. In the last few days, he had made many notes of targets to aim for and problems to overcome. He read them through then added Ivy Nolan's name to the list. She had been a homely girl when she was with Gerry and, although not disliked by the other women, preferred the company of a wireless to chatter at a soiree. She had worked as a nurse before their daughter Chloe was born. Chloe went in the Wrens and the marriage seized up soon afterwards. Once their baby flew the nest they had very little left in common. Sad, but that's the way life is sometimes. Now, as well as nursing, it seems she was trying her luck as a streetwalker.

"Ivy must have been so desperate," mused George, scratching an irritation under his stubble and looking for inspiration. "Perhaps we could employ her to look after Theresa," he thought. "Yeah, that's what the company's all about, after all."

Twyford plotted the rest of his day in order: a run over Hampstead, then a visit to Mickey's, followed by a telephone conversation with Irving, a quick call on Ivy Nolan and he'd have the rest of the afternoon to himself. He could look for a flat and a decent car.

He left his Mum's house at 6am. -it was pitch black. An air raid was warned but nothing had materialised. Having never been in London when bombs were falling it was hard for George to imagine it; the deafening noise and the fear, people flooding down tube stations in terror. Thank God he had missed it and, more to the point, thank God his family had come safely through it. As he ran, George thought how odd it was that he was too old to be called up, he didn't think of himself as any different. Twyford turned the corner and there, parked up, lights on, was a police car occupied by two officers. He ran past them and the engine started. They were facing the wrong way and so executed a one point turn then drove along next to him on the wrong side of the road. The window was open and the driver began to taunt, 'What's so special about you? They talk like you're a bit tasty, you look a right old mug to me.' George said nothing but altered course and ran along Rhyl Street, passed the school and into Litcham Street. To Twyford it was a street like any other but to the police it was strictly off-limits. Bobbies were often attacked and, unless there were three or more, they did not enter -even in a car. But this time of the morning was too early for its inhabitants to be up just yet so the officers drove through, enjoying themselves. 'I'd like to have five minutes with you round the back.'

George ran up into a block of flats facing the road; the car stopped at the curb. Twyford took an empty milk bottle from outside one flat, stood on the stairs, and peed into it then came back down with the bottle behind his back. George signalled he wanted to talk and bowled over to the open car window, then leaned on the door to thwart an early response from the officer. One hand poured the warm urine on the driver's lap whilst the other seized the officer's nose and jerked it hard, pulling his head out of the window.

From a second's delayed reaction at the shock of a facial attack *and* what he was sitting in, the Rozzer went stark raving mad. His partner jumped out and rushed around the car, brandishing a truncheon. George let go of the near side nose and made off back to the stairs. They pursued him up three flights then Twyford dashed the length of the balcony, running his empty bottle along the railings, making one hell of a racket. Lights came on and doors began to open. Voices.

"Ere, there's Bluebottles in the flats!' The cry went up.

Realisation dawned quickly; the officers were caught short and could be in serious trouble. Almost tumbling down the stairs they scooted back to the motor. George was adding to the pandemonium, jesting, 'Stop 'em! Stop 'em!' The next move was to damage the car and he lobbed the bottle with precision. It landed on the vehicle's roof and exploded while the two inmates were trying to start the engine. It had failed the first time and with more missiles hitting the bonnet and the boot they were now positively panicking. The squad car fired on its fourth attempt, revved loudly and flew up the street; Archie would have a blue fit at the damage. George stood on the third floor busting a gut with laughter. The people began returning inside, surprisingly not that put out at all, in fact, they probably considered it to be a good start to the day. Deeming it wiser not to continue his run Twyford sprinted merrily home. He breakfasted well with Alan and they left the house together at around a quarter to nine. Alan was going to school and George could take the same route. At the top of the street was a different police car but with the aforementioned two officers. George took Alan's hand and stopped next to it then tapped on the window until it wound down. The copper's scowl was a picture. 'If I'm strolling too fast and you lose me, I'll be in Leybourne road and he's attending Holy Trinity school.' Then added, 'Can I smell cat's pee?' The window rolled back up.

George stepped in front of the car and winked at them. It wouldn't hurt to have two coppers in tow just in case Ruben's men fancied their chances again.

They arrived at Alan's primary school and Twyford just had to go in on the pretence of meeting his teacher. In truth, he wanted to see if it had changed since he'd been a pupil there some thirty three years before. His name had been entered (several times) in the dreaded Black Book and he thought of asking if he might see it when a haughty tone interrupted his reverie.

'Can I help you?'

'Oh, I was miles away,' said George coming round quickly to

behold an hourglass figure that begged a second leer.

'I take it you are Alan's father, as I stated in my letter I am most concerned with his absenteeism.' She stuck her chest out as she propelled her voice, obviously theatrical.

Almost ugly with a pointed nose, a mouth that housed too many teeth, a high forehead and boggling eyes yet the ensemble was strikingly attractive. No wedding ring, either.

He ventured,' I've recently returned from abroad and this has come as a something of a shock. My name's George and you must be..?'

'Miss Poole.'

'Ah the terrible Miss Poole or may I call you, "Ma'am"?'

Ignoring his attempt to strike a more pleasant cord, she questioned, 'A shock? You have read my letter?'

Calmly, he strove to gain a footing, 'In fact, no. But if you have a copy…'

'Mr. Twyford, if you think I have nothing better to do with my time…'

She was actually telling him off, and shilly shallying was getting him nowhere, so he pounced,

'I'll pick you up tonight and we can discuss these problems in more depth.'

The flared nostrils told him a lot and before the expelled gasp could select pitiless words for the refusal, he darted in with,' Forgive my directness but the war has claimed the last four years of my life and I vowed if I survived then I would never again waste a precious moment of it and, simply, I find you incredibly attractive.'

Caught completely off guard, she inquired, 'But what of Mrs. Twyford?'

'Ah, you see, uh, we're not together and haven't been for some years but, from what I understand, her drinking may well be one of Alan's problems.'

'Oh, I am sorry to hear that. I had no idea.' Then surprised herself by announcing, 'I get off work at four thirty.'

George was pleased with his achievement. Mary had given no warning about Alan being in trouble with the School Board and had planned for him to suffer grief at the hands of Miss Poole, little knowing how come-hither 'Ma'am' looks.

The Butler dwelling was only two streets away and when Twyford got there he noticed the police car already parked by the bomb debris. Reaching his destination, and to add to their annoyance, he waved. The door was on the jar so he walked in to find the boys all hard at it; even Lestor was there.

'Where's the kettle?' shouted George, and they all downed tools. Over tea, he told them of his result at the school.

'Jammy bastard,' was Lestor Hogg's considered opinion. 'Where you gonna take her? Down the Bedford?'

'Na, too coarse. I want something a bit more tasteful than an old fart's music hall.'

Nolan threw in, 'And I thought your vision of a proper treat was carting her down the pie and eel shop then round the back of the bike sheds!'

Similar sarcasm assailed him from the others until Kit came up with (for him) an almost sensitive strategy, 'Drive up Hampstead, go in the Bull and the Bush for a drink and then try your luck in Jack Straw's car park.'

Yes. Everyone agreed that was far more refined.

Listening to Nolan reminded him to go and see Ivy. He stayed for another ten minutes but, having no wish to do any work and dirty his suit, decided to bid them *adieu* and crossed the road to the police car. Again the window rolled down.

'I'm going to Ryland Road and as you'll be following me, how about a lift?' The reply took two short words and the window rolled back up.

Out of the blue, Lucky appeared and walked with him a little way. 'About our chat the other night, I think that medicine is far more important than education to people in the Townships. Many children die from lack of medical help.'

George thought of the child, his child, that Malla was carrying but before he could comment the trailing police car made itself known and, remembering an appointment, Lucky altered direction into a side street. His parting shot was, 'I would make that my next priority if I were you.' George had been thinking more long term; with a sound education they could take care of themselves. Of coursc, Lucky was right; medical help was essential.

Ryland Road was a quiet backwater in Kentish Town for almost posh people. Ivy had rented one room in a big house split in to many similar sized lets, all to nurses by the look of it. She answered his knock in her uniform and without saying a word left the door open for him. He followed on to a room on the second floor and studied her in the daylight, all the spark had gone out of her. George flopped on the bed and Ivy sat in the only chair. 'Come on. Nothing's that bad!' he said, kindly.

Her voice was as dead as her eyes and she had the most hopeless expression on her face. 'I was prepared to try anything to get some money together so I could leave here forever. Without him, I don't want to live.'

'Who? Gerry?' asked George, stupidly.

'No.' She almost smiled then, going lifeless again, said, 'If he goes to prison it'll kill him and me,' and with that she wailed loudly and cried her eyes out. Wishing he hadn't stuck his nose in, in the first place, George moved over and awkwardly put an arm around her until she pulled herself together.

'Well if it's that bad,' he sighed, 'tell me all about it and we can both have a cry.'

It seemed that she went back to nursing some time ago and met a Doctor Howard Small who was nine years her junior. They worked together at the University College Hospital. The age difference hadn't mattered and they start a romance. For a while life was almost perfect then the situation disintegrated with incredible rapidity. Howard was one of those fine people who constantly bring their work home with them. In this case he was treating a terminally-ill patient and was suffering along with him. He administered as much morphine as could be spared but the chap was still in dreadful pain and begged for someone to end his life. The doctor went to his superiors and asked permission. It was refused, mercy killings are against the laws of God and Man, he was told. That night he worried it over with Ivy and the next morning put the poor old boy out of his misery. Howard was challenged with the 'crime' and saw no reason to deny it. The police took him in to custody and suddenly he had less friends and no one who would come up with the fifty pounds bail money. She thought at best he would be struck off, never to practise medicine again; at worst he would go to prison for manslaughter.

It crossed Twyford's mind to ask how much a prostitute could earn these days; maybe now wasn't the right moment. 'Where's he being held?' asked George, seeing the flat hunting recede to an unlikely event but getting the feel for a possible, long-shot investment; gullible, hard working martyrs don't come along everyday.

'West End Central Police station.'

'Right. Get your coat. Now, I'm promising you nothing but there might be one chance if this lot goes bo'side, tell me all about him as we go.'

They caught a twenty-four bus down to the West End and through the journey she talked constantly. It was very apparent that she worshipped him; in fact the young man sounded perhaps a little too saintly to be true.

"I don't think she'd have gone on the game to get Gerry out of trouble," Twyford pondered sadly, and gave Ivy the amount needed for bail. She handed across the fifty pounds and signed the necessary forms. Dr. Small was to report back on Monday morning. George was waiting outside for them when a taxi pulled up and two men sprang out, one wielding a large camera.

'Just in time!' said the photographer, taking the first snap while Ivy and Howard were coming down the steps. As he lifted his camera again George moved quickly down in front of him, gripped his arm and quietly advised his ear. The camera man stepped back out of their way and Twyford opened the cab door for the inseverable couple. The reporter looked to see why he was not clicking away and received a warning shake of the head. George got in after them and the taxi drew away.

'What did you say to stop them? They've been plaguing my every movement,' said Howard.

'I just gave him some guidance on negatives,' smiled George.

Fintan made his daily call to the Mornington Café. He ordered the rolls to take out and sat down at one of the tables to wait. The chap opposite was reading the paper and the racing page was lying open on the table. Bored, Fintan asked to take a gander and studied form until the food was ready then put the news sheet back down, collected his rolls and left. Ten minutes later, Frank Nash came out of the same café, with racing page *and* Fintan's note secured inside his newspaper.

The taxi dropped Twyford, Ivy and Howard at the Green Gate in Bethnal Green Road. Irving Jacobs sat outside in a black Ford V8 Pilot, his cousin Roy was at the wheel and would be their driver for the afternoon, that way they could talk without fear of being overheard. George and the lovers settled themselves in the back then Roy pulled out and headed towards Epping. They discussed the predicament and Howard gave his version of exactly what had happened to land him in this plight. Irving was really only interested in the details and conversations since his arrest but listened throughout, without interrupting, to familiarise himself with the complete episode. Ivy then described how she saw the situation. She felt the picture looked none too rosy for him but Irving urged them not to worry yet. He needed to research earlier cases of a similar nature and would give them his opinion in the morning. They travelled as far as Woodford then drove back to Bethnal Green, to a garage in Three Colts Lane where Roy got out. He specialised in the availability of cars with false papers for anyone with the cash and, on Irving's recommendation, George was at last mobile. He slipped across behind the wheel and accustomed himself with the controls. After use each night it would need to be garaged at the coal yard, out of sight, otherwise questions might be asked; the use of cars and petrol needed permission.

Thrilled with his new 'set of wheels', Twyford dropped Ivy and Howard at the doctor's apartment in Parliament Hill and promised to return the following morning. George had deflected their aggravation and though the relief may only be temporary, they were grateful.

He arrived fifteen minutes late to find the playground deserted and the school in darkness. A lone figure stood inside the gates, and what a figure! A smart coat and high heels complemented long, long legs, the rich chestnut hair which had been pinned up earlier, now curled down over her shoulders and the image stated the effort made; they would not be talking too much about Alan's truancy. She eased onto the seat and her skirt rose up over her knees. Still better, she left it there. The evening murmured promise.

The Bull and Bush was relaxing but their conversation, in parts, danced into fencing bouts and he was made to work for every half smile. At first he thought that perhaps she saw him as a kind of challenge and he allowed a few snipes to slip passed, responding by finding amusement at each cutting jibe. This only pricked her to intensify and it was soon very apparent that she disliked most things about him. He teased out insults and chuckled the more which drew her teeth and an undisguised sneer that was meant to pierce deeply, though only succeeded in stiffening an already erected penis. Back in the Ford and a kiss was refused, so Jack Straw's car park was definitely not on. He drove to her rooms at Swiss Cottage and managed to wrench a date for the following Monday. The school ma'am was shaping up into a fantasy come to life and he wasn't giving up that easy.

Irving and George arrived at Parliament Hill with the morning post. Howard had received a bunch of letters, held together with an elastic band. Twyford carried in provisions of eggs, bacon, sausages and tomatoes and handed them to Ivy, who looked ten years younger. While she prepared the food Howard took the letters to his bedroom, the first one already opened. George saw his head go down but sat about with Irving discussing Monty's lack of progress through Italy; they had agreed in the car their only course of action. Breakfast was soon ready and Howard had still not returned. Ivy found him sitting on the bed, hopelessly depressed again. The letters were lying open on the floor, the majority hate mail from ignorant fools; nevertheless they had a bad effect on the good doctor. George casually ripped them up and threw them in the bin. 'Come on or this feast will get cold.'

They ate together and although Irving came out with some cheerful anecdotes Howard and Ivy had gone into themselves. Breakfast over, Twyford sat them down and Irving told them of his findings. He began, 'The news isn't good. You're allowed bail because the charge is manslaughter and the police believe that there is no likelihood of you making a habit of it. Normally with euthanasia it gets upgraded to premeditated murder. Have you made a statement yet?'

'No,' said Howard, 'before declining the case my solicitor suggested I answer all questions with 'no comment', which was exactly what I did.'

'Good! Let me inform you of the facts, as hard as they may be to take. Be it manslaughter or murder both charges are life imprisonment, at least.' That piece of information just about brought Howard's world to an end.

On first impressions this may not have been the sort of man Twyford could flow with. However, he was certainly ideal for what George had in mind so he gave the bombshell a chance to sink in and then produced his lifeline.

'Forgetting about the little worries here,' he said, 'let me tell you where I've been for the last four years and then you might consider it. The Rand is lush, wild and untamed, the weather always hot and sunny. Maybe that's why the local inhabitants are happier than we seem to be. They are open, friendly and warm, but these lovely people have little money and no medical help at all. They depend on old, wise women with a few charms and herbs to make them well. The children die too often and too easily from illnesses that are quite curable here and their parents never make old bones. They live in townships with no clean water or schools and work in the mines. The occasional missionaries from one or other of the churches do what little they can, telling them that God loves them and that one day he'll help them and they believe it, they really do. That's probably the one thing that keeps them going. You could help needy folk like that and save lives. It must be a wonderful feeling to be able to heal people.' Howard was taking the bait. George continued, 'Sometimes uncontrollable things happen and from them something marvellous emerges.'

'I would give anything to be in that position,' Howard interjected, proudly. 'That's the reason I first studied medicine. I was young and bursting with all those flawless aspirations of going anywhere that I could make a difference.' then, more sombrely, added, 'It doesn't take long to have it knocked out of you.' He was talking himself in and out.

Patiently, Twyford began again to hoist his spirits from the cellar, gently coaxing him further by remarking, 'The only crime I can see is if you're forced to give up practising medicine.'

'Yes, you're right, I can't let that happen. If only we could get away from all this,' he said looking at Ivy and linking arms, 'think what we could do, or is it hopeless?'

Ivy sensed they were being lined up for an undertaking and seeing the response from Howard's uncertainty swing the right way, squeezed his arm in anticipation; George was getting them out, she knew it.

'If it could be arranged, would you be prepared to help them?' asked Twyford.

'Wholeheartedly!' came the reply.

'And so would I!' added Ivy.

"And about time!" thought George. 'Then let me work on it.'he said.

Twyford returned three hours later. He had already made the necessary enquiries and knew there was nothing immediate going to South Africa but he produced two single tickets from the London Docks to Las Palmas on a Spanish freighter leaving Saturday and connecting tickets to the Cape some days later. He gave them two hundred and fifty pounds as a year's wages in advance. They were nervous, excited and frightened all at once but the decision had been made and they must only look to the future. Ivy would write a letter to her daughter and a small note for Gerry, and George would see to everything. Howard gave Twyford a list of medical supplies that should be despatched as soon as possible. He had the letter of introduction to Father Colm together with a bank draft for the Township for more desperately needed funds. George would get them to the ship Friday lunchtime and once aboard there was very little chance of their escape being discovered. He left them with enough food for twenty four hours and in a golden state of shock.

Thursday afternoon, Twyford returned to his Mum's house around quarter to three and found Kevin waiting for him. He had finished work early and was having a cup of tea with his Nan. They went to shake hands and again George grabbed him in an affectionate bear hug. This time, Kevin squeezed back and kissed him on the cheek and George glowed. This young man made him very proud but with such a fine, fresh face it showed his feelings too easily.

'This is a lovely surprise,' said George, knowing why he was there and what he wanted to know.

'Dad, I'm a man now, I hope we can be honest with each other.'

'Of course we can, Kev,' George was even proud of the manly way he broached the subject. 'Please don't interrupt me until I've finished, Dad. I want you to tell me why you left, every detail. I promise not to say anything to anyone, this is just for me.'

Twyford knew he could not avoid it, Kevin deserved better than that, but he hesitated for many reasons not least of all Mary. No matter how foully she had treated him, she was still the boy's mother and it was Mary, not himself, who had always done what was best for Kevin, who loved him certainly no less than George and had brought him up to be the great lad that he was today. He searched for a way to begin, to tell the story and leave out one or two details in the hope that Kevin missed them.

'It started about four years ago, late November as I remember. We had no money for Christmas presents but you and the kids were not gonna' go without if I could help it. This particular day I had to collect our best wash from the Bagwash Shop in Castle Road. The girl couldn't find it and left me for a moment while she went to look out the back. On the floor of the shop was a lot of dirty washing and cleaning, piled in a heap, and on top were a couple of what I guessed to be uniforms. They were tied, inside out, in two small bundles but the police buttons showed through. I picked them up and quickly dropped them outside. The girl returned with our washing, I paid her and then left with the two bundles as well. I was right, they were police uniforms. From there we planned a bit of business which I thought at the time was a stroke of genius and wouldn't hurt anybody. We told the wives we had some work for a few days cutting down Christmas trees up north. Mickey Butler, Kit and Owen came with me and we drove to Scotland in two cars; one was a black Wolseley that looked like a police car and the other was a big delivery van full of empty petrol cans. Mornie had pressed and altered the uniforms to fit Owen and Kit. We checked everything as we went up, picking out-of-the-way petrol stations and garages, finding out who was open early and who stayed late. We did our homework well and plotted the route back, avoiding London and finishing at Plymouth. The idea was that Mickey would start off in the van with no petrol and buy a gallon at each stop, paying with a white fiver; he would get the change and go. We would arrive ten minutes later, as policemen in the black Wolseley. I became the plain clothed officer in charge because of my mastery of the Scotch accent. That sounds flash,' added George, with a grin,' but honestly I only needed to listen to them for ten minutes and I can't stop myself mimicking the local dialect. I would enquire if anyone had passed a white fiver recently, number so-and-so. When they produced it I informed them that it was counterfeit and hurriedly took it as evidence, leaving the garage attendant with a petty cash voucher as a receipt for the note and racing off in whatever direction he pointed us, promising to keep him posted.' George paused there and studied Kevin. So far he was smiling. 'We planned it like a military operation, zigzagging the country and catching everyone. It was a hundred percent perfect! When we got back to London we had stacks of money and enough petrol to last for ages, but we made two mistakes which nearly cost us. The first one was Mickey's cockney accent, although that on its own would only confuse our hunters who would be searching for a Londoner, a Jock and two I.P.O.'s (impersonating police officers). The second and more serious mistake was spending too much money. That caught the eye of the local Bluebottles who get the particulars of all open ended cases.' Twyford stopped, took the carving knife and cut some bread. He lifted it up to Kevin who shook his head, and George speared a slice with the toasting fork then held it in front of the fire, watching the flames. Now he was getting to the delicate bit. Kevin sat patiently waiting for the last chapter. 'Unlawful opportunities that were just too tempting would come along and, mug that I was, I'd get involved which finally got me known to the police. So once my description was circulated I was a candidate -and if I wasn't about, they couldn't get us. Without me the others were safe.' Now the swerve, he thought. 'It broke my heart to leave but I didn't have a choice, it was that or prison. I couldn't bestow you lot with the shame of that. I've been very foolish, Kev, thinking it was big and yet the only one who suffered in the end was me. I was deprived of seeing my family grow up; a lonely, stupid man. I vowed if I had another chance to come back, I'd never get in trouble again. You must believe that.' He said it with his eyes closed, praying silently for forgiveness for more lies.

'I think I understand all of that, Dad, but why was it only you that left?'

'Mickey couldn't leave Theresa, as ill as she was, so he had to take a chance, the other two were uniforms and didn't ever speak therefore had very little to worry about. Anyway, the only one who would be remembered was me. Mickey was just another customer, none of them were sure of what he looked like. I asked all the pertinent questions and planted the thought that Mickey was taller and older than he was. They urged us to move fast, thinking we were hot on his heels.'

Twyford did not want this to go much farther, but he knew Kevin was not finished yet.

'I've asked Mum this question; did Pops know about it and if he did, did he warn you?'

'If it wasn't for your Grandfather, I would never have got to South Africa.' said George. "At least that bit was true," he thought.

'But Dad, he hates you.'

'Perhaps he just wants it to look like that,' answered George. Kevin looked confused, Twyford continued, 'I promised him I wouldn't talk about any help he might or might not have given me. Don't ask me to go back on my word, ay?'

Archie Shaw was a brutal, wicked thug legalised by the uniform - but it would be incorrect to let Kevin know that; he must form his own opinion.

'No, of course not.' said Kevin, a little naively. 'But then, why aren't you and Mum together? How come you detest the sight of each other, what brought all this on, you must have loved her once?'

George took a bite out of the toast he had just buttered, giving himself time to think. He could not answer and there was no point in coming out with a lot of twaddle.

'No, Son,' he said, sadly, 'that's between your mother and me. I don't want to talk about it anymore tonight. If you really want to know, I'll tell you another time, I promise. Let's natter about something else now, something better, like how you're getting on down Spitalfield's?'

Archie Shaw worried the problem of George Twyford around in his mind, the man was like a little black ball of bad luck, bouncing back to haunt him. He had been so gloriously pleased after running that chiselling piece of garbage out of the country. It had to be done; the pressure point he used then was the threat of sticking anything he could down to Mickey Butler and locking him up. He guessed this was Twyford's weakness, knew he would never allow the Butler wife to be without her husband. So George went quietly, she would never have survived. Too bad, they shouldn't break the law, it's there to protect everyone, even them, and that filth had got away with it for far too long. Once Twyford was gone, that particular crowd of miscreants fell in to line. Now he's back and trouble's starting, Archie could smell it. Georgie boy would have to be re-persuaded and the sooner the better, who knows, perhaps that very night?

The children had all left for school and in Alan's case there was a fair chance he might arrive there this time. Mary had warned him that children who did not go to school could catch dyslexia. He kept asking what it was and she suggested if he went, he might find out. He was too like his father and it worried her how much influence George was already having.

Why couldn't she meet a man like her Daddy; strong and safe, somebody she could depend on. Richard was certainly a nice fellow, perhaps too nice, and that may be why Mary couldn't feel that special something to take him to her bed. She had been so long without a man. George was once the only one Mary ever wanted and she had made sure he was roped and tied; what a dreadful mistake. Were it possible to undo the tangled mesh and wipe him from her life, if she could plunge a dagger into his heart and never get caught, tomorrow wouldn't be soon enough. He was not worth making herself angry over. George Twyford only wanted things he could not have. He did not like her being with someone else, that was apparent, especially someone better looking. Good. Perhaps she could use that to render some serious damage.

The two firms of solicitors were meeting in the West End to finalise the sale of the seven properties. Benson was not in attendance; in fact neither party had to attend. It was basically signatures, deeds and a bank draft, and needed no more than fifteen minutes of anyone's time.

Ruben Benson sat in his office pondering the sale. The price hadn't really bothered him. The War had been a blessing, for he could not have got away with a fraction of this in peace time. He bought very cheaply and just collected rents. When a house gets bombed the structures of the other houses around it suffer badly, yet he had spent next to nothing on repairs. Yes, in that respect he had been lucky. What goaded him was that saucy bastard threatening him personally. Benson had been shaken before, but had always handled it himself and they never tried twice. He knew in his heart he had gone too strong with these bullying tactics and should have controlled the action better. Too late for that now, but in future he would chair the meetings once a week, get reports on all problems and have the final word on what was necessary. Ruben felt he'd been financially violated by the legal actions and was forced into taking the least painful way out. Win or lose that was business but nevertheless he wanted to punch

Twyford's head in. The attempt to run the man over was not meant to kill him, just break a few bones. It was wrong, had he died, no doubt these South Londoners, for he was now convinced that's who they were, would have started something nasty. Yet, had Ruben bashed the lights out of him, the deal could still have gone through and no one would have been too put out then, more importantly, Ruben's self respect would have been restored. That's why Benson had led him into the woods for a straightener. The idea was to get to a quiet spot and tell this Twyford exactly what he wanted to do, and may the best man win. He had expected George to understand and agree to it. The fucking fright he experienced when he turned the path in those woods, and surprisingly he had to smile. Reflecting on it now, it was a good move by them. The shock had nearly made his dinner pass through. "I definitely haven't heard the last of him," he thought. "Shame he wasn't working for me!"

At that moment, George was below him on the Underground, using half an hour to ensure he was not being tailed. He alighted at Kentish Town and walked through the Coal Wharf to check in with Lestor Hogg, who was too busy to even utter an imprecation. That side of the business was marching on at a furious pace.

Twyford arrived outside Howard's flat and noticed the curtains in the ground floor window twitch. He drove on for fifty yards and parked the Ford in a side street, got out and walked back; it wouldn't do for anyone to get his registration number. As arranged, the door was on the jar. He slipped upstairs and Howard pumped his arm warmly. He and Ivy were so excited; they had packed and been ready for hours. Twyford calmed them down and ran through some safety procedures. She was to leave with the luggage and take a taxi to Kings Cross. Howard and George would wait five minutes and then drive to the same destination and collect her; that way, no one could know that Howard had jumped bail. By Monday morning, they'd be long gone. Any of their letters from Karinna would be routed through the office. They understood but George repeatedly drummed in the need for security all the way to the London Docks. He shepherded them on board and said a hasty farewell. They were holding hands and had been from Kings Cross Station. Ivy cried saying goodbye but she wasn't sure why, perhaps happiness. "Everyone deserves a chance of that," thought George. He left with a little billet-doux to Gerry in his inside pocket and wondered how Nolan would take the news. For himself, Twyford was chuffed at how well the move had worked and for such an inexpensive outlay. Admittedly it was a stroke, but a stroke of genius when all points were considered. Life imprisonment was a slight exaggeration; in fact a couple of years probation would have probably been nearer the truth but the happy pair were not to know that and, besides, the sunshine would do them good. The more his blinkered brain rummaged around the more convinced he became as to what a great kindness he had bestowed on everyone. Howard and Ivy were having an adventure, on top London wages making them wealthy indeed by South African standards, and the Township would now receive serious medical help. He cheerfully put it down as assisted kismet, logged it in the archives and mentally marched on.

The car sped through the East End to the Jago for his next appointment. He seemed to be having nothing but business meetings these days but his head was so full of schemes that he constantly needed to let some out. Moreover, if the house purchases had gone through, he anticipated that there would be a proper celebration that night.

When George entered the office Irving and Benny were waiting with three mugs bubbling over with creamsoda.

CHAPTER 16: 'DROP A LINE TO MY SECRETARY AND SHE'LL TRY AND FIT YOU IN.'

USSR: A German counter offensive launched yesterday retakes Zitomir and also forces the Soviets back at Korosten. Hitler brags of their impending world domination.

Churchill: We shall not fail or falter, we shall not weaken or tire, neither the sudden shock of battle nor the long, drawn trials of vigilance and exertion will wear us down!"

Even in the midst of wartime, the Soho Salon was a true treat and the six chairs were seldom empty. Treatments were speedy but never rushed and a cut could not be stylish without a vigorous Pashana massage. Piping hot towels softened the beard for that really close shave then a dab of eau de cologne around the jowls, a lighted taper to flick the ears and nostrils and a gentleman was altogether revitalised.

Jeffrey was younger than the other barbers but was already considered an artisan in the mastery of shaving. His third client of the day was a regular visitor to the establishment and, by the way the chap was usually pandered to, Jeffrey envisaged a substantial tip. Lively conversations of the war bounced around the busy salon and, with everyone adding their patriotic sixpenneths, the result was becoming a foregone conclusion. Tilted back in the chair, Donald Grogan shut his ears to the clatter but failed to put the near catastrophe of Birmingham from his thoughts. The crux was that his superiors had lacked the final confidence in himself and interfered in a painstakingly settled deal: -and the Brummie broker had mistakingly seen the new negotiators as nothing more than a weak French fop and a beddable woman. Consequently, his greed pushed his luck a tad too far that night and his murder might still heap unnecessary attention at such a crucial time in their proceedings. The soft badger hairs tickled lather over his face and neck and he became heedful of his pleasant surroundings once more. His nostrils were gently pinched clear and the cutthroat was smoothly gliding up the left side of his throat. A sudden laugh and the door bumped open. The young barber looked up and the finely-honed blade accidentally sliced the underside of Mr. Grogan's chin. In a flash, Grogan was bolt upright and glowering. The reaction came with such acceleration that Jeffrey stepped back in fright. The volume in the room tailed away and a hushed salon waited. Gingerly offering a towel, Jeffrey found voice and stammered an apology. A more relaxed man took the towel, settled back in the chair to dab his nick, and spoke easily, saying, 'Its okay, Laddie, first one's on you,' then paused before promising, 'next one's on me.'

Tinker was loading his cart with a dozen or so large boxes, each one full of bacon, ham, fish, eggs, dried eggs, sugar, jam, flour, a variety of fruits and vegetables, and a shoulder of lamb. He had been out collecting and delivering since 4 o'clock that morning and this was the last and most important load. They had had an astounding week and he was taking a little well deserved bonus to each of the lads. George had two because of his situation.

Before he could knock on Mary's door, Alan opened it and shouted out, 'Mum, it's Tinker!' then shot off up the street.

Mary flew out into the road and screamed at him to come back but he was gone.

'That devil's getting wilder!' she said. 'Come on in, Nathaniel,' she only ever used his proper name, 'Would you like a cup of tea?'

'Yes please, Mary, I'm spitting feathers.' he replied, and carried the box into the kitchen for her.

'Whatever can that be?' she mused.

'Open it and have a peep,' he suggested.

Mary was delighted. She could queue for hours with her ration book and still not get anything like this. The only food not in short supply was potatoes and carrots and they were sick to death of them. She gave him tea and plied him with questions about everyone. He had rehearsed his story knowing it might get awkward if she suspected that George had anything to do with it. But still he told her the good news about some of the lads buying their houses, and also of the gathering that night for a celebratory drink. When he departed he felt she had drained him of all knowledge.

George arrived at the Malden early. The band was setting up and he ordered a pint of Bass for himself and three halves of shandy for the minstrels. They would not take a strong drink until their work was almost over.

There were two young soldiers, still in uniform, 'fuffing' and 'blinding' at the bar a little too loudly to be sober. They looked over at George, one sniggered and whispered something quietly and they roared out loud. George was dressed as smartly as his wardrobe would allow and couldn't be bothered to pull them up. Anyway, he was in too good a mood, so ignored them. The barmaids started arriving and the squaddies soon got bored with him and turned their attentions to the shapely curves behind the ramp. Mornie and Lestor came in together to have ten minutes with George to discuss how the company's first week had gone. A few minor problems, but a strong roll of good luck had given them a cracking start. They had bought and sold plenty of tackle and were confident that the coming weeks would be double busy through to Christmas.

The soldiers were becoming a nuisance and had gone from being lewd to down right stroppy. Horrie had given them their marching orders; he told them, 'Drink up and fuck off!' and had walked down the other end of the bar, meanwhile the pub began to fill. As if on cue, Archie Shaw came through the double doors on the corner at the same time as an ashtray flew through the air and narrowly missed Horrie's nose. The soldiers knew, too late, that they had gone too far and a right good night was about to be ruined. People stepped away from the bar to let the big frame through. He walked at them, shot one arm out and gripped the first squaddie by the throat, then the second by the scruff of the neck. They were four foot apart and he crashed their heads together in one sickening blow; that dull thud of bone against bone. One remained upright, grasped by the neck still, but with buckled legs, while the other slumped forward, suspended by his collar, facing the sawdust. The big Sergeant walked to the door, taking the limp bodies with him. He moved up the alleyway next to the pub and repeated the treatment again, then left them in a bloody heap. They would sober up later and stagger off home, perhaps a little wiser. The two officers in the waiting police car continued to look the other way. Justice had been done. Why bother to arrest two drunks, lock them up for the night and then waste public money charging them at court the next day? All they would get was a slapped wrist, a small fine and sent back to barracks, whilst the police would be left the job of cleaning up the mess in the cells; justice had certainly been done!

George knew the reason for the police visit; Archie had come for him. The door of the pub opened and he walked back in. Tinker came through the other entrance and seeing the Sergeant's approach, altered course to the farthest point away. Twyford stood between Lestor and Mornie and carried on their conversation. Archie seemed to stop his face a foot from them. His complete presence was huge and intimidating. The other two each received a stony three second stare. They were meant to back away and leave but nervously stood their ground.

'I think it's time for our little chat, don't you?'

'Where's your manners! You don't rudely interrupt people like that. Who are you anyway? Do I know you?' demanded George.

'Don't get lippy with me, you slimy, little maggot!'

'Oh, it's you Father-in-law, dear. Until you murmured those eloquent endearments I didn't recognise you. Would you like a word with me?' Archie's top lip began to curl. 'Well, drop a line to my secretary and she'll try to fit you in.'

The lads failed to stifle a chuckle. Archie's eyes bore into George. 'I'm gonna smash you to pieces.' he said, quite matter of fact.

'No you're not. You're gonna fuck right off, now.' Archie started forward menacingly, his face closer still. 'Please, grab me by the throat like you did to those little boys. Go on, do it! You come in here and in front of witnesses threaten me with bodily harm. My solicitor would have your bollocks nailed to the wall in two minutes!'

'Right, that's the three of you,' he said evenly, pushing his great face into each of them, one by one, then turned and walked away.

George's voice followed him out, 'Stone me, he can count! No mug, him!'

Tinker came over, a look of alarm on his face. 'What ever did he want?'

'Oh, just a chat,' said George.

Lestor Hogg was blowing air and Mornie's shoulders had slumped with relief.

'S'truth!' was all he could utter.

'Take no notice', said George, feeling a mite braver now the threat had passed. 'He'll have me first, if he can. He'll have to be lively though, I'll tell you that.'

'He terrifies me,' admitted Tinker. 'He looks at me and I'm guilty, even if I haven't done nothing. That's the first time anyone's ever fronted him and got away with it.'

'You watch your arse from now on,' added Lestor shrewdly.

'Yeah. Still, who gives a carrot? Let's have another drink.' The bravado back in place and ready to swell.

Lestor suddenly started chuckling and the other three looked at him curiously. Frank Nash wandered across. 'You have to laugh,' said Lestor, 'He's done more damage in three weeks than the Germans have in three years, what with Ruby, Archie and even that Scotch bastard Grogan, back to haunt us.'

Mornie found no gaiety in the conjecture's final character. 'Now that cow-son scared the shit out of me, the same mad eyes.'

'No I don't think so,' replied George, seriously. 'To Archie, we're the opposite of what he stands for and he believes he's right. That Grogan makes us look like monks. One evil man who'd do anything that suited him. Look at that time in river crossing training when he forced Mickey to fall eight foot between the rocks and break his leg in two places.' Everyone silently remembered.

'Yeah, he hated Mickey,' agreed Lestor. 'That night we spoke of snuffing him, desperate times eh?'

Frank Nash had heard the story on many occasions but prompted them on.

'We had decided to tell him to leave us alone -or we'd kill him.' began Twyford, to get the annals flowing.

'Yeah,' added Lestor, 'It was rock climbing the next day. You have to support one another.' he explained for Frank's benefit. 'We had reached the top of some sheer tor and Grogan stood near the edge. He was the instructor and had to show how fearless he was. He still had the connecting rope round his waist and was dishing out the usual bollocking, calling us all the cowardly shitbags in the world, when Johnny Bass stepped near him to speak, then just pushed. He went over the edge backwards with a huge scream but there was only us to hear. We dangled him from the top, remember?'

Again it went quiet with those dark memories. Tinker retold the rest of it.

'George told him, "There's seven of us and it'd be easy to kill you: loads of opportunities for a fatal accident. Either stop the heavy treatment, especially to Mickey, or we'll let go of the rope now." He knew we were deadly serious. When we pulled him up if he had said one wrong word we would have thrown him off. He hated us for that but he learnt a precious lesson that day!.'

Mornie remarked, 'He tried to do you Georgie, sending you up in No Mans Land without support.' and asked, 'Do you really think he shot that flare?'

'Yes,' answered George, 'I'm positive he did.'

'Still, you got the medal for bravery.'

'Or stupidity. I ain't sure if there's a difference.' came the reply.

Lestor added, 'We were just kids but we were the only ones in that regiment who weren't scared of him anymore.'

'No,' corrected Mornie. 'Individually we were frightened but it showed him that our friendship was stronger than anything he had ever come up against, and it's still the same now.'

'Here, here!' said Frank, and they all chinked glasses.

'Come on. Let's liven ourselves up here. Where's Kit? We need a song.'

Kit was at the bar talking to a busty blonde by the name of Rita. They called him and the pub drooled as she came too. Slinking across the barroom like Mae West, she caught the attention of the drummer, who beat time with her breast bounce while her cheeks constantly battled to see which one could rotate higher. The words of a song came to mind and George quoted, 'That's not thunder beating dear, just my poor heart you hear -and it's applause.' He received a flashing smile; what a little darling. Kit left her with his "friends" and jumped on the stage, he was about to show off. With great timing he sang "Night & Day". She was smitten. Lucky bastard, they all thought.

Mary came in with Kathy and waved at Tinker, ignoring George completely.

'Did you tell her we were out tonight?' asked George.

'I don't remember,' said Tinker. He was such a nice fellow. 'She might have got it out of me. You know what she's like.'

Lestor butted in, 'She's murder, your old woman. Mary don't

miss anything! Good job she's not a copper.' Twyford was adding Archie to his sums and did not like the total. She had told her father where he would be.

The effervescent Kit loved the stage and lived for the attention; he followed up with "All the way" while George laboured along with Rita, keeping her warm for his return. Meanwhile the group swelled. Fintan and Bridgid arrived and stopped at Mary's table. The pub was jammed to the rafters.

'Is George here?' asked Fintan, after ten seconds of polite small talk.

'He's over there with the rest of the force,' said Mary, pointing behind with the back of her head. Fintan left the girls to join him …they didn't notice.

Mickey arrived next. He was so happy with his new house, just the upstairs to be decorated and everything would be done. His job now was constantly checking the security of their operation and the rest of the time helping Lestor replenish stocks to meet the incredible demand. George summed it up. 'We can earn enough this side of Christmas to cover us for the next twelve months. We all want to own our houses and buy a nice few more before this War's over. I don't want to get political,' he stated, 'and spoil the evening but, just to say, the ordinary people of England are gonna suffer for the next ten years, whoever wins. They're paying for this folly so we'll make our own luck and perhaps our families will do better than we did after the last one. Anyway, to the Company; to us.' Everyone toasted and drank deeply.

George had a quiet chat with Fintan; it seemed Ruben had suddenly decided to take the waters at Bath. He was away for a fortnight's break with his family.

Irving Jacobs turned up with Benny and about a dozen of his relations. A few of them had met the boys before but everyone was made welcome and Twyford mingled busily. The next target was Gerry Nolan. A word in his ear and he passed across Ivy's note, Nolan put it in his inside pocket. 'I'll read it later and maybe we'll talk in the week.' he said. 'Just tell me, will she be alright?'

'More than alright,' promised George.

Gerry smiled, 'Well, good luck to her,' then changed the subject with a joke about a sailor and a goose.

"Nice to be able to pigeon-hole things and bring them out another time." thought George. "I wish I could."

The Jewish crowd had a great sense of humour and as they achieved intoxication, Irving reaped Dutch courage and sang. Gifted with the worst voice in Shoreditch, he gave it everything he could. The girls supported him nobly by dancing erratically, in and out of the tables, to the missing rhythm of his distorted gravel. It was a splendid night. Even Horace appeared to smile continuously but most people put that down to a severe case of wind.

The Force, as they called themselves after Mary's crack, had intended to aim at the Café Luxor, but Charlie Gay, Kathy's father, was in the company and invited everyone back to his house for a party. No one noticed a stout couple who walked in and immediately walked back out again. Ruben's man Nobby had heard it was a good night at the Malden and decided to give it a try. He saw George sideways on and stepped behind his woman. Fintan was there, as large as life, laughing with him. Nobby grabbed his wife's elbow and left quietly.

Sergeant Shaw sent two Bobbies into the pub at twenty-five to twelve that night and cleared a crowded bar. Horace was in breach of his licence, allowing people on the premises after hours so everyone loaded up with booze and descended on the Gay's house several streets away. Archie sat in an unmarked car and watched them go. He could wait. He would have that bastard tonight.

Charlie Gay was popular with everyone and regularly woke his wife up with half of Kentish Town. She came down and made sandwiches and was more than happy to do so, just as long as Chas came home to her every night and not someone else. The Gay's piano tinkled into life and the singing began again. Fintan and Bridgid stayed for quite a while but were the first to leave, dropping Mary off on their way home. George left with Johnny Bass about an hour later and walked back towards the Square, stopping by Rhyl Street School for a minute. Both were in the middle of a pee and looked up when they heard a footstep. Archie came out of a doorway not three paces away and went for Twyford. Considering the amount of booze he had tipped down his throat, George's reaction was good. As the hand gripped his collar he turned and fled. His overcoat remained in Archie's tight grasp while George sprinted off, penis still protruding. Ignoring Bass, Archie dropped the coat in the urine and pursued him at an incredible speed. Hearing nineteen stone of solid muscle pounding after him Twyford ran faster. With the movement, his penis had worked its way back inside but was now being strangled by his underpants. They hared through streets and alleyways but Archie stayed with him. George's lungs were gulping down air and his heart was coming through his chest, yet still the big bastard was close. With all the ale sloshing around inside him, George knew he could not hold the pace much longer and had to find somewhere to hide. Archie was also grunting with the effort and the gap gradually began to widen. They were now ten yards apart, both dying on their feet, but neither would stop. The chase was about to pass the top of St Leonard's Square when Twyford saw the squad car coming down Malden road, heading straight for him. He altered course and lost a big advantage, his only choice was to run at the bike sheds in Shipton Terrace, a blocked turning. Archie made a final effort and shortened the gap. George knew with a good jump and reach he might clutch the roof's edge and use his foot high on the door to spring him up onto it. Pure hatred drove Archie to rip apart the piece of scum whose neck was almost in his grasp, just a yard away and closing fast. There was a "rizla" between the massive arms that reached out to grab him and Twyford's back as he leapt into the air. Fingers gripped fast, his right foot hit the shed with force and then propelled him high enough to roll across the flat roof. Completely committed, the Sergeant was at full pelt and could not stop. He thundered into a shed door while his prey escaped over the roofs. Raving with frustration, Archie stormed off back towards St. Leonard's square in case Twyford tried to creep home.

Johnny Bass watched the police car park down the Square blocking George from using that route and decided to keep out of the way. He returned to the party, Twyford's pee-riddled Crombie over his shoulder.

Sergeant Shaw went to Mary's house and threw stones up at her bedroom window on the first floor. After a minute or so the curtains moved back and, in the moon's light, she saw her father waving up at her and came down to let him in. He was still in a rage but, controlling himself with great effort, told her what he wanted and why. She saw him out into the garden, where he could wait and grab George if he tried to get home the back way. For that to happen, Twyford would first have to be let into the house. Mary decided to sit up with her bedside light on. It wasn't long before another stone hit the glass. She did it well and waited for one more before lifting the window up and peering out. George was desperate or he would never have asked her for help. She took delight in that.

'What do you want at this time of night?' she hissed.

'Just a small favour. Come down for a second, please.'

Long she glared and then shut the window. As she came down the stairs Mary could see her father from the landing, his breath giving him away. Without showing herself she opened the door just enough to let Twyford squeeze in. The passage was dark but he could see that although she wore a long flannel night-dress, her face was made up. "I'll look a right mug if Nero's here," he thought, following her upstairs and feeling wrong. She stopped at the landing window and opened it. He stood behind her, looked out and froze.

'Daddy!' she said in a stage whisper.

With no chance for thought, George dropped to his knees, shoved his head up her night-dress and sucked at the crotch of her knickers. She was leaning over the windowsill and, as his mouth locked on to her, she shuddered. He heard Archie say, 'Is he here?'

George sucked harder. She remained silent. He yanked her draws off in one movement and with his tongue buried inside her she could only manage haltingly, 'Tea, Daddy?'

Twyford heard no more. He twisted around and her thighs blocked his ears and firmly held his head. She shut the window then her fingers pulled his hair, holding him inches away from her luscious valley. She stepped a leg over his head and led him to her room, then lay on the bed with her legs apart for George to start again. They hardly touched each other, just his lips and tongue tenderly and rhythmically taking her up and she came quickly, shaking violently in repeating convulsions. He rested his head on her belly and watched the nerves in her legs begin to slow down; very aroused now he stripped in seconds, flinging his clothes anywhere. Without taking his eyes from her treasure he eased up her body, the scent of her numbing his sagacity. She sat up quickly and backhandedly smashed him across the nose with her elbow. The stinging blow took him completely by surprise, knocking him from the bed. His reaction was to pounce astride her and clamp her throat with both hands. She tried to knee him in the groin but his weight flattened her.

'Get off me! Don't touch me. Get away from me!' Mary spat it out as if he were the vilest of reptiles. He pressed down further on her air supply intending to choke the life out of her -then grudgingly reconsidered the outcome. He relaxed his grip, stood up and began grabbing up his underwear.

'What did I just do?' he asked the room. 'Was that nothing?'

'I take my pleasure from whoever I choose,' she answered, desperately regretting one senseless moment of weakness and immediately covering it with all the callousness she could muster. 'Now, get out!' Mary rose from the bed and adjusted her night-dress. George was half-dressed when she walked from the room.

"Mad bitch," he thought. He had one shoe on as he heard the

landing window sash go up. He grabbed his shirt, jacket and spare shoe and flew past her.

She was saying, 'I think he's at the front, Daddy.'

Twyford dashed out and slammed the door loud enough to wake the whole street. 'Explain your way out of that, you old crab!' he hollered, and began ducking in and out of the shadows, making his way to the coal wharf. Very happy to have escaped another near miss, he arrived at the yard and let himself in but the office lights were on. "What now," he thought, quite exhausted. There was nothing around except a bin of parsnips. He selected a large one to use as a weapon and approached the door stealthily then ran in fast with the parsnip above his head raised to strike swiftly...

Johnny Bass looked up from studying a nude book and remarked, 'The last time I saw that it was hanging out of your flies and travelling at a hundred miles an hour.' They both fell about laughing at how ridiculous it all was.

'What are you doing here anyway?' asked George.

'There's a squad car down our street so I went back to Charlie Gay's. They'd all gone to bed and this was the only warm place I could think of.'

'I should have known better,' said George. 'I woke Mary to let me in the back way,' and he told John everything. Bassy tried ever so hard to keep a straight face and then fell about again. George was laughing too and it became a silly half hour, just cracking jokes and taking the sting out of his troubled circumstances. The two of them had always been on a special wavelength and could say anything, ask anything of each other. George had never mentioned why he left. He had said recently that he had no chance to contact any of them before his disappearance and on his reappearance no one had pressed him to tell them why. Now was the time; John became serious.

'Whatever's up mate, you're home and things should be wonderful but instead you and Mary are at war with each other and you're living at your Mum's. I'd like to hear if you want to tell me.'

'Course I'll tell you,' said George, and he began. 'It was that bit of work we had with the fivers, doing the petrol stations. We'd been home a few days and my father-in-law carted me off to the

Station. Kept me in there for twenty four hours with a million questions about where me and Mickey got all this money we were spending. Now, Mickey was spending too much but I gave Mary all my share. So first, who told him about that? He knew it was us they were looking for. Some of the pump attendants had picked me and Mickey out from a photo he had shown them. Knowing Theresa's condition, he swore Mickey would go away for a long time unless I did what I was told. Theresa would die without Mickey, I couldn't let that happen. You must never let Butler know it had anything to do with him.'

'On my honour,' swore John.

'That nasty bastard made sure I saw that photo. It was the one Mary took of us three at your gate when we were all going hopping. There was only one photo and it was in my house in a frame. She must have given it to him. She may be a good mother but I'll see that witch burn in hell before I forgive her for that.'

John felt passionately sorry for his boyhood friend but you can't interfere between man and wife; all words are pointless. 'The sun's coming up,' he said, 'let's greet the morning by taking a jaunt in the jam-jar and get some breakfast.'

It was a fine, bright sunrise and they drove over the back of Hampstead Heath and walked through to Kenwood. They sat there for an hour and a half in silence, watching the last of the night's wildlife. Rabbits were having their final meal before hiding until the sun went down again, a heron rose high in the sky and a lone fox nearly stumbled into them, then bolted away. They walked through the woods, white with frost, towards the restaurant attached to Kenwood House.

'I reckon that fox must have had a cold,' surmised John.

'Hark at Doctor Doolittle! Perhaps you could kindly enlighten me as to how you came by this assumption?' asked George.

'Well, he should have smelt your overcoat fifty yards away.'

'You saucy bastard!' said George, sniffing at his sleeve. 'Is it that bad?'

'Not 'arf, it ain't! Thank 'Gawd the wind's blowing the other way.'

John ran for the restaurant and George gave chase, aiming a boot at his rear end. They burst in like kids and the place was quite busy. Everyone looked up at the intrusion so they tiptoed to a table by the window and sat down grinning. John asked for the biggest fry-up they could have and the manageress served them. When it arrived the treat was so disappointing.

'What, I reckon you stood on the roof to throw them mushrooms on!' complained John.

'I'm sorry the portions are small,' she said, 'but we just can't get the produce.'

Twyford was in like a shot, asking her all the obvious questions and, when he got the right answers, promised to send someone up who would call regularly with everything. They washed their breakfast down with four mugs of tea and were ready to face anything.

'What do you fancy doing today?' asked John.

'I'm easy but shouldn't you let Megan know where you've been, she'll be worried.'

'No, she won't,' came the reply, 'she's left me.' George was flabbergasted. 'She's gone back to Wales for a bit,' he continued.

'But you love each other,' said George.

'Yeah, I know. I just forgot to tell her.'

'What are you gonna do?'

'Nothing.'

'What do you mean nothing? Go down there and bring her

back.'

'Yeah, I will, but not just yet. You can think lots of things about what you didn't do or say when you're on your own. In a week or so, I'll make it right forever. I've only told you, no need for the others to know.'

'No, of course not. So, it's just the two of us, like old times.'

'Yeah, good 'innit? Let's go down Soho and have a look at the shoes and, while we're there, try that French cake shop we used to nick the eclairs out of when we were kids.'

'That'll do me.' And so they set off, just gloriously happy to be together.

Old Compton Street was always exciting: shady men, wild women and excellent shoes. Most pedestrians were in uniform -and the Americans were being served everywhere.

'There's money to be extracted working down here,' said John. 'They're conning these Colonials for fortunes.'

'That's cos they've got fortunes,' answered George. 'I'd like to get a few of them on the payroll.' They were walking down Windmill Street to Piccadilly when they saw a continuous line of Yanks coming in and out of a pub called "The Red Lion". George had to pop in for a drink to see what the attraction was. The Windmill Theatre was along the street and the Inn was second home to its comedians and dance girls when they were not performing. The Yanks were brash and loud, but not in an offensive way, and liked to expound on the War and life in general with anyone who would listen. In no time, the two of them were chatting with a great crowd. They were from an airbase in Cambridgeshire. Thank God Hitler did not decide to attack that day, it seemed the American army only protects from Monday to Friday during office hours. The rest of the time they were using stockings and chocolates and the like to get inside young ladies knickers. George suffered the conversations which started by them saying how they loved England and then, after ten minutes, hearing how nothing works here as well as it does "back home". He contained John from the obvious retort that formed on his lips more than once.

Twyford had been selecting one to approach for possible business. The fellow he picked was sharp for an American - and hungry! He was a corporal which probably gave him a lot more access to their stores than mere enlisted men. George asked him if they had all they needed back at Base.

'Well, we could always use a few more women,' came the answer.

'You've chosen the only thing we can't supply but, thinking about it, my Grandmother shows a fine ankle when her stocking's not hanging around it.'

'Tell me more; she sounds like my kind of gal,' putting his right hand out, 'Buckland Bonnet. Glad to meet you. They call me 'Bone'.'

'Why's that?' asked John. To say the man was skinny was an exaggeration, he was translucent!

'Do you know I've never been able to work that out myself.' His grip was firm and unexplainably his smile established him as straight forward. They spent a good hour talking and arranged to meet later that night to cement their friendship with a few drinks at the Café Luxor. Normally Yanks couldn't get in because they had a reputation similar to the Irish. George's theory was that, when inebriated, the Welsh thought they could all sing, the Irish wanted to fight, usually their friends or relatives and the Scottish wanted to fight anyone but, preferably, tooled up first. And the good old English let them get on with it as long as it didn't affect them. The only way to unite our Island Race was with a bloody, good war.

On the way home, Twyford spoke of his hopes of trading with the Shermans.

'We can never get enough spirits and tobacco; this might bring us nearer to the total service. I thought the long streak was all right.'

'I thought he was very polite.' George raised an eyebrow and waited for the remark. 'Not mentioning the aroma.'

'Fuck off! You'll give me a complex. I won't let you wear it tonight now, you've spoilt yourself.'

Spirits were high in anticipation of the coming night. George hadn't seen Radna for a week and decided he would try to drink less until the Café Luxor, then, on further reflection, realised he couldn't so he would have to go out an hour later. John just loved the place; the style and the elegance of it and agreed to do the same, reflecting, 'Funny, we might not have the bank balances of some but we don't hold back. I bet we must be his best customers, no wonder Tony laps us up.'

The day had gone somewhere and it was already getting dark when they parked the car in the yard, locked up and walked home. With an eye out for Sergeant Shaw and his merry men, they reached the Square safely and each went to their respective houses, agreeing not to surface until 10 to 10. It would do the world good to miss them for an hour. George had tea with his Mum and, suddenly weary, enjoyed a nap in the armchair. He awoke in a sweat having had a nightmare that 'Bounty' had been stolen, and all those endless possibilities were packing their bags from his heart. If the clock wasn't playing up, it was still only 8.15, plenty of time. Twyford dived into a thick pullover, grabbed a torch and made his way down the garden and into Mary's. The black-out curtains were still pulled across so, making no sound, George slipped into the dark outhouse. He heard a faint sniff and turned the torch on. Alan sat on the logs with his coat over his head, terrified.

'What are you doing here, mate?' asked George, quickly realising that the boy couldn't see who it was and that he had, unwittingly, given his son quite a fright. George hopped up next to Alan on to the old chest of drawers, gave him a squeeze and whispered, 'Why are you shivering out here?'

'It was them girls.'

'Who? Niamh and Mairead?'

'Yeah!' He could tell his Dad everything about what the horrible, old cows had done. 'They kept taking the rise out'a me saying I was scared of the dark, just cos I go asleep with a little light on.'

'Take no notice of them, son! They're just practising on you so they can be horrible to bigger boys. Girls are like that.'

'They said rats would get me if the light was out. I told them I ain't scared of nothing.'

'So that's why you're here is it?'

'Yeah. But they don't know so don't tell them, ay?'

'No, course not. That's good. You mustn't show that they're getting to you cos then they'll do it all the more. Just laugh at them, they hate that!'

'Yeah. I love you, Dad.'

'Me an' all mate.' They sat a little longer and then George lifted him down, turned the torch on and said, 'Hang on for a second, Al, I'm looking for something.' He went to the ballbaring scooter and the beam lit the floor all around it. The tennis ball was not there. Twyford tried not to panic. It must be there, somewhere! Perhaps it had rolled? He lifted everything up and stacked it in a heap by the logs. Nothing. Alan watched, sensing trouble.

'Can I help, Dad, what we looking for?' George stared at the empty space he had cleared.

'I'm looking for a tennis ball, Al.'

'An old one,' said Alan, knowing he was in trouble. 'It was useless, Dad; didn't bounce so I slung it. I can get much better ones for you.'

'No, no,' interrupted George gently, his heart in his mouth. 'It was a special one, Al. When did you sling it?'

'About a week ago. I wanted one to take to school but the inner tube had gone, you could hear it.' George crouched down and held Alan's hands.

'Don't worry. Nothing's gonna happen, if it's gone, it's gone, but do you remember what you did with it?'

'I just threw it up and kicked it.'

'What, in this garden?'

'Yeah.'

'Try and think. Where did it land?'

Alan looked around and shrugged his shoulders. 'I didn't look.'

'Let's look now.' The garden was overgrown and untidy with so many places that could hide it from view, including, in the yard, a drain with a broken grill. George investigated this first, while Alan looked with him, one torch between them. They were kneeling down, peering into the hole, when the back door opened shedding light on both of them. Mary stood there, hands on her hips and a curse on her lips.

'What the hell?' she began, 'Holy Mother of God!'

Words failed her and Alan said quickly, 'I lost a shilling between here and Nan's and Dad's helping me search for it.'

'We'll look in the morning, Al,' said George,' it'll be easier. No one's gonna get it before then.' And with that kissed him and walked away; Mary's scowl burning into his back.

Twyford went to his room and sat on the bed, blaming himself; this was his life's security. He knew this stone could easily steal his reason and its departure would be utterly devastating. Everyone he loved was safe under the umbrella as long as 'Bounty' was there. He tried to be positive, it had not gone far; the ball would be rotting somewhere quite close. He would break the area into sections and examine each one thoroughly until it was back with him, no matter how long it took.

CHAPTER 17: 'NOT THAT SIZE, I HOPE, OR THAT ATTRACTIVE!'

Dodecanese; Germany captures Leros and the Allies are forced to evacuate all the islands except Castelrosso.

Always punctual, Johnny Bass called for him at precisely 9.50. George had to laugh; he was wearing his purchase, it was a strong red cravat with a white shirt and a navy blazer. A nautical man, he was short a tattoo and telescope but actually showed a pipe in his top pocket. Any time he made a comment George screwed up one eye, touched his forelock and said, 'Aye-aye, sir!' They went up the road singing "Putting on the Ritz".

Arriving at the Malden, the two toffs pushed the door open and people almost fell out. Normally it was worth squeezing through the throng at the bar to see what talent was about but, in this instance, it was easier to walk around to the side entrance. They still had to do the sideways shuffle but the lads' position was nearer and already had three cases of pale ale with the tops off in their corner. Two pint jugs were produced and everyone clambered around to hear last night's adventure with that nice Sergeant Shaw. Shrieks of laughter went up as John described George's take-off from Archie's clutches. 'He was out of that coat like a greyhound out of the traps. Archie stood there stunned for a second, dropped the Crombie right in the urine and flew after him.' Twyford added comments on his father-in law's surprising speed and his own fear of being caught. But the noise level drowned out the band when John painted a verbal picture of Georgie running for his life, with his truncheon hanging out and Archie a foot from his backside.

'With that dangling I'm surprised you didn't pole-vault up on them bike sheds,' said Owen. More laughter as they all remembered trying to climb those sheds when they were kids, and credit to George he could still do it.

'I don't think I could make it,' remarked Stan Swindells, 'even if Archie was after me.' Stan was just a little overweight; he could afford to lose four stone and still be considered cuddly.

'I had no choice,' said George, 'it was that or the crusher.'

Never short of a suitable anecdote, Nolan gave a knowing look and voiced, 'Needs must when the devil drives.' Being such a know-all he could often grate on people's nerves but it always gave the others a chance to throw in the most ridiculous phrases that bore no connection to the conversation, provoking vitriol from Nolan and wonderful childish amusement for everyone else.

Mary was in the bar with Kathy and Pat and they were sitting opposite in one of the snugs with Nero and two others. She kept glancing over every time a raucous laugh went up, fully expecting that bastard to be blackening her name, but then relaxed when she considered he would only make himself look stupid into the bargain. The circle squeezed together again eagerly when everyone realised there was still more to come. George became the narrator and told them of part two in Mary's house. Stunned murmurs of shock and disbelief turned into widening grins as they hung onto every word. He would not tell them the personal parts so he changed it slightly to, 'She lured him upstairs in the belief of sexual favours and, once trapped, shouted for Daddy who was hiding in the garden.' While he spoke, from where he stood, he could see her peeping over. Most of the others had their backs to her, so he said, 'Don't look now but Mary's over there.' As one, they twisted around and gaped; it could not have worked better. She went scarlet. They turned back for the happy ending and he finished by describing himself as running out naked, with his clothes in one hand and his shoes in the other. Not exactly what happened but why let the truth mar the path of possible folklore...?

'I liked that ending better,' murmured John.

'Yeah. That part even surprised me and I was there,' whispered Georgie with a titter.

The hounds were impressed. 'I feel like a song,' he said with confidence, and waved to the drummer who played an introductory roll. Twyford climbed on to the stage and told the pianist what he had in mind then took the microphone in both hands; a strong fanfare led him in to 'Temptation'. His pals whooped with delight, whilst closer to home, Kathy and Pat smiled sheepishly. Mary just grinned nastily at him and he was struck by how much she resembled a cartoon shark.

On the first bell, seven of them left for the Red Lion in Windmill Street. Two cabs dropped them outside just at tipping-out time. Bones was there with two pals, introduced as Barker and Daley. Both wore Sergeant's stripes but were affable enough and seemed to agree with all the Corporal's suggestions. Daley was tall like Bones, a six footer, while Barker was smaller, but both were porky with cropped hair. "You could order this model in every size," thought Nolan, who didn't like Shermans much, but withheld his sarcasm for later. George had instructed one and all to look after the Yanks; they might prove very useful.

The walk to the Café Luxor wasn't five minutes, and although Lenny frowned and put a big hand on Bones' chest, George said from the rear, 'Good friends of mine, Len,' and to the Americans, 'Lads, this is Lenny; him and the boys here run the best club in London, but they don't like Yanks so you got to show him how well mannered you can be.' The three shook Lenny's hand and both Sergeants left it empty. Luckily Bones filled it with a piece of white paper, the international language. Much to Lenny's discomfort George kissed him on the cheek and showed everyone in.

The head waiter led the Twyford party to a table in pride of place opposite the stage. Bones was impressed and sat next to George, while the Sergeants sat next to each other, but chatted well with the lads and were soon at ease.

'I've put those two in the deal,' said Bones, 'they're in charge of stores and can sign for a lot more than me.'

'Lovely,' said George, 'you don't want to initial too much

anyway.'

Bones chinked glasses; he felt comfortable with George and always followed his instincts about someone. They talked for a while, outlining what was needed against what could be got. Prices were generally agreed and then skipped over. No point in heavy negotiations until they'd had a trial run; finer details later. They toasted future business and sat back to enjoy the evening.

Radna was singing and every man there daydreamed of winning a woman like that. She sang five good numbers before introducing a visitor she called 'Mr Rhythm'. It must have killed Kit to wait for the applause then he was out of his chair and across that dance floor: arrows have left bowstrings slower. Even the band liked him because he would always bring a fresh change to their style of swing. He began with "Pick yourself up", this was to give George and the lads time to scout for partners. By his second song, "The way you look tonight", everyone was tapping their feet. But the third and last was his best creation (or alteration). He jazzed up an operatic tune called "Cara Mia Mine". He had worked this to perfection with the Malden musicians and all of the lads knew their lines for the backing support they had to give him. The width of the dance area made it far more impressive with everyone's voices coming from different parts of the floor. The band excelled themselves and lifted Kit to new spires. When he finished, he was cheered back to the table.

Radna joined them for the break and draped herself across George. It was a good feeling to be spoiled for ten minutes then demanded more of his time to accompany her to another table right at the back, behind a jungle of green pot plants. Donald Grogan was ensconced there with three ugly looking characters and all rose as Radna came nearer. Donald welcomed Twyford like a brother, and two of the uglies gave up their seats immediately and stood between the plants and the table, ensuring them privacy. Grogan was charming, different from the other night, then it was business and he used those political contacts for his own ends, now he was more natural and had George not known better, might have liked him. Donald declared how fond he was of Radna and hoped they too could be friends. Radna made intelligent noises about the future and suggested to Grogan that George has a strong organisation and may be able to help him further his plans. Twyford felt she oversung his praises and the Glaswegian virtuoso could very well have expected more than he could produce. The nature of business was not discussed but intimated that it was highly profitable as long as you were prepared to take a few chances.

Before George became too engrossed a polished, glamorous woman joined them and Grogan fawned over her. Radna linked arms with the lady, while Donald had a complete personality change and became all la-di-dah, kissing her hand. She was introduced to George as the Donna Laura. With this new voice, Grogan pronounced it 'Low-ra', rolling his 'r's. Her hand was offered, they briefly touched fingers and it was withdrawn. She looked George over quickly, seemed to decide against and turned her attention on the other men present. After a few polite niceties the Senora sat and coaxed Radna down next to her, everyone else remained upstanding, awaiting the Royal Command. In a thick, husky, Spanish accent, she informed her audience,

'We live in the same block and I haven't seen her for a week. These hours are too hard for you, my dear.'

Without feeling the need to consult with anyone, George sat down jogging Grogan and his henchmen out of their immobility to do the same. Twyford studied her. Her jet black hair was pinned high, supported by a diamond grip. A few curly strands hung down around her neck. She had dark eyes and an aquiline nose with full red lips that pointed down, and was used to being obeyed. About ten years Radna's senior with, admittedly, a more voluptuous figure, she was certainly fetching but, in his view, no real competition; Radna was a goddess by comparison. The Lady further lowered his opinion of her by speaking to the Scottish contingent as if he wasn't there. It compelled George to be obnoxious so he leered at her protruding cleavage and contemplated the rudest thoughts. Sensing all was not well, Radna excused herself, 'Donna Laura, forgive us but I have to work. I will call on you tomorrow.' She kissed her on both cheeks. 'Good night Donald. Please call on me Wednesday evening.' He received the same parting pecks. 'Good night, Gentlemen.' Twyford tilted his head in a kind of bow and took Radna back to the stage. 'You're terrible,' she whispered. 'I'll see you by Tony's office when I'm finished.'

George rejoined the Force, only to see Bones had pinched his dancing partner and was showing her some new moves; his hands were travelling faster than his feet.

Too soon it was time to go. Twyford wished a safe journey on everyone and made plans to see Bones early the following Friday evening then walked to the door and tarried a while with Lenny.

'The Jocks were in,' offered the bouncer.

'Yeah, I met them.'

'All alright?'

'I'm not sure,' said George, 'but could you let me know of anything that happens that's to do with them?'

Twyford went to slip him a drink but Lenny refused, 'We're mates. That's on the house,'

'Thanks Len. I appreciate that.' Radna came to the entrance hidden inside her fur coat. 'Are you warm enough?' said George sarcastically, his teeth chattering as they walked along.

'Wonderfully, 'she answered. 'Where's your coat?'

'It had an accident,' he replied.

'I'll heat you up soon as long as you promise to come on Wednesday to meet Donald.'

'Temptress! How can I refuse?' and already hailing one, suggested, 'Lets get a taxi.'

The back of the black cab wasn't much warmer but at least it blocked out the icy gusts that blew up his trouser legs.

Twyford gave the name of the apartment block and the cabbie took them the long way round. They kissed as she wrapped him inside her Musquash and when he came up for air they were at the lights in Camden High Street. George checked his watch with the big clock outside the Black Cap public house. 'That's five minutes fast,' he said.

The fire in her sitting room had died sometime earlier but had valiantly managed to keep the chill at bay. She made two powerful scotch and hot milk nightcaps and they took them to bed. Their lovemaking started before the drinks were finished, with Radna dripping the potent mixture on his naked parts and licking it off. He wanted to impale her on himself but was made to wait and watch. She dipped her long, slender fingers again and again into the tepid drink, now letting it trickle from blood red nails over her erected nipples, decorating herself with trails of the beige liquid, dribbling it down her fabulous body. His lips pursued the elixir between the hollow of her cleavage, sucking hungrily at each breast and slowly moving lower, becoming intoxicated more from passion than alcohol. Entwining her fingers through his hair she directed his head securely between her legs, his hands gripped her haunches and lifted her to his mouth. His tongue tickled, tasted her piquancy and wrote a poem and her thighs locked him in until the last word of the final verse. Wanting further fulfilment her hands wrenched at his penis and reintroduced George to her moist warmth then wrapped her legs around him. Uniquely with Radna, her dominance revved him to the power of a racing car at clutch biting point, straining for the off. She yielded George his freedom only at the last possible second, finally unleashing the horsepower. Throbbing with intensity he drove his member deep inside her then thundered into a merged madness that engulfed them both. They detonated together and almost immediately gravitated into delicious slumber.

Twyford awoke two hours later with a strong heartbeat pulsating in his penis and this time controlled the coupling. He turned her over and entered her from behind, settled himself comfortably, then rode her slowly, sensually and thoroughly until, with vocal vociferation she reached her crest, which spurred George on to join her on her second peaking. This time he went out for the count and when he awoke it was ten in the morning and he was alone. George sat up and called her name but the flat seemed empty. He wandered from the bed, naked, walked to the sitting room and caught sight of himself in the long mirror; he looked good. The thought crossed his mind as to whether there was time to take her in front of it again, and that old stirring extended itself. He stepped into the kitchen and jumped back quickly. The Donna Laura watched his naked display over a glass of a mint tea. Her eyes were laughing.

'Sorry!' he said from behind the wall and then silently cursed himself for his good manners. Why do Englishmen do that? She should be the one to apologise for the intrusion!

'Radna will only be a moment. Please don't be embarrassed on my behalf,' she said.

"Condescending cow," he thought, and stood behind the wall, wondering what to do next.

She came through the connecting door and appraised him. 'Don't worry. I have seen them before.'

'Not that size, I hope, or that attractive,' he said, not giving a fuck now and openly reaffirming his dislike of her.

She positioned herself in front of him, took his penis in her left hand and squeezed firmly, at the same time biting into his chest. Her teeth sunk in him. He liked the strangeness of it but flinched with the pain, nevertheless. Lustfully, one hand gripped her hair, while his other squeezed her breast as hard as he could. She made no sound, only intensified her bite. The pain was too savage. He pulled her head back but her jaws were locked on, forcing him to yank her away from his body. It felt as if she'd taken a chunk of flesh and for a second his fist bunched. Showing contempt for his weakness she pushed her face forward, daring him to punch her. This woman was begging for a good right-hander. Still holding her hair vicelike in his grasp, Twyford smeared her lipstick all over her face then laughed loudly and roughly shoved her from him.

'Listen, you snobby, fat freak, you can strut about with a bit of shit stuck under your nose and impress the likes of Grogan but I find you twisted and ugly. Now, fuck off before I do hurt you.' Rendered motionless from a mixture of hatred and shock, his stinging vilification released her and she ran from the room. His words saw her out with, 'Don't come around when I'm here. I hurt women or men; it's all the same to me.' The back door slammed and he walked away to find his clothes. Radna returned some time later through the same fire exit door. She'd been upstairs with the hard-nosed bitch and George had never seen her so flappy

'The Donna?' she said, close to tears, 'You? What happened?' George took her in his arms, but she would not be comforted and pulled away.

'Radna,' he said, 'She got everything she deserved. Look at this…' and undoing his shirt, showed the deep ring of teeth marks on his chest.

To Twyford's surprise, she was not shocked at all, just kept repeating, 'But the Donna...no one ever... not to her.'

'Well, someone has now!' he said, getting annoyed, 'And tell the old dragon, she can think herself lucky I ain't *Saint* George or, by now, she'd have a lance up her 'Arris an' all.'

'No!' said Radna sharply. 'Men worship her. You must go to her, apologise, ask her forgiveness.'

Twyford could not believe what he was hearing and tried to control his language. He failed. And,

after raving a tirade of four-letter abuse at her, stormed to the door vowing, 'Apologise to that randy whore? If ever we meet again, she can kiss my arse before I speak to her!' And George left with yet another door slamming.

He started the route towards Primrose Hill, but found his bad temper was making him walk too fast and look stupid. A black taxi turned out of the side street in front of him and he jumped in. The cab driver wanted to chat, 'He tickles me, you know,' he said.

Totally uninterested but naturally polite, George helped him out with, 'Who's that then?'

'Lord Haw Haw. He's the only reason I'm working today. I live local and I've just heard him on the wireless. He spouted the usual old tripe about how they know all of what's happening over here, and then he said the big clock outside the Black Cap in Camden Town is five minutes fast. So I jumped in my cab to have a look, he was right. He's a clever fucker you know!'

'Yeah, I noticed that clock last night, or this morning rather, still maybe it's been fast for a while.'

'No. I have a pick up in Belsize Park every morning so I checks it regular. It was right on Friday.' George thought little more about it and in no time was at the Malden. A few pints and he would soon forget about the row. Shame, but life's road has many bends.

The pub had only just opened and Twyford was the first one there. He ordered a pint of bitter and had a quick giggle with Rose. Then happiness came over in the shape of our genial host, 'Do you know how loud you were last night?' asked Horrie caustically.

'Now, would it be (a) very loud, (b) loud, or (c) no where near loud enough?'

'You were bleeding loud!' snapped Horrie, not at all jolly.

'That's (d), you weren't 'sposed to know about (d).

Owning the pub gave Horace the last word,' Grow up! You're not kids anymore, you know,' and before sauntering off he concluded the slight with a curling of his top lip.

Rose frowned a look of, 'I hope you feel properly chastised,' George made sheep's eyes and they both laughed. Horace ignored them.

Twyford was left to ponder, so he took his drink and broke another rule by removing a precious bowl of tiny, chopped squares of cheddar and, with this booty, sat in the snug farthest from the bar. He did not fancy company, unless it was his good pals. The rubberised cheese made his beer go sort of flat but it still tasted all right. The ruck with Radna came to mind. Normally, he would have taken the micky rather than take offence but he was not himself, probably worrying about 'Bounty' had made him too touchy. Where the fuck could it be? The only good thing was that it must be somewhere out the back, and that offered some hope. He might have to make out he wants to baby-sit. It was a long shot, but getting rid of Mary for an evening was worth a try then he could concentrate on the search. "Better not go down there today pissed," he thought.

'It can't be that bad,' said Bassy, from behind, 'At least you got your end away.'

George brightened immediately. 'So what happened with the freckly bird?'

'All the way to Richmond on the night bus and got nothing; it took me an hour to talk my way into the house. Now I told her, before we went, that I wouldn't be able to get back until the morning. Still the prat wants me to take her home. What would you think? I tried for ages but she wouldn't have it, just kissing, waste of time.'

'Not even a knee-trembler?' asked George.

'No,' answered John, 'I hate teasers.'

'Yeah, so do I,'

'I kipped on the settee and come home on the milk train. So what are you fed up for?'

Danny Curry arrived with Frank Nash and Kitchener Thorpe just in time for the story. He'd finished with Radna now and so could be really graphic. As he got to the scotch and hot milk bit there were a few loud whoops. Horrie looked over sternly but George had already set finger to lips.

'It's Horace's time of the month,' he confided, 'so let's keep it down a touch.'

The adventure moved to Donna Laura and Frank interrupted him with, 'That shapely beauty will haunt my imagination and accompany me to bed for many nights to come.'

'Yeah, I'll say!' agreed Kit. 'The breast was outstanding and the rump mouth-watering.' Then added, 'Better than that Icelandic wishbone.'

This fired the starting pistol for humorously insulting each other's past conquests until Danny Curry insisted they got back to what happened next. Nolan had only caught the last chapter and, with hand raised, begged for Twyford to begin again but was told to be earlier next time. All the Force were now on parade and kept interrupting with, 'What happened then?' and 'Why this?' but they all quietened down when he described the scene about the bite. At the final curtain, some looked at each other and nodded knowingly in disbelief. George realised it could be misconstrued as a tall story. They needed proof and he was only too pleased to bear his chest and display the wound. The circle of wide eyes turned into fly-catchers.

Owen broke the spell with, 'I hope she brushed her teeth!'

'Cor blimey!' said Bassy, hanging onto the last glimpse. 'Book me in and I'll apologise for you. I'd love an hour with that wench.'

Nolan snorted loudly at the "hour" then professed, 'I like the idea of trickling drink but I think I'd prefer champagne.'

'Who you, tight wad?' said Frank Nash, 'You'd swoon at the price of a ginger ale.'

Plenty more pints and twice as many insults made it a pleasurable Sunday morning. Kit was hogging the microphone, the boys reckoned he was shoving the old dears off the stage rather than let them sing a song, but he was in good voice and when he crooned, "Make yourself at home", everyone joined in. Good friends plus good music and worries are forgotten. The trouble was George forgot about not getting drunk and so went home for Sunday lunch with his Mum and a kip claimed the rest of the afternoon. Well, it's what Sundays are for.

That night, and not in the mood for a drink, Twyford decided to stay in and listen to the wireless but at seven o'clock Owen Esterbrook called and enticed him out with the showing of a George Raft film at the Forum. The idea appealed so he slung on two thick jumpers and they strolled up Kentish Town. It was a gangster film and both enjoyed it immensely. To avoid passing the Bobby shop they walked back through the coal wharf in the murky darkness and nearing the depot saw a light flicker briefly. Going quietly to the door in the gates Owen found it unlocked. The two friends slipped silently inside and waited. It wasn't long before a torch beam flashed on and was held to the lock of the tool shed. Someone fiddled with the padlock then turned the beam off and felt his way along the wall towards them, flashing the torch at the floor every few yards until he reached the gate. Their eyes had become accustomed to the dark and the night concealed their presence. As the intruder went to leave, Owen kicked him in the kneecap. The man yelped a second before George hit him somewhere in the face. He fell against the wall and they grabbed him. Owen shone his light on the prowler; it was Mickey Butler. He couldn't see who they were but his torch was lying on the floor, still switched on, and shedding light on a carton of tobacco. Twyford went berserk; he started punching Mickey about the head and bellowing abuse. Mick covered up but made no attempt to retaliate, he could have fought back and given as good as he got, but he didn't. Instead, he started to cry. Owen went between them and struggled to calm George down. He deflected the blows but couldn't stop the words that once uttered, could never be taken back.

'You mongrel! No good filth!' Expletives tumbled out. 'I've gone away for four years to keep you out of prison. You're rubbish!' George babbled with rage, 'You deserve nothing, how can you nick off us? Pole-axing's too good for you!' He thundered each word, 'Where's your fucking ethics? How could ya?'

Owen was holding his wrists, so he let fly with his boot and connected with Mickey's knee again. Butler fell to the ground rubbing his leg and blubbing about how sorry he was and what a fucking idiot he'd been. He did not know what made him do it.

'I just had to. I didn't mean it!' he said wretchedly, 'I'm sorry, I'm so sorry. Please!'

Twyford leant his arm against the wall and shut his eyes; he wanted to deliver a kick that would send Mickey's head over the rooftops. Owen said nothing. George went quiet and after a few more minutes of pathetic drivel, so did Mickey. Taking his keys out, Twyford walked to the office. Mick got up and limped after him, Owen gathered up the tobacco and followed. George switched the lights on and walked to the far wall then turned to face the thief. Owen came in, shut the door and leaned on it.

Starting to cry again, Mickey snivelled,' I can't believe I was stupid enough to have done it.'

'Nor can I!' said George, bitterly. 'Tell me why, after all we've done? We painted your fucking house, for Christ sake.'

'I know, I know!' That became his standard answer.

'You're rotten! A slag!' He could say nothing constructive, just more name-calling and Mickey agreed. Owen had not wanted to speak, these two went back to short trousers, but they were getting nowhere.

'We all know Mickey's a compulsive thief, he can't help himself; it's a sickness with him.'

'Don't talk daft!' said Twyford, shaking his head with disgust, 'Not off your own.'

'You won't understand, George,' said Mickey, 'and I can't explain. It's been making me go hot all day; I couldn't stop thinking about it.'

'But you ain't desperate! You've got good wages and your house is secure. All you have to do is work for the common cause to make us all safe. There's no excuse!'

'I'll pay you back, I swear to God I will. Please don't tell anyone, I'm so ashamed.' Tears were streaming down his face and his nose was running. He cuffed it away and sniffed back loudly.

George asked of himself, 'What the fuck am I gonna do?'

'Give him another chance.' proposed Owen, 'As far as anyone's concerned this didn't happen; he won't do it again.' Twyford was so hurt he couldn't think.

'Please George, apart from Theresa, our friendship's the most important thing in my life and I'll prove I'll never let any of you down again.'

Twyford knew there was nothing else for it. 'Blow your nose for fuck's sake!' he said, and gave him a squeeze. 'We'll never talk about this again. And now I'll swear an oath.'

'George, if I ever break my promise,' interrupted Mickey,' I expect you to kill me.'

'And you know I will,' said George in earnest. They walked home and, to change the subject, talked about the War, 'I still haven't seen an air-raid.'

'I sincerely hope you never do,' answered Owen.

'Yeah, there's a few more street lights on now. We soon forget,' added Mickey, struggling to walk at their pace, but happy not to complain and just be mates as before. They said good night at the Shipton and all shook hands. A silent pact.

George was in need of the punishment only a gruelling run over the Heath could produce. It was teeming down in stair rods and he ran faster, racing up Parliament Hill, provoking the burn that would engulf his chest. That was the best, collapsing in the mud, looking over London, feeling gloriously at peace with himself. The events of Sunday had shaken the foundations of his perfect state. Utopia and Shangri-La fell to earth with a bang, but were only dented. The longer he lay there and let his fantasies roam, the stronger his belief in what could be done. When he ran down, his determination was out in front, motoring him on again. On the return leg, Twyford saved his final burst of energy for St Leonard's Square. Just before the turning, he accelerated up a gear and came round the corner and down his street at an incredible speed. The local people must only see him at his athletic best.

It was 7.30am and just getting light when George went into his Mum's house, but did not stop, going straight out the back and across the gardens on that familiar trodden trail. No one was up yet and, if they were, the curtains wouldn't be pulled for at least thirty minutes so Twyford got busy. He plotted the garden out and marked it with half-bricks at various positions, splitting it into six sections, each one would be searched with great detail, morning after morning. George returned to his Mum's house with an appetite.

CHAPTER 18: THE FIRST BOARD MEETING OF THE ST.PANCRAS PROPERTY COMPANY

Off Bermuda: A live torpedo fired in error by a U.S.destroyer narrowly misses the battleship, Iowa- with Roosevelt on board!

Fintan drove to work. His instructions were to check in for an hour every morning and, if all was well with no sicknesses or absentees, he could take the rest of each day off until Benson returned. The last to arrive was Nobby, who greeted everyone in a friendly manner and made a full compliment of staff so Fintan departed. Once he had left, Nobby called the fieldsmen together and told them of his shock at seeing Fintan, with one of the South Londoners, at a pub in Kentish Town. None of them really cared much for the Irishman because of his privileged position with the boss, to a man they all felt this new crowd were muscling in and threatening their livelihood. A few hot heads called for him to be bashed up the next time he came to work but cooler minds had other ideas. The spokesman was Laurie Newman, a strange fellow, who never took a drink of alcohol but trained every day with boxing gloves and weapons. Super fit, he drilled himself to be completely aware. All his life, Newman had thought of nothing but fighting and had made a reputation out of never coming second, hurting people was an art; he gave no warning, no quarter and no chance for anyone to hurt him. 'Calm down and listen.' he advised, 'Before, they couldn't be found and we were on offer; now this is the first chance we've had of really getting them so let's do it right. Be nice to the Paddy, let him suspect nothing. Come Friday night, we watch the place and when they're in there, allow them about an hour to have a good drink, relax and slow right down then we go in, tooled up, and give it to 'em badly, and anyone with 'em.'

'What about Ruben?' said Nobby, silently wondering if he should have kept his mouth shut.

'Ruben's not here so we did what we thought was best. Or do you want to lose your jobs to these parasites?'

'No, no!' everyone agreed and, on that final note, it was decided to go straight from work this coming Friday evening.

George shaved, dressed and went for a walk up to Queen's Crescent Market, Owen was busy on the stall and his wife, Elsie, was helping out. They chatted between customers, murmuring low. 'Mick's in the butcher's shop with Kit,' said Owen. 'He's taking orders out the back, it was his idea. Fintan's off for this week and he's helping Lestor with despatch.'

'I like that word,' said George, and walked over to the butcher's shop.

Kit was lifting sausages out of the window display and banged on the glass to get Twyford's attention. He was laughing and pointing at his own eye, mouthing, 'Mickey had a fight with his brother. You wanna see the state of him.'

George grinned back in surprise and Kit stuck his thumb up and blew his lips, signifying how busy they were. Twyford returned the thumb and strolled to the depot.

The coal yard was a hive of industry; lorries leaving fully ladened and carts pulling up and immediately being unloaded and stored. It was beautiful to watch. Even Willy Roe himself was taking a load out.

'What, have you come to take your jacket off and do a bit of collar?' asked Willy, knowing full well he hadn't.

'Don't be silly, I'm the planner,' said George, 'How's the deliveries going?'

'Exceptionally well. The problem's not being seen to be this busy. Lucky we're tucked away and lost on the railway property, this site goes for miles. We're weighing and bagging everything up, putting it inside potato sacks, and then packing them inside coal sacks. Just needs care when delivering.'

'That's the ticket,' said George. 'I'll speak to Lestor now; I don't want to carry too much stock in case we get raided. If anything starts going slow don't buy anymore until it's clear. I'll try and line up another yard, just for extra storage. Might be best to stash the gear there and fetch it over daily as its needed. We should work to an order and delivery pattern. Order Monday, delivery Wednesday, something like that. That way we keep it fresh.'

'I told you I like your ideas, Son. See you later.'

'Yeah, see ya.'

Lestor agreed with George and had a lot of sound ideas of his own on how to speed up distribution. Other schemes were a little too far-fetched and involved building brick walls across railway arches with secret entrances. But it was true; another safe place was needed to hide non-perishable stocks.

'If really good parcels of gear come along on one-off deals,' said Lestor, 'we've got to be in a position to buy it, no matter what. The offers mustn't stop coming.'

'No, I appreciate that,' said George, earnestly 'and I'm working on it, believe me.'

Lestor Hogg went back to his stocks and Twyford reversed the car out and drove off, pondering where to look first. Generally, it was an unrewarding day but he did see another coal yard and thought of a possible buyout.

That evening, he was again late calling for the delectable Miss Poole but, when he rang the bell, she answered the door in a low-cut, black, cocktail dress that hung fabulously well and clung in all the right places and... beamed at him. She improved the effect still further by adding a deep, inward intake of breath, sucking in her diaphragm. George couldn't help the admiring look he gave her as her breasts left the flat several seconds before she did. Knowing she deserved it, Sally smiled and said, 'Now take me to meet some interesting people.'

The woman certainly looked mouth-wateringly devourable but Twyford was beginning to doubt her depth. He suggested a place where chilled wine and riveting conversation flowed non-stop and the beef was as rare as the complaints; an evening at the glee club followed by Gowan's fish and chips should take her down a peg or two.

These things never go quite to plan and where George had hoped that the chaps would give her a thorough verbal drubbing, the opposite occurred. They teased at first, going quite strong at times, but she answered them bravely with an amazing change of character that charmed and disarmed them one by one. They were won over with eyes, teeth and touches; most of all the touches. Her hand would rest gently on an arm, then her fingertips might momentarily brush a wrist and they were captured. The more they listened to her notions and opinions, the more entrapped they became. It was an exercise in subjugation and while she wasn't practising it on him George could see right through to the other side of her. What she lacked in experience of life, Sally made up for in the power of her designed personality. They left the pub early before anyone had enough alcoholic confidence to take her dallying seriously and make a pass, which would have been her crowning glory and ruined his night completely. The drive home started badly. She bubbled with views of his friends and surprisingly only mentioned the better looking ones. He sulked with one syllable answers and she had the cheek to accuse him of being touchy. That drilled a nerve. He stopped the car and blew his top, telling her, in no uncertain terms, exactly what she was and that she would never again get the chance to embarrass him. Flirts were off the menu therefore so was she. Not used to being spoken to in such a manner she was even more shocked when he ordered her out of the car. Flustered and mortified, she truly hadn't realised, and if her behaviour had offended him then she was most awfully sorry. In her own defence she was not accustomed to wine and if her merriment seemed over-friendly then he was to please accept her apology. She touched his hand, the eyes went to work and in utter disbelief he found his tongue being sucked into her mouth. Before he could get comfortable she suggested her flat might be warmer. The gear lever found top and George raced to Swiss Cottage but as they pulled up she came over quite nauseous and, with a tear in her eye and a hankie over her mouth, got out of the car and ran inside.

It was Wednesday morning and Alan cautiously looked around the playground. "Safe enough," he thought, and strolled through the kids towards the far end. His mates always met there to play 'three goals and in' against a chalked-out goal on the wall. He was gonna' have to up that Jackie Robinson; once he was floored the others wouldn't take the micky out of him anymore. This was all Miss Poole's fault; every time she saw him she started fussing over him, messing his hair up and things. The other day she even fixed his cardigan buttons that were in the wrong holes. She shouldn't be doing that, especially in front of the boys. He wondered for the hundredth time, what ever was the matter with her?

There was a copper on point duty at the corner of Camden Road and Royal College Street and he was useless, traffic was piling up in all directions. Tinker sat at the front of one of the halted queues and didn't cause any bother. He had a mixed load of fruit on his cart, hidden by a tarpaulin, and the last thing he wanted was to upset the Bobby and attract attention to his cargo, but a Bass brewery Dray with two big horses and two foul-mouthed trouncers was directly behind him and they were shouting insults at the officer, who in return pointed at Tinker to remain. The queue was made to wait even longer which provoked more curses. Completely indifferent to the abuse, the Rozzer sauntered across to Tinker and ordered him to pull in to the side. He had two choices; he chose the other one and cracked the whip on the horse's rump, setting the mare off at a pelt. The policeman began to give chase on foot and was loudly ridiculed from all over, while his absence from the crossroad's centre spurred the traffic to edge forward and choke the intersection. Girdled by complete pandemonium, he dashed to the nearest Police box and rang the station.

Tinker was well clear and slowed to a canter, still too fast but a car would be despatched from Holmes Road Police Station so he had to get to the yard before he was found. As the police car travelled down Kentish Town Road, Tinker's cart trotted along a parallel street in the opposite direction. Willy's yard was close to the station and seconds after he swung into it another squad car came roaring round the bend and past the top of their turning. A quick warning and all hands were unloading him at break-neck speed. Once it was done, Tinker knew he must go and get arrested to stop the hunt and, having no time to reload with empties, drove to the station and presented himself at the Duty Sergeant's desk.

'I'd like to complain about your officer on point duty in Camden Road.' stated Tinker.

'You saucy bastard!' came the reply. He was grabbed, had an arm forced up his back and frogmarched away to be locked in a cell, then through the spy hole was told, 'You'll wait there until we decide otherwise.'

Tinker was fine with this; he could stand any treatment they dished out. His only fear was if Archie Shaw got involved and began to ask himself, 'What if …?' then shivered the question away, not daring to think about it. He saw no one again until supper time when he was treated to a cup of tea and a water biscuit then informed that he was to be appearing in court the following morning.

'What charge?' asked Tinker, not really caring, just needing to remain inconspicuous until then.

'Dangerous and reckless driving, failing to stop at a red light,' came the reply.

He had given his real name, Nathaniel Woods, which shouldn't ring too many bells as few people knew it, he was Tinker to everyone.

The next morning he was being led out to a meat wagon as Archie Shaw was coming in. Tinker's head was down and he nearly got away with it. Sergeant Shaw felt the prisoner's fear and stopped the procession.

'Let's have a little look at what we got here. Well, my, my. Been a naughty boy have we?' and to the arresting officer, 'Bring him back in here. I want a word with this monkey.'

'But Sarge, he's up before the Beak in twenty minutes.'

Archie stared at Tinker who wilted. 'What's the charge?' The desk Sergeant told him.

'What load was he carrying?'

'Empty,' came the reply.

'Empty, my foot!' and he pushed his face down in to Tinker's. 'I'll be waiting for you when you come out of that court.'

Tinker's stomach turned over and he wanted to use the toilet, but went willingly to the Black Maria just to get away from that face.

By Thursday morning, George had covered half of the garden with no luck. He had yet to see Mary to ask if he might baby-sit for a night and detested having to entreat with her for anything. She was a spiteful, hateful bitch and in his opinion a clean shaven version of her old man; other than her stature there was very little difference...

Recently, Mary's father had become a lot more active and could now be seen walking through Queen's Crescent Market twice a day. Furthermore, whenever he neared Owen's stall or Kit's shop, he would stand and look until they saw him. He knew they were up to something the way they averted their eyes. Patience, and soon all would be forthcoming. He called at the local Inns and watering holes that George had previously frequented; they too would soon get the message, whoever encouraged Twyford encouraged Archie. St Pancras was too small a place to hide in but while he was not around, George's presence could not poison the streets. Short of murder, Archie Shaw would do whatever was necessary to rid Kentish Town of him. He likened Twyford to a pestilence that, unless rooted out, would become an epidemic.

His mother had named him Kitchener so that he would stand out. 'A namesake to be measured by' was her somewhat flawed reasoning. Sadly, from the first day at school, a shy, little boy was made even shyer by the baiting his name provoked from the other kids. Abbreviating "Kitchener" drew out the obvious rhyming derivatives that would be chanted on the streets or in the playground every time they saw him. And so he learned how to stand up for himself until, after many, many scraps and plenty of good hidings, he eventually earned the grudging esteem of a fighter.

That particular morning, Kit stood in his shop doorway, looking across the road, while his mind worked backwards a month to when he thought he would have to close. Rationing had put them on the proverbial breadline, but unlike the Northern Line, this one only had two stops; empty pocket to empty belly. George had changed all that; he'd had the foresight to plan it, the wherewithal to get it going and the cash to make it work. All at once people were happily paying sensible prices for black-market goods. They were sick of going without. The sun had started to shine in Queen's Crescent.

'Hallo Kitchener,' sang a female voice, bringing him back to earth swiftly.

'Hallo Rita! I was wondering when we'd meet again.' It was the busty blonde from the Malden.

'I've been to the country to visit my little boy. He's out at Brentwood with a lot of the other kids who were sent away. They're having a lovely time working on a big farm.'

'Oh, that's nice,' he said, 'I didn't think you were married?'

'I'm not,' she said proudly. 'I spoil my son terrible but I had no time for his old man. I kicked the useless bleeder out long ago.'

Kit grinned dopily. 'Do you fancy a drink Friday? We might finish up down the other End.'

She paused to consider then, with hands on hips and chest tantalisingly close, forewarned saucily, 'I'll come out but don't you think you're getting anything.'

'Amazing!' he teased,' That's exactly what I was going to say to you!'

But she got all serious, 'I'm sorry Kitchener, I don't think I fancy you.'

Her words deflated but turning up her nose as she said it, absolutely stung. Still, one more look at the Jane Russell stance and he was game as a bagel. 'Come out and we'll have a laugh anyway.' He reckoned she was worth a bit of extra effort. 'Outside the Shipton, about half past eight, alright?' Without answering she left him with a look that kept every possibility open, waggled her fingers in a wave and then wiggled her arse off up the road.

When Nathaniel Woods arrived at the court he found a Barrister waiting for him.

'I'll be representing you. Plead not guilty and let them prove otherwise. You have been incarcerated and so had no opportunity to provide witnesses. We will apply for a delay.'

'Whatever you say, boss,' said Tinker, 'only stay with me after the hearing. Don't let them take me back.'

'Fear not,' said the Brief. 'This is a favour for a friend.'

Irving Jacobs had pulled a few strings and the Barrister's reputation guaranteed a good result. The case was deferred but as Tinker came out Sergeant Shaw barred his path. The barrister was as good as his word and demanded to know why they were hounding his client.

Archie knew well the pecking order and grudgingly stepped aside with a parting, 'Look out for me, 'cos I'm gonna' be seeing you.'

Tinker was still shaking when he sat in the back of a taxi with his escort. The cab took them to Irving's flat and dropped Tinker off. He thanked the chap again and walked through the Jago to the office where George and Lestor were waiting. With the fear still apparent on his face, he told them word for word what had happened and added, 'I'm not going back for the horse and cart.'

'Don't worry, that's already been arranged.' said Les, 'Anyway, no damage done. Archie knows you were carrying something dodgy and he'll make sure we get no peace for a while. Tink, I think you had best do the same as George and keep out of the way for a bit. Make your collections from wherever but change over with one of Willy's drivers outside the manor.'

Gerry Nolan arrived with Stan Swindells and the first board meeting of the St Pancras property company was called to order.

George took the chair and said, 'We're here in Irving's office and he's with us so are there any ideas how to buy the properties we rent from the council?'

'The only one who can advise on that is Ruben,' suggested Tinker. 'He's got the right people in his pocket, have a word with him.'

'That's not as funny as it sounds,' retorted George, 'I might just do that.'

Lestor frowned, remembering the car incident, 'Don't let's stir up any trouble, eh?'

'Believe it or not, Les, I respect the old bastard. That night in Spaniards Wood showed how much pluck he has got. You scared me and I knew you were there.'

'Yeah,' said Les, grudgingly, 'but I don't reckon you're on his Christmas list. Think first, eh?'

The agenda moved on and Tinker proposed widening the service to spread outside St Pancras. It was a sensible suggestion and would make them less dependant on one operation.

'We'd need agents, working on commission; single operators who take orders in a particular area. Those orders need to be quite large to make the load pay but, undoubtedly, it could be done.' Everyone said, 'Aye' and the motion was passed to scout about for salesmen. Keeping to the positive side, Lestor Hogg rose and stated that he had deposited the first and rather handsome payment into the company bank account. He suggested that, while things were rolling well, after wages all monies should be converted to property as soon as possible.

Gerry Nolan piped up with a caution, 'I agree, and at the moment we're sitting on top of the world but remember it turns over every twenty four hours.'

'We're back to Ruben again,' said Twyford.

'I think you might be pushing your luck with Mr Benson,' remarked Stan Swindells. 'He's reputed to be a very vengeful man.'

'No-one with a morsel of a brain would even consider what you're contemplating.' added Gerry. George looked around the table for support but was outvoted by raised eyebrows and shakes of the head.

As acting Chairman, Irving Jacobs motioned, 'I suggest a meeting once a week. Can we have a show of hands?' Everyone raised in favour. 'Let's put the idea of George meeting Ruben in the waiting room for a decade or so.'

No other business was up for discussion and the meeting was closed.

The inns of Bethnal Green opened at five o'clock, half hour earlier than Camden Town for some strange reason. A few costermongers from Roman Rd. market joined the crowd for a swift half, George knew them from his days as a fruit salesman, and by seven o'clock everyone was piling into the back of two vans and driving from pub to pub. All through the East End, the alehouses got better, the barmaids excelled with every pint and the Force got severely inebriated.

Coming home in a cab, and after a wonderful competition of who could enchant the worst woman, George informed the boys that one very lively salesman had been selected and he was prepared to give it a try. From their pleasant state of intoxication, nothing was seen as a problem so, without knowing anymore details, 'despatch' confidently ensured the execution of all his deliveries. Apart from an emergency stop for Tinker to reacquaint with a gallon of brown and mild the taxi dropped them safely at the Shipton. Twyford didn't notice the two Revenue men, eating chips outside the fish shop. They kept their distance and followed his swaying figure down St Leonard's Square. Kirby would be delighted.

Mary peeped through the black-out curtains. What was he doing? She'd watched George each morning scrabbling about the garden on his hands and knees when he believed everyone was asleep. She thought at first he may have been hiding something but, each day after he left and the kids had gone to school, Mary scrutinised the exact same spots and saw nothing. She guessed that it must be to do with all this money he was purported to have. Perhaps the dimwit was burying it in the garden and, stranger still, son of dimwit had knocked next door and apologised to Mrs Selby for kicking balls over her fence. The neighbours were two elderly sisters and always scolding Alan for something or other, normally he would run a mile.

Twyford returned depressed from another fruitless search and made a bowl of porridge but couldn't fancy the grey, tumorous mass and pushed it away. Unable to settle, he wandered up to the paper stand outside the Mother Shipton, where Dicky pulled his leg about unshaven louts drifting around, frightening away the customers. The headlines were worrying. It had been suggested that Germany may have developed an A4 ballistic missile that could be fired from anywhere in Europe and launched against us. "That's all we're short of," thought George, seeing London as the obvious prime target. "Still, at least it's Friday."

Always the life and soul of any function, John Bass sat and absent-mindedly flicked the pages of his old New Gresham

English Dictionary. Usually he would select long words to slip into conversations at gatherings. It was expected and looked forward to, as were his party props such as false arms, dew-drop light bulbs up his nostrils and a dud training grenade guaranteed to clear a packed public house when it was difficult to get a round of drinks; but today he seriously missed his wife and couldn't concentrate. Perhaps it was how mothers train their daughters in the valleys; whatever it was, never was a man so spoiled. She polished his boots, run his bath and scrubbed his parts, seldom let him wash his own hair and, generally, smothered him with affection. From his side, he would often tell her that she had his permission to enjoy herself and to carry on. Then one row changed everything; a screaming match about getting in late, acting like a child and smelling of whore, in which he flippantly countered with something about… inside every old man there's a nineteen year old wondering what happened and he wasn't ready for the old folks home just yet! They'd gone to bed in a fury and in the morning she was gone.

CHAPTER 19: THE BATTLE OF THE MALDEN

Anzio on the west coast of Italy: The U.S. and British combined landing was almost thrown back by the Germans, with high casualties. Churchill said,"We hoped to land a wildcat to tear out the bowels of the Boche, instead we have stranded a vast whale with its tail flopping about in the water!"

The fieldsmen were all in early and Fintan McMahon felt there was something wrong. He couldn't put a finger on it except to say that the West Londoners were being friendly when normally they ignored him. Sensibly, Ruben employed heavies from off the manor to stop fiddles or favours for friends. McMahon left perplexed and set course for the coal yard. Once he had gone Laurie Newman ran over the plan again, he did not want any mad bastards spoiling the manoeuvre by dishing it out willy-nilly and allowing George and Fintan to slip away. Not everyone had seen Twyford so it was decided to make them all sure of who he was. One group would be watching from the parked vehicles while the other five were to be inside the Malden Arms when he came in, then someone from the cars could join them at the bar and point him out. That way they could see who he was with and also a layout of the pub with nearest entrances and fastest exits. It was a good plan. No one was to drink alcohol and they were to leave the bar soon after Twyford arrived so as not to draw attention to themselves. Patience was demanded, two cars would house their full complement and both boots contained enough weaponry in the form of lead piping camouflaged inside rolled up newspaper. There was nothing better to dull the blows and help prevent too much blood; it also adds an important foot to the reach. The collectors were so keyed up, they wanted it now.

Experiencing a touch of remorse, George went along to the butcher's shop to see if Mickey fancied a swim down at the local public baths after the lunchtime trade. They swam for an hour and then, over a cup of tea, talked of four years ago. The past had to be voiced and afterwards it was as it should be, their friendship fortified and welded. Walking home, Mickey announced that Theresa wanted him to get out with the boys more and tonight could be the night. Understanding his caution, George replied that everyone was assembling at the Malden and assured him that, apart from Owen whose lips were glued, no one would ever know of his slip. From there they would meet Bones for a late one. Just to mention the Café Luxor had them both animated and eager..

'We need him because he's made for this. You say Twyford's cunning and not to be trusted, good. Don't you see he's perfect, exactly what we've been looking for. This is his city; he dwells in the bowels of it. The complete consignment should all be in circulation long before the authorities understand what's happened. Can you imagine the manpower needed to slow it down, for it couldn't be stopped and must help tremendously to detract attention from stage two?' The speaker looked to the head of the table. A slight nod of agreement, a click of the heels, no further dialogue and the six other occupants left separately at three minute intervals.

For once, George was on time and parked outside the school to wait. His idea was to bed her early then steal a few hours sleep at her place before their planned night out at the Malden. A gang of boys were the first ones through the gates and he could see Alan among them, heading for the bomb debris along the street. Sally came out sometime later and where it was getting dark she couldn't see him until his lights went on and the engine started. 'Miss' flopped in and gave him her cheek to avoid smudged lipstick. The action caused her dress to ride suggestively high and his concentration barely took in her news while his imagination was wrapping those long legs around him and hand weighing each toned buttock. They went directly to her flat where he confessed to being tired and frustrated. She declined the canoodling to increase his frustration, and sleep was off limits because she meant them to be early, then pinched his bottom and reminded him of the promise to take her out and show her off. The hint was that coupling might be desirable if the evening went well.

Less than a dozen customers greeted their entrance and most of them stole a sly look at Sally, who met their favourable appraisals with a radiance that added to his own esteem. Whilst calling for a pint of bitter and a port and lemon, he noticed even the little trade that was about began to thin out. 'Miss' was amused; this wasn't quite how he had described it. She used the ladies and, left alone, he happened to glance towards the door; two customers were leaving and George could have sworn that the pair gave him a most unfriendly glare.

Ruben's men in the second car wanted to 'have' the South Londoner that very moment but Newman insisted on sticking to the plan. They had the layout of the bar and would enter from the corner and the side to take George, Fintan and anyone with them in a pincer movement. Those remotely near either of them must be considered as part of their crowd and would also suffer, women included.

Kit met "Jane Russell" at eight thirty and an arm in arm stroll brought them to the Malden at the same time as Mornie Quill and his wife. Violet Quill was a lovely girl but could be somewhat volatile and when she rucked, which was frequently, it registered on the Richter scale. The ladies were introduced and soon fell into comparing experiences of man's deficiencies in consideration.

Frank Nash turned up with Gerry Nolan and Stan Swindells. This trio strongly believed that Friday was lads' night out and women were nuisance value on such occasions…until eleven-ish when moods mellow. Tinker crept in with Mickey Butler, nervously keeping one eye out for Archie. All three entrances had a flood of customers coursing through them and the pub filled quickly as locals came to enjoy their regular weekend's entertainment.

Outside, Newman began to get anxious, so many bystanders and still no Fintan. It was nine o'clock and his keyed up squad were jumpy and needful of action.

Another two couples went in through the corner door and then he was spotted. McMahon escorted three smart looking 'things' and was all over one of them. Newman waited for the group to enter then synchronised with the other vehicle around the corner, in exactly ten minutes both carloads would move on the targets.

Lestor Hogg and his wife had met up beforehand with Johnny and Megan Bass, so as not to cause too much attention to Meg's return from the valleys. The foursome went straight over to George and he introduced them to Sally. Fintan followed in with Bridgid, Mary and Pat Passmore. Nolan was holding the whip and sorting out the drinks. Mary and Pat would be in the call and the company, even if she wasn't with George; that was the way it was. Kit had hopped up on the stage, showing off in front of his new pigeon, and started his repertoire with 'You made me love you'. She was too engrossed in scandal with a swelling group of gossipers to take much notice of his efforts to impress. Bridgid shook hands with Sally as Mary and Pat passed by, looking for seats.

Pat looked twice and then said, 'Hallo, Miss Poole, I didn't recognise you with your hair down. You look lovely.'

'Thank you, Mrs Passmore, and so do you. Here we are, Cinderellas gone to the Ball. How's your Cyril?' They exchanged pleasantries for a minute or two and then Pat joined the women at Kathy Gay's table.

'Who's that poor fool?' inquired Mary, with no embarrassment.

'You know who that is, don't you?'

'If I did I wouldn't be asking, now would I?' replied Mary, a might snappy.

'That's Miss Poole.' Mary's face was still blank. Pat helped out some more, 'You know, Alan's teacher.' It took a moment to sink in then Mary stood up, hands on hips and glowered at her. She pushed her way through the throng and interrupted Sally's conversation with Johnny Bass.

George was already getting an ear-bashing from Megan, who held him chiefly responsible for her husband's bad behaviour of late, but grimaced when he heard Mary's voice behind him saying, in no uncertain terms, 'So you're Alan's teacher! I want a word with you.'

'Mrs. Twyford,' said Sally nicely, 'I'd very much like a word with you, too. I was hoping you'd let me call on you one quiet evening after school perhaps.'

Mary had plenty to say to this woman but accepted that this wasn't the best time.

'I hope it is Alan you're concerned about and no one else,' imagining correctly that the school mistress took her meaning.

Sally touched her hand and leaned closer, 'It's you I want to talk about.' Misunderstanding completely, Mary recoiled, her face reddened and she began to push back through the crowd, but Sally came after her and spoke just loud enough for her alone to hear, 'I know about your problem. It can be helped.'

Mary stopped dead and turned, her mind racing. 'Problem?' she repeated. What had that bastard told this girl?

George closed his eyes and waited for the explosion but it came from an entirely different direction.

It was at this point that Kit's warning brought them up sharply. From his position on the stage he could see all who entered and, thank God, that night his instincts were keenly honed. Locking on to the last note of 'After you've gone' for as long as the human body would allow, he drew a deep breath to prompt the applause and saw them coming in. Strangers, a little too fast, heads down, each with a hand under his jacket. Then more from the far door. The microphone blared at Dan Curry who was nearest the danger, 'Danny! Tooled up. Six geezers going by you. Mickey, behind you, more of 'em!' Some of the old girls panicked and jumped up, looking for a way out, but trade had swelled to such packed proportions it hampered everyone. From the stage Kit gave a running commentary and his warnings were invaluable.

Fintan saw them pushing through the crowd and recognised the faces straight away. He called to George, then moved forward to meet the threat head on and struck the first one three times in the face, left, right, left. The punches packed iron but Ruben's fieldsmen were employed for strength and aggression. The thug's head rocked as it absorbed the blows then he swung the covered piping savagely at Fintan's head. Only his agility saved him. Weaving away, it glanced off his shoulder making him duck low before drilling a fist into the man's groin. As that one doubled up another reached across him to lunge at Fintan's face. To avoid that he leaned the upper part of his body too far back and went crashing over a chair. Two of them were on him in an instant, the strike from one found the bridge of his nose but Twyford's boot took the other under the jaw, his head snapped back and he dropped to the side, not moving. George, still holding his pint jug, lifted it high to bring down on Fintan's other attacker but someone from behind locked an arm round his throat. George dropped the jug and, using both hands, pulled the wrist inches from his windpipe then propelled himself backwards at speed, butting the man with the rear of his head. The nose bone crunched as it broke, Twyford's elbow hammered back into the same spot. Owen jumped in and pulled the big lump up off of Fintan then smashed a knee into the side of the man's head. Fintan wriggled away, sprang to his feet and was straight into the affray again; his opponent had fallen and twisted sideways then, in the same fluid motion, bounced back up at Owen with a shoulder barge that sent him reeling across the pub. The fieldsman came after him with something silver flashing in his hand. Everywhere you looked, brawling men were exchanging punches and kicks while flying bottles whistled and crashed all over the place. Frayed newspapers showing uncovered lead piping was rising and walloping down all through the crowd, laying men and women out. The floor was littered with bodies.

Danny Curry had had the advantage of Kit's warning and, with a great right hook, knocked down the last one to pass by as they went for George, who seemed to be the bull's-eye for this mob to aim at. He threw himself on top of the chap, grabbed him by the ears, spat in his eye and banged his head on the floor boards but the man still gripped his weapon and belted it across Danny's head. The first blow numbed and slowed Dan's performance, the second and third knocked him senseless.

Stanley Swindells had taken a brutal hiding. His mouth was a mass of blood but he'd held one of them in a bear hug and forced the man to the ground until some of the locals could kick the life out of him. Even the old boys were sparring up and getting stuck in.

The pub had been too packed, slowing their attack by losing the element of surprise and, as the first to sense it could go against them, Newman just hit out at everyone around him with the lead pipe. A show of pure viciousness was called for, which usually paralysed normal people with fear and always won the day. Following his example, two others fought through to join him in the onslaught.

Down the other end, George was rolling all over the floor with a gorilla who was too strong for him, each trying to strangle the other. The ape craftily loosened his grip momentarily and knocked Twyford's hands up and away from his throat then butted him in the eye. George's knee came in hard between the man's legs, barely in time to prevent his own jugular being ripped out. They returned to the double head lock and continued knocking tables over as they rolled. Nolan grabbed a heavy chair and swung it with all he had, but his timing was poor and it smacked into the wrong head knocking George spark out. His next strike was better and, as ape-man rose to stamp on Twyford's exposed crutch, it cracked down on his crown. He collapsed and lay still.

Frank Nash stood toe to toe slugging it out with one of the

raiders, while Lestor Hogg steamed in to another, twice his size. He took several serious blows before he could grab the other end of a lead bar. The man was bigger, heavier and younger and Lestor struggled to wrestle the weapon from his grasp in a tug of war. They tumbled onto the stage and off again to the sawdust; Hoggy was getting the worst of it. He clung to the pipe for grim death and then using the man's body weight, reversed the strategy and pushed instead. The thug struck himself in the throat, that was all the edge Lestor needed and he was on top in a moment, pounding him with a large ashtray. The next thing he knew, someone had lifted him off and flung him away like a sack of spuds. He lost his ashtray and his balance and careered into another battling couple. A strapping brute had Mickey Butler's head under his arm and was punching him in the face. Each punch was lifting Mick off the ground. On shaky legs, Lestor Hogg lined himself up and struck Butler's attacker twice between the eyes. It stung him and he dropped Mickey then grabbed Lestor by the throat and his fist began spanking the marrow out of Hoggy's nose. Gritting his teeth, Mick gamely clambered up and sprung on the assailant's back, trying to choke off the man's air supply with one arm, while clumping him repeatedly on top of the head. The blows had little effect against such tremendous strength, the man was like Colossus. He pinned Lestor up against the wall then, with his other hand, in one movement heaved Mickey over his shoulder and slammed him down on his back, driving all the breath from his body. Lestor flung an exhausted left at this giant but it lacked anything and ricocheted off. Desperately lifting an arm that grew ever heavy, he jabbed two fingers into the brute's eyes and felt the jelly squelch. The grip on his collar relaxed and he staggered out of reach.

Kit tilted the balance. After his directions could help no more, and he had emptied the stage of everything hurlable, he leapt down and ran into the core of the fight, knocking people aside with fists of concrete. Fresh, fast and uncommonly tough when the madness took him, he swung from the hips, right and left, with great momentum, and each blow exploded like a bomb on targets that swayed in front of him, taking him deeper into the hand to hand combat. His route went between Lestor and the blind Titan and he struck with an upper cut that started on the floor and finished under the chin, lifting the Cyclops up, off his feet, to bowl him over in a heap. With somewhat depleted ranks, the enemy were frantically battering people all over, but Kit's rage carried on through like a tank, mowing down anything that got in his way.

Fintan had taken too much punishment to be good but fought tooth and nail in front of Bridgid and Mary, guarding them with every ounce he had left. Many women had been hurt, some crawling from underneath the battle, where they had been cast down and couldn't get up. Others had taken serious strikes from coshes that were aimed anywhere. It was carnage.

Gerry Nolan was kneeling to revive George when a bottle, thrown from the other side of the pub, hit him, badly splitting his dome and rendering him unconscious. Twyford used Gerry to prop himself up then leaned on a table that collapsed beneath him; the prostrate Gerry cushioned the fall. George lurched up and stood on his face by accident, stumbled over him and, gasping a great lungful of air, went to get stuck in again. There were only a few of the raiders left standing and once they fell...knew to expect no mercy. Nobby sat slumped against the wall with his eyes shut; George kicked him in the head for luck as he passed. Most of the shouting and hollering was at the rear of the pub. Three of Ruben's men, still wielding lead pipes, had backed into the ladies with two women. Twyford pushed his way through while they locked themselves in. Johnny Bass turned and looked for him, his nose bleeding down his herringbone suit.

"I bet I get the blame for this lot as well," thought George, rubbing the pain away from his head. He reached the middle and was pleased to find a halfdozen bruised but friendly faces. 'How many's left?'

'Three of them,' answered John, wobbling a front tooth with his finger and thumb. 'They're holding two women in there.'

Twyford's stomach turned over, he knew there was more to be said. 'Is it Mary?' he demanded, suddenly desperate with worry.

A voice called across, 'George, she's safe enough.' Twyford turned to see Owen using the bar for support and holding a very blood-stained handkerchief to the side of his head nodding him on. George twisted further around and saw Fintan near the stage, almost dropping, fists still raised in the stance; Mary and Bridgid crying and cuddling behind him.

"Thank God," he thought, but by the look on Owen's face he still had trouble.

'They've got one of the barmaids and…Sally.'

Everyone looked at George; they would follow his lead. He picked up a pint mug from the floor and moved towards the toilet when Horrie the governor stepped in front of him. Horace put a hand on Twyford's chest and pointed a finger at his own lips, then spoke loudly to the toilet door, 'It's okay, it's all over. You won't get hurt unless you hurt the girls. I'm the governor here and you have my word there's to be no more violence. Now let the ladies go, sling your weapons out and you can piss off before the police get here. There's been enough trouble for one night.'

The room was silent; nothing happened for thirty seconds then a deep voice answered, 'They're alright. This has fuck all to do with us, now keep away and once we're clear… they go free. We don't want no bother.'

'Come on out, boys. Nothing will happen to you, but throw those weapons down to show you mean it.'

The door lock clicked loudly and it opened a few inches while an eye peeped about but most had moved away to give Horrie's peace talks a chance. George waited at the blind side of the door with his glass jug concealed behind the pillar he leant on.

'Okay,' said a voice, 'move back, we're coming out.'

Three long lumps of pipe were tossed out and the door opened wider. Newman stood behind Sally with a broken bottle at her neck. Her head was trying to stretch away from it at a strange angle, a muted scream of terror locked in her eyes. Another thug gripped the petrified barmaid by the hair, while the third scouted the ground warily. George readied himself, the jug still out of sight. No one showed any aggression and Horace said wearily, 'It's all right, boys. Put the bottle down, I gave you my word. Now, *please,* piss off quietly.'

Newman nodded to his oppo more confidently and they let the hostages go. The girls fled away. The broken bottle remained in his hand then, as they moved cautiously along the wall towards the side door, Horrie hit Newman right in the temple with a soda siphon that had been standing on a table behind him. The jug went to work next as George gave its savage message to a second thug moments later. Then everyone piled in. When they stepped back you could not tell who was who. Three faces all looked identical; one terrible bloody mess.

Looking at them, Twyford had no sense of victory, only sorrow that it had been necessary and, with a brief sigh, went in search of Sally. To say she was distressed was an understatement. Tinker had his arms around her, her head was buried in his chest and she clung tightly to his lapels, rasping down air like an asthmatic; the surrounding ocean of concerned faces had made her hyperventilate. George helped her outside with Tinker held fast and the cold night air slowed her breathing to near normal. With care, he took over and the stout Tinker went to find her coat.

'I don't suppose you fancy a trip down the West End, do you?' She answered by almost going in to shock. 'No, course not, I didn't think so,' he mumbled. With her head tucked under his chin, Twyford cuddled her protectively and watched Fintan gently ease Bridgid and Mary into his car. "I'll give Ruben a ring Monday," he thought, then went back to considering how he could get to meet the Yanks, and made a mental note not to keep checking his watch. An idea came to him; the Ford was around the corner and the fight had left him completely sober. He could load Sally in the back and run her home, then put her to bed with a stiff drink and say good night, nicely. Spend three minutes in her bathroom cleaning himself up, scoot off and try to catch the 'Shermans'. It seemed a reasonable answer.

Kit, the berserker, was calm, happy and alone, leaning on the windowsill outside the pub and about to light a cheroot. He had enjoyed himself tonight and was running over it all in his mind, savouring the recollections.

Rita came to him with a mooney look in her eyes, 'Take me home,' she said, dreamily.

'You all right?'

'Take me to bed!' The straightforwardness threw him, momentarily.

'I thought you didn't fancy me,' he blurted, stupidly.

'That was before I saw you fight. How you laid into those men, it excited me. It made me go all shivery.'

'Shivery?' he repeated.

'You know, hot.' He looked at her and she became more emphatic.' Sexy!'

"Stone me pink," he thought, "if only Nolan and the others could hear this." He looked around for them and saw Gerry being stretchered into an ambulance; "shame." But then with panache, he offered his arm and whipped her off down the road, a mite faster than they came up.

Bells had been ringing constantly as, one after the other, ambulances and police cars were pulling up. Horace had suggested that everyone should go home, but nobody took any notice and hung about outside the pub, recounting their moments of glory. The police insisted Horrie had to point out the offenders. He tried to wriggle, saying he would rather not in case they came back during the night and smashed his windows, but in the end he had to give in. There appeared to be nine strangers amongst the casualties, so they got the blame. Fifteen people in all were hospitalised over night, including two women. At least the same number were cleaned up, stitched up, bandaged and sent home: Nolan, Owen, Stan Swindells and Pat Passmore amongst the former. It was hardly past ten, the fight had spanned no more than twenty minutes at most. Oppressive policemen, using well practised badgering techniques, tried hard to take statements but everyone, it seems, saw nothing; it was all strangers fighting. Names and addresses were taken down and then most people went back into the pub to help clear up. Once the tables and chairs were upright and the floor swept clean of glass, the placc bcgan to resemble its old self again, with the odd tell-tale lake of red to be scrubbed clean in the morning.

The tenth stranger had concealed himself among the injured, still in the pub, and sat with his face partially covered until medics began assisting invalids to the ambulances, then he slipped out with them. Head down, Nobby circled the emergency vehicles, crossed the road and disappeared around a corner. No one saw his escape, except Mickey Butler. He knew the shape of him, if not his name, from the times he'd come on the knocker and stuck his foot in the door demanding money. Anger boiled and fatigue was forgotten, he darted across the road after him and, remaining out of sight, stopped in a doorway to study the collector's attempt at a nonchalant stroll along Queen's Crescent. Butler timed his dash to perfection and as Nobby approached the off-licence, sprinted the final yards and ran at the man with a force that caught him by surprise and totally off balance. Mickey careered into him in a low crouch and, using the momentum, lifted the body up through the plate glass window. Nobby screamed as large shards fell dangerously close to cutting him in half. He lay amongst the window display, not really hurt, but nicked and bleeding from a hundred minor cuts. A great slice of pointed glass hung above him like the Sword of Damocles and he dare not breathe too sharply in case sudden movement dislodged it.

'Talk your way out of that, you slimy bastard!' said Mickey and vanished.

Under normal circumstances Horace had a good understanding with the police and, with the cheek of the devil, asked the officer in charge if he could have a family party in the bar. The tills were taken upstairs and the officer waited until the other squad cars had left, then joined them for a scotch or three. The tills were brought back down the second he departed. A good portion of the earlier trade was still hanging about on the off chance so the doors were locked and they carried on serving till half past midnight. What with the tenner George donated towards the damage and the money he'd taken on the late one, it had turned out to be a rewarding evening. Sergeant Shaw may be a problem, but he did not return to duty until after the weekend and lots can happen in two days.

Fintan sat at the kitchen table in Mary's house whilst she and Bridgid cleaned him up. Ruben Benson was back on Monday and he had a lot of thinking to do, though, at the end of the day, the decision to join George had been made for him. Betraying Ruben did not lie easy with him and the firm's direction was totally unacceptable but, nevertheless, he took no pride in treachery. Benson had two heads and one was rather likeable.

Johnny Bass could not face another row with Megan so instead of going home, decided to remain at the Malden and drink to excess. To her credit, Meg stayed too. She went upstairs with Rose and Vi Quill to make sandwiches for everyone. The remainder of the Force waited hungrily in the bar, toasting their own valour and showing their scars. It was Crispin's Day all over again.

George had been soothing Sally with soft words since they left the pub and managed to get her home with no further trouble though she was still in a state and clung to him. He administered a strong night cap but it had little effect on her. She stared and stared and said nothing. Unable to leave his lady like that he put her to bed and lay with her, holding her close. Tiredness engulfed him and, not meaning to, he fell asleep with his brain dancing about, incapable of settling on anything that remotely made sense.

Kit and Rita reclined in a similar position, sharing a cigarette, both happy with their private thoughts. Kit felt that he had proven himself as a man and a lover; the lady need look no further. He was pleased with the way he had pleased her. She blew smoke at the ceiling and mentioned,

'Do you know what, Kitchener?'

"More praise," he thought, while she searched for the right words.

'You fight a lot better than you fuck.'

The slur stung for but a second and then he started to chuckle, she chortled with him and it swelled in to a real belly laugh.

George awoke in the dark and couldn't work out where he was. A warm lady lay next to him and she flinched as he sat up, then moaned softly and rolled over. Short of a jacket but still dressed, he slipped out from under the covers to find pen and paper. The moonlight glowed enough to write by, it also provided him with a fair view of cleavage. Perhaps he should dwell a touch longer for shock can appear in many forms then, for no sound reason that he could think of, found his jacket and left.

Theresa was already awake, as usual, when Mickey brought in her breakfast. Her eyesight was stronger some days and today, as he sat close, she could see the bruises on his face. She looked harder and saw the fat lip. Ready with his story, he told her that he came across one of the bullies who used to call for rent and had knocked his block off. Stating that he would not have worried her for the world, Mickey explained that it was one of those things he just had to do. She understood, as always, and treasured their happiness all the more.

Most of the lads were getting the same treatment from their wives; good loving then once they were softened up, the knife was twisted into George Twyford. It was his old proverb again; the tongue is the deadliest of all blunt instruments. He had returned and although there was more money in the purse and food in the larder, the women saw him as a threat. All this boys own stuff about mates forever; the best thing he could do was to go back to Mary and suffer like the rest of them.

George arrived at Lawn Road Hospital just in time to see Owen Esterbrook signing himself out. He had a huge plaster over his ear and a bandage wrapped around his head. This particular problem was news to Twyford. It seems Owen's ear had needed to be stitched back on properly; an open razor had separated most of it from his head.

'Oi, where's our wounded?' yelled George, making him jump..

Appearing to balance his head, Owen turned slowly and answered, 'Swindells's ribs are all strapped up and one bollock's black but, once the doctor's seen him, he'll probably be released.'

'Oh, that's a touch. Shall we go and visit?'

They chatted as they walked and soon reached Stanley's bedside. He was laying flat and told them he was in a lot of pain. They had given him an injection but it had yet to work. The doctor reckoned his spare tyre saved him from internal damage.

'How's Nolan?' asked Stanley.

Owen's expression got more serious,' Not so good. A flying bottle's split his head wide open and he's had sixteen stitches, but last night something happened with his vision and he was seeing everything upside down.'

'No!' said George, astonished.

'Yeah, straight up,' answered Owen, trying not to scratch his bandage. 'So they're keeping him in for observation.'

'Perhaps they'll manage to find out how he can open his mouth and still talk out of his arse.' remarked George, which set them all to giggling until Stanley started coughing. As the cough worsened, the bed shook and bounced him about.

'Don't fuck about, Stan,' said Owen, 'That ain't a trampoline, you know.'

His ribs were racked with pain yet while he choked and laughed at the same time, he still managed to utter, 'Fuck off before you kill me!' They left to find Nolan.

If ever there was a right miserable ward Gerry was in it. Some old geezer in the corner was shouting out to no one special and the nurse had a moustache. Nolan's head was swathed in bandages and two black-rimmed eyes peeped out.

'Can you see me or shall I do a handstand?' asked George. His reply expressed a similar sentiment to Stanley, except the wadding made the first word sound more like 'Buck'. The doctor arrived at the same time and Twyford took him to one side. He would not say too much until George informed him that he was Gerry's brother. Only then would he open up and express his concern at the optical images that Nolan's brain was receiving.

'It may just be severe concussion,' he said 'but we can't take the chance and a neurologist has been called in to be on the safe side.'

Twyford extracted the chap's private telephone number and would drive him mad for information. He then promised Gerry that everything was sweet and they would be back in the morning.

'He's in the best hands; people always say that, I hope they're right.' said Owen as they left.

'Please God they are!' muttered George and dropped him at the market to catch the last of the Saturday trade. They'd forgotten all about Pat Passmore.

It was time George paid a visit to the family. Walking along Marsden Street he saw Alan playing football in the middle of the road with a dozen kids of all sizes. Coats were down for goal posts and a serious game was in progress. Alan was belting down the wing and put a terrific ball into the area. Nothing came of it but, had duty not called, he would have liked to tarry a while and enjoy the match. Twyford knocked on the door of twenty-one and Mairead answered with a big kiss for him. He walked through to the kitchen, Mary narrowed her eyes but he was not in the mood to fuck about.

'Are you all right?' he demanded to know. It took her by surprise and she nodded. 'Did you get hurt?'

'No,' she said curtly, not wanting to make an issue of being knocked over, kicked and trampled on.

'What about Bridgid?'

'Fine.'

'How bad was Fintan hurt?'

'Worse than he said, I think, but he drove home safely; I'm seeing them at Mummy's later.'

'You're definitely all right?' He asked again.

'Yes!' she assured him, confused and a little off balance.

'Good. Tell Fintan that I'll see him before Monday,' and with that he went out the back and across to his Mum's house.

Kirby returned to Liverpool and spent a pleasant weekend with the family. Unlike his customers, with no thoughts of business worries until 9am Monday morning.

That evening he was tempted to stay in. Niamh and Mairead came over for an hour and it was refreshing listening to the problems of growing up and being girls. Unfortunately opportunities of meeting a contact like the American Corporal were few and far between so, with no real choice,

George decided to make the Red Lion, in Windmill Street, his first port of call.

Twyford dressed smartly to make up for a face that looked like a bag of nuts and bolts and prepared to go out alone but when he opened the street door he beheld the gypsy features of a handsome Danny Curry coming down the path.

'I couldn't stay in and leave you on your own, now could I?'

'Capital, Old Bean, fancy coming down the other end?'

'Yeah, why not?' They walked to the top of the square and a twenty four bus flashed past. With a mad dash they chased it away from the stop and managed to jump on the platform before it picked up too much speed.

The Red Lion was clogged with Shermans. No Bones, but the evening was young. They stood at the bar with frothy flagons of ale and watched both doors. The beer was barely savoured when he bowled in with an officer who was as pissed as a newt, saw George and Danny and barged across.

'Sorry about last night,' Twyford said in earnest, getting in first.

'What happened to you two?' he asked, laughing. 'Not fighting over gals again. Believe me, they're not worth it.'

'No! Some friends were in a bit of a scrape and we had to stay and help them out.'

'I'sh...important to help pals!' slurred the officer, who was sticking to his corporal and wouldn't be shaken off.

'Hey Captain, you're driver's over yonder,' said Bones, waving someone across.

The officer turned to look and slid sideways into them, Danny steadied him until friendly hands helped the Captain outside to his car. He tottered back in to say something but the words refused to be expelled, so he waved and staggered off.

'Always good to look after my betters,' said Bones, flashing a weekend pass. 'Where are you boys taking me?'

'Anywhere you fancy!' answered Danny, keen for the Café Luxor but didn't like to mention it. Bones suggested it anyway and George didn't mind, as long as he didn't have to fight anybody.

Lenny and his henchmen made some great comments about Twyford's bruises and a good mood was descending on the evening. He secretly hoped Radna showed remorse so he could blank her properly. Bones was gasping to get down there so Danny asked him if he had a meet with someone special.

'No! It was real fun last week. You guys do it; no one holds back, everybody joins in. Those bums at the base make a lot of noise but they're full of piss and wind; shouting about it, but doing "San Ferry Ann".'

Dan looked quizzical until George translated for him, 'That's a colloquialism for "sweet fuck all".' They were shown to a smaller table and Twyford sat with his back to the stage. Radna came on for four numbers then supported for two more; he seemed not to have noticed. During one of the breaks they spoke of business and Bones explained how useful the inebriated Captain could be, and mentioned his weakness for women. If George could arrange some girlfriends for him an open pass for Tinker might be obtained, giving legitimate access to the airbase. That way Bones could load him up twice a week with Scotch, chocolate, blankets, milk, petrol and boots.

"If it had to be done, so be it," thought Danny, and shrugged it off with ease. 'No problem for us,'

Twyford smiled in agreement, wondering how that might be accomplished. Still, the two Londoners gave off a confidence and a good impression of themselves. Bones might well be an even bigger liar than they were for this was all great in theory, though was yet to be proven possible. Regardless of that, the boys went along with it and made arrangements to sort the Captain out for the following Friday night. They were to meet in Bethnal Green at the Green Gate.

Business over, Danny had spotted four lovely ladies sitting together and a bottle of champagne was immediately dispatched. These ladies had a directness that shrank lesser men. The waiter was informed that they would only drink it if the gentlemen joined them. The message was well received and the lads found chairs and sat between them. As Bones went to squat, one of the girls put her hand on the seat and pinched him. With a shriek, he leapt in the air making everyone laugh and that set the standard. The bevy were so easy to be with that within minutes their table was the noisiest in the place. Hailing from Stepney, they were mad dancers and very saucy with it, nothing embarrassed them. Swarthy was singing a fast Latin American tune, and as George and Elena twirled, his eye caught Radna who, disappointingly, wasn't watching him. Bones had never managed two women before, never had the opportunity; maybe now his fantasies could well come to fruition. The young ladies were the straight forward type who, having chosen to be with you for the evening, couldn't be tempted away by Prince Charming himself. For their part, the lads were smitten and perhaps that too was only for the night. Be that as it may, the girls were fine company and George contemplated how he might do them a kindness by putting the Captain in. Rising even more in his estimations, the ladies demanded their attention and danced brazenly together as two couples, the smooching full of sexual innuendo. When the number ended the hall roared its appreciation.

Ties were hanging loose, collars open and enormous quantities of champagne had been quaffed until their pores were sweating pure alcohol. The music had abandoned them, the balloons were burst and reluctantly the guests began to leave; now it was time to pay the piper and George called for the bill. The waiter returned to inform him that it had already been settled. Twyford looked around for his benefactor and saw Donald Grogan, for the first time that evening, at the end of the hall. He waved George over. Extracting himself from the ladies, and promising to be back in two shakes of a lamb's arse, he joined Grogan and they shook hands.

'Thanks for the drink,' said George politely, 'that was most kind.'

'Think nothing of it, Georgie, my pleasure. Just needed you for a second, lets step behind here.' They moved through the jungle that grew in pots and once he was certain they were alone Donald handed George a white fiver. Twyford looked at it casually with a somewhat perplexed countenance. Grogan beamed and withdrew another one from his top pocket, like a magician producing a wonder to swoon at. Becoming keener, Twyford inspected the notes, the numbers were identical.

'All my own work,' said Grogan, with undisguised immodesty. 'Interested?'

'You said it,' replied George, eager to know more.

'Keep both and study them then meet me at the Savoy, Tuesday evening about eight. Okay?'

Twyford grinned, 'Look forward to it.'

He rejoined the gang, not quite so inebriated but merrily enlivened about the next page in life's ongoing adventure. They set off for Stepney on the night bus and walked through the back doubles from Commercial Road. Because of its close proximity to the London docks, the East End streets had been bombed even worse than Camden Town. Elena lived in a pre-fab, among five others, in King John Street, and never having been in one before George was surprised how warm and comfortable it was. Catching a second wind they arrived in great spirits and gin was compulsory on entry. With little regard for the neighbours, dance records were loaded onto the gramophone and the party went full pelt. Four girls to three men posed no problem for whilst constantly changing partners there was always a threesome, or Stepney sandwich as the ladies called it, where the lucky chap would waltz pressed between two pairs of breasts. Twirling until legs refused to coordinate with their top halves, the carousers finally got to bed as the sun was coming up.

It was three strangers who staggered out at eleven thirty on the Sunday morning, lost and dreadfully hung-over. They wandered around for half an hour, and by the time the trio found where they were, they had forgotten where they came from. More important, no one could remember how to contact the girls again.

'San Ferry Anne!' said Danny. But neither one had the energy to correct him.

Stan Swindells was released from the hospital, but should return in one week for a check-up. Tinker and Owen Esterbrook had helped him on to the back of the horse and cart, and instead of taking him straight home, decided to pop in to the Malden for a quick snifter. Unfortunately lifting him back off wasn't so easy and he cursed with every jerk, complaining, 'I need painkillers, not booze.'

Owen replied, 'Come on Stan, a couple of large brandies will start the engines a lot better than any aspirins.'

'My engines need a full service and me' battery's flat!'

'Well, consider this an oil change.'

Horace the landlord glowered when they entered the bar but Rose treated them to their first drink and wished the invalids better, too. Danny and George arrived for the last hour, and a hair of the dog. Memories of Friday night grew again as heroism was expanded, the youngsters would recite the Battle of the Malden for many years to come. Poor Pat Passmore had a fractured wrist and stitches in her face. The word was that she may be scarred for life, which took the edge off the merriment. It was not nice when women get hurt and no one could think of anything to say.

'We'll look after her, anyway,' suggested George, and made everyone feel better and okay to laugh some more.

The barmaid, Lynne, who had been one of the hostages, came in for a drink. It was the first time they had seen her since

Friday night. The boys started to sing, 'Oh dear, what can the matter be, two old ladies locked in the lavatory.' Everybody joined in and she took it in good part; nice to make her feel cared for. Horace came across and asked sarcastically if, by any chance, those louts were after George.

'Never seen them before in my life.' He answered, 'But, as they came at me, one shouted, "he's the landlord. Get him!" I thought I was standing up for you.' Horrie's eyes narrowed into slits and he was about to hiss like a serpent. 'Straight up, Horace!'

Unable to spit on the floor because he'd have to clean it up himself, he walked away in disgust and felt their silent mirth on his back.

'He's all right,' said George. 'I gave him a tenner for breakages.'

'A tenner!' the astonishment was plain to see.

'I know it's a company expense but did we have to be that generous?' inquired Lestor Hogg, hating to protest but ten pounds takes a lot of earning.

'He makes us feel wanted,' said Owen. 'That's what I like about him.'

'Ear 'ear!' They echoed together.

'You going soft on Mary again?' asked Johnny Bass, in front of everyone.

'Course not!' said George indignantly, 'whatever made you say that?'

'Just the way you flapped about when you thought she was the hostage.'

'Leave off! I hate her but she's a good mother, I have to admit that.' Not a soul among them believed a word of it and all started to take the rise out of him. Firmly, he quelled them with, 'No woman's worth the salt of my tears!'

Over Sunday lunch, Min told him that Kevin had called on

the off chance. His answers to his son's earlier questions had been squeezed through the mangle and the lad was bound to have more. Still, if luck was with him, he'd be asleep when Kev called back. He could never stay too long in case what's her name got upset. The boy was too young for all that courting stuff, George decided for the umpteenth time.

Twyford picked Mornie up, early evening, and drove to Kilburn to see what condition Fintan was in. Bridgid answered the door fresh as a daisy. The kids had toys covering the length of the passage and some of the bigger ones were sliding down the banisters. She was in fine form, the children did not give her enough time to fret and worry. Playground noises and tremors seemed to come from all over the house. "Fuck living underneath this lot," thought George, as they climbed the stairs to the front room. Fintan was bruised to a fetching purple and gold and every time he smiled his lip bled. He spoke oblivious to the noise and, with practised projection, his voice rose above it telling them of what he intended to do and how adamant he was. He planned to collect Ruben as normal and during the journey to work he would tell him everything, his feelings and his sorrow at having to resign but that the Mickey Butler treatment was, for him, the final straw, and as always he followed wherever his conscience guided. George knew to argue was pointless but he added suggestions and if Ruben was the man they thought he was, he might listen. Twyford's delicately worded ideas convinced Fintan that it couldn't hurt to try.

With bladders full of tea, George finished with, 'Hope to see you tomorrow morning.'

They had nearly reached Chalk Farm when a monstrous explosion shook the ground, the car convulsed and the sky in front of them lit up red and yellow.

'What the fuck was that?' yelled Mornie. 'That's the biggest bomb I've ever heard.'

And they decided to crawl along with the lights off and investigate. Fire engines were ringing bells and coming from all over to converge on Mornington Crescent. The Craven A building had been struck in its centre by some sort of rocket. No warning had been given and had it not been Sunday, anything up to a thousand people could have been inside working. As it was, three night watchmen were missing. Experts were sifting through the wreckage, while firemen at either end put out blazes and looked for survivors. Ruben's luck was way out, all the office windows opposite had also been blown in.

CHAPTER 20: E TENEBRIS VENET LUX

Gothenburg : The exchange of thousands of sick and seriously wounded British and German POWs began at Gothenburg this afternoon. Most of the British were captured in 1940 at Dunkirk; others, taken in last years raid on Dieppe, included Canadians. The Germans, mainly from Rommels Afrika Corps, were still in desert uniform.

Fintan arrived at the Benson residence in Frognal at seven thirty on Monday morning. It was a very large, happy house with many bedrooms. Ruben's wife died of TB years before and his youngest daughter had nearly suffered the same fate. Sarah was now a healthy young woman, but still lived with Daddy, his parents dwelled there too. Mum was a sprightly old girl of seventy five, if she was a day, but Ruben's father suffered from arthritis badly and needed a wheelchair to move more than a few yards. Benson's other three children, two boys and a girl were all married with children of their own, but the house was often full of them, Ruben's family was the most important thing in his life. The senior Mrs Benson answered the door to Fintan and asked if he would like to come into the hall. He was the only one who had ever been invited in and most times he refused, but today, he felt he would like to wait inside.

Ruben breezed by with a, 'Good morning, Fintan,' and a, 'Sarah, where's my green tie?'

Fintan wanted to get it all off his chest, but hesitated. Perhaps it was better to get him in the car, bare his soul on the way, and resign as they arrived at the office. He was not like George, planning it all, he just had to say it as soon as politeness allowed. Ruben came back, tie knotted in a Windsor, briefcase in one hand and overcoat over his arm. Fintan opened the rear door and Ruby got in.

He began to speak almost as they pulled away, 'Boss, I've got a lot to tell you. None of it's good.'

'Fintan, old son, it can't be that bad, either. Take your time; you know I'll help if I can.'

'No, Boss. You're not gonna like any of it, but I'd appreciate you giving me a chance to finish before you do your nut.' Ruben did not like the sound of this, but agreed. 'Boss, I've got to resign. I like you and you've always been fair to me. But I haven't liked what's been happening at work, and I was disgusted at the way we've been treating our tenants.'

'Not this Butler business again, that's all over!' interrupted Ruben.

'That brought it to a head,' continued Fintan, 'but Theresa Conroy's family grew up with my wife's family and they were good friends. It's much too close, and I've had to decide that I can't be a part of something as dishonourable as we're becoming.'

Ruben attempted noises to change his mind, not wanting to lose him.

'Don't decide now. Think about it some more. I'm making a lot of changes, believe me.'

'I'm afraid that's not all, Boss,' and dropped the first bomb shell, 'I'm going to work for George Twyford.' The name sent Ruben raving to the world.

'That no good mongrel from South London? That fucking parasite? That thief?'

'He's not from South London,' said Fintan, breaking the flow. 'He's from Kentish Town and he cares about the community.'

Another tirade, 'The fucking community! That chancer, that chisler! Let me talk to the cunt, I'll prove to you what a thief he is!'

'Would you really talk to him? Because I know he'd like to make the peace with you.'

'After what he's done? I bet he would, the fucker!'

Bomb hatch open for the second shell.

'Well now, he'll be waiting outside Chalk Farm Station. You

should speak to him. If not…' said Fintan hurriedly, 'I'll drive straight past and you won't be disturbed.'

Ruben's mouth fell open, 'You took the fucking liberty to meet him on our way?'

'No, Boss. Just say the word and I'll drive right by him, but I honestly feel you should hear him out. I'm your man until we get to the office, and you know that without asking.' Ruben understood that Fintan was saying he was perfectly safe and he knew that to be absolutely true. They were driving down Adelaide road, nearing Chalk Farm. Ruben hadn't spoken, so Fintan suggested, 'I'll drive straight on.'

'No,' said Ruben, 'stop and let him in.'

The car pulled up outside the underground and George hopped in the back. He was dressed smartly in a business fashion and offered his hand. Ruben Benson stared at it and, understanding his animosity, George withdrew it.

He began with, 'I know we haven't got off to a very good start for reasons we both know but, just for a minute, let's put that behind us. I would like to perhaps buy more property from you, the council, or whoever, for a fair price. And I think they're may be avenues that we might go down together, rewarding for both of us.'

'Here, hold on a minute,' said Ruben, 'before we all get comfortable in my car, how did you two get together?' Then to Fintan, 'Did you know him before or after he bought the houses,' adding, '"bought", that's a fucking joke an' all! Well?'

George went quiet. Fintan could answer this one.

'Well, you see, we're sort of related.'

'Related?' repeated Ruby.

'Well, he's married to my wife's sister.'

'You're fucking brother-in-law!' said Ruben in astonishment.

'She has three more sisters,' added Fintan defensively.

'That's charming, that is? I tell you what,' said Ruben crazily, 'why don't I marry one of them? Then we could all be related!

Wouldn't that be cosy?'

George sat quietly, making out he wasn't there. He was sure there was more to come. It would be

all falling in to place. Ruby sat forward, talking to Fintan's ear, while he drove calmly onward.

'You betrayed me! That's how he knows everything.'

'No he never,' said George.

But Fintan's honesty couldn't be quiet. 'My conscience wouldn't let me stand by and do nothing while you threw a disabled woman and her family out on the street *and* gave her husband a good beating. You went too far, Boss.'

'That wasn't neither of your businesses!' shouted Ruby.

'It was my business!' stated George, firmly. 'I left England for four years to keep that family together, and I'll be fucked if I let anybody hurt them now!' Wrong tack completely. It was all going rotten. Any second Ruby's temper would let fly.

'You invited this mongrel into my car. The man who beat up my workers, blackmailed me in to giving away a fortune in houses *and* even dug a grave for me over Hampstead Heath. You helped him do all that? You fucking Judas. He even threatened my family.'

'You were doing a lot worse to mine,' countered George.

'You ain't related to the Butlers.'

'Mickey's Mum took me in when I was orphaned,' said George, using outrageous lies to support his argument. Even Fintan believed it for a minute. 'Anyway, your men deserved what they got,' said George. 'If you'd have seen them on Friday night, you wouldn't have been so proud of them, smashing people to pulp with lead piping.'

'So that's where you got all the bruises!' said Ruben, smugly. 'Is that what this is all about? Frightened are you? Have they given you a taste of your own medicine?'

'No, but they tried,' said George, childishly hinting at the result.

'They struck old men with coshes,' said Fintan, 'cut women with bottles and razors.'

'I don't' believe you!' said Ruben, 'You're both lying!'

'It'd be very easy to prove it,' challenged George softly.

Ruben rose to the bait. 'Go on then,' he dared.

The trouble was they were already at the lights in Mornington Crescent.

'We'll prove it to you, but you might want to spend a few minutes at the office,' said George.

They rounded the bend and Ruben saw the bombed Craven A building; everything else was momentarily forgotten. He had dreamed of owning it, now half had been flattened to rubble. Fintan stopped the car and Ruby saw that all his windows had been blown in. Unable to believe in such bad fortune his face filled with despair. The three of them walked into what was left of the office. The clerks were tidying up as best they could but the immediate problem was four huge replacement panes of glass.

'Who's coming?' demanded Ruben. 'What have you fixed up?'

'Sorry, Mr Benson, but we can't get anybody to come out to us. What with the bomb and everything, they're in great demand. I don't know what we're going to do.'

Ruby asked, 'Isn't there anyone who'll do us a favour? We'll look after 'em.'

The clerk shook his head. 'We've tried them all,' he said sadly.

'Do the phones work?' asked George, lifting the receiver and hearing the dialling tone. He dialled the yard and of all people to answer was Mickey Butler. George spoke quickly and with urgency, 'An explosion's blown in all the windows at Ruben's offices. This is really important. Get Danny and bring plenty of glass.' He nodded and finished with, 'Good, we won't be here, just carry out all the repairs. See ya'.'

Thinking that this might very well prove a point, George looked up in anticipation of an appreciative word. Ruben could not bring himself to say 'thanks,' so he changed the subject and spoke to the clerk, 'Where's everybody?'

'We haven't seen any of the fieldsmen at all,'

A police car pulled up behind Benson's Humber and a plain clothes detective together with two PC's walked to the office door. George nodded to Ruben and said, 'Shall we go? I promise you, you don't want to speak to them.'

Ruben was no slouch when it came to avoiding the boys in blue. 'Tell them I'm out of town for some time,' he said to his chief clerk. 'I'll be back later.' And they left through the private office. 'I hate you,' Ruben said to George, 'and I'm gonna have you. You've been responsible for all of my trouble. I'd lay money you know what they wanted.'

'Probably to ask you about your fieldsmen, they were arrested Friday night, those that weren't kept in hospital.'

Benson somehow knew he was speaking the truth, this nightmare was never ending.

George directed Fintan to drive to Lawn Road Hospital and, between the two of them, they informed Ruben of what had occurred in the Malden. Benson knew his men were hired muscle, and villains in general, but he could not take in what he was being told, so matter of fact. Fintan added names as George described their deeds of brutality. He closed his eyes, "This was the end," he thought, and winced as Twyford's graphic description threw up a mental picture of all the terrified wives and bystanders. How could things have got so far out of hand?

They arrived at the hospital and Ruben began to worry about what he would see. Pat Passmore was waiting in casualty and rose as they approached. She did not know the distinguished chap in their company but was grateful for the lift home. Her arm was in a sling and her neck ached from supporting it. What was more apparent was the red and purple cut that ran from below her left eye, across her nose and through the corner of her lips. It had been stitched to look like a rail track and gaped open between the stitches.

"Blind Pew could have done a better job," thought George,

but smiled and kissed her after Fintan. She was more his friend and had never really been that pleasant to George.

'Do I look pretty?' she asked brazenly, covering her pain with tough bluff.

'This is a chum of ours,' clarified Fintan, 'It's his car we're using.'

'Thanks for the lift,' said Pat, shaking hands with him, 'I couldn't face going home on my own and the ambulance couldn't drop me off till after dinner.'

'Yeah, well you don't want the whole street blacking their noses when that pulls up,' said George dryly. 'We've got to see how Gerry is, then we'll be off, if that's okay?'

'Yeah, that's fine,' she answered.

Nolan had been moved to the sixth floor and the lift was busy, so Twyford suggested that they take the old stone staircase. No one was about and Ruben spoke as they began the ascent.

'You beat up two of my workers,' he said, 'you fiddled me out of my money and you've turned Fintan against me.' George went to interrupt, but Benson continued with, 'Let me finish, first.' His tone expressed how hurt he was and, as George listened, he felt belittled by the words. 'By all means threaten me, but not my family.'

Twyford wasn't proud of himself for that and could find nothing to say in his own defence. They had just passed the first floor when suddenly Ruben belted him on the jaw. It had taken George completely by surprise and nearly sent him over the metal banister, which he grabbed for support. Ruben then jabbed him with a right, under his kidney. Twyford ran off up the stairs hotly pursued by Benson, raving after him, 'Dig a grave for me, will you? Threaten me?' It would have been better to save his breath, for George wasn't going to fight and carried on sprinting higher; knowing that the older man would tire first, no matter how much hatred motivated his mettlesome limbs. A yard behind, Benson was desperate in his rage to get hold of him. At the sixth floor they ran on into a ward and Twyford dodged behind a patient on a mobile bed, being wheeled through by two porters. Ruben couldn't stop and bumped into it, recovered in a flash and feinted first right and then left. George countered by darting the opposite way each time, keeping the bed between them. A woman's voice shrieked an order to stop, but Benson sprang forward and dived across the patient, catching the tail of George's jacket. Hospital staff, hearing the commotion, came from all directions and, much to Ruben's frustration, stood between them, forcing them to cease their wild behaviour. Big, strapping nurses held their arms like bouncers, while the two men hoovered air, too breathless to speak. An old Sister berated them, mercilessly, for what she took to be horseplay that had got out of hand.

'It was him who started it!' puffed George, telling tales and finding it amusing.

Ruben bounced the blame back and Sister gave them a severe, three minute tongue-lashing. Then, after she had established what they were supposed to be doing there anyway, sent them off, under supervision, to the ward that housed Gerry.

When they reached the bed, it was screened off.

'Here, what's all this?' asked George, making himself busy.

A nurse stopped his protest and ushered them away until the specialist had finished.

'Doctor will see you now,' said the Sister.

A chap far too young to be shaving came over and introduced himself as the neurologist then gravely explained his findings. He compared the optical nerves with an old cinema projector that sometimes shows the moving images upside down or over to one side. Further in-depth detail lost them completely but the summing up was that Gerry's vision has been distorted by the blow from the flying object striking his head with such force. Damage had incurred internally and Nolan must be moved to Moorfields Eye Hospital, where the best specialists in the country could look after him. He tried to give off confidence, but it fell short.

'Can we visit him down there?' enquired Ruben.

'Not right away I'm afraid; he'll be in intensive care.'

'He will be all right, won't he?' asked George.

'I'm sure they'll do everything they can,' came the reply. Twyford's stomach became suddenly empty. They walked back to the stairs together; Ruben had calmed down and was quite chuffed with himself. He had planned to do that over the Spaniards and now he had shown the bastard. Neither had since spoken to each other and, as they descended, George rubbed his jaw, knowing it pleased Ruben. If he saw pain had been successfully inflicted, it may dissuade him from bothering to do it again. Twyford had no wish to fight a fellow ten years his senior, though had the roles been reversed, he would have wanted to do the same. It was natural and he was beginning to appreciate the man's values.

Once at Casualty, George repeated to Fintan and Pat the worrying news and by this time, the smell of hospitals was cloying at his throat. Strangely enough, Ruben took over and shepherded them into the car then left them for a short while. When he returned, he held Pat's hand and asked if she would let a friend of his in Harley Street take a look at her. She agreed at once and thanked him for his concern.

Benson wasn't short of contacts and had arranged two immediate appointments in the most famous medical street in the world. Fintan parked outside while Pat and Ruben entered one building and were shown up a precipitous flight of stairs then met at the top by an old boy with wild grey hair and pince-nez perched on the neck of a red bicycle hooter. Ruben greeted him as an old friend and left Pat in his capable care.

A hundred yards further along the street Benson beckoned George into another large house that smelt of ether and an identical receptionist took them through to a ground floor front office that faced out onto Harley Street. A rather handsome man in a very expensive suit welcomed them in. The consultant, Leonard Blackburne, was most cordial and, as George explained what he understood of Gerry's dilemma, the chap nodded knowingly. Mr. Blackburne specialised in sight and held a clinic at Moorfields twice a week. Allaying their fears as best he could he explained that, in some cases of this nature, vision was only temporarily impaired and may return to normal in a few weeks. He would take over the case from today. They thanked him and left. Whatever he was going to cost, would be worth it.

When they returned Pat Passmore was still in the examination room and the surgeon brought them through to show how he could vastly improve on the work already attempted. She was tilted back in a padded chair with a glass screen in front of her face which magnified every pore, but there was something about her body's positioning that aroused, in Ruben, an old, forgotten friend. Directing his attention back to the wound, he saw it was still fresh and open in parts. The expert was detailing every step of a possible operation, if they agreed to it, and stated that the sooner he began -the less chance of permanent damage. He would undo the earlier "disgraceful darning" and spoke of 140 tiny stitches taking anything up to eight hours on the operating table. This should guarantee at least ninety percent free of scarring; if they could leave her there he would make all the arrangements for time was of the essence. Pat was crying; she wanted him to start now. George agreed to it, and she graciously thanked Ruben. Benson made little of it and kissed her hand and her cheek, a few smooth words rolled off his tongue and the receptionist saw them out. Having no experience of Harley Street, Twyford wanted to ask, 'How much?' but Ruben walked him away before he could embarrass them.

'It's vulgar to speak of money here,' he said. 'The bill will be enormous, so what?' He was enjoying himself watching Twyford sweat. 'It had to be done and thank God you can afford it, George, you're about to find out why surgeons really wear masks.' Then added, 'I think that's very generous of you.'

'If I'm such a good fellow, why did she thank you?' queried George, in a low murmur, but the wily Benson was already striding off to the car.

Fintan wasn't exactly sure of what was happening but drove them back to Mornington Crescent. They hadn't actually uttered anything remotely friendly to one another, but at least the cursing had subsided and each seemed to reluctantly accept the other.

'Let's have a butcher's at the Craven A,' suggested Twyford and Ruben felt a depression coming on. He had gazed at that building every quiet moment knowing he had more than enough contacts to become a significant supplier, helping the War effort with government contracts, all gilt-edged. Now the place was in ruins, he would have to set his sights elsewhere. It was such a crying shame.

The building itself was the size of a normal block of houses. The two ends were still intact, but the central section was flattened through four floors and from the pavement you could see clearly to the basement. The three of them walked over the rubble and Ruben thought how damaged it looked, how beyond repair while George conceived how it could be rebuilt with improvements: the skeptic and the dreamer. To modernise the place would have taken major surgery anyway. Now, a ramp could be constructed and every inch below ground-level could be utilised for parking, deliveries, machinery, even a work place. The insurance assessors were finished and they chatted with them for a while. The mood in the city was worrying, had Germany now found the power to destroy London and the Home Counties with guided, unmanned rockets?

'Who would we speak to with a view to making an offer?' asked George. Everyone looked at him with different degrees of shock. The assessors reacted first by fawning over him, and instantly whisked him away from Ruben and Fintan, whilst assuring that the owners would be most happy to discuss anything he had in mind. They took down his details, promising to be in touch within the next twenty four hours. Ruben felt that old dislike rising again.

'What the fuck are you doing?'

'Well, you weren't saying too much.'

'Do you have any idea of the value of this building?'

'No,' said George, honestly.

'Then how can you make a bid?' asked Ruben.

'I've got twenty four hours to get an educated guess of how much it would cost to rebuild it with an architect to make sensible alterations. Once I know the asking price as it stands, minus the value to rebuild it, we get somewhere near the first offer.'

'And you can get this kind of cash!' jeered Ruben.

'Let's not talk here,' said George. 'I want to sit down and hear exactly what you've got to say. You've obviously thought plenty about it.' They crossed to the office. The windows were taking shape and would be installed by that night. 'Hope you've got some cash for these lads.'

Ruben grunted in acknowledgement while George used the phone and spoke to a builder he knew, who promised to take a look at the site early the next day. Sitting together in the repaired office, Benson valued the building at around twelve thousand as it was before the bomb, and for that money they would never have let it go.

'That's the beauty,' said George, 'Time costs money, the owners might want to knock it out rather than spend to rebuild. All the while that's non operational, the insurers are liable; they've got to do their sums quickly and take it on the chin. If it's cheap why don't you buy it?'

Ruben thought for a while and then decided to tell him what he must already have guessed, anyway. 'I own almost four hundred houses, all producing a profit. But to buy them, I borrowed heavily from the banks, putting some property up as collateral to borrow money to expand on more property. The houses are paying off the loans against them and covering the wages but not a lot more yet, I haven't got the lump I need to buy a warehouse.'

'And the banks won't lend you any more?'

'Not until they've had a big chunk back.'

George nodded understandingly. 'Let's talk tomorrow when we have more detailed information.'

'What about me?' asked Fintan, a trifle hurt to be forgotten about.

'You're still working for me,' said Ruben, commandingly, 'I'm not accepting your resignation.' Fintan rose to the challenge but Ruben changed tack swiftly and put an arm around him. 'I have always thought of you as being under my wing, almost a son as it were.' It was a pack of lies though he did think a lot of Fintan and would not lose any more ground to Twyford out of principle.

George smiled and went along with it. 'Why not leave any final decision for now, Fintan. You've got it off your chest and we've aired a few views between us. Stay with Ruben until after Christmas then you two may find there's no need to change. Let's just see.'

'That sounds like sensible advice to me,' added Ruben, tilting the balance in his favour.

Fintan shrugged good humouredly. 'Okay, but no slipping back to the old ways.' (Ruben had told them, without expanding on it, that big changes were coming whatever happens.)

Twyford was kindly dropped off at the Shipton and trudged down the Square. It had been a long day and though he could not admit to anything physical, he felt worn out. Kevin was asleep in the armchair when Twyford entered the kitchen and, accepting that more questions were inevitable, gently woke him. He came round with a jolt, shook his head twice and stood up, not fully awake.

'Sit down,' insisted George, 'I've got the kettle on.'

'Hallo Dad. Are you all right?' the voice full of concern.

'Yeah, of course I am, mate. Why shouldn't I be?'

'I heard a band of flatnoses dished it out to you lot up the pub Friday?' It was a question, and he waited for an answer.

George tried to expand on the reasons and results of the evening, hinting at the stupidity of it all, as he tried to work out what was worrying him. It became rapidly apparent. He wanted to go with his Dad and sort them out. George stopped the rambling and pulled him to his chest. Kevin was not embarrassed at all and returned the hug like a man. His reasoning was the seriousness of what he believed to be the situation. If anyone was threatening harm to his father then they would be dealt with. Now his father was home, he, Kevin, would ensure his safety; the protection of the family came before anything else. George was more proud of this boy every time he opened his mouth. He was a man. Once again the guilt rose, only to be appeased with the thought that Kevin had had to take the role of protector, and he did it splendidly.

'E Tenebris Venet Lux,'(out of darkness cometh light.) said Twyford to the air. Then to Kevin, he said, 'There are no returns and nothing to worry about, son. They tried their luck and came unstuck. A lot of people got hurt and it was all unnecessary. It's now best forgotten. Come on, let's have that cup of tea.' Kevin was convinced and relaxed as George told him a few good jokes. He in turn did the same, and pretty soon they were enjoying themselves to the point where they decided on a pint and a game of darts at the Glee Club, better known as the Monday night loan club.

The morning papers all ran major articles on the explosion at the Craven A. It was pure speculation, because no official statement had yet been made, although the general consensus of opinion was that Germany had a rocket capable of turning the tide.

Sally awoke Tuesday morning and the first thought that crossed her mind was the letter she had given Alan to take home with him. Hopefully, when he arrived in class today, he would have Mary's reply. She was sure her problem could be helped; it must be terrible to be so weak and alone. George, in part of his descriptive characterisation, phrased it coldly but probably correctly when he said her best friend was a bottle of booze, in fact her only friend. "How sad," she thought, "and how upsetting for the children." Mary Twyford may not know it but at least with George and herself, she had two real friends.

Kirby came out of the court room with a cold smile of satisfaction. His superiors had given the required support and quietly withdrew, leaving him alone with his enjoyment. Although considered unsavoury with the Revenue hierarchy he functioned remarkably well for them; he was ruthless, greedy, and totally without compassion, the perfect qualities for a man in his profession. It was said that Scrooge and Shylock both failed the interview. The judge had granted him a search warrant and the power necessary to execute it. He and six investigators, with local police in support, would raid 16 St. Leonard's Square NW5 at 4am this coming Thursday morning. It was the known residence of one George Twyford. If any evidence was discovered which could implicate Twyford, he would be placed under arrest by Kirby of the Revenue, who together with the security forces, had been granted special powers, far exceeding the local Constabulary. They could hold him without trial for their pleasure and for this action the police force would be under his orders. He still felt flashes of fear whenever the huge Sergeant crossed his mind but now the boot was on the other foot and if that belligerent lout interfered in anyway, he, Kirby, would have his stripes and his career.

Sergeant Shaw listened to every snip pertaining to the Battle of the Malden and knew there was much more to unearth before he could get to the truth of what it was about. The day previous, he had been driven all over St Pancras calling on anyone that witnessed the incident; a chat in private with Archie generally improved memory-loss. Now it was the middle of the night and he waited for his team of four to find their no.1 snout and hope that he had some of the answers. Even Archie didn't know the man's identity but their agreement was, in an emergency, the fellow need only produce a dented fob that played a certain hymn and he would be protected; he was that valuable.

The Sergeant had to be careful and appear unbiased, just doing the job, when in reality he had two daughters and two sons-in-law thickly involved. Although he had to admit the trouble was started by outsiders, the reason for it must appear in time and believed the facts would eventually prove that the cause was of Twyford's making. Archie would see his daughters last of all. If only he could turn back the clock and they were young girls again, safe at home with their mother, and he would sweep the rubbish from the door.

Alan stood at the back of class, before register, with half a dozen other lads sitting around him. He was repeating his father's stories of the War, and added a bit to what had already been added to. He was saying, 'You see; only the bravest could get in the Black Watch. Know why?' Silence came from his audience. He waited for them to shake their heads then continued, "Cos when they marched into battle, they wouldn't wear steel helmets or trousers.'

'What about jackets?' said one argumentative soul.

'Course they wore jackets or you couldn't tell who was a Sergeant, and that. They only wore Highland bonnets and kilts, and when the bagpipes played, the troops believed they was invincible, and all the enemy was scared of them 'cos they'd heard they were barmy.' He made the last bit up because he'd forgotten a little and that seemed to finish the story quite nicely, which was just in time as Miss came in and the class took their seats. The register was called and everyone unearthed their books for the first lesson. Alan closed his desk and found Miss Poole smiling down at him.

"What does she want now?" he thought. "Oh yeah." He ran his hands through his pockets and pulled out a somewhat creased note and handed it to her. It was brief but said that Mary was in after school if Miss Poole wanted to call. More than a little offish but Sally was prepared for that.

She stooped low with her hands folded in her lap, and said to him in her nice voice,

'I'm coming to see Mummy this evening, perhaps you'd show me the way?'

The look on his put-out little face showed, "Bleeding Hell!" but he nodded moodily and sauntered off with his head down. Sally straightened up and smiled sorrowfully as she watched his unspoken protest wend its way out of the room.

Mary was made up to look her best and had convinced herself it was for Alan's sake, she could not embarrass him in front of his teacher but secretly she wouldn't like to be outdone by this younger woman. The school ma'am seemed intelligent, so whatever a refined young lady like her saw in George Twyford was a mystery. He was trouble. You could tell the difference around the area in the few weeks he'd been back; those tax devils were spying on her family, the hospitals were filling at a rate of knots and the police were always down the Square. She knew poor Daddy was worried sick and asking for information everywhere.

The knock was light and Mary cast a quick eye around the room, looked in the mirror over the fireplace once more, touched her fringe without moving it at all then, getting in the mood, swayed elegantly along the passage to the street door. Sally had arrived at Mary's house still holding Alan's hand, much to his disgust. She had insisted on doing so to cross Prince of Wales Road and since then had held on regardless. They appraised each other as the meaningless words of greeting changed places. Alan was released as they shook hands and was out of sight before his farewell had reached them. Mary held the door and her open palm directed Sally down the passage. She was a good six inches taller and from behind, Mary could study her long legs. "Damn, but she was a fine looking girl."

Sally was nervous now she was there. At home, she had reasoned out many different ways to broach such a delicate subject, and a strong backup argument if Mary tried to deny it or take the other path and defend her actions with aggression. Either way Sally would be firstly supportive and sympathetic then gradually persuade her to a more positive direction. After all, the welfare of the children must be their prior concern but, in the cold light of day, suddenly she could not justify her interference.

Mary poured tea and then left her to make the conversation with no assistance at small talk. She must soon come to the point, which could only be for George to have more access to the children, but that did not explain her earlier remark to Mary's 'problem'. She had some trepidation that perhaps he was using the teacher to get the children from her and had good reason to put nothing past the conniving bastard. Still, all would soon be clear.

Sally began with her rehearsed patter about the ordeal on Friday night but Mary just nodded with no dialogue. There was nothing for it but to plunge in. 'Mrs Twyford, I can quite understand your actions, the stress of wartime puts additional pressure on us all but I would like to help really, we both would.'

'Who's we?' quizzed Mary.

'George and myself,' answered Sally, 'and before you say it, let me reassure you that he does care what happens to you. None of us want to see you in one of those homes.'

'A home!' she shrieked, 'The bastard's trying to have me put away?'

'It's not like that. His shoulders are very broad, but you must see that there are limits to what even he can do.'

Mary stared at her, "She's mad," she thought, "that's what it is."

'We understand why Alan stays at home and looks after you when…'she trailed off, but began more confidently with, 'I'm here to tell you that you have two true friends and we can help you to help yourself. If they're getting too much trouble somedays, let the children stay with their father, take time for yourself. You can beat it.'

'Beat it?' she repeated, not sure now who was mad. 'Beat what?'

'I think we both know what,' said Sally, a little too condescending.

'Will ye stop talking shite and spit it out!' said Mary, raising her voice to break through the fog.

Sally could see she was about to lose her reason and so took a deep breath and said it.

'George has told me all about your drink problem.'

Mary sat down, speechless. They sat in silence, surveying each other with pity. There was no need to scream and shout; the poor girl was taken with the swine. He had made up a complete pack of lies and she believed every word. Just being the wide boy, using women and never stopping to think who he was hurting. 'I take it he doesn't know you're here?' asked Mary.

'No, he doesn't.'

'Let's leave it like that,' she said shrewdly. 'Please don't tell anyone.'

'Of course not!' replied Sally, 'I wouldn't dream of it.'

'I'd like to have you as a friend,' professed Mary. 'I tell you what, I'll not take a drink if you come and see me every week. We won't tell a soul.'

Sally gladly agreed, happy with the idea of a secret friendship. They gossiped for an hour about people they both knew whose children went to the school and then Sally left, promising to return the following week. Mary was not quite sure what she was doing but a plan was forming to crack him like a filbert.

Twyford, unaware of all the goings-on around him, drained his cup, tea grouts and all, and folded the newspaper. His Mum liked to study every line at leisure after work. She was still given three months employment each year working at Mansell's Bon Bon factory. Min had known most of the other girls for years and although she had to be fast rolling the Christmas crackers there was always plenty of time for a chat and a laugh. George hoped to be as active when he reached her age.

He flopped a coloured silk handkerchief half out of the top pocket of his suit jacket then distributed a comb, a bunch of keys, small change and a petrol lighter about his person. Twyford had not smoked for years but it was always useful as a stylish introduction to women who did. He was running low on spending money and while counting out three hundred quid from the briefcase decided that the rest of the hoard should be deposited into the four bank accounts. Everything appeared to be kosher, with no reference to himself so it might as well earn some interest as to be under the floorboards, plus it would be one less thing to worry about. He wasn't seeing Irving and Benny until Thursday and he reckoned it was safe to leave it hidden until then.

Thunderstruck at the photograph in front of him and never accepting coincidences, Archie Shaw crosschecked against the missing persons file on Dr.Howard Small and the mystery surrounding his disappearance. A lady friend had stood bail for him and he was to have appeared at a preliminary

Hearing to defend himself against a probable charge of manslaughter, but was now believed to have absconded rather than face the music. The original press photo had caught the couple, descending the steps, outside Albany Street Police station and had been enlarged to give a much clearer definition of the suspect's features; it also showed someone to their rear who bore an uncanny resemblance to George Twyford.

CHAPTER 21: RUBBER GLOVES YET NO WASHING-UP?!

Britain: An RAF Photographic Reconnaissance Unit (PRU) today brought back a photograph of what looks to be a German 'flying bomb' launch site at Abbeville in Northern France.

Stripped of clothing and trussed up with wrists secured to ankles, on his knees in front of the mirrored wall, Donald Grogan watched the door behind him with expectation. One bout of her caning had already engraved its message in parallel lines across his buttocks and with a promise of "dressing up" she had left him to imagine what could happen next. The mere thought of her sadistic deeds could anaesthetise his senses and hold him feverish on a finely tuned line between desiring the almost unbearable and the dread of beyond that. The door opened and she appeared from shadow, naked and fabulous but for a harness strapped around her waist from which extended an extremely large and proud phallus, stitched in black leather. Holding it with both hands, she stood over him and explicitly described exactly how much it was going to hurt and how he would wail and plead with her to stop -then beg her to start again! Her expression was a fusion of lust and bestiality and he knew she was moving out of control.

'Mercy!' he yelled. It was the key word. She always stopped at the key word: -but not tonight. He was there to violate as she wished and nothing would stop her tonight. Positioning herself behind him, she implanted the appendage into his sphincter then with strong propulsive force entered his anus, each vigorous thrust delved deeper. He cried out, 'Mercy!' over and over, but she was far too aroused and rode him with crazed exuberance, swearing she would only disengage when he had given her 'weapon' a name!?! Nearing insanity, repeatedly he shrieked, 'Mendoza!'

She had him!

Gerry Nolan was petrified. Without the use of his sight, he couldn't believe how helpless he was. When his eyes were uncovered, he saw the room from angles, upside down and then flashing on and off and his complete equilibrium was gone; the body trying to rectify the vision by balancing levelly with the apparent horizon. As a result, it created a type of sea-sickness that made him throw up and he could only lie down for fear of falling over. The odd thing was that just using his weaker left eye he could make out shapes reasonably well but the two couldn't work together and refracted the image incorrectly. So both had to be bandaged up, for light entering through one affects the other and stops the healing process. He needed to depend on people for every little thing. One of the saddest instances, as he explained to George and Mornie Quill, was being led to the toilet with your hand on someone's shoulder and then never knowing if you've cleaned yourself properly. Other senses strengthen to help the body, especially smell, and he was forever sniffing himself for unwanted odours. The bandage had to remain intact for fourteen days, apart from the specialist's inspections with a pencil torch in the dark when he would apply drops to both eyes then cover them again. They tried to raise Gerry's spirits by promising that everything would be mended in a fortnight's time but he was nowhere near convinced.

From Moorfields, Twyford drove to Mornington Crescent. With Ruben's permission, his builders were using the office as a base while they moved to and fro gathering information. It would be another full day yet before they would be in a position to give a sensible estimate. Plans of the building and surrounding area had arrived from the owners and Twyford's architect had drawn a pretty picture of the building re-built and surrounded by trees. George had told him his ideas and it wasn't for a Gainsborough, no words were minced on where that could be hung. Benson was interested in all the details, unreasonably hoping to be amused by the plan's failure.

Back at the yard, George filled up with the usual mixture;

seventy percent petrol and thirty percent TVO. Petrol could be sold on the black market for double the outlay, and tractor vaporising oil cost half the price of petrol, so as long as the mixture had no more than a third TVO in a full tank it was a great little earner. The only give-away was the dark smoke sometimes emitted. Twyford had recently come out of an ale house just in time to see two police officers, over the back, dipping all the tanks of parked vehicles in the car park, underhandedly checking for illegal fuel, which carried a heavy fine. In his haste to exit, George rushed the ignition and gave it too much choke, flooding the engine and causing them to take notice. He shoved the choke back into an engine that refused to respond and had to sit and watch their approaching steps through the rear view mirror until they came level with his boot. With little hope of deliverance, he tugged the starter, touched the throttle, the motor roared and he shot off leaving them to asphyxiate in a cloud of thick, black murk.

The car was never left in the same place twice and today it was parked around the corner in Belmont st. Twyford still looked for shadows but, unless they were getting better at it, he was safe for the moment. As he walked past the fish shop Timmy Gowan came out of the door. Nicknamed Timmytoonice for obvious reasons, he had lived above the premises when they were boys and his parents still owned it. They had been good friends but Timmy was quite the boffin and had won scholarships that eventually earned him a place at Cambridge. Their paths had probably crossed only ten times in twenty years. Tim recognised him at once and called out but his tram was at the bus stop and wouldn't wait. They promised to raise a glass together at the weekend. George wandered down the Square, speculating about his meeting with Grogan later, this could be the best touch yet. He didn't like to coax others out on an evening that was normally a 'stay in with the family' night, but dropped it in conversation that he would be partaking of a pleasurable drink at the Savoy, if anyone fancied it. No one took the bait so, apparently, he travelled alone and readied himself to leave early. The meeting was for eight but it didn't hurt to look the place over first. Whilst brushing his teeth, a caller hammered the knocker. Min answered the door and found Stan Swindells standing there like Burlington Bertie.

'Come in and don't break nothing,' she warned him. He weighed over twenty stone but constantly forgot it, and leaned on things like everyone does.

On his last visit he'd sat on the extension flap of the kitchen table and snapped it off then said to Min, 'It's all right for you. I bet I've got a splinter up my arse now!'

She threatened him with her toe in the same place if he wasn't more careful, but having such a lovely manner he got away with murder. Twyford came down and was pleased to find that Stan was out with him. They took the car and drove along the embankment, parking on the north side of Waterloo Bridge, and walked in through the back entrance of the Savoy Grill. George wandered into the different bar areas and then went to Reception to enquire if Mr Grogan was staying there. The receptionist checked and answered in the negative but on giving his own name he discovered that there was a message for him, 'Balmoral would be in the residents bar.' Nice touch, Balmoral was the name for the Highland bonnets worn by the Black Watch. Twyford was escorted upstairs and found Donald, sitting alone. The bar was quiet but George recognised one of the two men at a separate table from the Café Luxor. Another fellow stood at the counter and was also a good bet to be part of the tartan army. To Grogan's credit, he was cautious. Donald called for G & T's and they chatted until the drinks had been served, neither mentioning Radna, then it was down to business. Grogan had no deal with anyone in London yet and, if he was to be believed, wanted one agent only here in the South. Was George in a position to handle the volume? Twyford stated that it all depended on the price. He could go to work, but he would have to sell it in quantity and there had to be a margin in it for him. Grogan spoke as if the price was settled and there was no need for discussion. It was twenty pounds for twenty, minimum order four thousand sterling, which brought twenty thousand pounds worth of forged notes. George argued it was too dear to move the required quantity and took out a pencil and did some figures on a napkin.

'If you can't raise the money there's not a lot of point in carrying on,' said Grogan, playing hard to get.

Twyford looked up from his sums and ignored the jibe by answering with, 'Ten thousand cash for one hundred thousand notes, which works out at two shillings each.'

Donald took the bid as an insult. 'Are you mad?' he asked. 'A fiver for two bob?'

'Let's get that right,' corrected George, 'Ten thousand pounds cash for a sackful of paper which has no value the second the authorities realise they're about.'

Grogan desperately needed an order like this but could not be seen to let them go for that price.

'I'll not haggle. If the order's that big, I'll serve you two for a pound. That's it.'

Twyford craved to be the sole distributor and, had he trusted Grogan that they were all as good as the sample, may have bid closer to the offer.

'No. I've got to sell them for less than that,' he said, coldly. 'Whatever stock I finish up with when it gets out, I've got to burn. That's the bid. My time's too important to fuck about.'

The finality in his voice unsettled Grogan and he nibbled his bottom lip. The man at the bar stepped in front of their table and eyeballed George. Grogan nodded him away. He thought for a while as Twyford waited patiently.

'At this moment I am not prepared to quote any less. If we get to an agreement, when can you have the money ready?'

'Don't worry, I can get the money. But before I part up with any of it I must know if any notes have been released in to circulation.'

'None whatsoever,' came the answer. 'The success of this deal must be timing.'

'I agree,' said George, 'and I have your word on it that if it comes to pass, I will be the only one in the South.'

'You have. Another distributor operates in the north of England and myself in Scotland. You've got Birmingham down, if you want it.'

'I would insist on it,' said Twyford, who would have been happy to accept anywhere south of Luton.

'Now make me happy, George,' said Grogan, in a much more affable manner. 'Increase the bid sensibly and let's shake on it.'

'I'm not being difficult,' replied Twyford, a little softer. 'My arithmetic leaves me at two bob. I can't move.'

'And neither am I when I say I can't reach you. Well, let's leave the door open, take a few days to think some more and meet Friday night at the Café.'

'That's probably a good idea,' agreed George, standing up and smiling in friendship. 'I'll see you around midnight under the swaying palms.'

Donald arose and shook hands, treating Twyford to his most sincere expression.

'Look forward to it, Georgie,' and they parted, each enjoying derogatory thoughts of the other.

The large bar area was empty, apart from seven or eight Wrens sitting together in a corner. Stan went in and ordered a bottle of champagne while George wandered the hotel. The barman gave him one glass and one bottle, both chilling in an ice bucket. Normally Stan drank rather quickly and not wanting to get too boozed, too fast, meant to sip his drink until George did his business and they could have their night out.

One of the Wrens came to the bar to buy a round for her friends and, eyeing the bottle, asked pleasantly, 'What are you celebrating?'

'I've won the slimmer of the year competition.'

She snorted with laughter, and then saw he was serious. 'Sorry,' she said instantly, 'I thought you were joking.'

'No,' he answered, letting on she'd upset him. 'Everyone thinks that, but I've lost five stone.'

'Oh, that's very good,' she said, trying to make him feel better.

'It's all right,' he replied, gently, 'most people laugh. I've never had any real friends, that's why I drink alone, unless, no, I couldn't ask you to..?'

'Of course I will!' she said at once. The barman produced another glass and she toasted him. He drank it straight down and she did the same. He filled the glasses and told her to excuse him if he drank fast but she made him nervous.

'Don't be,' she said, and again they drained glasses. Her name was Janet and, as they chatted, the bottle emptied. The girls had begun with the Vera Lynn songs when one of them came over to ask why she wasn't joining in. Janet stated that she was with her new friend. He suggested that she was just saying that and didn't really mean it.

'Oh, I do!' she declared.

'She does!' insisted her friend, then to Janet, 'Bring him over. The girls won't mind.'

He ordered another bottle of Bollinger and the two ladies grabbed an arm each and frog-marched him to their table. Janet introduced him to her group of gentlewomen as 'Slimmer of the Year'. Supping pints of beer and cider they lifted their jugs in his honour. He asked them shyly to carry on singing, saying how much he enjoyed their voices, then bashfully mentioned to Janet that his dearest wish would be for someone to sing to him. She put her arms out and sang him a love song. He was great at getting people at it and he hinted to her friends that she didn't really mean it 'cos she wasn't singing it with feelings.

One girl shouted, 'Show him you care!'

Another added, 'Put more heart in to it!'

If George lived to be a hundred, he would never forget what

he saw as he walked into that bar. Stanley was sitting all forlorn with a pretty Wren, down on one knee, holding his hands and looking in his eyes, surrounded by half a dozen more, and they were all serenading him. Twyford stared in astonishment. Stan saw him, stood up and copied the look, then made great show of excusing himself for a moment.

'I can't believe this,' he said to the audience,'It must be ten years!' and whilst hailing George and pumping his arm like mad, murmured, 'Play along. You're my only friend in the world and I haven't seen you in donkey's years.'

Twyford liked the role and went into action. They talked out of earshot while the Wrens, already half-cut, watched them attentively. Stanley persuaded him over and the girls did the rest; they hung on to each poignant moment as old friends met again. Both lads insisting that this wonderful occasion must be celebrated. Champagne was called all round and the lads skipped over each other with fascinating lies of their youth. Now, some people prefer women to dress femininely but this crowd were all in naval regalia, the hair pulled back from the face in the compulsory bun, with the usual thick black stockings. Women in uniform stimulated everything, even the plainer ones gave Twyford a swelling. It had all the makings of a glorious night.

They rolled out of the Savoy sometime later, trying to work out how to load seven girls into the car. Eventually, Stanley sat in the middle of the back with one on each knee and one either side of him, squeezed between the doors. The other three sat along the front bench seat with George. They drove to their trainee base at Greenwich, singing all the way and the car didn't labour at all. Twyford parked in a back street but the noise the Wrens were making would wake the dead. Janet stopped and pulled them in to line for if they were to get the chaps inside some trick would have to be contrived. The camp was policed by women only, one main entrance which was through two security barriers either side of an office. The girls would arrive and gather around the window. With seven girls talking at once, the two guards must take the time to quieten them down before letting them in. The rest of the base was asleep and quite dark, with only one light outside each separate hut. George and Stanley were to crawl between their legs as close as possible to the office. It was all for a laugh and the plan worked. When they were in, the Wrens walked en masse blocking any view of them from the security box. Proceeding extra quietly, the group reached their cabin and ushered them inside. It was twelve to a hut but their shipmates were not yet back, so Stanley and George made themselves comfortable. They paired off with two girls and before they would go any further, others replaced the first two, and as everyone's clothes came off, the girls changed again. Two cannot be divided by seven and the women became more demanding. Poor Stan was naked apart from his bandages, and these Wrens were getting rougher. It was difficult for Twyford, but even more painful for Stanley as they bounced all over him, jostling for position. One had hold of his penis and nearly yanked it off as she was pulled away by two others wanting a chunk. The more Stanley howled, the more George laughed. A pillow fight broke out and soon they were piling on top of one another. Twyford was pinned down near the bottom when someone bit his arse. He shot up and accidentally butted the girl above on the nose, which bled like mad. Stan begged them to watch his ribs but they were hollering drunkenly and drowned him out. The door opened and the lights went on.

A brace of MPs, questionably female and brandishing white truncheons, marched in. The girls immediately dismounted and stood by their beds, while Stanley and George tried to cover themselves with pillows. They were taken away and locked in the shower hut with the remnants of their clothing and held in custody until the following morning.

The lads slept sitting against the wall until at 6am and, still dark, were roused out and paraded before a Naval Security Investigation team. The poker-faced officer in charge carried the rank of Major and repeatedly looked at his watch while the antics of the night before were read out. As the Military rigmarole ensued, his escort of six took up anti-escape positions about the room and two Wrens, who could have boxed for England, stood guard either side of the door. With such security measures you would think they had stolen the Crown Jewels.

'Can we get on with this?' said Stan, tiredness in his voice. 'Only I'm supposed to be meeting Admiral Canaris for lunch.'

'Don't get funny with me, fat man,' said the Major, threateningly. 'You can go only when I'm satisfied there's no threat to Naval security.'

'There's no need to get personal,' said George. 'He never called you "baldy".'

The Major darkened and directed his anger at Twyford. 'I don't need my manners questioned by a common, flash Herbert like you, Poppinjay!' Flecks of spittle decorated Twyford's head which prompted him to request an umbrella then exaggerated mopping his brow with a handkerchief.

'One more word from either of you and you'll both be incarcerated for the duration.' It was aggressively warned, but they realised he meant it. Neither answered back, thinking to give Il Duce his big moment and hopefully they would be released shortly afterwards. But he had to push it. He began again, 'So, fat man and flash, I put the questions and you'd better have the right answers.'

Then, looking Stan up and down, scornfully asked, 'Why are you so fat?'

'Because every time I fuck your wife she bakes me a pie!'

The answer came so quickly it stung the officer like a slap in the face. The room held its breath, trying valiantly not to laugh, but George spontaneously roared; escaping air gave the others away. The Major glared from one face to another, each smirk stopped with the silent confrontation.

'Take them away!' he commanded, fiercely. 'I want their pockets emptied and I want their life histories, everything there is to know about these bastards.' The transgressors were frog-marched off and, after an ear shattering grilling, were strip searched painfully then hosed down with cold water. No towels were allowed them and they were made to get dressed wet then tossed out of the barracks. It was carried out to test their evident sense of humour and was meant, with good providence, to induce pneumonia.

They looked a sorrowful pair that day, two bedraggled souls, damp, miserable and cold. George had lost a sock and limped, where his shoe blistered his heel, and in their haste to undress Stan some one had ripped all the buttons off his shirt, which now flapped about exposing his belly. They wandered around trying to remember where they left the car.

'I didn't mind being naked, even though my old chap has shrunk to a shadow of its former magnitude,' mumbled George. 'I thought they'd just look us over...until I saw the pair of rubber gloves and no washing up.'

'I knew we were in trouble,' said Stan, 'when that guard in the miner's hat turned his beam on.' Smiling at each other, they had to laugh. What a night!

Twyford drove into St Leonard's Square, turned the car round to face the top of the turning, and went in to Min's. The problem was that Stanley had walked out last night after a basinful of arguments. His son, Brendan, who was only fifteen, had got a girl from his class in the family way. Her parents had come to the house to discuss a marriage. Mother and wife, Olive came from a devoutly, religious family and immediately agreed that it was the proper thing to do, but Stanley had sat and talked the subject over with Brendan and now knew only two things appealed to him and he was not going to see the boy's life ruined for a pair of thrupenny bits. The more everyone forced the day-naming, the more adamant Stan became against it. So, he went upstairs, put on his best suit, and with a 'kiss me elbow!' left them to it. That was why he came to meet George and was now deeply in trouble with his old woman. Unless they could find some buttons to stitch on his shirt he could not go home and, even if that was forthcoming, how could he explain staying out till now?

The answer was not a problem to Twyford, with those famous last words…'Leave it to me.'

Up until then Stan was coming to terms with his fate, preparing himself for the misery awaiting him. Suddenly nerves plumbed new depths.

'Just make yourself something to eat and I'll be back in fifteen minutes.'

Stan began to argue, he needed to be convinced but George was out of the door and gone. He heard the car rev up and pull away and, although the frost still shone on the windowsills, Stanley found that he was sweating.

Twyford drove to the Swindells residence and thumped hard on the door. Olive answered; her face dark and thundery. She was only tiny but put the fear of God into her husband when her dander was unveiled. Luckily, George was ready for her.

He gripped her shoulders and said, 'There's nothing to worry about.'

Her countenance flashed to fright, 'What's wrong? Where's Stan?'

Twyford spoke, as if to a child. 'It'll be all right. I promise you there's nothing to worry about.'

She wanted to believe him, even though she didn't have a clue what he was going on about. 'Tell me what's happened,' she demanded.

'Well, it was lucky I was there,' began George, 'we were walking up the pub when he came over dizzy. I sat him down on a doorstep and gradually moved him to the car; you can't be too careful. He had bad pains in his chest so I shot him up the hospital. I thought it was the best thing.'

'Oh yeah!' she said.

'They done loads of tests 'cos they reckon some sort of worry can bring it on. I was asked if I knew of any anxiety that might be troubling him. There hasn't been anything, has there?' queried George, watching her closely. Her head shook slowly from side to side, as if she was trying but couldn't think of a thing. 'You ain't been rowing, have you?' he probed, answering himself with, 'No, course not, not with him just released from hospital. Anyway, listen, I've come to prepare you. You know what he's like, he didn't want to worry you but the doctors thought it'd be best to keep an eye on him over night, so I stayed with him.' He rubbed his stubble for effect and tried not to dwell on his own brilliance, but Mesmer could not have done any better; she took in every word.

"Best speed it up now," he thought, and kept her on the wrong footing with, 'So if you could get him some underwear and a clean shirt, I'll have him back home in a brace of shakes.' She nodded and retreated into the house to do his bidding. George mused on how impressed Stanley would be and oh so grateful. He would tell the boys and, with no bragging from himself, another great deed was born for the Bards to sing about. But it was a different Olive that returned with the clothing. An Olive full of fortitude and resolve who marched passed Twyford and stood at the passenger door waiting for him to open it. He said, coolly, 'You don't want to drag all the way up there. Stay here and put the kettle on and, before you can say Jack Flash, we'll be back.'

It was a suggestion that could not normally be disagreed with. Not normally.

'He's my old man,' she said flatly, 'and he needs me. Open this door.'

"Oh fuck!" thought George, trying to collect his wits. He couldn't argue without giving the game away, so she sat in the car and he drove them to the hospital in Hampstead. He would have to bluff and feel his way.

They pulled up in the car park and George jumped out to take the clothes, but Olive would not let go of them.

'Stay here and look after the car,' he said, 'While I go and fetch him.'

'No,' she said firmly. 'You stay here and I'll get him.'

"That's really fucked it!" he thought. He was sure she believed the story but was now intent in flushing out her guilty conscience with a show of responsibility. 'Go on then,' he dared her, 'but hurry, in case we're blocking an ambulance and I have to drive off.'

He was bobbing and weaving in all directions but she started towards the hospital. Twyford sat at the wheel and watched her go into Casualty. She would find out he was not there and then thunder bolts would crash around the heavens, great pits would open up in the ground and cities would fall into them. As George pictured Doomsday, she came back.

'I feel such a fool.' she said. 'You didn't tell me what ward he's in.'

Twyford was in fast, 'He's up in…what d'ya call it, oh give us here; I'll be quicker than you.' And with that, he snatched them out of her hands and ran off towards the hospital. Once inside he paced about in the lobby for ten minutes considering a taxi down home and back with Stanley, but that would not work, far too long. More bluff was needed. He ran back to the car and slung the shirt in the back, jumped in and started the engine. 'He's stormed out. Said he was cheesed off waiting and he's going home. I hope he's not making himself bad again.'

'This is all my fault,' she said, as George broke the speed limit. He was worried Stanley really had got fed up waiting and would be there when they arrived back. The car pulled up with a jerk and Olive sped out and inside the house. Window down, Twyford sat tensely behind the wheel, engine ticking over as he finely balanced clutch and throttle.

She came to the door like a headless chicken, 'He's not here!' she shouted.

'Must be walking,' cursed George, 'I'll find him, wait there and don't worry!' Then stamped on the accelerator.

He walked indoors and Stanley was asleep in the armchair; Twyford dropped the underwear on his head and sat down. As the story unfolded, Stan trembled slightly but prompted in advance covered his end well when he came face to face with his wife by being more worried for her than for himself. Olive asked few questions but promised that nothing would trouble him until he felt better. George and Stanley agreed, when all was said and done, it had been a useful exercise; she had seen the error of her ways and was now the remorseful and dutiful partner he so richly deserved!

Twyford returned home and dumped the breakfast washing up in the sink then made a list of people he knew, some he hadn't seen for years who, on past history, could afford and might like to be involved in this scheme. It would be to release into circulation half a million pounds worth of forged notes within the Christmas fortnight. Approximately twenty outlets were needed to handle between ten and fifty thousand a piece. His list finished with thirty two possibles, some of which could be in prison, others might be dead for all he knew.

His first call was to the Arches in Bethnal Green. George was a stranger there and no one had ever heard of Roy Morrison. He left a message that should anyone of that name turn up, George Twyford would be passing back this way in ten minutes. He disliked using his own name, but guessed it was safe enough there among the warrens of the Arch Pirates; a battalion of tanks could be lost and dissembled here without anyone noticing. A rum and black in the Salmon & Bull and he returned fifteen minutes later to find Roy lounging about on the corner. The dialogue was short and sharp; his people could buy plenty of motorised machinery from official main dealers for cash and drive away deals. The tractor and H.G.V. industry had suffered badly with the rationing on petrol and were crying out for orders. All Twyford had touched on was the possibility of converting a lump of cash but secrecy was second nature in Roy's line of work. George would soon be in contact, using the name 'Balmoral', they parted and the next stop was Roman Road Market.

Steve Roper was supervising a woman and a young fellow on his stall and since their last meeting Tinker had already made two big deliveries to him and orders were coming in from everywhere. He remarked that the gear sold itself, vetting the customers took the time; how well Twyford knew that. A ten minute break in the café and George sounded him out.

The intimation was digested easier than the stale rolls and without needing to say much more, he declared, 'Reckon me. Tell me the finer points when you're ready.'

He was surprised and a little disappointed at his next port of call. The Jacobs brothers were now his partners but as they listened to George, who could only see the rosy side of this venture, Irving stopped him in mid-flow.

'Professionally I can't be a party to this, please excuse me, I must leave the room.'

Benny, on the other hand, stayed and when his brother had shut the door, observed, 'That's the way it is with all solicitors, a different understanding of legality to the rest of us. They could be knowingly wrong in a litigation yet still ruin some poor bastard and think nothing of it but sitting in a room discussing tax avoidance, in their warped minds, may be conceived as a conspiracy to defraud. Anyway, tell Uncle Benny all about it.'

George detailed exactly what had happened and explained his ideas in great depth. For one reason, Benny was good at seeing extra angles and, for another, he worked for plenty of shady characters and the more solid operators they had, the easier to spread the volume. In his mind, every outlet had to clear its stock of notes before the New Year. Benny listened intently, making no comment whatsoever until George had finished. The feasibility excited him; percentages flashed in his mind and threw out half a dozen names of big investors who would love the opportunity to be involved. The offer might have to be raised a tad but George was confident Grogan would take the bid, like all good girls, he didn't say 'no', just 'perhaps'. As the firm's accountant, the finances were constantly on top of Ben's head and Twyford still had in cash roughly six thousand pounds plus the dollars. His advice was to make the American notes part of the deal, unlike sterling, dollar bills attracted too much attention. If the bid was accepted, the exchange would take place in early December, which gave them a couple more weeks to organise the loan. Benny saw him out and George, always self-assured, felt ecstatic about this back passageway to fortune. The outline of his plan was to sell most of it in smaller lots, trebling his outlay, and retaining about thirty thousand in forgeries to use locally in London. Twyford reckoned that the firm would be pleasurably hard-pushed to spend it all.

CHAPTER 22: FEEL FREE TO PLANT EVIDENCE!

Italy: Guns fall silent along entire Italian line. The Brit. 56th Infantry Divis. attacked Monte Camino, a barren 3000 ft. mountain which the Germans had covered with mines and booby traps. At the halfway point, they faced a series of counter attacks from 15th Panzergrenadier Divis., but held on. They were finally forced to retire through sheer exhaustion!

The telegram from the Revenue, marked 'Private and Confidential', arrived on the desk of Superintendent Barry Hunt at Holmes Road Police Station at 8am on Wednesday morning. The Super read it and handed it to the desk Sergeant, who passed it on to Sergeant Shaw, all within eight minutes. Archie would instruct four Constables to assist and may be on hand himself, purely in a supervisory capacity. The big Sergeant walked out of the station and along to Kentish Town Road, where his presence would always strike fear into the local thieves and shoplifters, working the busy high street pavements. He had often broken fingers and wrists of those he had apprehended, and once crushed a pickpocket's hand in the police car door, by accident of course, yet people felt much safer when he was about. He was the law and took no decision lightly on the protection of decent folk; even scum like George Twyford should have his rights. Whether he came across this fabled sum of money legally, or not, it should be verified by a professional investigation. This way, he was guilty until proven otherwise; that was not right. As he came to a bus stop, a number 63 pulled up and he hopped aboard. The conductor touched his forelock with respect, Policemen were never expected to pay the fare and he alighted at the Southampton Arms in Highgate Road. From there he walked along Gordon House Road to the bom-bom factory and spoke to the floor manager, who thought, for a dreadful moment, that it was to do with missing stock. With great relief, he guided the officer upstairs to the tea room which had just been vacated by the ladies returning to work. There was probably over a hundred women employed by Mansells and nearly all of them, unlike their husbands, thought Sergeant Shaw was a hero, a John Wayne figure. The manager showed Min a docket, delaying her until the others were gone then pointed her towards the empty canteen where Archie waited, meanwhile he stood at the foot of the stairs ensuring privacy. No one else knew of the conversation and four minutes later Sergeant Shaw was back on the beat and Amelia was at her conveyor belt.

George Twyford was under surveillance and had been followed from the Savoy. His meeting with Grogan was enough to make him interesting to a certain party. A car followed the Twyford hareem to Greenwich and the watcher pointed him out, as he was ejected from the base the following morning, to the new eyes who were to take over for the next twelve hours. They were a couple in their late fifties and used an old Morris Cowley to trail him, parking it at the top of the Square. When the target left the street alone, they followed, guessing that he had been in his large friend's house. This pair had worked under cover for many years and kept Twyford's car just in sight as he raced from one place to another. At the hospital, one stayed with the Morris while the other followed him in; he acted peculiarly by doing nothing. From his nervous dalliance, the watcher surmised that he knew of the shadow but changed her mind, when he flew into action again and returned to the car, driving away at speed. Then it was back to the original house, collecting the large one, and off again. After the pursuit had brought them back to St Leonard's Square the third time it was decided to be too risky to follow any further and so, on this fourth sojourn, the watchers remained stationery. He reappeared that evening and went inside the house. During their inactivity through the day they recorded the description of another car parked in the Square itself. The driver had not moved for several hours and then left the street on foot when another took his place. A police car also showed interest by circling the blocks several times and slowing to a snail's pace each time it crossed the top of St Leonard's. The amount of spectators that viewed one small turning caused the watchers to park further away, though the Square's entrance and only exit was constantly in their sight.

A light hung low and shone down on the table, the room was very dark and the twelve people seated around it could not be seen by each other unless they sat forward. Grogan was partially visible when he gave his report and seemed to speak to an empty room. Two sheets of notes were in front of him and he referred to them at intervals. He stated the facts coldly and precisely, not attempting to influence either way, and the details given would affect the next step in the operation to be determined by the decision makers at the other end of the long table. It was not his place to volunteer an opinion unless requested to do so. A man and a woman in turn asked questions,

'Was Twyford stretching himself by offering to deal in such large sums of money?'

Grogan considered that to be the case by the way he refused to increase the price per note. The next question was from a female voice,

'Did he show signs of doubt or hesitation when he mentioned the authorities discovering it?'

'On the contrary,' answered Grogan.

The man again, 'Is it only greed that motivates this man in our direction? And if it is, could that make him careless and therefore dangerous?'

'No. Although he said little to suggest it was nothing more than simple business, I think that the high risk, big profits excite him and feels he is declaring his own private war.' Grogan could not explain this last statement as anything but intuition, though the senior people there knew his judgement to be shrewdly deduced and often priceless.

The lady with a final question, 'Does Twyford believe that you are the only source of these forgeries?'

'Absolutely. His fear will be that I cannot deliver and that perhaps I might try to swindle him out of his stake money; that alone will keep him sharp and on the very edge. His distrust of me clouds out looking for anything else. He doesn't want to know who prints it, just that I can deliver.'

Grogan and three others were then asked to wait in the other room and were called back twenty minutes later; they were given instructions and dismissed. The table members left at short intervals until the final three sat in private. One opened a bottle of Jack Daniels and poured the drinks. They stayed another hour to mull over the latest affairs then departed together through a side door.

Sally was surprised to find George parked outside the school when she came out. He told her he was passing and thought to save her legs for better things. She accepted the lift but left him frustrated, on her doorstep, with little more than a peck and a promise. Wondering whether sex with her, when it was finally achieved, would actually be worth it, he dropped the car at the yard then walked briskly home with his collar up. He had to pass Mary's and, on impulse, hit the knocker. Niamh answered and pulled him inside with a cuddle. He tapped politely on the kitchen door. Mary was listening to the latest propaganda, telling us how well Monty was doing. She had company in for tea and biscuits (supplied by the boys, she refused to believe it had anything to do with him). Two friends, Nell Higby and Kathy Gay, sat with her, wearing snoods over curlers and were obviously not expecting company.

'You shouldn't have gone to all that trouble just cos I'm coming round!' said George.

Both ladies without make up coloured naturally. Mary's eyes narrowed dangerously so he asked for an envelope and beat a hasty retreat to the girls' room. Mairead looked up from reading, kissed him, and asked what two separate words in her story meant. She loved books but struggled with a lot of it. He read the passages out giving her the gist of each sentence, encouraging her to discover the meanings for herself, then sat with them for a while to keep abreast of the characters in their social life. When it was time to go he filled the envelope with fifty pounds and told them to give it to Mummy when he had gone. As he put his coat on, he saw Kevin's box camera on the sideboard. He picked it up, opened it out and walked into the kitchen, clicked a picture of three unsuspecting models, who covered up too late, then was through the back door and half way to his Mum's when Mary called out, 'If that devil's over there, tell him he should be home right now!' She had to find something to ruck about. He thought then how amusing it would be if the film came out.

Alan had been waiting for ages and they had a precious ten minutes together before the girls were ordered over to march him off. Min had his dinner ready in a brace of shakes. It was liver, chips and peas, and one of his favourites. The meal rounded off with a mug of tea and Min timely mentioned, 'I saw Archie today.'.

George waited for it, 'If we had more room, I'd do a cartwheel,'

'Now don't be like that. I know you two don't get on but listen to what he had to say. It was meant as a message for you.'

'Did it begin with 'Good will to all Men'?'

'You hold your tongue!' she snapped, 'It's frightened the life out of me so listen and it might do you a bit of good.'

'The last bit of good he done me cost four years on my own,' he retorted sharply, at once upset with himself for raising his voice to her but she was not finished by a long chalk.

'Have you got money here? Cos if you have, you'd better move it,' she said, watching his reaction like a hawk. 'The Inland Revenue are coming with a search warrant and a police escort to raid our home during the night.'

His expression showed nothing, but his heart was pushing its way out of his chest.

'Sorry I shouted Mum but I don't trust that man. Please tell me word for word what he said.'

'I have. He told me not to be frightened by them and he's instructed his men to look after me and make sure they don't damage anything. I was wary, I'm not stupid. I asked him why he was helping you and he said he couldn't care less what happened to you. He reckons you can't stay out of trouble and you'll get your comeuppance sooner or later, but he doesn't want to see anything happen to me. They've already had a go at Mary, you know. Archie said the Governor was a nasty piece of work.'

George nodded thoughtfully while his Mum rattled on. Was it a bluff? If he tried to move the money, was the clever Sergeant waiting outside Mary's? He could not take the chance but, if he was going to act, he would have to decide soon. Just then Kevin came in through the back door and George and Min overdid the relaxed look; seemingly, he didn't notice.

'Alan said you was in. Fancy a quick pint, Dad?' asked Kevin, kissing his Nan.

'Its half past nine, you'll be dropping off in your beer. Anyway, I thought you'd be courting whats-her-name.'

Kevin smiled. 'I don't think you like her, do you?'

'Course, I do!' said George, too swiftly. 'I only wish you'd go out with your mates a bit more.'

'Well, we've had another row. Every time I go round there she's moaning and it's getting right on my wick. So she started crying tonight and I just walked out.'

'Ah, beware of tears, women's wonder weapon that weakens the foundations of mankind.' then thought, "God, I sound like Gerry Nolan."

'After those pearls of wisdom, are we having that pint?' asked

Kevin, again.

'One thing we ought to do first,' said George, 'Wait for two just ticks…'

He slipped on his overcoat, removed the briefcase from its hiding place and explained to Kevin what he wanted him to do with it. George then took an old suitcase from under the stairs; Min looked on silently. They crossed the gardens and walked straight through Mary's tea party; the women saw what George was carrying and all three cheered. Kevin took the money upstairs and, with the light off, watched from a front window. Fully expecting to be grabbed Twyford came out, case in hand, and wandered across the road looking in all directions; sweet. He signalled his son to join him and they hurried to the yard.

Kevin hadn't been in that many cars and none of them as good as this. They drove to Shoreditch and parked near the police station then entered the Jago. Each block of Irving's flats was guarded by dark characters in the shadows which, until George elucidated, made Kevin particularly uneasy. The door stood ajar and the Twyfords stepped inside to see that the apartment was full of the family, they were in every room, eating, drinking and listening to the wireless. Made welcome as usual, Irving guided them next door for a bit of privacy and took the briefcase for safe keeping. Kevin relaxed and listened as George primed Irving as to what he was expecting this night. Irving was more concerned by how the money seemed to be common knowledge until George mentioned the Revenue's earlier visit to Mary and assured him that it had to be a tip-off from Southampton. Lightened by knowing the raid would now be a farce, the Twyford's each accepted a glass of home-made porter to 'warm the cockles' and they departed. The car was returned to the yard, and father and son had their pint together, then Kevin went home and Twyford walked around the block to the Square, imagining enemies everywhere.

George wanted his Mum to go across to Aunt Lou's but she wouldn't hear of it. If she wasn't in when they swooped it might be construed that someone had tipped them the wink, and that wouldn't do anyone any good, whereas this way they might leave them alone once and for all. Twyford could not argue with her reasoning and worked on his part; to be or not to be? He would feign hurt dignity, that way they would know he was taking the piss but couldn't act on it.

3am at Holmes Road saw a bored set of Bobbies listening to the talk on how to prepare a raid. The house in question was owned by an elderly lady and her son lived there with her. The Revenue men would be searching every room looking for a large sum of money. Normally in these circumstances there was not expected to be any violence but the police were required to be on hand in case of trouble. All the Bobbies knew it to be the house of Sergeant Shaw's son-in-law. On his orders they'd been keeping an eye on it already, so this came as no surprise. Unfortunately for George Twyford, two of the officers had a large debt to settle over a bottle of urine and one damaged squad car.

Archie Shaw saw the resentment his men felt for the Revenue boys; they drew twice the wages with none of the risks, so there was no casual banter between the two forces as they drove down St Leonard's Square quietly and positioned themselves in the front garden. The Sergeant knocked on the door loud enough to be heard, but not to wake the street. Kirby wanted a full frontal, headlights from several cars fixed on the front of the house and a team that hammered the door open, making a grand entrance for him. But this part of the operation was police jurisdiction and, as the occupants were well known as local citizens, their civil rights would be respected.

A trace of light shone from an upstairs window and a curtain was pulled back for a moment, then footsteps were heard and the front door was opened by George Twyford. One of the Inspectors held out a piece of paper and informed him of why they were there. The police entered the house and took up strategic positions on the landings and further outside into the back yard. The Revenue men worked the back garden first then entered each room and began to search thoroughly. Kirby brought up the rear with a smug look of conquest. Archie Shaw stayed at the front door with another of his officers. George was doing an impression of a penguin, flapping from room to room, trying to watch everyone at once, warning them that he'd know if they nicked anything. A few minutes passed and the Sergeant entered the passage with his hands behind his back, strolled slowly through the house, looking in each room and making the odd suggestion about putting everything back tidily if they found nothing. George kept well out of his way.

Kirby thought his authority was being flouted and began pointing it out, clearly reprimanding the Sergeant. Archie said not a word. Made stronger by the policeman's silence, his voice was raised for all to hear. Sergeant Shaw turned and looked at him but the Revenue team leader marched blindly forward. George stopped complaining and fell silent as Kirby altered the dressing-down into a threat. He was the last to hear the growl that came from somewhere deep. The work and movement stopped as the sound reverberated. Quite suddenly, Kirby felt the heat in his head as fear returned. The others felt it too, if one had run from the house that instant, a stampede would have begun. Archie's eyes had reached the point of madness, Kirby backed away, ready to flee. The berserker was nearing the surface. Min took charge.

'I'm sure you didn't mean to say that, dear, now did you?' Her voice came unexpectedly and tension eased a fraction as Kirby responded,

'No, no! Please forgive me,' he stuttered. 'I've been under a great deal of strain lately.' Archie was still immobile and, as Kirby spoke, his eyes looked in every other direction rather than at the Sergeant. The rest of his apology faded to a whisper, then louder, 'If anyone needs me, I'll be out in the car.' He walked softly from the house and the search continued though a little more subdued.

Sergeant Shaw went out into the back yard and inhaled deeply of the frosty night air. He knew the danger of his temper and would wait for his muscles to relax and stop the rush of blood that rose up behind his eyes. He could actually feel it descending back down, cooling his head.

In the house, George's voice had returned to full flow and he was again arguing and harassing them, demanding that each turn their pockets out before they leave, remarking to an officer, 'This lot 'ud nick anything, shifty bastards! I wouldn't trust 'em with a woodbine.' Enjoying himself immensely, he suggested, in a stage whisper, 'Feel free to plant any evidence, I'll turn the lights out for two minutes then stuff as much money as you can down the furniture and in the drawers.'

Archie had disappeared and his other officers had aught to do but wait. The Revenue search squad studied wall panels and skirtings, removed stair-rods and carpet, even lifted every roll of lino but no cache was forthcoming. Knowing they would discover the loose floor boards in the scullery George had wanted to plant a dead rat there but again it would have said too much. Min poured gallons of tea into the best crockery, saved for special occasions, and George took it round. He carried two hot drinks to a couple of Bobbies in the garden and, only then, realised who they were. He put the tea down on the wall for them and moved away, when the younger one said,

'We're gonna nick you, Twyford, and when you're in the cell we're gonna give you the biggest hiding of your life for what you've done.'

'I'm glad you said "we",' retorted George with a smile. 'Just so's I know, what you gonna nick me for?'

'Don't worry about that. We'll sort something out.'

George became nettled with this game and his pent feelings found their vent, 'It's people like you who abuse your position with the force, just to throw your weight about, bullies in uniform; no wonder decent people won't have you anywhere near them. You'd nick your best mate for promotion, still I suppose that arresting mentality qualifies you for immediate entrance into the Gestapo when they get here.' The younger Bluebottle came aggressively forward but his wiser colleague pulled him back. George, unmoved by the threat, sniffed the air and said, 'That tomcat's been round here again!' The young one strained to get at him. 'Any time you want to take that uniform off, I'm your man,' said George and went into the house. The two officers dwelled amid the hardy weeds and indulged in the reiteration of schemes for falsifying evidence so that Twyford's, or his mother, could be arrested. They would secure him eventually and hurt him badly. The tea was tipped on the floor and a cup was stepped on before the officers went back inside. The Sergeant's dark figure emerged from behind the air raid shelter and watched them go, shaking his head with disgust.

Nothing at all was discovered and Kirby left before his men finished up. Fuming over the whereabouts of that money, he was more resolute than ever to find it and in the process make sure Mr Twyford suffered with maximum punishment. Kirby was a vindictive man and had already worked out a report to his superiors on the basis that the Police Sergeant should never have been included due to family connections. That should create serious problems for the Neanderthal brute and that was just the synopsis; the main charge sheet was yet to come.

George saw the last of them out without receiving anything like an apology for being awoken in the middle of the night and put to such trouble. The whole street now formed their own opinions as to why the Twyford residence was searched but what rights have the working class? Who could they complain to for being trampled all over by Government departments? No one! Min had no such objections, what was the point? She was asleep as her head hit the pillow. George, on the other hand, was wide awake and the night's stillness enlarged his problems. He was guilty, but of what? Having money? They were investigating him because he was believed to have a large amount of cash. To their knowledge no crime connects with the money, but still they would hound him out until it could be legally confiscated. It was unbelievable. The gauntlet had missed the floor and struck him in the eye and he was ready for the challenge, anxious even. Let battle begin. He would earn enough with these forgeries to pay for a voice. The voice would have power and would express eloquently what needed to be said on behalf of the muted and, if necessary, could summon enough British phlegm to spit in the eye of any bureaucratic big-wig that stood in front of them. Life's lessons fed him full of hate -a diet repugnant to his nature; only action could clear out the confusion.

The Heath was magnificently white with frost and enticed George to run further into its midst covering half as much distance again, but the only strategy he could come up with to balance the worry of Bounty's loss was to go at everything with all the energy and resources that could be called on. There was no time for a back-up scheme. If (A) went wrong, it stopped at (A). He compiled a list of people to see with the assurance the deal on a half a million pounds worth of reproduced bank notes was in his pocket. It could all collapse at the Café Luxor but for now he would continue to prepare in a positive manner. The list began with Ruben and the owners of the Craven A and finished with that night's meeting of the Force. He would not move without their approval.

Out early and smartly dressed in a dark grey flannel, double breasted suit and sporting his old school tie, George Twyford caught a trolley bus to the West End. He sat downstairs, next to the platform and as the bus pulled away from the lights at Camden Town, jumped off and disappeared down the tube. A train to Euston brought him back to Kentish Town, secure in the knowledge that no one was following he walked to the yard. Lestor Hogg was organising delivery notes for the making up of orders to be executed that day. More help was needed but for now he was managing - just.

Watching him scribble furiously, George made a pot of tea and requested that everyone be at the Queen's for an urgent meeting around seven. Blaming increasing business Lestor countered with a suggestion of nine. That agreed, George drove to Ruben's office and pulled up seconds behind Fintan, he needed a good hour with Mr Benson. In a nutshell, Ruben wanted the Craven A and that would be the dangled carrot if his plan was to succeed. Twyford spoke of having two possible deals on the go but could only go with one of them. He put it to Benson that he would restore and improve the Craven A building in exchange for fifty percent of Ruben's property company. Benson feigned astonishment at the thought of a partnership but, in truth, was strongly in agreement with the idea. They sword-fenced for a while, each covering the seven entrances into the body. George had sworn for the umpteenth time that he had purchased the Craven A and only awaited the paperwork to become the legal owner. He also took an oath that the builders were set to go in at the drop of a hat and that money was already in place. Eventually convinced, Ruben finally shook on it and Twyford left shortly afterwards. Alone and stimulated, Benson wandered to the window and gazed across the road.

The next next port of call was Irving Jacob's office, if anyone could buy the bombed building for the right money, he could. It took George five minutes to explain the estimates and valuation reports then instructed him to bid four thousand pounds to the agents acting for the owner, with the authority to go as high as six, if really necessary, but purchase it he must.

In the scheme of things, Benny was now a separate entity and details of their surreptitious enterprise was conducted next door. To secure the agreements, Ben had had to open up to his contacts about the offer. Of the six certainties, one had surprised him by dropping out but five were ready to commit for two thousand pounds each. Half the money would be left with Benny and the balance ready on the hand-over. The problem was that Ben would not part with any of it until the goods were produced. Twyford understood his caution and didn't blame him in the least. If something on this scale goes wrong, life becomes cheap but at least part of his risk would be narrowed down into hours, rather than weeks. The rest of the day was spent visiting selected traders across London, he promised delivery and they guaranteed the cash would be ready. By the evening, he had definite orders for sixty percent of the load and could now take time to ease prices up as he widened the area.

It was good that his meeting with the boys had been made for later for, as always, he'd tried to squeeze two extra hours into the day and, try as he may, it wouldn't work. Twyford had considered every angle he possibly could and had tramped home from the yard satisfied. He wanted to see the girls but Mary refused him entry, shoved envelope and contents back in his face, then slammed the door on him. Oh well, he'd expected as much, "Ungrateful mare!"

Min was making the most of her weekly box of assorted delights and tonight they dined on boiled bacon, sadly, he had eaten so much that indigestion wrestled with his first pint of Toby. The others trickled in up to nine thirty looking knackered but happy. The business was certainly demanding but was producing the best from everyone involved and would continue to do so whilst the golden rules were kept sacred. Partners were content as long as they were fed well, exercised and taken out occasionally; these considerations seemed to quell any need to pry.

Kit arrived late, suited and booted. He seemed edgy and excited that Rita was coming there to meet him for an all night grapple.

'Let's bring the meeting to order,' suggested Johnny Bass, with mock tiredness. 'Kit's got that right soppy look on his face, so the sooner we get shot of him the better.' Everybody observed him and chuckled: the silly grin was chiselled in. The Queen's Arms had a back room off of the Saloon bar used regularly by the St Pancras Pigeon fanciers Association but tonight it was theirs. George waited for everyone to take their seats then began, 'It's very important to meet tonight 'cos something's come on offer and it could be the best thing that's ever happened for us.' No one spoke, he had the floor.

'I don't think things are going too bad from what's been set up so far, have they?' Agreements all round. 'Well this would mean sticking all that we've produced and everything that can be sponged, stolen or scrounged for one big deal that might put us straight for the rest of our natural.' He shuffled papers in front of him to let that sink in for a minute then continued, 'To be that successful, obviously there are risks.'

'Before you tell us anymore,' said Danny Currie, 'we appreciate that without the money you started us with none of what we're doing would have been possible. Is this anything to do with where all that come from, or is it still a secret?'

George had not anticipated the question and considered for a moment without answering. He had never discussed the incident in Karinna that led him to be standing there and although he was sure it would be safe, and even correct, to tell his close pals the truth of what happened, the timing had never been quite right. Sensibly, they would have to know to be in a position to let his children understand, if anything bad befell himself or it all came out, and so he wavered.

'I will tell you all about it but trouble is… we're running against the clock.'

'We've got all night,' said Stanley. Everyone looked at each other and nodded.

George felt the meeting just went down the wrong turning and South Africa was on a crash course with Scotland. He tried to swerve, 'I'm trying to make you rich,' he joked, 'and this story's longer than the Old Testament.' They knew him too well for that one.

'Come on, bore us!' said Owen; each prompting coming from a different member.

He had to do it. 'All right then, no fidgeting, an outline only, as it's too involved.' Groans. 'That's all you're gonna get for now so belt up.' He began, 'You know I worked as an overseer for a big mining company, well, all of us were white and we had a reasonable life. The mine workers were black and that colour meant you had very little privileges. Their existence was at best miserable, and normally down right pathetic. They get ill but haven't got doctors to tend them. There's medical people at the mines but only for the stronger ones to keep them fit for work. Old people and kids die every day and nothing changes, until you see it, you can't imagine how bad it is. When I arrived at my interview I was warned not to befriend black people or I'd lose my job, so obviously the first thing I did was become friendly with a couple of lads from one of the townships and I spent some time with them. About two hundred people lived in this Kraal, and one white, Catholic priest. The Catholics have no great presence in Karinna and I think he was posted there as a punishment. Anyway, I got on quite well there and finished up a regular guest at the head man's table. Afterwards, if it was ever questioned, I was visiting the priest. Most of the overseers treated them badly and I had to appear to be doing the same; but that was our secret. Anyhow, to cut a long story short, the head man's son was provoked and did something bad for what he would have been punished, well, executed, actually.' The others listened intently without interrupting. He carried on, 'Being white, and the only one with any chance of being believed, I tried to cover up for him with a fairly well invented tale but a Dutch copper wouldn't leave it; like he had a cold and no hankie, sniffing around everywhere. Father Colm, who I've mentioned before, reckoned that to halt the investigation I had to disappear; that way, it couldn't be proven otherwise. The priest would then tell anyone who asked that I'd received bad news from home and had to leave suddenly. No matter what he'd suspected, without answers the detective was up a blind alley then, if he put pressure on the family, they could accuse me. The timing was perfect and one night I slipped away to Cape Town and boarded a boat for England. Extradition can't be easy during wartime but, either way, it was better than what would happen to the township. The work would be withdrawn and the people would starve, apart from the death sentence for at least one of them.'

Nolan, his head akin to an Egyptian Mummy, piped up with, 'There had to be a lady involved.'

The others had thought as much and were not surprised when George answered, 'Well done, Pharoe!' adding, 'It's a pity they didn't bandage your mouth up an' all.'

'Where'd the money come from?' asked Frank Nash.

'I'm coming to that. As I went to leave 'Old Cor Blimey', that's what we called the head man, took me in his hut and gave me a pouch of precious stones. For years his people were finding the gems and swallowing them. We searched several of them every night, you were taught what to look for: a limp, a diverted eye, a smile too friendly. I dreaded catching anybody 'cos of the punishment meted out. That's why I used to grab the people I knew, throw them in the back room, make a lot of noise and then let them go.' George began to see the funny side of it as the memories returned, 'Nevertheless, back to the story…'

'Who was the girl?' persisted Nolan.

'She was special and I've got to save her for your next week's entertainment. If I can carry on about the diamonds? He gave them to me and just said, "Help us".'

'So you helped yourself!' laughed Nolan.

'No,' said Twyford, becoming serious. 'I told him I didn't want the responsibility, there was obviously a fortune there and if I lost them, or anything came to grief, it would all be my fault what happened to those people. But he took a bit of fruit, it was like a little melon that grew in the dust, and chopped it in half then handed one piece to me and he kept the other, and said 'fifty fifty', and that's all he had to say. So I've used half and the balance I've invested for him; I've had enough bad luck to last me a life time and I ain't tempted to nick one penny of his bit. Well gentlemen, that's my story. Now, I'll swear you all to secrecy and then carry on with the good news of the night.'

'One question,' said Owen. 'How'd you change them up, and was that why the Revenue raided you last night?'

'First of all, that's two questions. The answer to the first bit is that I changed them up in Casablanca . Father Colm, who must have had a very murky past, knew people there and I got in touch. Nearly got my throat slit, but that's something else we won't go in to now. And yes, when I went through Customs they discovered the cash but couldn't nick it off me so the swines must have grassed to the Tax people; that's why last night's raid came about.

'Oh, it's anything but dull!' sung Stanley Swindells, as he stood up to go for a pee.

'You fucking amaze me!' said Mickey Butler. 'You must shit sticks of dynamite.'

'Yeah. I'd like to know what you consider a normal day?' added Owen.

George had no answer but the meeting had obviously reached half-time as Johnny Bass and Lestor Hogg took the trays to get refills. The remainder chatted around the table about the unidentified rocket bomb that was still frightening the country, until the beer arrived, then settled down for part two.

'I can't wait for this next episode,' remarked Tinker, 'It's like the serial at Saturday morning pictures, i'nnit?'

Twyford stood again and handed round one of the two fivers he'd been given. Each member looked at it, turned it over and passed it on, while the second one travelled the other side of the table. The two met at Mornie Quill. 'So what're we looking at?' he asked, studying them. 'Oh,' he said, and showed the pair to Lestor Hogg. He looked straight at the numbers, passed them on and looked expectantly at George.

Kit had them but his mind was elsewhere. 'What?' he asked. Johnny Bass took them from him and saw the obvious.

'Exactly the same?' asked Mickey Butler, from two seats away. John nodded.

The audience waited in anticipation.

'I'm trying to buy the lot!' said George with great enthusiasm. 'No one in the South has even been offered them. Just imagine in early December, Christmas shopping, buying saleable goods, getting the change, earning almost a fiver on every note.'

'How much do they cost?' asked Danny Currie.

'He wants ten bob each. I've bid him a lot less than that. If he takes it, I've also pre-sold enough to cover our stake money in 48 hours then everything else is pure profit. It's perfect,' he added.

'Not perfect,' said Lestor Hogg, shrewdly, 'or you wouldn't have two with the same numbers.'

The others thought about that but Twyford carried on quickly, 'That's why they're so cheap. The last numbers go from nought to nine hundred and ninety nine then back to triple nought, and as long as no one carries the same numbers at the same time, it's sweet.'

'It sounds 'triffic!' said Mickey, eagerly.

'Too good,' said Bass, 'now give us the bad points.'

'The bad points are he hasn't taken the bid yet and may not. The other one is we're doing a one-off deal with the devil.'

'Who?' asked Frank cautiously, knowing he wouldn't like the answer.

'Grogan,' answered George, 'And for you who didn't serve under him, he's a very, very nasty man.'

'A wicked bastard!' added Mickey, unconsciously feeling the leg that Grogan caused to break and still gave gyp every winter, the hatred for him as strong as ever.

That took the edge off it somewhat. Tinker, Mornie and Kit all knew what he was, a man without a conscience and capable of anything. The last thing needed now was for someone to mention the flare at the Somme, but up it belched and they were going in the wrong direction again.

George parried and countered with, 'If it doesn't worry me, fret not. I'm the only person dealing with him and the only one who can get done so I'll plot each step of the hand-over, double checking everything. When we know where and when you can be close, just in case. The money stays with me until I'm satisfied everything is as agreed; I just want you lot to watch my back.' Everyone was leaning his way and it only needed a further nudge to draw them in. 'The safety factor is that all the people on our side have been vetted by Benny and myself and within two days of the exchange we'll be in front, then it's spend, spend, spend all the way. After Christmas, it'll be dangerous. Once the notes have been banked, and they realise how vast this is, emergency measures will be taken but by then we'll be clear and substantially richer.' The smiles broke out and they all toasted that.

Bassy nearly put a spoke in it when he said, 'So far what we've done hasn't appeared to harm anyone, in fact to the opposite. We've made it a lot nicer for our customers and we've earned - but someone's gonna get hurt with this.'

Once again it made George appreciate what a sensitive man he was.

'Only the Bank of England, John, and they've got bundles.'

'Are you sure?' he asked again.

'Yes! They've got to honour them. It would be impossible to trace who paid in what at Christmas with all that shopping. In the New Year white notes might very well be withdrawn from circulation, but that won't bother us, by then we'll be so rich it won't matter what we spend.' The finer points of who would do whatever could come nearer the time. Tomorrow was the all important meeting, and on its conclusion would rest their future. So, for now, they would take a drink in the public bar and talk pigeons until closing time.

The lads came out from the back room chatting and no one noticed the old, dumpy couple sitting against the wall. He had a pint of bitter in front of him and she sipped a glass of Guinness. The barman called Kit over and gave him a message. His chin dropped on his chest and he visibly sunk two inches. Rita had waited and gone.

'It's for the best, Kitchener,' said Nolan with glee. 'She'd have only kept you awake half the night with gymnastics and all kinds of weird demands.'

'Yeah, and my Nan says it makes you go blind,' added Johnny, touching Gerry's bandages.

'It's all right for you lot,' Kit moaned, sadly. 'You don't chop meat all day. My right hand cramps up about midnight.'

Their group had almost reached the fish shop when Kit saw her. She was leaning on the lamp post, legs astride with a split up the back of her skirt that reached heaven, eating a bag of chips.

'Perhaps she don't realise the client has finished and fucked off,' said Nolan, which caused everyone to fall about.

'Tell her you've got a headache,' suggested Owen.

'Yeah, see how they like it!' added Mornie, with such zest his private life was suddenly spotlighted. Kit chose to ignore them all. His chest was sucked up and he was striding off in front to reach her first. She was barely five foot and he had to stoop to kiss her. Her arms slid around his neck and the cat-calls began.

'Leave him alone!'

'Yeah, pick on someone your own size!'

She gestured a charming little two-finger salute in a most unladylike fashion, then hooked his arm and away they strolled totally absorbed in each other. The lads carried on shouting after them but it's no fun when the targets take no notice. The world was put to rights once again over a bag of chips then loud farewells echoed the street. Tomorrow evening could not come soon enough.

CHAPTER 23: NO WONDER THEY 'NICK' ALL THE WOMEN

Norway: Some 155 bombers of the U.S. 8th Army Airforce today raided the Heavy Water Plant at Vermork. Although the plant was not damaged it is hoped that it may help to slow down their Atomic Bomb programme?!

Sally pulled the bed covers around her then reread the note and pondered the old ground. She knew with looks and a brain it was easy to entrance a room full of men and she frequently did so purely for the conquest of it. It was fulfilling to make each of them feel he had been individually selected for favour then switch her interest in a moment and savour the nettled reactions and pathetic perseverance. Wicked perhaps, but the perfect suitor eluded her and the attentions of those that didn't fit the criteria produced the cruelty and evoked such vitriolic volleys that could cut a man to shreds. She even appreciated how much hurt she bestowed, however, her virulence was spontaneous and instinctive and therefore not to be curbed. The question was, having no real target to allure, how long could she keep George Twyford keen without granting that which he desires. Something about him irritated, though, with no one else spending time and money to win her, she may have to lower her sights and consider his eligibility. Unattached, he was quite presentable but let himself down with his occasional coarseness, fun on a date despite the fact that he could be too domineering and sometimes quite patronising. He had an annoying, easy going disposition that would have to go, in fact, there was plenty to change which made him something of a challenge. In his favour, he was pretty well-oiled and reasonably generous, without which he would face immediate disqualification from any possible value as a husband. On a final note, she balanced his wife Mary's position against her own future requirements and decided to take him. His divorce from Mary need not be mentioned until he was fully committed to her, and then she would supervise it herself.

Daydreaming of his coming good fortune, George had a lie-in. Alan sneaked up and jumped on him and they had a five minute wrestle before he went off to school. Unable to lay there any longer while his head was alive with glorious schemes, he hopped out of bed, dressed swiftly and walked to the paper stand. His plan was to breakfast at Queen's Crescent with Owen and Kit, then get the car and drive to Shoreditch. At the top of the Square, he was hailed by Timmy Gowen and they talked for a while. Tim confided that he was an advisor at the Admiralty, but joked as yet he had nothing to advise on. Nevertheless Twyford was impressed and said so, for Timmy was still the same likeable kid from the fish shop the leg-pullers used to make up rhymes about; they swore to take a drink at the Malden around nine. George purchased a paper and strolled to the Crescent to meet Lestor Hogg. The market was busy but luckily a table was secured in the local café and fry-ups ordered all round; Fatso, the proprietor, was turning out to be one of their best customers. No money would change hands at the meeting tonight but Twyford wanted a presence at the Café Luxor and proposed six lads as the correct sized party, not too big to attract attention, yet enough to guarantee a force, if that were necessary. It was to be Kit, Danny, Owen, George, Frank and Bones. Definitely not Butler, as he and Donald Grogan hated each other, nor Bass, because he was the one that pushed Grogan off that rock -and the Scotsman would never forget a thing like that. Twyford wanted everything on a nicer footing, an enjoyable evening, and if the deal happened that too would be quite pleasant. If not, it was not a tragedy; if not, it was a fucking disaster! But Mr Grogan must sense nothing at all. The seven envoys, himself included, would venture off from the pub, sober, at approximately ten thirty. George didn't notice the solid looking workman squeezed on the end of the next table and, luckily, the general hum-drum drowned out their conversation from anyone who might want to listen. However, his stroll to the yard took him through quieter streets and he became conscious of a tail. Twyford ambled straight by the depot, into the coal wharf and along the railway tracks towards Kentish Town then passed some old rolling stock, circled it and came up behind the man. His tracker wore stained white overalls and seemed immune to the cold. George's eyes took in the wide shoulders and muscled back; perhaps rather than fronting him, he might do better to lose the man. He ducked back behind the railway carriage and made his way into some rundown shacks that were dotted about between the lines. The roofless buildings were barely standing, but among the rubble George found a large wooden beam, gripped it like Little John's staff, and waited to see if his follower came looking. He was a patient fellow and after some time was rewarded with a creak, that was enough for George to remain hidden and ready. Several minutes passed and a brick grated somewhere closer. Catlike, he came into the doorway almost soundlessly. Twyford stepped into view and struck him in the forehead with the beam. He staggered back but kept his footing well. George followed up with another, only this time, the chap caught the wooden plank and twisted it past him. Twyford clung on, stumbled and found himself on his back, on the debris, unarmed, looking up at his adversary, who now towered and glowered. The blood dripping from his head made him look maddened; the timber held fearsomely in his hands. Scrambling away, Twyford used the wall to rise and face the danger but when he turned, the man wasn't there?! George seized a busted piece of brick in each hand then moved stealthily outside, expecting, at any second, to be hammered into the ground; but the stranger was gone, no tricks.

With the utmost relief, he thought,"How queer? Should have beaten the life out of me when he had the advantage." The man was obviously combat trained, George hadn't seen that move since his army days but who was he and what did he want? Apparently not to harm him; Twyford puzzled his way out into Kentish Town Road. It was too chancy to go anywhere near the yard now and, to give himself more time to think, took the tube to Irving's. The odd mark hadn't responded like a Londoner. Even when struck soundly, he didn't utter a word, not a sound. But then why would a foreigner be interested in him? Evidently not a robber, an observer perhaps? For whom? The Inland Revenue, the police, Grogan? None of it made sense. Except, George was now positive the man wasn't English. That left him with a foreign soldier who bested him with ease yet did not harm him, would not harm him. Muttering to himself, Twyford verbalised, 'Why? Because he was ordered not to, until….until the deal was done. Maybe that's it. Follow me, watch, learn my habits, and then when the goods are paid for, kill me and get back the notes. Yes, that's it. Maybe. No. Why bother to wait? The fivers would have changed hands. If Grogan planned anything like that, it could be done before the change-over, once he's sure I have got the cash with me.' It was guesswork and not probable, but possible, either way it was a warning of how tricky this might become. He thought of Baden Powell, a great man with one motto for life; "Be prepared!"

He travelled the underground to Old Street station and walked past his old school, it seemed exactly the same, solid and safe. On reaching Irving's flats he looked at the upper floors of the blocks he passed. "Perhaps they did it with mirrors," he thought, and, making sure he was not noticed, climbed the stairs two at a time. As always the door was open and Ben was pouring his tea. George refused to mention it, just sat down, picked up a newspaper and began to read. Benny placed the cup in front of him and patted his shoulder, which was tap language for 'never mind'. Irving came in looking more harassed than usual, with a big wad of files under his arm.

'We're not on,' he stated flatly.

Twyford looked up, hiding his disappointment and thinking that for some indefinable reason by acting surprised he was pressing Irving to work harder, the suggestion being that it was a foregone conclusion the bid would be accepted and, if not, why not?

'I was there all afternoon,' answered Irving, defending himself from the unspoken cross-examination. 'They started much higher but came down to seven and a half thousand and would not budge. I was told emphatically that there was no need for further discussion and to only contact them again if we accept. So, after I was shown the other side of the door, I went to the Black Cat to see for myself. That building will be worth at least twenty thousand pounds when the War's over. The gamble is will it last the War, with no more destructive bombing? The area flattened would probably be worth four thousand, so it's not so much of a risk.'

George listened to the advice gravely. This was creating a loaves and fishes exercise on his lump. Seven and a half thousand, plus at least fifteen hundred pounds for the renovation, takes his outlay to nine, which translates to half of Ruben's business, and would have to be agreed as soon as possible.

'Irving, go there. Tell them only as long as it's finalised today.'

'They won't want to do it that fast!'

'Of course they will! They want the cash and we need the deeds in our hands for Ruben, in case he decided to renege.' Jacobs looked tired so, to liven him up, George twanged his thick, elastic braces. Ben saw him out and as they looked over the balcony, Twyford said, 'Get me some figures urgently, Ben, buying the Craven A has slaughtered the cash I had for the deal. We may be able to cover it with the Company money, and the deposit accounts, but I don't think so. Look, you've got five thousand coming in soon then a slight delay before the second lot arrives.' Benny went to interject but George talked on, 'Hear me out. I'll give you cheques to cover five so if all goes bo'side, your down-payment's safe. It might very well wipe out everything else but that way you're sweet.' Benny agreed to that but warned of no further spending until funds were coming back in, because if called upon to meet his immediate outgoings, George was insolvent. The accounted figures could be ready for Monday morning and, on that promise, they advised each other not to worry and Twyford left him to his calculations.

Riding a bus to Old Street, and another for Euston, he walked through Somers Town to a builders yard opposite the Lord Somer's public house. It was lunchtime and the staff and management were all in the pub for a pie and a pint. George joined them and after two pints had his jacket off for a fight with the boss of O'Brien Construction. Most of the labour was Irish and to get their best price, you have to accuse them of taking you on, which goes without saying anyway. It is always broken up before a punch lands, but then they know to go steady; otherwise, they'll rob you blind. Arabs barter while Irishmen fight; to each his own. The electrics and the plumbing were deducted, as Johnny Bass and Lestor Hogg could do both easily enough, and finally a rate of a thousand pounds cash was agreed, sealed by swallowing a pint in one on the strength of it. Twyford left with a guarantee that, when instructed, the labour force would start immediately, work for weekly wages, with the balance paid when the job was finished to his satisfaction.

Arriving home, George tried to snatch forty winks but sometimes worries keep a mind from relaxing. He looked at the ceiling for an hour and gave up when Tinker knocked with the cotchel. The stout fellow had successfully brought another load out of the American base and, with it, a message that Bones would be at the Malden that night. "For his money, no doubt," thought Twyford with a smile. "But good luck to him; he'd been as good as his word." Tinker carried all the necessary passes and Bones had him loaded like clockwork twice a week. It was nice dealing with good operators.

The Malden was lively when John and George walked in. Both treated the bar staff to an appreciative once-over and advised Horace on which barmaids to keep and whom to lose. They could have been chaps for all Horrie knew and to save him a job, a sensible suggestion was... why not let them give the interviews? Surprisingly he declined!

Within no time there was a full compliment of the Force. Lucky had just taken the stage when the guest of honour arrived and to introduce his return, the band struck up a little ditty and the whole pub sang, 'Timmy Gowen sells fish, three ha'pence a dish, don't buy it, don't try it, it's smells when you fry it.' He went red, like always. This man was such a nice fellow that everyone went out of their way to speak to him and he was genuinely interested to know how each of them had fared. He said very little about himself but delighted in being back with the boys, listening to the conversations and the stories. Another hour went by and they only awaited Bones. Sally came in dressed to kill and caused an awkward moment. George was devastated at having to disappoint her but business arrangements had been made and, as tempting as her suggestions were, he must soon be leaving. She pouted persuasively but he was resolute; she joined them for a drink anyway and Twyford introduced her to Timmy. Sally loved to chat and he was an excellent listener.

Bones narrowly made it but was in a great mood. He had taken the Captain to the Green Gate on the off-chance, only to find Eleanor and the girls were already there and looking out for him. His senior officer was now safely in their tender clutches. One last drink all round and it was time to go. George felt worse about not taking Timothy with them than leaving Sally to get home by herself, but they were happy to stay on for a while and he promised to see her safely back.

The lads made good time and arrived just after eleven. Lenny stepped in the foyer with them and had a quiet word in Twyford's ear,

'The Jock's been in twice this week,' he said, 'and you'll never believe who he left with last night.' Before George could venture a guess, Lenny confided, 'Connaughty, the Yank.' Teddy Connaughty was a wealthy American industrialist who always seemed to be in the news with the Washington decision makers.

'That's a turn up for the books, Len. I knew he dabbled in politics but I didn't think he'd reached that level. Are they in tonight?'

'No, not yet anyway.' Twyford shrugged, nonchalantly. 'Watch him, George,' Lenny warned, 'he's a wrong-un, take it from me.' And with a classic wink, returned to the door.

A well positioned table had been reserved for them and Twyford was pleased at how many people showed out, nodding or waving across. The plan was to keep it low profile but what was the point? Within ten minutes Kit had allowed himself to be coaxed on to the stage and sprinted the last five yards. The band was superb and supported him through three numbers made for swing. Radna followed him on and joined in the applause as he returned to the table. The lights dimmed and her love song transfixed the hall, there was only one man not looking. George sipped his drink and studied the entrance to the bar. Eventually, the lights went up and Frank called his name. Turning towards the beckon, he saw the Donna Laura patiently waiting to speak with him. She wore a bright red evening dress that started an inch above her nipples and clung around her waist and hips, then down to sweep the floor. Twyford stopped his mouth from dropping open.

She began, 'I hope you are no longer wild with me. I take nothing seriously and deserve to be chastised but I would never have wanted to be the cause of a quarrel between you and my Radna. She has been so upset, I humbly apologise.'

"Well, fuck me ragged!" thought George, with a grin.

A hint of fun gleamed from her eyes as she continued, 'I believe my punishment is to kiss your arse.' The last word rrr-rolled from her tongue. 'May my penance be changed to your face?'

He admired the manner of her speech, how she added impudence to the sincerity. She was ready to kiss either end, he decided.

'One cheek's almost as good as another,' he tossed at her,

casually, and turned so the side of his face was her target. The full mouth came nearer and he could feel her breath. A swift twist of the head and their lips met. She pulled back startled then quickly giggled at his well worked ploy. George rose and took her hand, he hated aggravation and would always rather accept an olive branch. A few quiet words of conciliation were murmured between them and she moved on. Without warning, Twyford spun around guided by one of those strange, protective feelings. He looked straight at Grogan, who stood against the wall, away from the lights. Caught off guard the Scotsman was too slow to change his spiteful gaze. George stared across, forcing him to make the first move. Donald pointed at the far end to the cover of the potted jungle and walked towards it without looking back.

Twyford spoke to the boys *sotto voce*, 'We're on. Keep awake,' and followed after him, steering a route through the tables. There were eight to ten separate areas spread out under the leaves and private if speech was guarded. Grogan already sat at a central table, and apart from four recognisable Jocks dotted about, they were alone. Both intended little or no small talk, giving the appearance of take it or leave it.

Grogan began with, 'I saw you talking with the Donna Laura so I didn't interrupt.'

'Yes,' said George, adding no more.

'Fine woman,' continued Donald, daring him to say otherwise.

"Soppy, daft bastard's jealous, and he can't hide it," thought George, cursing her silently for knowingly, or not, getting Donald's back up. 'I'm sure she is, though I don't know her well enough to pass a comment, really.'

Grogan seemed satisfied with this and proposed, 'Anyway, George, to business, we're both very busy. What's your final offer?'

The directness gave Twyford little chance, 'Sorry, Donald, I want to trade, that's why I'm here, but the bid has to stand, I've got no leeway.'

The silence was broken by a Jeeves lookalike, carrying a bottle of Jack Daniel's and one glass on a silver tray; they watched him disappear passed them into the foliage. He turned back only to see Donald stand. 'George, I've tried. You've had the first offer, I can place them all. I will now do it, perhaps another deal, another day.' Said as a consolation, Donald held out his hand, 'It goes without saying, I'd appreciate it if this meeting never happened.'

'What meeting?' said Twyford, trying to gather his thoughts and not panic. He couldn't afford a mistake, for he would never again be this close to a fortune.

Grogan picked up his briefcase and walked away. George could smell the distinct aroma of piped tobacco wafting in from somewhere. Another yard and Donald would be lost in the forestry. He could not let it slip away, not now. The excitement of it all, the organisation and the adventure; he wanted it so badly.

'Donald!' he called, sharply. Grogan stopped and looked back to see if the return stroll was worth the effort. His expression looked doubtful. 'Relax and sit down for fuck's sake,' said George, persuasively. 'I haven't earned enough tonight to pay my bus fare home.'

Grogan held the high ground and pushed it. 'George, I can't be messed about with your insulting bids.' His voice with the correct amount of tiredness, pressuring Twyford's new offer.

'Three bob a note and that's it.'

Donald leaned forward angrily, 'That's only one fucking shilling more!'

George, equally wild, replied, 'That's five fucking thousand more, you Scotch cunt!'

Grogan's neck muscles bulged out either side of his large, intimidating head as he strained to push his face further at him. They were almost nose to nose but even so Twyford still looked poised to go for his throat. Another waft of 'Old Shag' passed between them and they sniffed like the Bisto kids. Grogan sat back and started to chuckle. Unable to see anything to laugh at, Twyford smiled anyway.

'You were always a tough bastard to handle, Georgie.'

'That's the final offer, Donald, I won't walk away to come back. It's a simple yes or no.'

Grogan considered his expression like a poker player and said, 'The answer's 'no'...' then paused for effect, '…but, or should I say 'yes'… but…'

'But?' asked George flatly, masking any feelings.

'I'll accept three shillings, but it's got to be for a minimum quantity of 200,000 notes. That translates to one million quid.'

As if George needed to be told that. One million, the figure bounced around his head, "Was there that much money in the world?"

Donald was grinning, 'Are we on, Georgie?'

"I want it, I want it," is all he could think. "But how to get thirty thousand pounds?"

'I'm tempted, Donald, I'll admit, but I'll need about half hour, okay?'

'George, you don't want to miss this one.'

'You've just doubled the stakes, that's far more than I calculated for and all I've seen is two notes. I've only your word for it that you've got this much.' Twyford was looking hard into his eyes but could only find confidence beaming back at him.

'Trust me, Georgie, I've got the notes.' My, but he was cocky now.

'Why not? The last time I trusted you, they gave me a gong!'

Donald's face changed and abruptly left him with, 'I'll see you back here in exactly thirty minutes.'

Twyford sat alone for a while, playing with numbers. Who could double up, what other big players could be introduced into the equation? He had stretched himself too far with fifteen thousand, knowing that if the chips were really down, he could use the Townships money, lying to himself that it was a good investment for them. But even with all that, he was short, considerably short. They now owned the Craven A, which he did not regret, it was a good investment, but it just left the pot a little emptier. He spent ten long minutes, working out simple arithmetic that came nowhere near, becoming more apparent that fifteen was not really manageable without stripping every account. "Bounty, you bastard, where are you?" he cursed himself for his blatant stupidity. "It could have solved everything," he thought, then not so sure, "perhaps….?" These precious minutes had to be used wisely, but other things kept popping into his brain. If there was no deal, Grogan might well decide that George knew too much of his business and have him done away with. He knew if the situation was reversed he could not do that, wouldn't think of it, but Donald had a different set of values. All this madness wasn't helping. He could not make the deal, but he couldn't lose it. Seven minutes to go, no point in running to the others for advice. Bones maybe, though too much pressure might frighten him off. No, the decision had to be his, "What if…" and he pursued an intermediate possibility. By George's 'Thomas Kettle' watch Grogan was two minutes early and all smiles. Twyford rose to the occasion, 'Thank you for that short break Donald, I needed to adjust a few moves. Now I can agree your offer.' His manner was positive as he described how it would be carried out. 'I will only deal if the notes are as good as the sample.'

Donald nodded matter-of-factly.

'The number sequence is unfortunate, but acceptable.'

'That's the only reason they're that price,' growled Donald.

'I appreciate that, but I want to get all the rules correct and on the table.'

'I agree. We don't want any unforeseen problems.' There was that underlined threat again.

George continued, 'There will be two exchanges. The first…'

'No!' interrupted Donald. 'Definitely not.'

'Donald, I wouldn't trust you with a packet of fags, let alone thirty thousand pounds. So hear me out because it's this or not at all.' Grogan sat back but continued shaking his head. 'The first exchange will be for fifteen thousand sterling, checked by you or your appointed inspector, against a hundred thousand notes with a paper value of half a million. When we're satisfied…'

'We? I thought you said you'd do this alone. I can't have any exposure.'

'We'll both have the same number of assistants, probably three each.'

'Why three?'

'One driver, one inspector and one scout. My driver doubles as an inspector too because it'll take us a lot longer to check half a million. You and I can take a drink or a stroll. I suggest the money's examined in my car and it remains locked there until your's is examined. You and I return, exchange keys and you walk away with my fifteen thousand and I walk away with your's.' Grogan made no comment but didn't stop him and that was a good sign. George carried on trying not to pause. With sensibly thought out points, he had to convince Donald that this was the route to take. It just could not be financed in one hit. He changed tactics slightly, not letting him settle on any one detail. 'Can it all get in one suitcase by the way?'

'Yes, with room to spare.'

'We'll return same time the following week and do it all again. I need that week to place all the stock to pay for the second consignment.'

Grogan's face was granite but he could not have been more pleased, this was exactly the way his superiors had orchestrated it. Twyford had to be stretched to breaking-point, making him desperate and completely dependent on the second consignment. Every single note needed to be spread and counted on to do the utmost damage to the economy. At the same time that Twyford began to spend, smaller quantities would pop up as far a field as Canada, Australia, even Easter Island, and by the New Year every national newspaper would blast the story, panicking world opinion into losing faith in sterling. Grogan could not be seen to capitulate too easily and so, sounding incredulous and for good measure, he threw in, 'Is that your final offer?'

'That's it, take it or leave it? Your choice, there's no more.'

'I'll take it, Georgie, and I'll shake on it. But first, let *me* make things clear. Don't mess with me, boy. You'll take the second one exactly seven days later 'cos you wouldn't want me to come looking for you. And don't think of using any of my masterpieces to pay for the next arrival. I wouldn't like that either.' His accent had slipped back into broad Glaswegian.

'Don't be stupid!' declared Twyford, with hurt dignity. 'I deal straight. I'll have knocked out the first lot for peanuts and I'm depending on that second consignment to make the proper money of it. That's the earner.'

'We understand each other,' said Grogan and held out his hand.

They shook on it and George blessed their union with, 'We both want the same things, it'll work like a dream.' He relaxed and finalised the details. The exchange would be the next Friday night at one of three destinations picked by George, but Donald would confirm which one an hour before. Telephone numbers were exchanged and Twyford would ring twenty four hours earlier to check for any delays and to pass on and receive the licence numbers of the cars to be used. There was no room for error, it would be planned and screened like a military operation. When they were both satisfied, Grogan walked him to the edge of the potted plants and summed up the last agreement,

'George, I look on you now as one of us and my other outlets will ensure that no money gets into circulation until you get the second delivery. But from midnight that night, it's spend, spend, spend, and every man for himself.'

'That'll suit us perfectly,' said George. They clasped hands and Grogan's bone-crushing clutch was meant to express his sincerity. Twyford walked back to the lads who, instead of being alert and ready, were half-pissed and having a jolly good time with pretty maids all in tow. Stan was the first to notice him, the thrill lit his face. George nodded imperceptibly and looked down, he didn't want to dare think about it. He'd actually agreed the deal: it was astonishing, magnificent, glorious, there were not enough adjectives to describe it. Stan mimed a swoon and passed a nod onto Bones, Bones to Frank, Frank to Danny. Not a word was spoken.

Kit rubbed his hands together and announced, 'I think this calls for a song!'

The ladies present bubbled and though George was wedged in amongst excellent company, he felt aloof, detached by a great distance. He poured himself a very stiff gin and tonic and drank deeply while his brain soared, swooping from place to place. The glass was empty and his hand still trembled slightly as he poured another. The drink helped him to unwind and steadied the flight back to earth, when a voice from behind caused a landing with a bump.

'Would you think me precocious if I asked you to dance?' Radna had come to him. The whole table looked, beyond his outline, at her: the men leered lustfully while the girls looked on with critical envy and then at George, reappraising, as he stood slowly and turned. He tried to seem unsure but his grin gave him away.

The music was slow and romantic as they drifted across the floor. She danced closely with her hand as light as a feather in his palm, her other arm gently draped over his shoulder, her cheek softer than a peach. The mood was perfect, no words were spoken and he restrained himself from holding her tighter. Gradually she began to press against him, her fingers dug into his back, forcing him to crush her in his arms. She ooed, aahed and purred in his ear. He was utterly aroused. The slow dance ended to make way for the Latin American and she had to return to work.

'Will you wait for me?' she asked, not letting his hand go.

'Do you want me to?' he answered seriously, acting the scene out properly. She could not talk and as she looked in his face, her eyes filled with water, her jaw wobbled and she nodded, frightened that one word might release the tears. He kissed her hand and said, 'Go on. I'll be here.' She blew him a kiss and hurried to the stage. He watched her lithe body climb the few steps and Rex King caught his eye and his expression. George gave him a thumbs up and Rex made a fist back. The band struck up and Swarthy began to "Begin the Beguine" almost before she reached her place.

Happy to be alone, Twyford walked to the bar and ordered a drink. Tony Mavropoulous was having a word here and there and at that moment was making a fuss of a large man whose expensive suit tried, unsuccessfully, to cover a few years of good living. That same smell of shag tobacco caused George to look in their direction and 'Big Stuff' was smoking the only visible pipe. Tony wandered away from him and, after two more stops, arrived at George. He showed interest in Tony's wide circle of acquaintances and asked casually who the man with the bone in his mouth was.

Tony lowered his voice with reverence and said, 'He is a very important man. That's the American, Teddy Connaughty.'

'I bet you a fiver I can guess his tipple.'

'Ha ha!' said Tony, 'I bet you a fiver I can guess it for nothing.' He was good at getting into the sporting spirit of his customers and lost Twyford at the first hurdle.

Numbly confused, George said, 'It's Jack Daniel's.'

'Pah! I could have told you that. I think compulsory it must be for all Americans to drink that brand.'

'Yes, that's true,' agreed George. It may be a coincidence, still he stored it. Tony passed on and Stan Swindells toddled over to hear the news then returned to the lads soon after with a word-to-word summary of the deal. Twyford managed to hide the fact that a super human effort would be necessary to raise the first fifteen thousand, forget the next dainty little steps danced between superb success and utter financial ruin if he failed to upheave the second fifteen . George had this vision of Stanley skipping back to the table, throwing daisies hither and thither. Within two minutes Danny was across to confirm the same statement, hearing it second-hand wasn't enough. Twyford asked him to send Bones over; it was important, he was the one George was least sure of. It was their first chance, that night, of privacy and Twyford began with, 'Did Lestor Hogg pay you the outstanding balance?' Bones patted his pocket and smiled. 'We exchange contracts next Friday,' said Twyford, looking everywhere. Bones did the same and, comfortable in their privacy, began to give George the details he anxiously needed. The two Sergeants they had met collected the wages from Bury St Edmunds every Friday, the bank handed it over in one lump and it was mostly white fivers. Each serviceman receives five pounds, two shillings and sixpence in their wages every week.

"Christ almighty!" thought George, 'No wonder they nick all the women.' He said the last bit out loud.

'No, that's good looks and charm,' laughed Bones, 'but it helps.'

Twyford had to admire his nerve for he wasn't the least bit daunted by the prospect.

'How many on the base?'

'Ten thousand bodies, plus or minus a few.'

'Fifty thousand in one hit!' The excitement rose up in him. 'Can it be switched?' The Corporal's smile said it all. 'Bones, my lovely boy, we're on the way. Wait!' said George, immediately foreseeing a problem. 'When do they get paid?'

'Every Friday,' replied Bones, missing the point of trepidation.

'Morning?'

'No. The money's collected at three o'clock in the afternoon and back to the base in thirty minutes tops.'

'Fuck me, if we have to depend on that we're cutting it fine. Still, no matter, with that in place, we're…we're…' He daren't say anything that might put a curse on it.

'Flying,'said Bones

'Right up there in the clouds. No second thoughts?' asked Twyford.

Bones smiled and shook his head. 'This is the big one I've been hunting for, George. You only get one of these in a lifetime.'

They grabbed hands. 'First class tickets on the gravy train!'

'Shorter prayers!' willed George.

He was still at the bar when the Café Luxor closed and having drunk his fill only now showed a dash of mellow. The Force trooped over, some in company, and said goodnight. Bones left with a right doll and could hardly contain his elation, strolling off with her trailing two paces behind.

Radna changed swiftly and joined him for a last scotch while the waiters cleaned up around them. She wanted to hear where he had been, eager to know what dangers her hero had swashbuckled his way through. He dazzled her with hazardous exploits and spoke of the Battle of the Malden, describing the fight scenes that men love to brag about and girls really don't care to hear, though manage to appear interested. He told her about the bomb on the Craven A and how in a strange way it had done him a kindness, for he had purchased the site cheaply and hoped to modernise it for government contracts.

Chairs stood on tables, the lights started going out and the journey home had to be faced. There were no taxis to be had so they braved the frozen wastes of Regents Park. Radna remarked how sweet the Donna Laura had been and they laughed at her bold but well meaning apology to him earlier. No mention was made of Donald Grogan or his business, they had plenty to tell each other without that.

At her flat, Radna left the lights off and pushed him into the bedroom. In seconds she had him naked and pressed backwards onto the bed where he sprawled out over the pillows and, in the darkness, became her audience. Silence, while seconds ticked away for the act to begin, then a match struck and George watched as a flame licked up the stem of a long, thick candle, kissing its wick to illuminate and exaggerate the shadows. With the grace of a ballet dancer she began undressing, bending from the waist to caress her legs from the ankles up to the tender, white area between stockings and panties. Pieces of underwear were peeled off and his concentration locked on to her fingers as they brushed her breasts then moved tantalisingly downwards. He held his breath while she took a pose and applied lipstick artistically to both sets of lips then, just remembering to breathe, he exhaled a moan as she approached the bed and climbed aboard. Her knees moved slowly either side of his head. The glimmering lips drew his and his tongue parted them and explored. Dominantly, her fingers tweaked his nipples making him gasp and work deeper then, purposely leaving him lustily simmering, she glided down until their bodies aligned. Nerves danced and quivered when sharp, white teeth nipped at his earlobe and nibbled his neck; her kiss tasted hot and whisky-flavoured as she pulled him beneath and ground him into her. Locked around his hips she began rhythmically tightening and releasing the muscles inside her, forcing him into pumping, pelvic thrusts that marched him onward, and she rode him up the great hill to ecstasy, madly peaking in a gushing orgasm for them both. Shivering spasms were jerked free and drumming hearts beat to diminuendo until, in her arms and a state of perfect contentment, he passed out.

Dozens of kids were kicking footballs about when, with a pounding head, Twyford crossed Primrose Hill and stopped at the top to check that he was not being followed. He left the park without noticing an insignificant little man in front of him on the other side of the road. He arrived home to find his mother was out, probably still shopping at Queen's Crescent Market. George also intended to go there but first changed in to a pair of corduroys and decided to do some figure work, feeling that he had to put on paper the rough arithmetic of how they stood. He was no accountant but drew comfort from figures and began with the six offshore accounts now opened, two for South Africa, two for himself, one for the housing and one for the trading company. The South African accounts consisted of two deposits; one with eight thousand on a monthly roll-over and a smaller account with just two thousand earning overnight interest. From this account, one monthly standing order of two hundred and fifty pounds had already gone out to Father Colm. The housing account had started with a thousand and he had spent three hundred and fifty pounds, leaving approximately six hundred and fifty. The trading account had built up to almost a thousand net as all costs and wages had been paid out first. Two offshore statements for George showed a thousand pounds in each. Ben held cash for him of six thousand sterling and five thousand dollars (roughly four to the pound). And one way or another, there was about a thousand pounds floating around being used for out of pocket expenses. In brief, South Africa had nine and a half thousand, George had two, Benny held six thousand plus twelve hundred and fifty equivalent in dollars. Nineteen thousand, less the cost of the Craven A knocked the total down to eleven thousand five hundred. Add a straight thousand from the trading company and six hundred and fifty from the housing, bringing it to just above thirteen thousand sterling. They were still two thousand short and every account would have been emptied. Even though it was only needed for just over a week, it was still a daunting thought to put every shilling at risk and still be short. On the plus side, Benny had sold ten thousand pounds worth at four shillings a note and held half in advance already, that cleared out two hundred thousand in forgeries. Bones had done another ten thousand notes but the money for them would not be available for next Friday. Steve from the Roman and the other traders had called on one hundred thousand pounds worth at four bob a note, which could bring them in the five thousand pounds needed. So, if everyone was as good as their word *and* on time with the readies he might just have fifteen thousand cash by next Friday and a hundred and fifty thousand of forgeries for nothing. It should have looked much better than that but the real killing would have to be made with the second consignment. For now, two thousand pound cash was the immediate worry and George could brood about that problem on Monday. He heard the street door bang against the wall and jumped up to see who it was.

Before he could get to the passage Min called out, 'Is that kettle on, Georgie? I'm spitting feathers!' Then after a graphic description of where the bitter wind had been blowing, she mentioned. 'By the way dear, did you see there's a letter come for you this morning, it's on the hall stand in the passage.'

Retrieving it, he saw it was an officious looking, typed envelope and guessed who would send him his first correspondence since coming back. Apparently, he was summoned to a hearing at ten a.m. this approaching Thursday with the Inland Revenue at their offices in Kings Cross. That horrible little so-and-so wasn't giving up, he left it where he found it to remind him, then John and Mickey called and the three of them walked to the Crescent. As they slipstreamed along the market, Lestor Hogg and Frank Nash were on Owen's stall chatting between customers. With yet another excellent reason for a swift half they settled in the nearest warm alehouse and George admitted in his estimations they were two thousand short. Lestor reckoned it had been their best week in the trading company so far, with bigger orders from the same people. That operation was strengthening all the time but that business only worked with a strong cash flow and had nothing to spare. George would have to look elsewhere.

An hour before the lads were due to meet that night, George pulled the car out then drove back the same route. No one was following. 'Getting paranoid!' he told himself. Sally was no where near ready and asked him to give her an hour. He decided to give her the night; saucy prat!

He parked across from the pub and flipped young Joey Gay a shilling to keep an eye on the motor then looking him up and down joked, 'Come round my house, I'll give you a cheese sandwich; it might build you up a bit.' To say he was thin was an understatement, the boy was a spindle!

'Nah, your daughters fancy me too much, they drive me mad.'

Twyford's clip missed his ear and he stood there, tossing the coin in the air like George Raft. He was a smashing kid.

The bar was already busy. Fintan was doing the honours and frothy pints of bitter were being passed across. Mornie brought Nolan in, still with both eyes covered.

Owen inquired, 'Can't you do something about that and cover the rest of his face, an'all.'

Nolan countered with, 'I'm back to Moorfields on Thursday. Thinking about the sight of you lot, I might request a patch for each eye.'

Mary and Kathy Gay came in and nodded over, and then, surprise surprise, not two minutes later in walked Nero and the fiddlers three. Most of the wives were out and settled in the snugs and a rare old evening ensued. Stan and Olive were the last two to arrive and as he walked her over to the girls, the band played "Ain't Misbehaving". The bar laughed. Lucky was on the stage and crooned "Don't get around much anymore". He always got the biggest applause, not because he was the best, everyone just loved him. Then Kathy Gay sang "You made me love you". That got the men up with their arms stretched out to her. The Irish crowd called Fintan for the "Fields of Athenrye".

'Forget the Bedford,' said Lestor, feeling the mood early, 'This is proper entertainment.' The songs got better and better, lifting the crowd up as the drinks went down. By the time Kit was 'on the air', Lestor was dancing and hopping about on his own, and by the second number, Stanley was dancing with him. The band finished that night with Ada Butler singing Vera Lynn's 'We'll meet again'. The noise level doubled as the whole pub joined in the chorus. A tiddly host collected outside on the pavement to say their goodnights when a distant droning began in the dark skies. The conversation stopped and everyone fell silent as it grew louder and nearer. Careless cracks of light went out everywhere and low-cloud continued to hide the moon yet the sound seeped through the darkness, becoming louder still; its ringing penetration fixed to grate on nerves. People stood like statues while something sinister slowly passed above them. It had probably taken no more than a minute to fade into the mist but had redelivered the chilling fear that, until then, was a rapidly, diminishing memory. Whatever it was, given a choice, no one wanted to hear that twice. A little less merry, the crowd splintered and made for home.

Little Joey was waiting at the car, 'What do you think that noise was?' he asked, not in the least bit frightened.

'Search me.' said George, 'Maybe another of them rocket bombs gone wrong.'

'George, you've had visitors,' added Joey. Twyford's ears pricked up. 'Three fellas in a big, old, fancy Austin stopped and looked at your car but they didn't touch it.'

'Did you know any of them, Joe?' he asked calmly.

'No, I've got their number though.'

George saw he was proud of himself and took out a pen in readiness, 'Good boy, what was it?'

'There it is,' said Joey, pointing a torch beam at the pavement and scrawled in chalk was 'UEB 121'. Twyford made a note of it and gave the lad another bob for luck.

It was so dark, since the droning, that it made sense for George to drop him home and Joey was already making himself comfortable in the back.

'Cor, this is smashing, George. Want me to drive?'

'How old are you now?' asked Twyford.

'I'm thirteen. My Dad lets me reverse the fish lorry out of the yard.' They pulled up at the Gay residence and caught Kathy in a clinch with one of the fiddlers.

'You should have been home ages ago!' she said, pushing him in the door, and then,

'Thanks, George. See ya.'

'See ya.

CHAPTER 24: AND A HUNDRED BEAN BAGS FELL OUT

Med; An Hs293 glider bomb hits the British troopship, Rohna off Bougie in Algiers; 1115 are killed.

After being spoiled with breakfast in bed, George came down to the kitchen and turned on the news but nothing was mentioned about the buzz-bomb. That was its new name for obvious reasons and everyone was talking about it. He could hear girls' voices singing a little ditty, punctuated by a steady beat, and went to investigate. In the garden he found Mairead with her skirt shoved into her knickers, against the toilet wall, bouncing a ball in a stocking between her legs and either side of her head. Niamh stood to one side accompanying her as the song sped faster. For a magic heart beat, George thought they had unearthed Bounty but, on inspection, it was just another tennis ball. They had time for a briefest of hellos and then the ditty chant began again as Niamh took her turn. Trying to talk to them just drew head movements for the recital was too important to interrupt. He gave up and prepared himself for the Sunday lunchtime quota.

That same evening, George went around to collect Alan. There was a war film on and they were looking forward to it. Nell Higby answered the door and asked him in, which was not unusual in itself, she was often over with Mary. She and he had been pretty good friends when they were kids. He remembered when Nell and Pat Passmore were 12 and had been the first to grow breasts. They were a year older than George, and he and his mates would run up to swing out of them. Perhaps that was why Pat had never liked him. How peculiar. These recollections of an earlier life spanned but seconds. No, what was unusual was the sad look she gave him, a look that said words were pointless so he followed her through to the kitchen. Mary was consoling her younger sister

Orla, who laid across her lap and sobbed her heart out. She sat up embarrassed when she saw George, then rose and ran to him to lose her head in his chest. Mary glared at him. For interrupting? For being there? Or maybe just breathing. Orla had grown since last he had seen her. Then she was Niamh's age and height, and now she was a woman, small and pert, like Mary. He mouthed,

'What's happened?'

Mary spoke with an emptiness that only the unarguable finality of death can bring to speech. 'Her Peter's ..gone. Killed in North Africa, somewhere called Mersa Matrux.'

'Oh darling. I'm so sorry,' said George. They were already engaged and had planned to marry when all the madness was over, now, another young life had been tragically wasted and another young heart crushed. Hundreds of lads were being killed every day, joining clubs called Freedom and Justice, and the figures made you numb to them until your free membership arrived. Quite suddenly the war film did not hold the same appeal.

The railway arches began on the Brick Lane side of Spitalfields and stretched through Bethnal Green and Globe Town to Mile End. The narrow lanes and blocked turnings followed the railway above through some of the roughest parts of the East End. Scores of legitimate, small businesses worked in this maze of industrial chasms, but 'things' could be lost or found: vehicles and machinery could be destroyed or created, cookers might enter one archway and reappear in the sunlight dressed as a coach. Visitors were not welcome. If a stranger entered any of these yards he would probably be seen off by axle-wielding grease monkeys, smothered in oil and unidentifiable again. It was in this labyrinth of secrecy that Roy found his living and a right regal one it was, too. He knew everyone and lived on their endeavours. If someone needed a lorry for a job, see Roy. You want your car to disappear, leave it to Roy. A tractor engine can be swapped for print machinery, he gets it done. He paid no rent on arches or lock-ups but knew who had what for sale, and more importantly was trusted by them all. Since their last meeting, Roy had been very active and without committing himself, had spoken to close associates in many types of businesses. The arch dwellers lacked cash but never contacts, people who knew people. With the absence of commerce outside of war supplies and ancillary, emergency services, some industries were against the wall. Vehicles and machinery of all types could be purchased cheaply for cash and, without paperwork, collected from the back door. Roy had made plans, by using the forged notes and passing them out on trust, his people could buy commodities for half the normal price and still turn them over easily to make a nice little profit. On average for every five pound spent, Roy and George should get a return of twenty five to thirty percent. Unfortunately no cash could be put up front but every note should convert to between one pound five shillings and one pound thirteen shillings and sixpence. George thoroughly agreed with the trust involved, you do not knock your own. The only thing that could go wrong was if someone tumbled the numbers and even then it would be conmen trading with crooks and so the deal may not go through but it was doubtful that the police would get to hear.

At that meeting on Monday morning, Twyford drew encouragement that fifty thousand pounds worth of white fivers, costing one thousand five hundred pounds should turn into twelve thousand five hundred pounds the worst way; two and a half for Roy as the agent, and the rest in the kitty.

'Don't let's be greedy.' warned George in earnest. 'Tell them to buy and sell for cost, we'll work on twenty five percent and your people do the same. Do the deals, get the readies and disappear.' Roy nodded at the logic of cashing everything in as quickly as possible and shook his hand; he would collect from George, on Friday night, fifty thousand pounds worth of crooked money.

For his next meeting, Twyford drove to the Jago and as usual parked near the police station in Shoreditch. His tea was ready as he walked into Irving's office. Benny's face betrayed nothing as he mentioned, 'When you left the Arches an old grey Morris-Cowley followed you out, it had been parked all the while you were with Roy. He just rang to warn you,' added Benny in answer to the look of astonishment.

'They must have been bloody good,' said George, not completely surprised but comfortable that no one could know who he met or what was discussed. The kitchen often doubled as a private office and had two doors, Ben closed both of them and joined him at the kitchen table. He took a ledger from the sideboard and ran through the accounts. Twyford listened intently as he added them in reverse order and back to front. He started with the updated figures in each account first, which was all George really wanted to know, then followed with expenditures and his bottom line was the original starting figures but the point was, although these figures were five hundred pounds higher than Twyford's, the simple reason for this being that Irving, against his own understanding of the deal, had managed to buy the Craven A building for seven thousand pounds thus saving a monkey - and making George forever grateful in the process. They still had to find one thousand five hundred pounds cash to complete and, though a considerable sum, was not insurmountable. All that Benny could hope for was to try again with the one client that had refused his earlier offer. George suggested selling them at pure cost just to get the cash up front and reminded him that the whole deal hung on his success.

Irving knocked and passed through, repeating loudly, 'I'm not listening, I can't hear you!'

Once they were alone again, George asked why he couldn't get his brother interested in the deal. But Benny's smile was discouraging. 'He won't even talk about it. Believe me, I've tried. It's breaking the law and he wouldn't consider it.' They sipped a last cup of tea pensively, then Twyford headed for the Roman Road.

Steve was holding an auction with all manner of household goods and George arrived in the middle of it. He came across very well and gave the impression that although he was selling his wares to lose money, it was done with a good heart and they lapped him up. The performance finished with a parcel of sprouting Dutch onions offered out as daffodil bulbs and sold with the promise of a stronger fragrance every year. Twyford wanted to applaud. They went 'backstage' to the Needlegun pub and outlined the latest moves. Steve spoke for his people, saying that they would be pleased to double up. He was prepared to go at it hard as long as the credit could be extended until after the Christmas holiday. He guaranteed base price plus but getting upfront money was an impossibility. Twyford was heartened; he needed dependable outlets like these market boys, where good sums could be quickly and safely dispersed.

Quite a productive day had given him the flavour and the Queen's drew him in for 'Glee Club' night. The Loan Club was paying out on Friday and a few of the boys were clearing their back debts. During the evening Frank came in and mentioned that he thought he saw Sally going down Marsden Street towards Mary's house.

'I shouldn't think so!' laughed George. 'I can't imagine those two having much in common.'

'Oh, I don't know,' remarked Owen, holding his forefinger and thumb out, barely measuring an inch.

The old couple were there again and though sitting rather close to the chaps remained unnoticed. George felt a little tired and left early. No streetlights lit his homeward journey and turning right through St. Silas st., he switched off the torch and stood quite still then waited for slip or sound. None came. He thought how daft he must look to anybody coming across him and would probably frighten the life out of them. Yet still he shivered in the shadows for a few minutes more then gave up playing cops and robbers and jauntily swung off home, the epitome of 'Jack the Lad'.

Sally left Mary's house after ten. It had been a long day and she wearily walked to Chalk Farm for her bus. They were becoming good friends now. Sally understood that Mary did not get out much and loved to hear all the news. Tonight she practically drained her of gossip and had even been interested in George and his meetings; more importantly she was not drinking. Sally took a certain pride in that fact.

Tuesday morning, the squad car carried Sergeant Shaw to the station early and he was in a hurry to get started. The word was out that St Pancras was being swamped with black market gear and none of the usual busybodies or grasses could impress him with their knowledge. Mouths that might know something were shut tight and plain clothes officers, trying to mix with the local community, were too easy to spot. Among others, Archie had considered George Twyford, but he had been watched any time he was in the borough and been seen to be doing nothing at all, which in itself was suspicious; but then, by association, had arrived at Tinker. Now he could not wait to pull out the case file and study what he was doing to be arrested and why he broke the law in the first place. The desk Sergeant coughed loudly as he strode in and nodded behind him at the Super's office, Archie sighed and entered without knocking. These two seldom spoke in front of others at the station but such was their respect for each other that a strong understanding had developed over the years. Basically, Archie did whatever was necessary to combat the ever-present crime and violence in the area while the Super turned a blind eye, covered him completely and gratefully left him to it. No permission sought or given. Archie stood in front of the desk and waited. A letter on Inland Revenue notepaper was turned upside down to face him and pushed across. Without picking it up, he read it thoroughly. It was addressed to the assistant Commissioner of the Metropolitan Police and was a very serious complaint against himself. Among other things he was accused of warning his son-in-law, George Twyford, of the search warrant. He finished the letter, stepped back and waited. Superintendent Hunt rose, walked to the window and said, 'I've spoken to the Commissioner himself over the seriousness of this correspondence.'

'And?'

'I've informed him that, in my opinion, the Revenue have made one almighty cock-up and are now looking to pass the buck, and if we accept this as an official complaint then how can we expect our men to ever co-operate with them.'

Archie waited. 'Is this gonna take much longer?'

'Yes, it bloody well is!' said the Super, annoyed at being hurried.

'Only, I have got a lot to do.' Archie tailed off.

'Don't you want to know what he said?'

'Yes, I do.. really.'

'He said to file it properly.' Now the Super was happy, 'Would you like to do the honours?'

Archie understood a smile was called for, 'May I?' he said, then screwed it up and dropped it in the bin. The Superintendent waved him away and he strolled back through the station and upstairs to the 'library'. The file on Nathaniel "Tinker" Woods was signed for then Archie withdrew to his private office downstairs and shut the door. Reading through it quickly he listed the points that stood out. One; the cart was loaded when at Camden Road and empty a short while later when he gave himself up. Two; why give himself up? Three; how could he afford a top brief to defend him? Archie took out a map of St Pancras and circled the short journey then studied the area as he mentally moved along each street.. The coal wharf was positioned to the left of, and slightly above, the police station. It was just outside the circle.

Tinker left the Americans with another full load. It was like

Aladdin's Cave, they had so much of everything and no one went without; what a difference. Normally a happy-go-lucky sort of fellow, life amused him, he enjoyed meeting strangers, some may be interesting and engrossing, friendly or offish, but he chatted to them all and he was a good ambassador. Nathaniel Woods spent long periods on the road with just the sound of Ginger's hooves and often pondered on the complexities of the people he came across. Take Bones for instance: wouldn't stop scheming, carried a lot of responsibilities, yet always had a smile and a pleasant word for everyone. In Tinker's opinion they didn't come any shrewder than Bones. Today he appeared to be organising the whole Base, had Tinker loaded in no time, gave him two messages for Lestor Hogg and still remembered another little present for George; thinking of that he took it out from under the blanket and felt it in his hands. It was heavy and rattled around in its box, Tinker became more curious by the minute. Ginger had a fine sense of direction and quite often he could nod off and wake up when she stopped at a junction or traffic lights coming into London. A very intelligent animal was Ginger, so he set her reins to automatic pilot and examined the package; it wasn't sealed, just folded in at each end. Nice man, Bones, nice gesture. A quick peak couldn't hurt so he opened it from the top and found a woollen glove wedged in with the fingers full of bullets. Tinker tipped the box up and out popped a small pistol. He quickly slid it back and squeezed the glove in after it. He shouldn't have looked. "What does George want a gun for?" More important Tinker thought, "If it's found on me, I'm in real bother." He shoved it under his old raincoat and tightened the string around his waist for safety.

Twyford's bedroom was on the first floor landing and faced the back garden. He looked down on the skeletons of two apple trees, planted by his father years before and probably destroyed by George and his mates, constantly picking the fruit before it had a chance to grow. He watched his cat crouching on the air raid shelter roof, preparing to spring at a robin. Bob,bob,bobbing was a good description, as the bird hopped about the garden below. The cat sprang and the robin flew off; no chance.

Mary came between the gap in the wall, dragging Alan by the scruff of the neck. In fact, he was being pushed, pulled and dragged along all at the same time. George couldn't hear but Mary was shouting something at him and, as he spoke, she swung him a blow that bounced off the back of his head. George heard his holler though, and saw his hand go up automatically in case another of similar force followed.

"What's he been up to now?" mused Twyford. It had to be serious or Mary wouldn't be coming to him. He buttoned his fly and adjusted the waist band of a new pair of trousers Mornie had made him and went downstairs to intercept. She held the shoulder of shirt and jumper bunched in her hand and shook him once more for good luck, then shoved him in front of his father. George looked down at him sternly but he wouldn't look up.

'Tell him what you've been doing!' she demanded. But Alan wouldn't speak: she was so furious. 'Tell him!' He still would not answer. 'You bloody little liar!' she shrieked, and struck him round the head again. Her logic sometimes amazed George.

'How can he be a liar if he hasn't spoken yet?'

That was all she needed. 'That's it!' she screamed. 'Take his side, why don't you. I'm only his mother!' She was almost delirious in her rage. 'You're the reason he's never at school, the little liar!' she repeated and raised her arm yet again but this time George withered her with a look. She flushed for a second and stepped back; even her breathing was laboured.

'You've been bunking off.' A statement. 'Why?' Still no reply. 'Are you a dope, is that it? Can't you keep up with the other kids?'

Alan shook his head but still would not look up. George took that to mean he could keep up and that was not the reason.

By the tone of his voice, Alan knew his Dad was really annoyed, but he wouldn't speak, not in front of his mother. Dad would understand when he explained. George held him firmly by the arm and took him into the front room. It was never used accept for Christmas and always smelt musty. Mary followed them in. Twyford pulled back the curtain. It was twenty to eight and the street was quite busy with people leaving for work.

'Do you see all these men? Look at them, not a tie between them. Do you know why? 'Cos the poor bastards are going to graft in factories and the like, that's their only way to get a living. No education and if it was available they were too pressed to find work to take it in. You think you're hard done by at school, they're lucky to get a week's holiday a year, hopping. Is that what you want, to be just another mug with no future?'

Alan's head was still down and he tried hard to keep the tears in as he shook his head.

Mary transferred her weight from one foot to the other, showing frustration at not being able to put in another fourpenneth. George knelt down and held him close to look him in the eye, but softened his approach when a tear fell on his hand. He turned Alan round and walked him past his Mother, out into the passage and up to the bedroom, calling back, 'We'll be down in a minute.'

Mary bristled, she felt dismissed and shouted up the stairs, 'When you've sorted him out, you get the little devil to school. I've had enough!' And with that she stormed out. They watched her from the bedroom window as she stamped across the garden, seething. George grinned broadly and Alan cuffed a dew drop and smiled too.

'Sorry if we sometimes come down a bit hard, son, but it really is for your own good. Schooling's necessary to teach you all the basic things you need to survive. Use the teachers to help you learn more than anybody else, so it make's a difference in your life. When others are queuing for jobs as van boys or packers, you're being asked to advise the Prime Minister, with a big house up Hampstead and a chauffeur.' Alan started to like this bit. 'Have all the education on offer. It's free, and it's the only good thing you'll ever get for nothing. I'm telling you, Al, give it a chance, get loads of it; there's a million interesting facts to find out about and you'll love it. Never be embarrassed about being clever, that's a gift God gave you. Other people you'll meet will always have an angle for themselves, everyone has, except for me. The one certainty in your life is that I'll never put you wrong. Hang on to that and don't ever forget it; I'm the one who wants you to have everything.'

Alan's eyes welled up again. Perhaps he knew how critical his Dad thought it was and wanted to make him proud by doing it immediately, at his age everything had to be instant. His reasons for playing the hop did not seem so dire now but he felt Dad deserved to know he was not just being lazy. 'I never went in 'cos all the other kids take the mickey out of me. Well, it's her fault, 'innit?. She keeps fussing round me and it's only 'cos she loves you.'

'Brainless cow,' said George, not meaning it to come out loud.

Heartened by this, Alan sniffed, 'Yeah, I know,' and stacked more wood on her bonfire by adding, 'I hide from her but she finds me. And then in the playground, Whitely and Richards and them all wait at the bottom of the stairs, laughing and singing soppy songs about me.'

'I thought Derek Whitely was your best mate?' asked George.

'No. We had a fight last week and I upped him, and I ain't been back since.'

'Listen. Don't fall out with your pals over a dopey teacher. I'm sorry, mate, I'll have a word with her.'

'No, it's all right, I can manage,' he said, very grown up. Twyford got his coat, he would take him nonetheless. Before they walked in, George freed a little penknife from his key chain and gave it to him; it had two blades and a bottle opener. He was so pleased, you would think it was the Crown Jewels.

The other children had just sat down and Ms Poole was about to call the register. She looked at the door as Alan bowled in and her face brightened when she saw who was with him. Perhaps blowing her out Saturday night had done him a favour!

Knowing when to be nice, Sally came outside the classroom and said, 'This is a lovely surprise!'

Rather bluntly he explained why Alan had not been in; she was deflated and took it badly. Probably because her legs were so long and her stance was wider apart than most women, he softened, and cogitating all the wrong thoughts, helped her back with, 'You know how daft they can be at that age. You see, no one's ever made a fuss of him and I suppose it came as a bit of a shock.'

A complete pack of lies, but she jumped aboard and sailed into, 'Of course, I should have seen that. Whatever was I thinking? I should have eased into our friendship gently. I hope I haven't frightened him off, he's such a sweet boy that sometimes I just want to cuddle him.'

'Well, practice on me till he gets a bit bigger,' suggested George, with perfect timing.

She laughed and squeezed his hands, pressing her nails into his palms and they began whispering like two conspirators,

'I want to kiss you,' she said.

'Well you'll just have to wait,' he answered. Then, on second thoughts, and confident that all now would bode well for Alan, he pulled her behind the stock cupboard and opened the door to hide them. As they embraced, a hundred beanbags fell out.

CHAPTER 25: DISAPPEARING TAILS OF ELUSIVE BLACK CATS

Italy: The 8th Army clears the area north of the Sangro; the 5th Army mounts diversionary attacks to precede another assault on Monte Camino.

Wednesday morning, George ran the heath. It was freezing cold and the rain-soaked ground was icily dangerous underfoot but once the pounding effort of his movement had warmed him, he found the wind to be quite bracing. The smell in the air promised fog. He reflected on how it must have been when the bombs were falling all over the capital and the people prayed for thick, smoky fog, or on clear nights waiting for the air raid sirens then grabbing your valuables and running for your life to the nearest underground station.

His thoughts jumped to the South African Press who had suggested long ago that England and America had allowed Germany to strengthen, as the political puppeteers of both countries saw an industrialised Russia as a threat to their grip on world trade. America, it was said, financed the Germans to go against Stalin, but Herr Hitler had other ideas. He took it all and signed a pact with Russia, then smartly trampled across Europe. There was probably more than a bit of truth in it, as the Astors, Asquiths, Mitfords and even the Duke of Windsor, were mostly more pro-German than pro-Russian. It was rotten. Crooked politicians, backed by power-crazy capitalists, decided on a conflict where worker went to fight worker; working classes who began the war with nothing and would finish with even less, no matter who won. What price an English life, eh? How much was Orla's Peter worth, did he produce enough to show a profit before he was killed and still merit the cost of a wooden cross and six feet of dirt in North Africa? These warmongers should be put against a wall and stoned to death, shootings too good for the bastards. It was good to run.

His mind was rambling again, dreaming of how he could sort it all out and everyone would live happily ever after. He was out of Parliament Hill Fields and running along Grafton Road when a car horn frightened the bloody life out of him. He jumped on to the pavement as a police car slowed to a halt next to him.

'Well, if it ain't Wetleg and Piss-Me-Quick!' said George. 'Been waiting long?'

PC Devlin smiled, 'We don't mind, plenty of time. Nearly got your Mum for shoplifting in the Crescent, Saturday. If she'd been on her own, we would have done.'

'I wish I was as tough as you two, dishing out beatings to old women and little boys. Keep it up and Archie might make you into milk monitors.' With that he jogged on.

They drove alongside with the same officer promising, 'We'll have you, you flash bastard! Then see if you can smile without any teeth!' George didn't grace them with a glance but signalled in the fashion of the English archers after Agincourt and they pulled past and accelerated away. He ran through the streets and sprinted the last few hundred yards to his door.

The most important meal of the day was swallowed in one lump and washed down with a mug of tea before George scrubbed, spruced and suited then called for Mornie Quill and Gerry Nolan. They had to be at Moorfields by 10am for the 'unveiling'. The boys caught the tube to Old Street and sat either side of him in a comfortable, busy carriage. Gerry was obviously mentally strengthening because he pontificated ceaselessly. His opinions were always a bit extreme and for fun they disagreed with him over this and that. Perhaps the bandages impaired his hearing because as he argued, he raised his voice to drown out their opposition. The train filled at Euston so George and Mornie gave their seats up and moved away, Gerry was still ranting on and didn't notice. His adjacent fellow travellers thought him quite mad but, like all polite English folk, appeared not to notice his ravings. By the time they reached the Angel, he realised he was the only one speaking and felt either side of him to make sure they were still there. He touched the arm of an elderly gentleman and relaxed, then tensed slightly as he felt the knee of a young lady, whose frozen face coloured as she watched Nolan's hand hop further into danger as he too froze, then swiftly crossed his arms tight against his chest. Further along the carriage George and Mornie were bouncing about soundlessly, almost weeping with laughter.

The lads helped him off at the next stop and were cursed soundly. He carried on a barrage of expletives while they made their way onto the street, blighting their ancestors with vehemence. They reached a small island in the middle of City Road and left him there. The tormenting sods stood on the side of the busy thoroughfare, directing him to step forward or back depending which looked more dangerous. Each time he ventured out, the hooter of a bus or lorry had him retreating quickly backwards. He swore obscenities that damned them and their offspring for ever. George and Mornie passed a pleasant ten minutes that way until two old dears eventually helped him to safety.

Moorfields Eye Hospital had a dreadful smell of fear about it as they sat in front of a young doctor and waited while he unwound the mass of bandages that were encasing two-thirds of Nolan's head. The boys had made light of it all along but now was the moment of truth, they were there to support him, whatever happened. Gerry faced a dark area for obvious reasons and tried to give himself courage. His last examination hadn't been so good, in fact he'd seen only darkness and was told that it was one of two reasons; either a tiny, undetectable blood-vessel may have passed across the pupil or... he was now blind. His head was freed and he prepared himself to face the rest of his life. He opened his eyes and George and Mornie held their breath. Two seconds passed and Gerry looked and saw nothingness, then a pinhead of light that quickly grew to an egg and a Television screen that became a cinema. Elusive black cats disappeared from the edges of his vision, as their fleeting tails slipped out of sight. He blinked several times, trying unsuccessfully to remove the tiny clouds that sailed from the centre -but he could see. With a shaky voice he described the view and his friends delighted in his swelling joy. The three of them jumped up and down and the doctor warned against jolting. They danced around while he attempted more advice.

'Don't get bumped or banged, stay out of fights, don't drink too much, a fall could be dangerous.' But they weren't listening. Gerry was okay and it was great to see the swagger coming back into him. They left in a clamour of laughter and bad language.

Nolan, Quill and Twyford came out of Mornington Crescent tube station and into Ruben's office. They were shown upstairs and, after knocking politely, entered. He was sitting on the desk while Pat Passmore reclined in his big chair, both seemed in excellent form. Pat had small stitches showing across most of her face and, although they were caked with dried blood, the improvement was obvious. She courteously acknowledged George for his financial help with the operation then warmly took Ruben's hand and, for all to see, gave him her heart-felt thanks for everything. This time it was Twyford's turn to feel put down. Nolan gave a snort of laughter that was meant to deride Pat for her uncharitable manner. It struck home and George appreciated the gesture, ungrateful mare.

Ruben rose above it and introduced himself to the other two, remarking how pleased he was that Gerry had recovered so well. He sat them down and ordered tea. Pat stood and Ruben took his seat while she positioned herself behind him, her hand resting on his shoulder; Twyford had never seen him so affable. They talked of the Craven A and the property company, everything was going through smoothly. He made pleasantries and encouraged the conversation. This was a sunnier Ruben; a quixotic man who, every so often, reached up to feel her hand. They couldn't stop touching and, had George not have known the other side of them both, it would have been rather nice. Benson even enquired as to Archie's health using the Sergeant's Christian name prompting George into asking where he knew him from. Ruben was in a reflective mood and with an old fashioned look, began, 'I knew him before you and Fintan were born.' George looked incredulous. He continued, 'It was in the second year at Cantelows School. We were a pretty tough gang, most of the kids were scared of us. He joined as a first year and being that twelve month younger, generally they look smaller and nervous, but not him. Archie was as big as what we were and knocked about with two small mates, one of them was an Arab or something. Anyway, he was the one the boys often picked on. This day they were chasing him around the playground for fun but the kid was terrified. Archie came out just as they had him on the floor. He stood in front of the kid and pushed my mate Davy James away, telling him to pick on someone his own size. Jamesy gave him a dead leg and Archie punched the fuck out of him. We couldn't let that happen so five of the boys gave him a kicking. I watched like everybody else and ashamed as I am, I thought he deserved it for sticking his nose in. Anyway, that night as we came out of school, he was waiting there. He was gonna fight Jamesy and, if the others wanted to, he'd fight them one at a time, afterwards. They all rushed him and this time gave him a real, good hiding. The next day Jamesy wasn't at school, no one thought anything about it. He came in the following day black and blue but by this time Archie had had another one of them and given him the same. He'd watched their houses in the mornings and ambushed them on their way in. The boys gathered the gang together and chased him home but he got indoors before they could grab him. Bugger me, if by the next morning he hadn't done a third one! He got all five in the end, hurt them too. After that people steered clear of him, he was an oddmark all right, there was something really unhealthy about him.'

"He's still the same horrible bastard forty five years on," thought George.

Their attention had been absorbed with the story and Ruben gave them a moment to ruminate then added, 'You can't stop him. If he's after you, you'd have to kill him.' He looked straight at Twyford when he said it and George responded with a shrug. It was true, but people dared not think it, let alone say it out loud.

Pat joked it away by saying, 'Oi, that's my mate's father you're talking about.'

Mornie continued it, 'Yeah. She could bash us up on her own.'

'A proper little Messerschmitt,' accorded Nolan, and changed the subject.

They chatted on for a time until Fintan came in, he smiled a friendly acknowledgement to the boys but spoke directly to Ruben, 'The car's ready, Boss.' Benson swept Pat off, looking into her eyes with his good side.

'Any chance of a lift?' asked Twyford, following them out.

It was a polished, 'Fuck off, George, there's a good chap,' and a, 'Oh, you'll be glad to know number 24s run every six minutes.'

'But we're partners,' chided Twyford, arms outstretched beseechingly.

'Not where the ladies are concerned, we're not.'

Three frozen turds found the bus stop and, while stalactites formed on their noses, deliberated on Ruben and Pat. She had been hard work even before her husband died - he was a fireman and was killed in the first week of the bombing - and Ruben has only ever been stern, coarse and gruff. Now look at them, undeniably taken with each other and it made them lighter, gentler, more approachable. The trio smiled at the pleasing description then as the first to recover, Mornie said, 'Mugs!' and the other two quickly agreed. They boarded the bus and when they alighted at the Shipton Kevin was walking towards them, laughing to himself. He spotted his Dad and brightened even more.

'Tell us then?' said Mornie, 'What's so amusing?'

'Oh, something said today that keeps coming back and making me giggle. It's a trade thing, you see. We sell wooden barrels of grape from Canada, and when they're fresh they're worth money. Trouble is the porters break open the slats on the bottom and pinch a couple of pound then shove newspapers in to keep it looking full up from the top. A customer complained today and I said it was definitely a fresh arrival.

'Oh it's fresh all right!' he said, 'I knew that when I found yesterday's Sporting Life in the bottom.'

George chuckled too; those porters had more strokes than the boat race. 'I remember once asking one of the barrow boys why he couldn't pay his bill that week. He said he'd had a fire on the stall and all the paper money got burnt.'

The lads advanced on Min's house for a cuppa and listened while father and son swapped more market stories. It passed a good hour. Kevin went across the gardens and Mornie asked if he was leaving the trade.

'Why'd you say that?' questioned George.

'He said to me that's the one thing he'd miss; the laughs. I thought he might be coming to work for you.'

'No,' said George, quite mystified.

After an early night, the morning found him running to Primrose Hill and back before breakfast. He tried to prepare himself for his Revenue enquiry. Twyford had no idea what questions to expect, except the obvious - where was the money? He did not doubt how difficult they could make life for anyone; they were official thieves, robbers with authority and as such should be treated with respect. His naive but honest stupidity must be glimpsed by them and show through the interview gradually. He arrived five minutes early and was pointed to a waiting room full of 'expectant fathers', chain-smoking and nervously marching from wall to wall.

"Well, at least I'm not on my own," thought George, as he casually brushed ash from a wooden chair and sat down. He watched the six other occupants; they varied from anxious to full of dread. Saying nothing was the sensible policy. A smartly-dressed man paced about and threw the other fellows glances of alarm, needing them to return sympathetic looks of agreement.

'Calm down,' said Twyford, addressing the walker but speaking to the room. 'They want you to be worked up and flapping, that's why we'll all be kept waiting. Give it half an hour over your appointment and if you're still here, knock on the door and tell them you've got to get back to work. You'll see how fast they move then.'

'Do you really think so?' asked the hiker, then, 'Yes, of course they do,' he said, answering himself

Everyone nodded, wanting to talk.

George spoke airily, 'They never know as much as you think they do. Don't offer anything just answer the questions as briefly as you can.'

A little bald man, who looked as if he carried his money in a purse, piped up with, 'Yes, I was warned by my accountant; the more you say, the bigger the chance of hanging yourself.' then, 'Sorry, bad choice of words.'

Everyone began to chat and George could see them composing themselves, preparing rather than panicking. He pondered on trying to pick one who might want to invest fifteen hundred pounds, some of them may need to lose some cash; this was probably a good area for recruitment. The door opened and his name was called, he left them with a smile of assurance and boldly walked through to meet his next hurdle. The corridor led past many closed doors and up a flight of stairs to a corner office overlooking Euston Road. Almost albino, a younger, tall and slim, white haired gentleman with a pink face and rimless glasses, remained seated but shook his hand and introduced himself as Priest. Funny thing with names, he could have been the local vicar. Kirby went through the same ceremony, though his hand barely showed interest. The guide said nothing, just took a seat at the wall and held pen and paper at the ready. The room was comfortably furnished, more like a private office than the interrogation cell Twyford had imagined.

Kirby began, 'I think you know why you're here.'

'I'm afraid not,' answered George, 'unless it's to receive an apology for the other night.'

'Don't come the clever Johnny with us!' said Priest sharply.

It took George by surprise, this was not how it was supposed to go. One should be disagreeable and then the other takes over, in a much friendlier manner, and in him you confide. These were the Brothers Nasty.

Priest continued, 'And you can wipe that smirk off your face! You're in a lot of trouble so you'd better answer these questions truthfully, or else.'

'Or else, what? Who'd you think you're talking to?'

'You, little man,' said Priest, leaning across the table, 'and I can make sure that you're locked up for a long time.'

'What charge?' argued George.

'Do you doubt I can do it?' said Priest, rising to the challenge and reddening all the more. The room paused, but Priest must have liked the threat, because he repeated even louder, 'Do you doubt I can do it?!'

George did not doubt, so raised a hand to stop him and with dignity swerved into…

'I have come here in answer to your letter. I try never to be rude and I expect people to be civil to me. Be sure I shall not remain here if you're not. Now, shall we start again?'

The vicar looked as if he'd dive for Twyford's throat and Kirby could see this was going to get out of hand. He should be free to play it his own way but Priest was London's senior man.

'Perhaps we should all relax and have some tea,' he suggested.

The clerk lifted a phone and ordered refreshments. Kirby began again, 'Mr Twyford, we've had information that you carried into this country a large sum of money.'

'Yes, that's correct,' said George.

'Well?' said Priest aggressively.

Twyford ignored him. Even Kirby's face showed exasperation as he continued, 'We want to know where that money is now.'

'I've no idea,' said George.

Priest jumped up and walked several long paces away, making loud tutting noises. Undeterred, Kirby doggedly pursued his objective, 'What did you do with it when you left Southampton?'

'I took it to London. I couldn't hand it over until Monday when the embassy opened.'

'Which embassy?'

'The South African, I was asked to give it to a Mr Te Pas.'

'And who might he be?'

'I've no idea, I have never laid eyes on him before.'

Kirby could feel the wriggle. Priest stormed back and leaned his fists on the table. 'We want that money and we'll bloody well find it.'

'Why?' said George. 'It's not yours.'

'Oh yes it is! Or rather, it's our duty to ascertain who the real owner is.'

'Then I suggest you go to see Mr Te Pas and he'll put your mind at rest. What I did,' added George, 'was a favour for some people in Johannesburg. I should think England would be pleased with foreign investors prepared to spend money here.'

'If that was straight money it would not be in cash.' Kirby stated the fact. To his mind, any cash was dishonestly come by and, therefore, open to a claim on all of it by His Majesty's Revenue.

'The reason it's in readies, as far as I understand, -and it's not my business to comment really, is that the investors wish to remain anonymous for pretty clear reasons.'

'You don't really think we believe that!' sneered Priest.

'I personally don't care what you believe,' retorted George, seeing more than a fraction of red and controlling it with difficulty.

Kirby spoke again, 'Unless we get a satisfactory answer from…' looking at his notepad, then continuing, '…Mr Te Pas, we may very well hold you responsible for the undeclared tax on that money. Whether you gave it away, which I doubt, or not, technically you were the owner so you're responsible for tax avoidance. We can bring in penalties that can wipe you out for this life and the next.'

The door opened and the lady carried in a tray of refreshments. The two Inspectors amazed Twyford by abruptly stopping work and attacking the victuals in case they missed their share of the biscuits. As she put the tray down, Lily Hall looked away quickly and closed the door behind her, but not before George had caught her eye.

He thought of their duet on his first night back, "Now there's something I can build on,"

Although there was a spare cup and saucer, he was offered nothing and wouldn't have accepted if they had. After the tea break the questions and threats began again but he had decided his strategy and would say little else. He was given forms and indemnities to fill in allowing them the right to search bank accounts and anything that was in his name. They could look up his arse if they wanted, they wouldn't find anything; Naval Security could vouch for that. Priest demanded his passport but, as no mention of it had been made in their correspondence, he had purposely left it at home. Eventually he was allowed to leave and ordered to return in a week for a second 'grilling'. He was directed to another exit but instead made a point of walking back through the waiting room. Only the little bald one was missing, those 'waiting to die' greeted him like a hero. Not wanting to make too much of it, he simply warned to take no notice of the threats,

'They only want your money, the rest is drivel,' and left thinking that it was a funny place to make new friends. Twyford had not fared too badly this time but heaven help anyone who has possessions in their own name. Kirby was a parasite and Priest an animal, even that fell short as a description. "Piranhas, that's what they were! These people could strip a man to the bone in seconds."

It was necessary to ring Grogan to exchange car numbers and monitor each careful step. Donald was that full of beans, he was either feeling cleansed by a deep religious experience or was set for a bout of excessive sex. Twyford gave the licence number 'JLO 751', which was the laundry van the lads frequently borrowed from the bagwash shop in Castle Road. Grogan gave 'UEB 121'. This was the car number little Joey had chalked out on Saturday night and it seemed to answer the questions of who the hell had been following him. Tomorrow, George would call in one hour before the meet and give three possible rendezvous points. Grogan would pick one.

CHAPTER 26: CAGNEY COULD LEARN A LOT…

Netherlands: Anton Mussert, the Dutch Nazi leader, says 150,000 Dutch Jews have been deported to Eastern Europe.

Horace stood back and his eyes did a head count. The pub was beginning to fill already and it was only the second Thursday night that he had put the three piece band on. He'd had sleepless nights over whether it was a waste of money what with Christmas so near, and even the few who earned good wages were spending it on presents. Yes, a big gamble but, as long as he was covering now, when the Loan Clubs paid out it would be as busy as weekends.

Rose watched him and saw his head nodding slightly as he tallied. "Would he ever be satisfied?" she wondered, then the corner door swung in and the professional smile took charge and welcomed the next wave of customers.

It was around eight thirty and a couple of the lads had just finished an incredibly, hectic day collecting for Ruben then helping out at the yard. It had needed every spare pair of hands to make up the orders and the last load had finally left the depot. The others would arrive over the next hour as each 'department' checked stock and closed for the night. Some of the boys had been there since five that morning for the trade was excellent and no one complained about that. It had been a collective decision to meet tonight and finalise everything for tomorrow evening's epic deal, where the fortunes of some of the inhabitants of St Pancras could very well change forever. Lucky was at the bar, flashing his beaming white teeth at them and calling two pints.

'How is it you're always happy?' asked John, who'd forgotten to tell Meg that he'd be late and fully expected when he eventually did get home that dinner would meet him halfway up the path. Lucky just chuckled his infectious, dirty laugh.

'If you had white hair you'd look like a pint of Guinness.' observed Owen. George came in and joined the conversation as Lucky recounted one of his preposterous yarns. Very soon the full compliment was present and correct. It had been an effort for some to shake off the tiredness but a dose of good music lifts everyone's spirits

Mary arrived with the fiddlers and smiled hallo to everyone but her gaze seemed not to reach where George stood. Nero came to the bar and chatted to John and Owen while ordering his round. Twyford had to agree he was quite charming, always knowing the right thing to say. He carried the round of drinks over while his friends tuned up on an accordion and a violin. Leaving Mary to sit alone, they joined the band and Nero took the stage to sing to her.

'Croons well,' said Danny Currie, winking at Owen.

'Yes he does.'

'D'you think so?' Twyford queried with indifference.

'Oh, he's very polished,' agreed John.

'Ask me why I'm such a good performer?' said George, and before John could finish the question he interrupted with, 'Timing.'

It was a quick remark to bring a little humour and it got a few chuckles.

'He should sing professionally,' remarked Lestor, applauding loudly after the first number.

'He ain't that good,' argued George, not willing to appear bitter but unable to keep his mouth shut.

They had him now.

'Good looking fellow,' said Rosie, who had stopped collecting the empties to join in.

'Who him?' queried Twyford, quite aghast. 'You want to collect some proper glasses and wear 'em a bit more!'

'Oh, come on George, you have to admit he's quite a dish.' she continued, 'He's got it all, really.'

'For crying out loud,' said George, looking for support. 'He's got a face like a starting handle!'

Everyone seemed to disagree then Gerry sent him soaring with, 'A proud eagle.'

Stupefaction couldn't describe his expression. 'Proud eagle?!' he repeated loudly to rise above the music which stopped abruptly a second before he yelled, 'A fucking vulture, more like!'

The outburst caused a busy pub to hush and look towards the shout. He stared at the floor and when he raised his eyes saw his friends collapse with merriment.

'You bastards!' he grinned, 'You rotten bastards!'

The lads had drunk far too much and sang most of the way home, crucifying "The White Cliffs of Dover". As always, the plans were left to the last minute and were discussed while they stood having a pee around the back of the bike sheds, before saying good night and splitting up.

Friday morning and the sun was up long before Twyford. A visitor was using the knocker to smash his way into George's brain. He got to the door in slow motion and found a triumphant Benny bouncing about.

'Why don't you get a telephone and save me a bleeding hour getting here?'

He left the technical fastening of the door latch to Ben and glided slowly to the kitchen, trying not to move his head about too much.

'It's on order, but businesses get priority so I've got to wait,' whispered George. Words seemed to club the inside of his dome and the echo ricocheted around it. Benny slammed the door on purpose and bellowed out his good news, 'The deal's safe! I sold three thousand pounds worth for cost, but it means we've got the stake money!'

Twyford smiled and put a finger to his lips; the relief of not having to rush about today was tremendous. Ben quickly recited the collections of the moneys, adding them together as he went along. It was a bad day for George to try and keep up.

Ben could see it wasn't going in so ended his summary with, 'Just leave it to me. Can't stop, people to see, but I'll be here about four this afternoon with the dough. Stay in and lock the door, eh?' As he spoke, he constantly shoved his jacket back from his collar, whilst thrusting his chin forward like a chicken; the perfect Spiv. With shoulders swivelling he ambled out, pulling his jacket together at the waist and holding it between forefinger and thumb.

Before they parted George remarked, 'Cagney could learn a lot from you.'

Benny paused for the imaginary camera to flash then grinned a,'Not many, he could!'

The hangover began to subside and, thinking some fresh air might sweep it clear, Twyford made his way to the paper stand outside the Shipton where Dicky the News was stamping his feet, trying to keep warm. They jawed for a while and George turned homeward studying the pathetic news sheet for anything Dicky might have forgotten to mention.

Timmy Gowan looked down from his bedroom window opposite and thought of Sally. He'd thought of very little else since that marvellous night they were introduced. If he had any courage he'd ask his old friend about her and if George was sincerely courting the lady, then Timmy would put her from his mind. But what if he wasn't serious, say he didn't care? If there was the slightest chance and he'd not known and someone else stole her. He was driving himself mad. She probably wouldn't be interested and yet they were so natural together. And when she looked at him, her eyes captured his attention, held it and made him want to lean forward and kiss her and he imagined Sally responding sensuously. Her hand would find his and rest on her breast... Timmy wasn't fully clothed or he'd ask right now. He hastened to button his braces but would have been quicker with the trousers off. He buttoned the back first, then dropped forward from the waist and flipped them over his shoulders. Catching one he stretched it down to fasten and levelled a swift glance at the paper stand. Twyford was wandering across the road towards home.

'Sod it!' he thought, as it twanged free -then vowed to pose the question at the very next opportunity.

In the warmth of his kitchen, Twyford scanned the rest of the paper then leafed it backwards in case he'd missed anything. God, he was bored or excited, even on that subject he wasn't clear. Needing to be moving no matter where, he decided on a visit to the site. Quickly dressing smartly, he strolled to the top of the street and Timmy Gowan was at the bus stop.

"That's a stroke of luck, he looks to be going in the same direction," thought George. Exactly the same notion crossed Tim's mind as they hailed each other. Timmy watched his friend's approach and saw the bus a good way off. It was then he noticed the old couple behind him, they'd been leaning against the pub wall earlier when Twyford was speaking to Dicky.

Timmy just had long enough to say by way of a greeting, 'You're being followed, old chap.' and the number 24 pulled up.

'Get on, but watch what he does, I'll dwell here.'

Timmytoonice hopped aboard and the bus pulled away. Without glancing around, George sprinted after it, catching up easily as it slowed to cross the lights. The old couple turned with surprising agility and rushed off as Twyford swung into the long seat downstairs, too late to get a good look at his pursuers. Timothy remarked on the coincidence of seeing them behind him earlier and again just then. He described the pair as best he could then inquired why anyone would want to follow him.

'Search me,' said George, and jested, 'Probably Archie in disguise.'

'How's Sally?' asked Tim, as calmly as he could.

'Fine.'

Timmy went suddenly very red. 'I hope you don't mind but can I ask you if you truly care for her?' He knew how stupid it sounded. His heart beat stronger as he waited for the answer but Twyford was so taken aback, he couldn't think of what to say. 'Because I do. I know I have absolutely no right, but I think she's the sweetest, most intelligent, beautiful girl I've ever seen... met...' George opened his mouth to speak but Tim pressed on, 'She may not feel anything for me -and who could blame her? I probably bored the pants off her.' Words were gabbling to get out and override the gut-wrenching reply he expected but didn't want to hear. 'She wouldn't be interested in me, would she.' He made it a flat statement then when Twyford still hadn't answered, versed it as a question, 'Would she? Do you think..?'

George was delighted, he considered that Sally was made for Timothy: plus, he had to admit he felt very little when they actually kissed and also sensed tentacles inching around him. This was kismet, and someone should be cuddling that body on cold nights. Had it been any of the Force that had showed interest he would have said, with panache, 'She's your's; my gift.' They frequently passed girls about. Unfortunately Timmy was a different barrel of beer entirely. 'I reckon you're perfect for her,' he said, 'and I would love to see you two together but I don't think she's the sort of girl who would stand being casually swopped. So, if you want her, you have to do this my way.' Timmy was so happy he would have agreed to anything. Twyford pointed out that the plan might seem a bit slippery. Business had forced him to let her down several times already therefore Timothy could meet her Monday evening, explain that George had been delayed, then take her up Hampstead somewhere, on the pretext of meeting him, and work on her to see how he got on. Mornington Crescent came into view and Twyford readied himself to jump off; the finer details had to be left in the air.

'Knock for me Sunday morning and we'll sort it out,' he called back. Timmy gave him a thumbs up and then reddened again as he realised, by their looks, his fellow passengers had been a party to the whole conversation.

More of the Craven A had been demolished as unsafe brickwork was smashed down. The mad O'Brien was storming around the site, shouting orders and cursing everyone. He greeted George good-naturedly and swung his boot up the arse of a hod carrier who wasn't moving fast enough.

'Is this the Irish way of getting things done?' enquired Twyford, quietly impressed.

The big red neck sung in his Kerry accent, 'If the work is not done to my satisfaction their remunerations remain in my pocket 'til it is! Any gentlemen not liking it can choose to try and take it out of this.' and pointed at his nose.

'How's it coming on?' asked Twyford.

'Well...' and he sucked air through his teeth. George recognised the action as a bad sign, where previous cowboys are blamed for faulty work and the price rises for having to correct it.

'Now pack that up!' said Twyford, before the Irishman could "try it on". 'We've got a deal.'

O'Brien laughed, then spat on his hand and held it out. George did not flinch from what had to be done; he gripped the wet, dirty palm and squeezed firmly, careful not to wipe it afterwards on his suit trousers. As they strolled over the hills of rubble, O'Brien's batman followed with a wheelbarrow full of bricks and tools, stopping when they stopped.

'Will you have a cuppa?' asked O'Brien, patting his hip flask. They entered a basement storeroom that was being used as site office; it was worse than the bombed area. 'Spider!' was all he said, and the batman released the barrow and found three cups. George didn't mean to stare but Spider was worth a second look. He was older, below average height and build, and wore navy dungarees. But his bottom lip was large and mauve and hung down by his chin; the weight of it kept his mouth open. The only time it closed was when he spoke, his lips locked together and clipped words came from a gap on the left side of his face.

"Ugar?' Twyford nodded dumbly and took in the spindly arms which extended someway out of his overalls, dangling the biggest hands of bananas that swung around his knees. Each finger joint was like a pork sausage and a cannon ball could easily be lost in his palm. Dirty great feet kept the whole body in balance and these were contained in enormous wellington boots that must pay ground rent. Spider held the chipped mugs under a tap riddled with algae and rinsed them out with his dusty fingers, muttering to himself as he worked. "Ucking lazy bleeders!' The 'f' lost in the wind and spray, as his mouth made a tunnel up near his left ear. George had this mental picture of Spider, standing like a Cyclops on the white cliffs, lobbing handbricks at the German Navy and shouting, "Uck off, you 'ucking bastards!'

O'Brien added a measure of poteen to the tea. The mixture certainly had a piquancy but Twyford decided against inspecting it for survivors. He sipped and perused the mysteries of life…"What about his birthday, how does he blow the candles out?"

Cups drained and the niceties were over. O'Brien asked, 'First payment next Saturday, roight?'

'That's what we agreed,' said George.

'Lovely man! Spider, back to work!'

Twyford spent ten more minutes around the site; the work was all preparation. Weak walls were being knocked down and damaged concrete ripped out, but it would soon start taking shape. He crossed the road to Ruben's office. Fintan was coming out and gave George a rueful look.

'What's up mate?' asked George.

'Orla slashed her wrists last night.' Twyford screwed his face up and mentally prepared himself for the worst. 'Archie came home late and saw her light on. He found her unconscious in the bath.'

'Will she live?'

'They think she will, if she wants to.'

'Thank God he found her in time.'

'Boss says I can use the car to round everyone up. Do you want to go down there?'

'Yes please, my friend. Let's go.'

She had been taken to the Elizabeth Garrett Anderson on the Euston Road. It was a maternity hospital, but the nearest with plenty of doctors twenty four hours a day.

'This is a good omen,' said George. 'Alan was born there.'

The family had already assembled in the corridor, outside a ward on the top floor and Twyford worried that his presence might not be welcomed. Realising this, Fintan stayed with him and they stopped on the edge of the group. Mary had four sister and two brothers, only Eamon was missing and he was last heard of with the SOE in Northamptonshire somewhere. On the few occasions of a home visit, he'd never spoken of what he was doing; very hush hush. Josie saw them first and came to them, her eyes were red but she was composed and confident. God had seen fit to save Orla. It would all turn out well, she would see to that. The twins, Tess and Kathleen, were in a dreadful state and Archie sat between them with his arms around them both. He noticed Twyford but looked away. Mary waited with Bridgid and four or five cousins George knew but couldn't remember their names. Only one family member at a time had been allowed in to sit with her. The ward door opened and a jubilant Morgan came out. 'She's awake!' he announced, 'And hungry!'

Archie looked to heaven and groaned with relief. He reached the bed first and noted a healthy tinge returning to her complexion. The others filed in behind him and gladly awaited their turn.

'Sorry Daddy!' she sniffed.

The big man's gruff voice said, 'Get well now for me.'

'I promise, Daddy,' she answered, and he stepped back for Josie to fuss over her.

She sat by the bedside and held her hand while the others came in order; Mary, the eldest, Morgan next, the twins and then Bridgid. The relations with Fintan and George came to the other side and grinned down, nodding like village idiots. 'You look funny,' she said, hoarsely, and sobbed, 'I'm sorry to cause all this..' But now the heads shook in unison. They wanted no apologies, only her will to recover.

Twyford relaxed a little and Fintan finally went to Bridgid, leaving him alone. The room was bursting with love, it was so infectious that he lingered to savour it with everyone else. Mary looked across and made her way over. He became the intruder again, wanting to shy away.

'Thanks for coming,' she said, civilly. 'I'm sure Orla will thank you herself once she feels stronger.' Her next words had the effect of a cold shower, 'In the meantime, we would appreciate the least people knowing the better.'

George forced himself not to retaliate. A sigh, full of disdain, relayed so much more.

'I think I'd best be off,' he said and stepped away from her then caught Fintan's eye and mouthed, 'I'm going. See you later.'

Fintan gave a thumbs-up and George left the room.

'That was very unkind, Mary.' She turned to respond to her brother's words but Morgan was already following Twyford out and caught up with him on the stairs, he linked arms and cheerfully suggested a pint. Unlike his sister, he was a very warm person and as this was the first time they had seen each other in four years, George wholeheartedly agreed to join him. Over a drink Morgan relayed what had actually happened. Orla had decided to end it in the bath, so as not to make a mess, and had fallen unconscious through loss of blood. Archie saw the light under the door and checked her. Acting with the speed of lightning his competence definitely saved her life. He bandaged her wrists while she lay there, then wrapped her in thick blankets and ran with her in his arms to the hospital. Through the alleyways of Somers Town, it was probably less than a mile. Had he waited for an ambulance, she would have been dead. Another pint toasted her complete recovery. George apologised for not being able to stay, for he could see Morgan was in the mood for an all-day session and any other time Twyford would have instigated it, but today was so important. They left together and walked towards Josie's house when Fintan pulled alongside with a car full and beckoned them in. Morgan hopped across on laps, but George saw Mary and declined.

'Thanks, but I'm going the opposite way,' he lied.

The car moved out of sight and he corrected his direction and caught a bus home.

CHAPTER 27: AND THERE STOOD A SOLDIER

German raids reveal Allied Mustard gas! Bari, Italy: Frantic attempts are being made to conceal the inclusion in an Allied ship's cargo of a consignment of mustard gas, which is causing the deaths of troops and dock workers alike, after a surprise German air raid here today.

Benny swanned into the kitchen with all the class in the world and fifteen thousand pounds in a creased up, brown, carrier bag, rolled over tightly at the top. The bottom half showed the words 'Co-operative Society'.

'It's all there,' said Ben.

'Are you sure?' asked George.

Ben weighed it on one hand, 'Exactly right,' he confirmed, then flopped into the armchair and made himself at home.

'Couldn't you have put it in a brief case or something?'

'No, course not! Who wants to rob me of an old Co-op bag?' The point had its merits; in the Co-op bag it would remain. Benny, meticulous in all things (he even rolled his fags with a machine), asked for a summing-up. George had gone over this a thousand times in his mind, but once more wouldn't hurt. He, plus three others, would arrive with the money and reverse into the darkest part of whichever car park was picked. The car must be facing outwards.

'Two of us case the area before we switch the engine off, keeping at least ten yards away from their car. Nobody bunches, we space out. Grogan and I meet and leave. The back doors are unlocked, six bags of washing are unloaded and our money will be counted by them in the back of the van, then left there and relocked. We inspect the forgeries in the boot of their car. If acceptable, we take their suitcase and accompany one of them to our van. He takes the carrier bag, we load in the suitcase and cover it with the bagwash. Then leave, sharpish.'

Benny asked questions, adding suggestions. 'Who departs

first? Make sure you do. Don't all exit in the van. Blow one tyre and you're trapped. Take weapons but, if there's any fighting to be done, the one with the money must run. Two of you leave with the van; the others fade away but stay close and watch what Grogan's pals do.'

George nodded, detail was everything. He withdrew and loaded the automatic pistol and polished it with his hanky. It was a beautiful little thing and fondling it gave him a strange pleasure. The name shone up at him - Fabrique Nationale.675 Belgique.

'Let's hope that's not necessary,' remarked Ben, getting his coat.

With at least two hours before he made the phone call to Grogan, Twyford deliberated over the three choices. He would suggest the Spaniards car park which was probably the darkest, the canal mooring area behind the brewery stores in Camley Street and the railway ground circle by Somers Town potato market. The last one would be the quietest because it doesn't come to life until 11pm. But perhaps they didn't want it too quiet; it was their choice.

George washed and soaped up with the shaving brush, stropped the razor and had scraped the right side of his face to a shiny pink. He was just about to attack the left when the knocker crashed down so loudly, he inadvertently nicked a chunk from his chin. He stared in the mirror, willing the flesh not to bleed. Min went to open the door and he heard her gasp, 'Oh, my God!' Then quieter, 'Oh Lord, no!'

The gash, which had waited until he looked away, released a tidal wave of blood that burst forth and cascaded down like Niagara. He held a towel over it and rummaged for a plaster whilst calling, 'Who is it, Mum?' then moaned at his dripping chin, 'Poxy nuisance!'

'Oh George, come and see!'

He couldn't tell if she was happy or upset so, with more concern, came downstairs. The visitor had settled in the kitchen determining that it couldn't be anything too bad. He opened the door and a dozen different reactions shook him rigid. There stood a soldier; a handsome young man in uniform, and George wanted to cry. Speech wasn't possible yet. He stared at his son. Whatever had possessed him to join up? The right words were essential. His brain screamed caution.

'Kevin!' he faltered.., 'your forage cap's on wrong. Tilt it to the right, that's it.'

Kevin was excited and George could see he was impatient to share it with his Dad.

"Oh Lord, what could he say?" Thoughts raced past; "He can't go to war. The Germans would try and kill him. He's a baby, he's too young! He must have lied to the draft board. I can get him out of it, he's only sixteen. I can prove it to them."

His mind searched for keys, trying all the doors, looking for a way out, while his face belied it all. His expression tried to mirror the pride that was stirring strongly inside him, knowing it was what Kevin wanted to see. But a smile couldn't mask the uncertainty he felt and adding it to the hardly disguisable nagging fear, he was left with the bemused look of a half-wit.

'I was struck at how much you look like Grandad Graham,' said Min. 'It's the uniform, of course,' she said to George, sniffing, 'He's so like your Dad.'

George could only nod like an idiot (he was getting good at that) and strained to stop a wet eye from smarting. 'Have you seen your mother?'

'No Dad, I thought I'd show you first.' Twyford shuddered at what she would say. Kevin did not notice; he was living his dream. 'I wanted to join up ages ago but there was no one to look after the family; now you're back I can go and do my bit for King and country.'

'Don't say that to Mary, please,' said George, bewildered at where to begin.

'Dad, I know you're a bit shocked but don't worry, I'll come back safe. Everybody's volunteering.'

'How did you get in boy, you're only sixteen?'

'Oh, they need more young men; I told them I was seventeen. They don't ask too many questions, they know right enough.'

'Oh, of course they do.' said George, then warned, 'You do realise why more men are needed?' He left it in the air, then followed on with, "Cos the others didn't make it.'

Kevin agreed but didn't seem to care. Twyford's biggest worry now was not that he'd go - his course was set - it was that he'd go with the wrong ideas. In George's experience, the only ones that got through understood the dangers and were aware. Soldiers are taught not to think and the kids that follow the flag regardless are used as cannon fodder. He approached the debate, that had to be said and listened to, in slippers, no stomping over the boy's "current" ideals. Hopefully he would get it all fermenting before Mary could use her hobnailed boots.

'What regiment takes you at seventeen, Kev?' asked George, with controlled curiosity.

'The 58th at Bovingdon; it's an armoured training division. My grammar school certificate got me accepted; some of the lads there went to public school. The Sergeant said I could be officer material.' He threw that in with casual scepticism but George could see that statement had hooked him. It would be difficult to cool his spirits while he was this fired up.

'This is the biggest decision a man can ever make because your life's at risk. Should you be lucky enough to come back, what you do there will stay with you for the rest of your natural. If you kill another human being or be responsible for a friend's death, it'll haunt you! I knew a brave man once who deserted because his grenade fell short and killed our own! You have to live with all your actions. Very few soldiers look in the mirror and see a hero. It's great when you're marching off to war, the drums are beating step and the pipes lead you on to glory, there's no feeling like it. But when you're lying in a crater half full of water and mortar bombs are exploding all around, ripping your friends into little pieces, it seems like the end of the world has come; then you know fear and believe me, there's no atheists in a bunker!' Kevin looked at his Dad and could see he had a lot to confide, the youngster had never known him to be this passionate about anything before. George carried on with a story, 'At Passchendaele it rained without stopping for four days, the stupid bastards sent us marching into valleys made of mud and, as it rained, the mud slid down and bogged all around us until we were wading chest high in it. The gas bombs come over and fell in our midst. You couldn't run, you were stuck in it and I saw friends slide beneath trying, too late, to get their masks on; more died by drowning than bullets that day.'

Kevin smiled, 'Dad, I know you're saying all this to put me off, but you're not going to convince me. You were a hero, they gave you a medal.'

'Son, believe me, that was temporary madness and we were lucky. I wasn't trying to scare you, I love you and I want you to come back safe and sound BUT there's no need to throw your life away attempting valiant deeds of derring-do. This ain't like playing runouts in the streets. You get no second chance in war. Your mates can't tap you on the arm and up you get to play soldier again; one bullet and Ting Tang Tommy's over for good.'

'I know that Dad. I'm young but I'm not stupid.'

George had hurt him now and tried to reconcile his words. 'Kevin, you're anything but stupid and I'm so proud of you that I'm the one frightened. We left too many in far flung corners of foreign fields the last time around.'

Kevin tried to explain, 'But I want to be like you. I think I'm brave and I'll earn a medal of honour if I can, then I can tell people about my Dad. For all the heroes I've read about, you're a real life one.'

George had to get up and leave him sitting there while he walked up the passage and opened the door. It gave him time to blow his nose and clear his eyes. 'There's no one there,' he said to Min sitting back down. 'I could have sworn I heard a knock.' Then he looked at Kevin's beautiful, young, open face and gave him his last bit of advice, 'You will make new friends and stick together, but not all of them will have your wherewithal. Remember, officers are unapproachable and your lives won't be their first priority, so the boys will become your responsibility and they'll look to you for guidance. The usual pattern is that orders for the next day arrive in the evening. Show interest in them, let your superiors see initiative; they'll lap you up! Then make your own plans 'cos you ain't gonna win the war on your own! Study the area you're advancing in to. If they come unstuck you'll know, better than anyone else, -the way out! If it's a retreat, don't be the rear guard. Don't volunteer for anything and always keep on the right side of your Sergeant; he holds your life in the palm of his hand. You're going to be a soldier, train hard and be a good one -and always look out for your mates.' ("That way," thought George, "You might be more careful yourself.") He studied the clock on the mantelpiece; it looked really classy encased in dark wood but kept terrible time.

'Have you wound that up, Mum?'

'Yes, that's exactly right.'

She would not have anything said against it, his Dad had brought it back from somewhere. If it was right he had a couple of hours before he had to ring Grogan.

'I think we should go and face your mother, Kev.'

Kevin grinned and nodded. Father and son crossed the gardens, guided most of the way by the light from Mary's kitchen window. She had company, Nell Higby, Nero and second string, the foursome were going out together and Mary was 'dressed to tempt!' They could see in, but could not be seen and so arranged that George would enter first to prepare her then shortly afterwards Kevin would appear. Yearning to be anywhere else he went through the back door, mounted the three stairs to the kitchen and knocked gently.

Mary's voice rang out, 'Come in.'

Noting the bored tone that said she knew who it was, he stepped inside.

'It's only me,' he said and thought his phraseology was almost an apology for existing. 'Could I have a word?' he asked nicely.

'We're on our way out so can you make it snappy.'

'Not really!' he said with overemphasised patience. The trio of guests seemed to enjoy the discourse. George had their attention, 'It's about our son so it might be better in private.'

Three heads moved for her reply. 'Giving your school Ma'am trouble again, is he?'

'Wrong son.'

The Wimbledon crowd looked to see Mary receive his block. The backhand returned, 'He can look after himself.'

'I hope so,' said Twyford, guardedly.

She stopped talking and George won the point. '15 – Love,' said Nero.

Bells of alarm sounded in a mother's head, 'What's happened?' she asked, warily.

'I'll let him tell you himself.' George raised an arm and Kevin came up the few stairs. The boots sounded like a battalion. When he marched through the door she went ghostly white and held her stomach. Twyford looked out into the darkness, he did not want to witness this, but still saw the reflection in the window panes.

'Hello Mum, what do you think?'

'Oh, my God! My God, sweet Jesus, what have you done?'

'Mum, I'm a soldier,' he said firmly.

'You're a child!' she shrieked. 'Take it off!' She looked slowly from face to face silently appealing for help but there was none. Nell stepped forward and held her in case she fell. She began to wail like a dying banshee and her legs weakened to a crouch. Kevin tried to cuddle her but she stared passed him at

George and sucked strength from her hatred. The words came through bared teeth, 'This is all your idea to take him away from me.'

He shook his head sadly, 'I've tried to talk to him but his mind's made up.'

'Come on, Mum,' said Kevin, persisting with the gentler approach. 'I'll be training for months before I go overseas.'

She only took in the last words, 'Overseas? To War?' Her wide eyes had remained burning into George. 'You knew this and you said nothing.'

'I've only just found out ten minutes ago.'

'Liar!' she screamed.

George looked at his son, 'Tell her please. You know she's not all there sometimes.'

Kevin spoke the words, but she was only talking to one person, 'And who drove me mad? You, with your frigging lies: leaving your children, starving them!'

'You need a psychiatrist, you're a raving lunatic!'

Kevin was getting no response from his mother so he explained to the others, who all answered at once, trying to find the right phrases to calm the situation while Mary and George yelled at each other, things that should have remained locked in the past.

'You deceitful swine! You've brought nothing but trouble on this house. You made him join the army. You wicked, blackhearted devil!'

'It's my fault, is it? It's always my fault!' George was losing his logic along with her. 'You drove him out, you drive everyone away!'

Nell put herself in front of George and attempted to soothe his end of the quarrel.

Kevin held his mother's wrists to get her attention and explained that the decision was his own. The other two milled around generally in the middle but the altercation was plummeting downhill at great speed. Accusations and misdeeds that had festered in two tormented minds for four years were hurled about.

She questioned her hearing, 'I drove you away?' The mad look of the Shaw's was coming into her eyes. 'Liar!' she screamed again. 'You abandoned us like the selfish cur you are!' Kites can be reeled back in, flying words cannot, and the secret Twyford never wanted known, all the pain and betrayal spewed out. Everyone including Kevin caught part of it.

'I would never have deserted this family,' then in a rage, 'What about the photo, you treacherous whore?' He froze momentarily at his own utterance. With another wail she ran from the room, knowing he would follow her. On her bedside table was a large pair of tailoring scissors, she would lure him in and stab him a thousand times; with no witnesses it would be self-defence. George came to life and dashed after her. Alan, keeping out of the way, was playing football along the passage when they charged at him. He knocked the ball against the opposite wall, avoiding their feet, trapped it on the rebound and dribbled on. Mairead and Niamh flattened themselves against the banisters as they flew past them up the stairs. Mary ran in the bedroom and shoved the door on him, but his body barged it open. He stood there and a hushed insanity embraced him. He would kill her; one powerful right-hander on the chin would rid him of her for good. He watched as she darted towards the bedside table and came back at him with a giant pair of scissors. She dived forward, straight-armed, to spear his Adams apple. His wrist swatted her arm up with scorn. The points drew blood as they skimmed his cheek, but he hardly felt a thing. She tried again with a downward stab at his heart, but he swung his arm in a great back-handed blow that knocked her across the bed and the blades from her grasp. He fell on her as she struggled against his weight. Only her head was free and she strained with all her strength to bite his bleeding face. He saw the viciousness in her eyes: her sharp, white teeth. And, he saw the lips, cherry red lips, full and shapely. Before he knew it, he was sucking them hungrily. She wrestled and fought against him but he held her fast. After what seemed like a long time, he desisted and rolled off the uninhabited body beneath him. Her mouth was open and limp and he felt disgusted with himself, forcibly embracing that witch of all people. God, what had he done? He stood up and, whilst she lay in the same deathly still position, feebly half offered a hand; she recoiled from it as if he might yet strike her.

'Sorry,' he said hopelessly.

'Get out!' she spat. 'Don't you *ever* touch me again.'

He shook his head in disbelief at what he had done and withdrew from the room.

Kevin sat on the stairs and had been listening to them. Twyford trudged down to the street door stroking his son's hair as he passed by. Kevin grinned to himself, and the smile that appeared was a replica of his father's. George arranged to drive him down to Bovingdon and have him there for nine o'clock Monday morning; but for now he had a phone call to make.

He knew to obey her; one wrong word and the "therapy" could be revoked, again. The lashing had delivered him wholly into the treatment and the cultured pain was singing through his body like the echoing twang of taut piano strings.

'No more for now,' snapped the Donna Laura.

'Please!'

'How do you address me?' she demanded.

'Mistress. Please, Mistress,' he pleaded.

She thrived on his need. 'I said no!' Spoken hard and sharp.

'Please, Mistress!' he repeated.

'Didn't you hear me?' He detected no weakness in her tone and could not hold in his panic. 'Beg me,' she ordered, jerking his head up by the black linen mask. ' Or shall I call ..*him*..?'

'No! No!' he cried, then, 'Please, please Mistress. I beg

you…please!'

He hung on to the last word in anticipation and waited. Two...three...four seconds.

He was at the pinnacle of his craving. 'Mendoza!' she yelled.

'No!' he cried, then, 'Now! now!' And she thrashed the cat of nine tails cruelly across his back, directing her aim to the red weals already proud and burning. With a shriek of detonated release and a deep gasp, Donald crumpled over the desk he was strapped to. She walked from the room to change, leaving him to recover. He always needed a while to savour the descent to normality.

The Spanish lady undressed and hung up the uniform. When she returned she wore an elegant short, black, collarless jacket, pencil skirt and a plain, bright red, silk blouse. She unbuckled the straps on his wrists and he remained still until she untied the cord at the back of his neck and freed his face. The mask and straps were put in the desk but the whip was left out. It was her comfort. She enjoyed its presence and often fondled it without thinking.

At the hall mirror she studied her reflection intently then slipped on a lavishly, expensive mink coat and, with care, placed a mantilla on her head. As she made to leave she called back, 'See yourself out, I'm late for Benediction.'

Fintan was driving the laundry van and George sat next to him, Danny Currie and Frank Nash sprawled on the bagwash in the back. They parked beside two telephone boxes outside Chalk Farm tube station. Twyford looked at his watch for the umpteenth time then readied himself. The station clock reached nine. He walked across and loaded 2d (tuppence) into the box and dialled the number. The other end answered and George pressed button 'A'.

Grogan chuckled down the line, 'A phone box! Don't worry, Georgie, you'll be able to afford your own exchange soon.'

"The bastard's calm," thought Twyford and tried to respond

similarly. 'Let's see, where can we meet?' He was wary because bored operators occasionally listened in but gave the three suggestions and asked if Donald could get to another phone. The answer was positive, and he passed over the new number. The telephone in the next box rang two minutes later. 'That was lively,' said George, answering immediately.

Grogan chuckled again. 'Ease down, Georgie, it's all sweet. See you in the Spaniards.' The line clicked off.

Fintan drove straight to the old Inn early and dropped off Frank and Danny with half an hour to spare. The van would return after the Jocks had parked, insuring they could be at least ten yards apart. The area was surrounded by woodland. Grogan arrived right on time in a huge, black Austin Princess and parked amongst several other vehicles, the lights were turned off and the four Scotsmen remained in the car. Danny watched them for a couple of minutes but they made no move to alight. He stayed hidden and circled back to Frank Nash, who was concealed on the other side. The two emerged from the undergrowth further along Spaniards Lane and waited outside the pub. 'Castle Laundry' pulled up and they advised Fintan of exactly where to park, then walked in behind the van and stood either side of it. The interior light of the Princess came on as the Jocks stepped out. Torches were flashed twice and Donald led them over. They shook hands and Grogan asked with amusement, 'Is this really necessary, Georgie?'

'Trust me,' said Twyford.

Donald shone a torch on his vehicle.'A laundry van! You're unbelievable.'

'There's a lot more chance of you being stopped in that flashy brothel. This van's always seen delivering around here.' Grogan nodded in admiration. 'Let's give you another laugh. The money's in the back in an old co-op carrier bag, under six bagwash.'

'Are you serious?'

'Take a look', suggested George.

Just then, a spring from one of the parked cars emitted a loud ping. Frank and Danny shone their torches and bathed it in light. A pair of heads popped up in unison and the car creaked again. Two of the Jocks, with incredible reactions, raced over and wrenched the doors open, each pulling a half-dressed occupant out and banging them on the ground. The torchlight showed a frightened man, who beseeched them to let him go, and a prostitute, who had no intention of being pushed around,even if she had been nicked, 'Oi! Get your hands of me, we're married!' then became saucier when she realised they were not of an arresting nature. 'Piss off and leave us alone!' she yelled. 'What are you up to anyway? I'll call a copper. Pulling decent people about…'

A clump across the mouth soon silenced the lady and terrified her 'husband', who tried to offer them money. A big hand threw him on the car seat and she was shoved in the other door.

'Dress yourselves and be away. Now!' The last word was pronounced 'noo' and roared out. Hubby started the car and sped off. A torch beam followed them out and saw the lady raise two fingers on either hand. The men relaxed and seeing the funny side one Scotsman remarked, 'With endearing qualities like that, I can see why he married her!'

As arranged, the bagwash were unloaded and, apart from the spare wheel which was bolted to the wall of the van, all that remained was a rolled-up carrier bag. Donald and George walked to the pub and Fintan stood by as the money was checked, while the other four spread out through the wide area. Customers that drove in were directed to the south end of the car park. Once counted and agreed, the money was placed back in the carrier bag and locked in the van then Fintan joined Frank and crossed to the Austin. The boot was opened, showing not one but three suitcases. Two were lifted out and the third was unlocked. A heavy dressing gown was taken from the top of the case, revealing a vision of loveliness. More money than had ever been imagined smiled back at them. They emptied it out into the boot and with haste, took ten bundles each and counted them out. Every one had fifty notes. The lads stacked them back four to a thousand, ten high. The cases were checked in the same way and although one only contained a hundred 'thou.' and two dressing gowns, collectively they were correct; half a million in forgeries.

A Scotsman came to the window of the pub and beckoned Donald and George. They drained their glasses and walked to the door, Grogan leading. Twyford felt the comfort of the automatic pistol in his right overcoat pocket. The three suitcases had been placed outside the van and as Fintan unlocked the back door Grogan himself reached in and pulled out the carrier bag. His checker gave a slight nod and he wheeled off to his car. The Jocks backed away behind him, the Princess revved into life and they were gone. Cases were flung in and hurriedly covered with bagwash, the lads had not anticipated Donald's speedy exit and were now concerned that a tartan army might at any moment come out of the trees. While Fintan drove out George withdrew the automatic in readiness and held it in his lap, covering it with his other arm. Danny and Frank ran alongside, looking in all directions, until the van was clear of the car park and gone. No one pursued them and the two relaxed somewhat, they had one telephone call to make and then could enjoy a well-deserved pint.

Roy and Benny sat in the cab of a flatback lorry outside Chalk Farm.

'Couldn't you get a decent car?' scowled Ben. 'I look a right ponce sitting here among the oil cans in my Sunday best!' then reflected, 'Why do the insides of lorries always stink to high heaven?'

"Cos some people, unlike you, have to work and sweat for a living.'

'Yeah, but this is unwashed armpits and its making me want to throw up.'

'Perhaps this might help,' said Roy, lifting the left cheek of his arse and letting rip with a loud fart.

'Oh thanks!' said Benny, flipping the hanky from his top pocket and holding it to his nose. 'That's much better!'

'Don't mention it, cousin. Only too pleased ..' The reply was made with some satisfaction.

The telephone rang and Roy dropped softly from the lorry to answer the call. Athletes Foot had kept him out of the army and his 'plates' were still very tender, which was why he wore a pair of moth-eaten brown check, bedroom slippers. Ben watched him waddle along the pavement. Their family ties were very close and they loved one another dearly but, as opposites, took the rise out of each other at any opportunity. This particular night Roy was dressed in a pair of flannels that did not quite meet around the waist, his Dad's elastic snake belt kept them hoisted up. A frayed blue shirt was without the detachable collar and over this he had an off-the-shoulder and opened brass-buttoned railway waistcoat that also didn't go the distance. The ensemble was rounded off with a green cardigan, knitted by his Mum years before, complete with smart gaping elbow ventilation. He prided himself in his appearance and always carried a comb, with half its teeth missing, in his cardigan pocket.

As he raised the phone from its cradle, Benny shouted, 'If that's the palace, tell them to leave the pickled herrings out and we're on our way.'

Roy gave him a weary look and said into the mouthpiece, 'Grease-proof.' He listened for a moment and replaced the handset then pressed button B, just in case he could get any money back. Benny had wound down the window and with the aid of extra large nostrils was depleting St. pancras of oxygen.

'We're to meet George at the yard,' said Roy, climbing back in. During the drive through the side streets of Kentish Town, Roy lifted his cheek and fired off another round that fair ripped the air.

'Will you stop aiming them at me!' demanded Ben, winding down the window again, 'You'll wilt my carnation.' Then, with his head outside the cab, enquired, 'You'll have this money shortly; I hope you spend it wisely.'

'Tentatively, I've sold tractors to the Irish.'

'Tell me?'

'Combine harvesters I've bought, and self-propelled threshers. I've given nothing for them. With cash they're so cheap.'

'And how will you get them delivered?'

'I'll drive them of course.'

'They only go at about ten miles an hour; it'll take you weeks.'

'So, for the money I should complain?'

'True,' said Ben. Even sitting down, he pushed his lapels back. 'What's the matter with you, anyway, you've been miserable all night?'

'My best customer died today,' said Roy mournfully.

Ben felt his pain, 'I'm sorry to hear that. Who was he?'

'I should tell you my best customer?' They both laughed and Roy turned into the coal wharf.

Fintan held the gate open for them to drive straight in then locked it behind him and remained there. George came from the office, 'Come and give your eyes a treat!'

The sharp little Spiv and the big cuddly scruff stepped inside and stared. Three cases were opened on the floor, the dressing gowns had been removed and there neatly majestic was a King's ransom and the end of all worries.

'My quest nears fulfilment,' stated Ben, quite poetically.

Roy was agog, 'It's like a dream. I've seen nothing so beautiful.'

Ben remarked, 'Shame it's not real,'

'You're never satisfied!' said George. 'It still represents a first-class ticket upwards in the world. I'm just happy we got it back here safely; Grogan is a devious, artful bastard but far worse than that -he's the most dangerous man I've ever come across All at once Ben was business-like again and in a hurry. Twyford saw his agitation and said, 'Take that one. It holds two hundred thousand but don't release any until we've got the second arrival.'

Ben nodded, closed the suitcase, shook hands with George and left. Roy would take twenty five percent, the rest Ben would use. It was decided that Fintan must look after the second two hundred thousand and George could mind the lesser amount. Once Bones and Steve had fifty each, one case would be cleared and one batch of seeds sown. The overall deal was already a winner. Even if one operation came unstuck, which was highly unlikely, the success of the other results made it infallible. The minute the notes changed hands, each scheme became unconnected.

Fintan secured the yard from inside then joined Twyford for a large Irish whiskey in the office. They sat looking at the money and kept their own thoughts. After a while the Irishman observed, 'We can do an awful lot of good with this, and I don't just mean for us.'

'Yes, I was thinking exactly that,' said George. 'If you saw those poor sods in that Township, you'd give it all to them. This way I'll be able to send out money and medicines every month and it will be seen to have been donated from the Catholic Church. You'd like Father Colm, if ever there was a renegade... I know he spent some time with the Foreign Legion and God knows what he was up to before he joined the church but, if those shady Casbah cutthroats were anything to go by, I'd lay money he's got secrets to make your pubics spike. I arranged an English doctor and nurse to move out there and stay with him. They must be arriving soon and hopefully should make an enormous difference, working purely for our Township.'

Fintan refilled the glasses and didn't miss the 'our'. 'What about the girl? Who is she?'

'I hoped you might have forgotten her.'

'Some chance!' laughed Fintan. He had picked the time well and could see his friend was in the mood for confessions.

'Her name was Malla and she was the daughter of the head man, Captain Bligh. Colm had read them several books and 'Mutiny on the Bounty' was his favourite. He understood English well enough but spoke a sort of pigeon. When he used to introduce himself, he would say, 'Captain Bly - me'. So, I nicknamed him 'Cor Blimey'. He was saying it in the right context too, before I had to leave. It was imprisonment for white people if they were caught having sex with Negroes but, quite outrageously, she chose me and who was I to refuse a lady? No whites ventured near the Townships after dark, that's when I used to visit her. We stole many tender nights together. Giving me pleasure seemed to please her.'

'Never got a headache?' enquired Fintan jokingly.

George continued with the verbal portrait, 'Her looks would tempt a saint. I think sex always has more bite when it's forbidden and the danger of getting caught builds the excitement.'

'What really happened to bring it all to a head?'

'An overseer was murdered, and murder it was, even thought he deserved it.' George said flatly. 'He was a very, nasty man, not just a bully. I thought quite a few of the white staff were mentally twisted, but he was probably the worst one. He used his position to terrify the workers. He'd treat the men with contempt and degrade them in front of their women, then maul and manhandle the women on the pretence of searching them. Filth would roll from his mouth while he abused them. Built like a bull; he was one of the vilest men I have ever come across, barbaric and depraved. Anyway, perhaps it was lucky I was there that night. He arrived at the Kraal very late. I was asleep on Malla and kept me' head down. He was going off on a hunt and had come to collect beaters. The trouble was he'd been drinking and flayed a few of them who declined his offer of work. He would have got away with that, but he took a fancy to a young, teenage girl, who was promised to Malla's brother and had gathered with her family to see what all the noise was about. He threatened the parents away then dragged her by the hair into a hut. The brother grabbed a machete and ran in after him; some of his friends found their courage and went in too; they hacked him to death. By the time I got there he was in a terrible, bloody mess, my God he was! When it calmed down, a group of us took him out in the bush and secured his horse, then left him for the beasts. Pretty soon hyenas found him, they scent the fresh blood, see? Anyway, they feasted on Will'm for a bit until the cleaved flesh was gored away and we shot one, frightened the others away, and brought what was left of the two carcasses back.'

'Was that a believable story?'

'Oh yes, hyenas are vicious bastards, they'll attack anything if they're hungry enough and bagging game was the normal pastime. Every weekend I spent with Malla, my colleagues at work believed me to be hunting. My story was that we were tracking together and split up. I heard no sound and only knew when the beaters called me to the body. They killed one of the wild dogs but it was too late for Will'm, that was his name, Willyam van Lancer. I told our bosses that he'd been drinking and, aware of his habits as they were, everyone believed it, except one detective named Kruideneer. He began to haunt me with questions so, considering what was best for the Township *and* me, I decided to disappear. The idea being that my absence would direct suspicion to me and save the Kraal from some pretty terrible retribution.'

Fintan loved a happy ending and said, 'So the jewels were your just reward?'

'Not quite,' answered George. 'I think old 'Cor-Blimey' was beginning to trust me and would have suggested a partnership. He had the stones but no one who could get a decent value for them. If you think of it like that, the incident, so unconnected, half way across the world, actually paid for all this,' and the arc of his arm swept over the suitcases.

Fintan heard a noise and swiftly turned the light out. George closed the suitcases and concealed them with the heap of dressing gowns.

'It's sweet,' Lestor Hogg's voice whispered clearly. 'It's only us night larks.'

Johnny Bass and Owen Esterbrook were with him. The lights went back on and when they were inside, Twyford said, 'Hey Presto!' and whipped away the robes.

The suitcases were opened and their eyes met Grogan's masterpieces.

'Forget Mickey Angelo,' said Les, 'I'm gonna paper my ceiling with these.'

After the compulsory ceremony of touching and flicking the notes, they relaxed and passed the drinks around.

'George has just told me some of the Karinna story, and I'm afraid he's gonna have to repeat it for you.'

Without complaining, he ran through it again having fully decided that they should be informed of everything. When the South African saga was eventually finished, he began to mellow and suggested having one more drink before locking up. Fintan refilled the glasses while Twyford stood and paced around the room, holding his drink.

'If this goes wrong, and I don't see there's any reason why it should but, just in case, every one of you has more to lose than me.' The boys didn't comment either way and George continued, 'Let's have an understanding now, all the blame gets loaded on me.' Fintan began to argue. 'No, no!' said George. 'It has to be this way. Don't worry, you lot aren't getting off lightly. If I go down, or if I get the chance to go on the trot, the responsibilities I carry get lumped on to you. Not just my family, and there's enough of them, but there's the Township and Malla. By the way, she's carrying my baby so there's another Twyford to look after. I'm also responsible for Ivy Nolan and her fiancé being out there; they've all got to be taken care of. I think these counterfeit beauties are gonna make us fabulously spoilt for the rest of our lives, but remember what we've amassed that can't be touched. We've got fifty percent of Ruben's business, seven properties of our own and, most of all, this highly profitable trading company here. So, as long as you're careful, the future looks safe.'

It was Lestor's turn, this time, to rise. 'George, I struggle to understand you sometimes. This is the best touch we've ever had and you talk of prison! Once these notes are spread it can't fail, you know that. For every note that gets spent, three shillings becomes a fiver. A pint of beer becomes a week's wages. I'll tell you what, we'll buy Hampstead Heath, build a wall round it and all live inside in big mansions.'

'Yeah, yeah!' they cried. It inspired the room to a final toast.

'Gentlemen,' said Lestor, 'Health, wealth and fantastic sex!'

His self-assurance was immense –but controlled. He set the meets and the play and players –all under his control. No-one called him to task, he was the Asset. He sold people for money, and lots of it. Friends and acquaintances had their moments and, with no conscience whatsoever, he priced each job accordingly. They went down, he got richer; money was his euphoria. Realistically, and with much less strain, he was about to make himself very wealthy indeed. Something of consequence was beginning, all the signs were there. People with plenty to say were a little less vocal, jokes weren't quite so loud and heads went down during conversations when an acquaintance might stop for a word. The eyes gave them away and alcohol will always loosen tongues. He now knew who and patience would deliver what.

CHAPTER 28: 'GOOD CHIPPERS, ARE THEY?'

China: Japanese aircraft raid Kunming as a strategy to weaken the Allies prior to an attack on India.

New Britain: Japanese forces moving against the Arawe beach head reach the Pulie river, east of Arawe.

Saturday morning and Twyford awoke with a wonderful feeling, everything was looking better. "Tonight you will be making love to Radna." She had filled his thoughts a great deal since last week. The lady was a prize; he could do a lot worse than to make a future with her. He stretched and daydreamed; his schemes were forming patterns and taking shape. Next week would be the big one and, learning from the first change-over, his plan was to keep it very similar but, perhaps, just a little tighter.

Sally would be one of those annoying missed opportunities that frequently haunt the memory, nevertheless he could not wish Timothy a better bed warmer. Benny, Steve, Bones, whoever he thought of, gave him the same glow. The only real worry was Kevin and before dropping him off in Devon, he would fill his son with as much advice as possible and pray to God it was enough to keep him safe.

Mary flashed into his brain like an advancing thunderstorm, all broody and threatening. Two of his friends popped up in his contemplations and, like switching on the sun, she evaporated. He considered John and Mickey and how, until now, he had concealed their presence from Grogan. Donald had been as good as his word, so far, but all that heavy behaviour irritated George. He thinks like a bully so perhaps tonight might be the time to give his two pals an airing. Grogan hated them both but he was also wary of them, either one would have volunteered for the firing squad had Grogan been the target. He stuck that particular piece of bubble gum under the table for now and would savour its flavour again later.

Alan was at the kitchen table when Twyford came down for breakfast. He sat in the armchair and pulled the lad into his arms, they liked having a cuddle together. He was an affectionate boy and George was pleased about that. 'I've been listening to Lord Haw Haw again, he mentioned us,' he stated, proudly. 'He said "Even buggy Litcham Street will fall under the might of the great German army." '

'Fancy that? Round the corner's near enough to be us,' said George. 'Where are you off to today, Al?'

'Saturday morning flicks; I'll have to go in a minute.'

'Has your mother seen you all right?'

'No, that Richard's there again. So I came over here for my breakfast.'

'Did he stay the night then?' asked Twyford, keeping his voice toneless.

'I don't know,' said Alan. 'They made me go to bed early.'

George moved him onto one leg and dug his hand deep into his pocket, pulling out some change.

'Thanks Dad!' he said, gratefully. George ruffled his hair and he went out counting the coins.

Lestor Hogg drove the car down the Square with Tinker riding shotgun. Twyford came out and got in the back. 'How come you got the day off?' he laughed. 'Good behaviour?'

'Nah, my understudy's in charge,' said Lestor. 'And I must say Gerry's doing a first class job with the paperwork. He can't lift anything yet so he suggested doing the stocks. Some people run a mile from a bit of responsibility but not him, he excels at it. I'm well pleased!'

'What about you, Tink, this must be luxury for you? Still, once we get a brand new lorry, then maybe we should all eat that nag of yours.' His wife's pet name was 'Ginger' too, so the legpullers often teased him with double meaning comparisons but today Tinker couldn't be drawn, he was too worried about Sergeant Shaw. Archie had called on Ginger (the wife) twice and left messages for him to go to the police station.

'What am I gonna do?' he asked.

'Keep right out of the way for a week or two,' said George, 'soon we'll sort you out a proper job with cards and everything. Then, just deny any knowledge of anything he asks you and refuse to speak without a solicitor.'

'I don't think I've got the guts. Can you imagine saying that to his face? He won't have to kill me; just a look from them eyes and my heart would give out. Feel my forehead, just talking about him and I'm sweating!'

George could only waffle, 'I'll have a word with Roy and between all of us we can cover you; trust me. Now, how do we get to the Sherman's base?' Tinker directed Lestor and they were soon out of London and driving down bright country lanes. Bones would be waiting to take the money from them and with each mile, the future grew rosier. They had passed very little traffic when suddenly bells were clanging. Lestor had been driving much too fast and looked in his mirror to see a black police car surge up behind them. They came alive and George made the decision, 'Lose them!' Lestor dropped down to third and stamped the accelerator to the floor. He swung around a long blind curve, speeding up all the time, then hit the brakes, skidding off the lane and across the grass verge outside some sort of farm. Had he not, they would have all died, for in their path was an enormous tractor attempting to pull a hay trailer clear of a muddy field. George wound his window down in a futile effort to wave the police on. The squad car halted behind them, blocking their exit, and sat there. A furious farmer came out, shouting about mad bastards trying to kill his geese and churning up his lawn. The tractor driver jumped down and while opening and closing his mouth like a goldfish, gestured wildly, waving his arms in Suffolk sign-language. Everyone got out of the cars and George explained to the tractor driver how they had thought the police were trying to pass them in an emergency. Tinker commiserated with the farmer over his lawn, whilst two large ruddy-faced policemen came either side of Lestor

Hogg. They looked like father and son.

The elder one jotted down the licence number in his notebook and asked, 'Is this your car?'

'Yes, well it's owned by the department. I'm in charge of it.' said Lestor helpfully.

'Would you mind opening the boot?'

Twyford edged closer to the younger officer whilst still talking to the tractor driver. Lestor fiddled with the keys and tried the wrong one. The Bobbies waited while he tested another. George had now worked his way into a position to the right of the target and readied himself to swing a punch into his solar plexus, which should incapacitate him long enough thus making it easier to deal with the other one. The boot opened and the solitary suitcase was its only occupant.

'Going on holiday are we?'

'No.' said Lestor and added, 'my wife ran off with a copper, years ago.'

'Why did you accelerate when you saw us?' asked the younger one, deadly serious.

'I thought you was him bringing her back.'

It was unexpected and brought forth real mirth that made them nearly normal.

'Can you tell us why you were driving so fast?' It was asked in a much lighter vein.

'We have a very important meeting at the American air base,' said Lestor gravely.

'Oh,' said the officer, nosing for details.

'I'm sorry but security forbids me to tell you more than that.'

George used this moment to close the boot, covering his action with, 'Not a good idea to let everyone see that we're carrying a suitcase.'

'Perhaps you can tell us what's in it, sir?'

'I'm afraid that's not possible,' said George. 'The American Colonel has the only key. We, ourselves, have no idea what it contains; our job is just to deliver it.'

Twyford could see the senior policeman, understandably, was not happy. He represented the law in the area but wasn't party to anything that involved national security.

'Have you any identification, sir?' He was becoming impassable.

'We never carry any. Constable, we're lost and late and need your help; would it be possible to guide us?' He seemed to take them into his confidence, 'It is vitally important that certain people…' then said no more.

The officer warmed to this approach and welcomed their request for aid. Both enjoyed nothing better than alarming the countryside with peeling bells.

'Righto,' he said, 'Follow us.'

The cars sped off as the farmer queried too late, "Ere, who's gonna pay for my ruddy lawn?'

The squad car stopped outside the perimeter of the base and watched Lestor drive to the barrier. Tinker produced his pass and they were waved inside. The 'Rozzers' drove off content in the knowledge that they were genuine for their vehicle would not have been allowed through had they had been anything but.

Bones welcomed them as if he was Manager of the Waldorf. He jumped on the running board and guided Lestor between the huts to a group of converted farm buildings. These housed the offices for the non-commissioned officers and Bones ran the base through these people and on their behalf. Any queries, only one corporal could answer them and that was the man with the clipboard. It was his camouflage and cover story. Carrying it, he became a blur and his actions were never questioned. He was undoubtedly one of the finest operators George had ever come across. The car parked behind the offices and they entered through a back door and into a secured storage area. Now confident they wouldn't be disturbed, Tinker opened the suitcase and the Corporal swooned. He took a wad at random, pulled a note from its centre and examined it. It was real to all intents and purposes, they had the perfect article. He held another to the light then rubbed it between his thumb and forefinger. The quality of the paper and the ageing of the notes were faultless. He took a white fiver from his back pocket and compared it, there was absolutely no difference.

George watched him check different wads and when he was completely satisfied, asked,

'Anything wrong?'

Bones shook his head and scrutinised one more for luck. Only then did he notice the similarity of the sequences. He withdrew more; the only flaw he could see was that the numbers were the same, apart from the last three digits. The machine printed from SK7958000 to SK7958999 and back again. His emotions were aroused and needed no persuading but Lestor still reflected, 'It took you five minutes to notice it and you knew they were forgeries. None of your squaddies will have enough in their wage packets to spot it.' He saw them to the barrier. They left him tangoing for joy and using his clipboard as a tambourine.

'Next stop the Roman,' said Lestor, driving from the base with a little more caution.

Once the route to East London was found, they journeyed in silence. The earlier ordeal had sapped most of their energy and they were left to reflect on what nearly came amiss. Had the case been opened, the dream would have been shattered. Tinker pictured four green walls and a small, barred window up high. George imagined having to fight and overpower the officers and the farm workers, then get the car past the tractor and immobilise it back across the lane, gaining valuable time for their escape. Lestor visualised stealing the squad car, racing though fields, around hair-pin bends and finally dumping it in East London; crazy endings to a situation that shouldn't have been created.

'I think we've just been very lucky!' sighed George, at last.

Lestor agreed, 'I don't want to think what could have

happened.'

'Just let me get through the next two weeks,' said Tinker. 'My nerves are packing up and leaving. I'll have a nerveless body that my eyes watch as it rots away in a cell, and a tortured memory that can't forget how good life was when my body used to work.'

'That was a sunny, little oration,' remarked George, 'I love that wicked, devil-may-care...'

'Where's the end of my tether?' asked Tinker, suddenly, 'I've probably lost if for ever.'

'What, your tether? Never!'

Lestor won the prize with, 'It's whether I could endeavour to say something clever, if only your name was Trevor!' They clapped and jeered like school kids as the relief was joked out of them. They could laugh now but it had set each of them to thinking just how easy things can go awry. The main factor in their favour was that the car could not be traced to anyone.

Being Saturday, the Roman Road Market was busy and about twice the size of Queen's Crescent. Lorries and vans lined the approach roads so they had to park a fair way away and troop back single-file keeping Lestor in the middle; the suitcase made him look like a fly- pitcher. Steve saw them among the throng of customers and nodded at the Needle Gun public house. It was a better plan to be drinkers; they definitely couldn't pass as shoppers. He left the queue at his stall to his staff, and came through the crowd carrying a shopping bag brimming with potatoes. All manner of deals took place in the outside toilets at the back bar and no one asked questions. The 'Gents' chucked up a smell of stale beer, vomit and bleach, not surprisingly the business was carried out swiftly.

'Is it all there?' asked Steve, pulling a folded shopping bag from his apron.

'Fifty thousand exactly,' answered George, watching through the high windows above the long urinal. The case was opened and Steve transferred roughly half to the shopping bag, tipped potatoes on top, overfilling it then stuffed the balance of the notes into the original bag, tipping enough of the potatoes back to cover them too.

'What if one bag bursts while you're walking along?' asked Tinker, perturbed by the coster's calmness.

'I'll have plenty of new friends,' answered Steve, apparently unruffled by the huge fortune he carried.

His remarkable attitude robbed them of anything to say, but Tinker proved invaluable as always when he uttered, 'Good chippers are they…?'

The empty suitcase was given to a member of the bonfire community that survives on the edge of every street market and they drove home. George had warned Steve to be prepared and, full marks to him, he had been.

Two lorries, full to capacity with wooden pins of beer, rolled down the ramp from the railway loading dock above Bass brewery depot and up to the barrier to get checked out. The paperwork was correct and the drivers pulled out into Camley Street to find themselves beset by Rozzers. Srgnt. Shaw watched as six men were hauled from the vehicles, cuffed and removed, and was amazed at the preposterous front of these thieves. The men were all known to the police yet the leader, still in the stolen uniform of a Railway Supervisor, created merry hell that a grave mistake had been made and demanded their release. This chancer had actually gathered British Rail employees from other loading duties and ordered them to give these lorries priority. What's more, they would have got away scot free had it not been for this morning's information from the Four's Asset.

Donald placed his notebook on the table and related his full account of the happenings of Friday night to the panel sitting in front of him. The questions would begin only when he had finished. Grogan was confused but showed nothing in his face. Some days he felt accepted almost on equal level then at these weekly sittings, they acted as if he were being interrogated. The Frenchman began and asked Donald whether he thought Twyford was to be trusted.

'Only as far as he wants the balance of the forgeries and will cash in his first consignment to finance the second.'

'Again we ask, does he suspect that you might not be the printer?'

'He doesn't look that far. His main concern is that he expects me to cheat him out of his stake money, and takes every precaution against this. The more I appear incautious and offhand about the arrangements, the tighter his plans become. I believe he expects me to lure him in and rob him. He will not think past me. This is his one big opportunity to alter his life forever.'

Another member changed the direction, 'Does he pass any remarks about the war?'

'No. It's as if it's someone else's war and the outcome doesn't affect him.'

'Interesting,' said the Frenchman. 'He seems quite capable. I think we can rule out national loyalty, and you know where you are with a man who works purely for financial rewards. Could he be useful to us?'

The four panel members looked at Grogan. Donald wanted absolutely nothing to do with George Twyford, so delayed answering.

He was assisted with another option, 'Well, when this is over, would you recommend a discontinuation?'

Grogan hedged his bets, 'I think we could have a couple of possibilities after next Friday's exchange. One would be to offer him enough money to work through me, keeping him at arm's length or, to make him an offer which, if he refuses, we then terminate our relationship.'

The other gentleman needed more before he agreed to a step like that. 'You are confident that all this money will get into circulation?'

'I am,' stated Donald, with utter certainty.

Sensing his colleague's misgivings and not wanting to take responsibility for the decision on his own, the Frenchman back-pedalled and suggested, 'I think we must ensure the success of Operation Bernhard and leave our options open for discussion again next week.'

The panel were in accord and Grogan was dismissed. He gave a curt tilt of the head and left.

Kevin ambled along Marsden Street and as he came close to the house he could see a man half in and half out the doorway. Mary didn't see him as he waited to pass inside. She stood behind the partially-open door and was saying goodbye to Richard, and each time he leaned in for another kiss, she closed the door a little more. An inch or so, and he would be decapitated.

'Can I disturb you two?' asked Kevin, after a while.

Richard jumped in surprise and his head rebounded off the wood and the wall. Mary opened the door wide enough to let him slip through and made embarrassed signals to Richard that she had to go.

'I'll see you about eightish,' she whispered, not looking, but turning to watch her son she accidentally crushed Richard's head as he tried for one last peck. 'Oh, I'm so sorry!' she said, healing his aches with a stroke of her hand then closed the door. Mary came into the kitchen to make his tea and noticed that Kevin was reading the paper with a grin that she found oddly disturbing.

Richard (Nero) Falco walked along the street wondering if he was wasting his time. Mary was a damned fine woman, good to be with, and he loved the saucy way she spoke her mind. But she always had a good reason why they could not be alone together long enough to make love. He admired her for holding out when she seemed to want to give in. She allowed him enough passion to keep his ardour on the boil, but turned off the gas before the relationship could fulfil itself. He had thought that maybe she still cared for her husband but if last night was anything to go by he had nothing to worry about on that score. "Dear God," he thought. "Why are women so strange?"

Heaven's answer came back at him, 'That's what makes them so interesting.'

Before the car was driven to the yard and locked away for the night, the boys knocked for Mornie Quill. He came to the door with a tape measure round his neck, a waistcoat full of pins and a length of black cloth over his arm.

'Come in. The evening suits are coming along. If we have the fittings Monday, I'll try and have them ready for next Saturday.'

A voice complained from upstairs, 'Answer the door, I'm making the beds!'

'I already have!' he said.

'I can't do it!' she shouted back, taking him up wrong. 'Does it look like I've got two pairs of hands?'

'Nah, but you moan enough for two tongues!' he mumbled then yelled, 'I said I already have!'

'Who is it, then?'

'Mind your own business,' said low enough not to be heard.

'Who is it?!'

'Customers!' he yelled.

'Are you fitting them for suits?'

'No! They only come round so I can draw chalk marks all over 'em!'

'Ha, ha, very funny!' she said, caustically and appeared at the top of the stairs. With the first look, her eyes became slits and the boys waited for the burst of flames to belch from her nostrils. But instead she hissed at them, 'Playing run-outs today are we? Or is it 'Knock Down Ginger'?'

She moved away out of view and Tinker, on behalf of his horse, said 'At least it's better than "Kiss-Chase", yuk!' She was back in a flash and staring accusingly down.

Lestor and George immediately pointed at Tinker, who cowered.

Twyford took skate and chips in for his Mum's Saturday night treat and found that Kevin had left a message.

'He wants to know if he can bring his young lady to the Malden, with your crowd, tonight.'

'Course he can, Mum, he hasn't got to ask,'

'Pop over and tell him before you go out, love. I'm getting ready at Lou's.'

Tonight everyone else would be with their wives and he and Gerry had arranged to be out early. They crossed the gardens to sort out with Kevin about welcoming him, and his merry maid, into their company. Mary was in the kitchen, far from ready, when she heard the back door go. She wore no make-up and her hair was still in curlers. The young couple sat ready and waiting for his parents' seal of approval.

"Kevin seems to be enjoying this," thought Mary, annoyed at being caught looking less than her best in her own house by, of all people, her estranged husband. The knock at the street door was timed to save her blushes and as Gerry and George entered the kitchen, she barged through them to answer it. Kevin introduced his young lady as Jackie, but she barely responded then reverted to staring at the floor. Twyford saw her doleful demeanour and thought selfishly of what a cracking evening there promised to be with this bundle of laughs.

'Come up with us,' he suggested to the two of them.

Kevin looked at Jackie who decided, 'We'd better wait for your Mum.'

"Sod ya!" thought Twyford, but was pleased at not having to suffer her company for too long. 'Okay then, we'll see you later.'

In the passage, Mary was being passionately embraced by

Nero. George showed nothing and the clinch uncoupled when it was apparent that they had an audience. Nolan and Twyford passed between them.

'Good night, Mary,' said Gerry.

'Good night, Dick,' said George and before he could reply, Mary called after them,

'It's Richard, actually!'

Twyford ignored her and continued walking; he felt nauseated but could not understand why. Apart from the loathing, he had no feelings at all where she was concerned and yet it seemed he didn't want anyone else to have her.

Gerry thought the night was ruined before it had started and said, 'Dare I hope you didn't see that?'

George turned to him and chirped merrily, 'Perhaps I'm rid of her for good!' Oddly, Nolan did not seem convinced.

The Malden was still quite empty and a clarinet player was tuning up with the three piece band when the two friends came in. Ten pounds was placed in a jug to begin the night and the lads settled themselves at the back, next to the far snugs. George was facing the wrong way, and as Gerry nudged him, he turned to see what everyone was gawking at. There, looking around from the centre of the room was the bold O'Brien, Spider stood close behind him. The big Irishman's gaze fell on Twyford and, with a broad grin, bounced over. His unruly mop of red hair was somehow flattened down either side of a centre parting, probably with axle grease, and the number of tiny bloodstains on his collar told of the effort he had made. His sky-blue suit had to be twenty years out of date and must have fitted him when he was at school, while the yellow tie that dangled from around his neck had, obviously, shrunk in the wash and now begun and ended halfway between Adam's apple and waistband. Even his building site boots had seen a lick of polish; the word 'smart' did not do him justice. The lesser sized Spider, on the other hand, wore a suit that could only have been made to measure. Extra material had been used on the arms and although cut to the correct quarter of an inch above the shirt cuff, he looked like the Indian rubber man and could have served himself by reaching across to the optics, without being at full stretch. They looked quite a formidable pair and Horace thought them trouble before an expletive had been expelled. George called a pint of mild for O'Brien and a sweet sherry for Spider. He handed them their drinks and noticed that the sherry glass wasn't visible in Spider's hand. Meanwhile, O'Brien swallowed three-quarters of the pint in one huge gulp and, with a drinker's finesse, still managed to protrude a pinkie. Twyford enquired how the work was coming on. O'Brien hadn't meant to talk business, but, as George had broached the subject, thought it best to mention a slight hiccup. It was nothing to worry about, but Mornington Crescent tube could be shut.

Unable to see the connection George enquired, 'Well, that shouldn't affect our work, should it?'

'Well,' O'Brien stretched it out. 'Well…slightly.'

Twyford began to get worried. 'What have you done?'

O'Brien thought how softly to describe it and held his finger and thumb, showing a little gap between them. 'Twas a small, nay.. tiny accident.'

Spider supported him nobly with, "Ucking nuishance, that's what it is!'

'I had the lads flat out, I did, and they were happy to be of service to your good self; working like Trojans.'

"O'Brien is smiling. It will all be okay," thought George. The Irishman checked that he still had their attention. 'Tell me exactly what you've done,' said George, calmly.

The Gaelic face contorted into all manner of expressions as he chose his next sentence. 'We've dug a little too deep, so we have.'

Spider chimed in with, '`Hink they're 'ucking miners, they do!'

O'Brien continued, 'Some of our concrete foundations fell through to what 'moight be, and I only say 'moight be, the

Northern Line.'

'Oh, fuck me, no!' chanted George over and over.

O'Brien let it sink in then furthered the story, 'Well, I peered in and it looks like an underground chamber, al'roight.'

George had visions of the complete Craven A building disappearing through the floor in a great cloud of dust and whipping off on a train, through to Clapham Junction. Twyford closed his eyes for a moment and when he opened them again, O'Brien had his arm proudly around Spider's shoulder. 'This man here is our safety officer, and he informed the railway people straight away, fine man!'

George closed his eyes again and asked, 'And they did…?'

'Closed us down, boss. Best t'ing to do.'

'How can it be the best thing?' asked a stupefied George,whose forehead had heated to fever level.

'Well. If there was a n'accident with one of dem ol' tube trains, you'd be in rare ol' trouble, boss.'

"Ucking right!' agreed Spider.

Gerry broke in before Twyford could explode. 'It's not too bad. If there's a chance of an accident, they route the trains direct to Euston on the City Line and bypass Mornington Crescent.' George knew this to be true. Nolan continued, 'Have they said it definitely is the underground tunnel?'

'No,' answered O'Brien. 'They're checking it out over night and we'll know Monday morning.' He looked very happy now he had imparted all the bad news and got it off his chest.

Gerry turned back to Twyford, 'Worrying's not gonna help. Monday we'll all be the wiser and, if we've made a hole, we'll secure it properly. It might be for the best.'

The rational recommendation dismantled the detonator and prompted George to think only of tonight's revelries. He looked at his professional builders and couldn't help but laugh. He articulated, '`Uck 'em all!'

Spider finished the phrase for him with, '`Astards!'

The music struck up and Lestor Hogg waltzed his missus over. 'I think he's getting in practice for later.' She said, as he spun her to a halt next to Gerry. 'Here George, why ain't no women allowed down the Cafe Luxor?'

'Can't say 'cos it would spoil the surprise we've got planned for you girls on New Year's Eve.'

'Oh yeah?' she asked, not believing him, but interested all the same.

The clarinet's introduction led Lily Hall into "All the things you are". She finished the song and pushed her way through the growing throng to Twyford. He hadn't seen her since the Tax Office and had already worked out words to bribe her help, but it was unnecessary.

'George,' she asked' 'you seem to be bang in trouble while me and my hubby could use an extra few bob right now. Can I oblige you in any way?'

Fintan had hurried Bridgid to get ready then collected Ruben and Pat. In all the years they had known each other, this was the first time Benson had socialised with them on a Saturday night. He was relaxed and what a difference it made! They came in the Malden and Fintan made the introductions. Everyone knew who Ruben was but none of them had witnessed his charm, in no time he was enjoying himself and the centre of attention. Mary, Kathy Gay and Nell Higby had joined them with the fiddlers close by. George watched on and marvelled how he kept everyone in the conversation, seeming to talk to each one individually. Pat stood by his side and hardly took her eyes off him. His finest touch was when he made a point of meeting Mickey Butler and to everyone's surprise, including Mick's, they got on splendidly well.

Kevin and Jackie found a little nook close to everyone, but drunk on their own. In truth, she hadn't sipped her gin and lime, just stood with it in her hand and her head down. That wasn't how Kevin had hoped tonight would go. He thought that Jackie would take her place among the women, with Mary to help her into their assembly, while he would drink with the men and receive advice and good stories and be like his Dad. He had told her of his intention to join up a month ago when his father had returned. She had been hard work to be with since then, but now he was going off to do his bit and she couldn't even brighten up for his last few days at home.

'You're making tonight into a right drudgery,' She looked up from the floor but didn't speak. He carried on, 'I wanted to be with nice people who laugh; this is my one night to have a drink with my Dad. He's been away for four years and I may be gone for some time.' She started to sniffle and her eyes welled up. 'Don't turn the taps on again for crying out loud,' he said. 'Surely you can cheer up for a couple of hours!' But she just looked in his face and sniffed some more. In disgust, he shuffled a few steps to be nearer George, and she followed the same steps and stood with him again.

Twyford studied the happy couple thinking, "He should have spent tonight with Mary and me. God, I'm glad that's in my head and didn't come out my mouth." He knew that he meant being with himself and also with Mary. Again, the words would have been misconstrued. Anyway, tomorrow the lad could have had Jackie at Mary's for the day. Unfortunately, it was too late for that now.

Kevin finished his pint then with a sharp, 'Come on, Happy!' They slipped out the side entrance. She knew he was annoyed but this was her scheme. Tonight she had no intention of sharing him with anyone, no matter what he wanted and when he saw what she had in mind he'd leap at it!

From outside, once again, the Malden gave the impression of jumping in time with the music. The wonderful songs performed by excellent singers echoed up and down the street and by ten o'clock when it seemed you couldn't have squeezed anymore people in, Bones turned up with the Captain and the East End ladies. Frank Nash added their drinks to an already long list of thirty five plus one case of light ales with the tops off. That way he only had to lift his arm and the whole round would be called again. The barmaids were in top gear and no one waited too long to be served.

It was Twyford's turn to sing and he gave them a Hoagy Carmicheal number called "I get along without you very well"; a fine song but a bit too melancholy for this particular night. The performance must have been reasonably good for the pub yelled for more, albeit mostly his friends. By popular request, his second tune got them all singing, it was "Make someone happy" and that song always sounded better with a cockney accent. Eleanor and her girls were next on the stage with "Keep young and beautiful". Stan Swindells supported with a decent impersonation of Oliver Hardy dancing on tiptoes up and down. Timmytoonice was there to make sure George hadn't changed his mind and was enlisted for the advanced party to the Café Luxor later.

John and Megan were acting oddly strange; every few minutes she'd come over and kiss him, then return to the ladies. Vi Quill, for a laugh, did the same and frightened the life out of Mornie. Gerry Nolan was more like his old self and flogged everyone with sarcastic comments. As usual Owen and Kit joined forces and fired back some hilarious retorts but were no match for Nolan's mockery. Always taken in good part, his insulting witticisms destroyed them and people that didn't know often thought it was about to get out of hand.

Mary and Nell Higby moved through the men on the way to powder their noses. As they neared George, he saw Mary and looked around for his son. 'Where's Kevin and Joyful?' he asked her.

'God, isn't she jolly?' declared Mary. 'Do you know, I felt embarrassed when people spoke to her, she just answered with a nod or a shake of the head.'

'Tell them she took a vow of silence.'

'Holy orders? I think marching orders might be better.' They stiffened at the realisation of having a conversation. 'Bye,' said Mary hurriedly.

'Bye,' said George, abruptly turning away. He gave it a few seconds, then casually glanced around to make sure that no one had noticed. Fintan and Bridgid looked across sweetly and raised their glasses to watch him act out a cringe.

The comperes for the night were Dan Currie and Lucky and either one hopped on the stage after every act and introduced the next. Olive, Kathy, Ruben, Tinker and Ginger were all called while Kit's repeated efforts to book a song were frustrated on purpose. Eventually he was allowed on stage and in his rush to get to the microphone, tripped up the stairs. He sang to Rita, who danced a solo Samba in front of the footlights with her eyes closed. She slunk about with one hand raised in a dance pose and the other rubbing her belly. The lads stopped drinking to ogle and Kit won the joust.

Time for a last round before some of the Force deserted their womenfolk for 'business' up the West End. The pub staff always responded quicker for Frank Nash and tonight was no exception. He leant on a pillar and smoothly raised a finger; it was rewarded immediately by one of the barmaids. She prepared their next round of drinks and, had it not been so busy, would have trayed them over herself; women seemed to find him quite masterful. Frank was tall and wolfish, yet with a cool sophistication. He sported a waxed moustache that 'tickled' and could be smutty or vulgarly suggestive yet women would never take offence, usually coming back for more. His wife, Leonie, was beautiful, interesting and had never been seen in a bad mood, tonight he too would be on manoeuvres.

Lestor Hogg looked at his watch and his wife looked at him, he glanced up and she tapped her wrist in warning. The gesture probably wouldn't make any difference to what time he got in, like the other lads, he was too keyed up and excited. From the few remarks dropped to fend off their questions and interference, the women were aware of something good in the wind and, quite unusually, refrained from pushing too hard.

The stage was full with the resident three-piece band; the clarinettist, Nero and his accordionist, plus the fiddlers. He sang an old 'un from the thirties and his impression of Rudy

Vallee was wasted as Mary and her friends sat with Pat Passmore, listening to Ruben's little anecdotes. Since he had arrived in their company, the women had gradually positioned him between them and tittered correctly to his winsome wit. The brave fool marched on, exposing his character for complete inspection. They were recording points and logging details. Pretty soon they would have him catalogued and, if acceptable, Pat was the box he would be filed in.

The oratorical O'Brien, with the poised pinkie protruding from his sixth pint of mild, climbed up and asked the band if they knew 'The Minstrel Boy'. The pianist played him in and, poignantly rocking, he sang. It was the finest performance of the evening receiving enormous applause and he revelled in it. O'Brien stood there lordly and took a big swig of his drink then bowed from the waist and gracefully descended the stairs. The noise level was rising still, aided by George's high-pitched whistling and Spider's hands banging together like thunder claps. The Irish man had redeemed himself; his earlier demolition of the Northern Line temporarily forgotten.

The 'men only' expedition left the pub as Min, Lou and Cissy were rousing the crowd with the Maori boat song "Now is the hour".

"Kevin should have been here for that," thought George, as he faced the bracing wind.

The Force listed; Lestor, Dan, Frank, Mornie, Stanley, Bones, Owen and Tinker. Along with George and Gerry, they would have an hour at the Café Luxor. Kit was to have been in that number until Rita licked her lips slowly at him and changed his mind. Twyford had purposely left out John and Mickey, who were to be put in the 'waiting room' until Friday night. That way, George surmised, the deal happens and if it proves to be necessary, Grogan would get an unsettling jolt to overcompensate in their favour. Timmy Gowan was outside with his coat on, taking the air, when they came out, he, too, was press-ganged and heartily welcomed.

The Café Luxor was decked out with the foremost London

fashionmakers. Beautiful, stylish women and high-level, influential men displayed their presence in a Christmas setting to surpass Broadway or Hollywood. Twyford and the Force meandered to their table and were stopped all along the way, a word here and a joke there, as people prided themselves on the familiarity and Timmy Gowan was impressed by their popularity. He, himself, through the Admiralty, was quite well connected, and recognised colleagues, mostly out of uniform, enjoying some relaxation.

Toot Robinson knew his audience. He saw the Force without Kit and let them settle, then played three tangos in a row assisted by Swarthy. Within no time the lads had selected partners and were on the dance floor. The singers changed and Radna was magnificent, the lights dimmed and she slowed down the music. George walked his latest partner back to watch and appreciate her performance. She shimmered with radiance and again Twyford considered the idea of settling down with this gorgeous creature. She sang them to the break and he met her at the foot of the stage, took her hand to support the high heels with their descent of the final few stairs then led to the bar. Her hand was soft and warm and refused to release his, though her mood was unusually quiet. George asked if everything was okay and she replied with a smile that was quiet. They sat on bar stools and he chatted away, hoping to get more response. Her eyes searched his face, never leaving him. Rex joined them and she lightened up for the end of the break, then *he* walked her back leaving Twyford to wonder what was wrong.

"Perhaps she wants to cool it down," he thought, wistfully, "It never works to show you care, they prefer it when you're horrible." Oh it would be a great shame, but he'd cover any show of feelings by enjoying himself with other company. On that thought, he wandered the greenery looking for Grogan. He wasn't to be found there and Twyford returned to his guests. The lights signalled the band was ready to swing. George sat and Donald rose from the very next table and came over. He was the politician once more and to deny him any advantage Twyford stood while they made conversation and tried to get a look at who he was with. No one was familiar but most appeared well to do. Grogan established that everything was in order for the following meeting on Friday night then faced the Force and looked at them like a hungry wolf studies a herd of goats. He was never short of self-assurance but this night his bearing declared him to be the master, and was there anyone to claim otherwise? They weren't ready and faltered slightly as his gaze fell on them and his mouth watered, even Nolan was empty.

Grogan turned back to George and said, 'They don't change, eh Georgie-boy? Speak to you Thursday.'

Twyford watched as he walked, not back to his table, but to the woods behind the bar.

'Oh well done!' said George, and each one took his meaning. "Bollocks!" he thought, Donald had stamped his authority on his own, Radna had gone cold on him, the first of his celebrations was knocked about somewhat but not a complete disaster. 'Fuck it!' and 'let's get pissed!' was the best he could suggest. He twirled with lovely ladies, making half-hearted meaningless conversation, drank but couldn't get back to the right mood. The evening ended flatly for him but the others seemed quite buoyant and made their plans to meet on Sunday morning. George felt the wise move would be to take advantage of the moment and whip one of the girls off home but, instead, he waited at the bar half-hoping to repair his relationship with Radna. He sipped a last coffee and prepared to leave alone when at last she came out. She took his hand but her mood hadn't changed. They walked into the cold night air in silence. He was the one to speak first, 'Tell me what's wrong? I'm sure I can make it right, even if you only want to hear me say "goodbye". '

She let go of his hand and walked a little apart from him. 'I hate jealousy in anyone,' she said, 'It's an awful quality.'

George sprang to his own defence and questioned, 'What

have I done?'

'Why do you have to do it? Have you not thought how I might feel seeing you dancing and flirting in front of me?'

Twyford understood he had been at his thickest tonight. 'I'm completely at fault.'

'George, everyone knows I wait for you. I understand I'm just your after-thought but I accept it, and remain patient until you decide to see me. I'm happy with what little of yourself you give but don't blatantly make a fool of me in front of the band, please.'

He put an arm around her and squeezed. She stopped walking and accepted the proffered hug.

'I'm really sorry, because the dances meant nothing. I didn't think it would bother you; I certainly didn't mean to upset you.'

'I'm not upset,' she said firmly, then still locked within him, admitted, 'Yes, I am upset and I don't want you to hold anyone but me.'

'It was a dance, nothing really.'

'Dancing is holding, so only dance with me.' He tilted her chin up and kissed her and her arms moved around his neck. They embraced for an age and his bum was getting cold, but every time he tried to break away she pulled him closer. Luckily, a gust of wind blew his hat off and they had to chase it towards home. She had his promise not to flirt with anyone else and, by the time they reached her block, she was her old self. Between drinks and embraces, they talked for hours. He told her of the good fun he had had with the boys and O'Brien's attempt to dig through to Australia and the consequential closure of Mornington Crescent Station, whilst she described quiet nights alone, wondering what he was doing.

'When you leave me you forget me easily,' she said. 'One phone call for five minutes would be so nice.'

'I never know when you're in.'

'You little fibber!' she cried. 'I make a point of telling you every week when my nights off are.'

'Yeah, but I've got a terrible memory, perhaps you should write it down.'

'Perhaps you should take it down,' she suggested, offering him the clasp of her dress -and as the zip went down so did he.

He awoke in sunshine and in panic and couldn't find his watch. A cup of tea had gone cold on the bedside table and Radna was not in the flat. He washed and dressed with speed and as he tied his laces, the backdoor opened and she breezed in.

'I hope you weren't going without saying goodbye.'

'No, but I'm ever so late.'

'While you were snoring, I've been upstairs for coffee,' she informed him. 'The Donna Laura has a full house. She must have twenty visitors this morning.'

'Was Donald there?' enquired George, delicately.

'Yes, he arrived as I was leaving to come and cook you your breakfast.'

'Honestly, thank you, but I haven't got time, really.'

She flicked his eyelids and said, 'I've sprinkled magic on your eyes. You will only ever see me.'

He left with her kiss still burning, keeping him warm across Primrose Hill.

As if proving the dictum that certain pleasures can make one's eyes go out of kilter, Srgnt. Shaw stood outside the Police station and stared bo'sidedly into the distance. He was reliving recent successful Trials where the Judge, before handing out custodial sentences, would call for the case files. Inside the folder there was always an unsigned document, carelessly left in, listing other crimes they were suspected of -but had yet to be proven; and they went down hard! Deserving every day of their punishment. Without the Asset, many of these felons would still be around to prey on the local community and the Sergeant gave silent thanks to the team for nurturing the man and safeguarding his identity.

CHAPTER 29: AN INQUISITIVE UMBRELLA

London: Viscount Simon, Britain's Lord Chancellor, told Parliament today that not if but when we gain victory severe justice will be meted out to 1000's of war criminals. He said, "We shall not establish sanity in Germany without a considerable measure of sanitation. War criminals must be followed to the uttermost ends of the earth!"

George arrived back at St Leonard's Square with enough time to change *and* make the Malden for midday. Sunday hours were twelve noon to two p.m., therefore each minute was of the utmost importance. Min came from the kitchen when she heard the front door open and guessing her appearance heralded a newsflash he waited expectantly at the foot of the stairs.

'I'm so glad you're early, Georgie, we've been invited to Sunday dinner with the family. Don't look so surprised, Kevin popped in earlier to say he would love it if we could have lunch with them. Mary agreed it so we're sitting down at ten past two. Don't you dare be late!'

'Did she say that?' said George, ready to cop the needle about any conditions she may have laid down.

'No, I said it!' his mother snapped, 'It's Kevin's last meal with us for a while and he's really looking forward to it.'

'That's different,' said George, 'and I think it's a lovely idea, Mum. I'll take him out for a few pints first and be back spot on time.'

'Please don't let the dinner spoil, eh love?'

Kevin was ready when he called, though only wore his uniform; he would sooner freeze than cover it up. It was bright but frosty as they walked along Malden Road. George pulled his trilby down against the bitter gusts and turned up the collar of his Crombie. "The boy must be balmy!" he thought. "Oh to be that insane." The pub was warm and packed with noisy people and they pushed through, saying hallo to every second person and found the Force to be in good cheer; the only one missing was 'Ten to two Mornie'. Everyone that knew Kevin wanted to buy him a drink before he went warring and Twyford had to refuse many on his son's behalf, having no wish to be carrying the boy home to look down the barrel of his mother's wrath.

Timmy Gowan, now somewhat of a regular again, planned, with George, the strategy for Monday evening's operation 'Sally'. He should arrive a quarter of an hour late and then it would look more 'last minute' and she would appreciate the effort made. After that, he'd have all night to woo her. Timothy had never before been a part of a 'swap' and was having more confidence losses than surges, but the prize of winning her was worth the trickery. A neighbour interrupted George and passed on that his children were outside asking for him. 'An escort guard!' he laughed and took them out lemonade and arrowroot biscuits. Little Joey Gay was showing off to a crowd of kids who preyed upon their Dads enjoying a Sunday pint. He was riding his sister Kathy's bike up and down with no hands and combing his hair at the same time, they all thought he was marvellous.

Last orders and Lestor Hogg took the microphone and prompted a Kentish Town chorus of 'We'll meet again' in Kevin's honour. It was men only on Sunday morning but the barmaids came and fussed over him and made him embarrassed.

Operating on the certainty that excessive alcohol makes for loose tongues, the Asset had been drinking with a crowd he knew quite well at the Malden and always spent money near closing time. "One for the road," was when the juicy titbits slipped out and it was as he was being rudely refused, by Horace the governor, that one of the company had muttered, 'That's alright, you miserable bastard, after next Friday we'll buy the pub and sack ya!' It was murmured just loud enough to win him a few sniggers and a sharp kick on the ankle. The utterance was sufficient but the ankle tap confirmed so much more for the Asset to know that, from the gift of one easy throwaway remark, providentially, he was once more gainfully employed.

Danny invited the whole pub back for a game of cards, George and Kevin declined and a bowlegged Kit left with them. He had been devitalised and devoured and couldn't wait to get home for some more, but out of sheer fatigue had to cadge a saddle down the hill. He did look choice, perched on the back, suited and booted with his feet sticking out and hanging on while little Joey peddled like mad.

The Twyfords sang as they walked and when they reached home the street door was open and appetising odours drew them in. George trailed behind the children, a little uncertainly. Dinner was being dished up as they entered and his place was at the opposite end of the table to Mary. A delicious offering of piping hot sprouts, parsnips, swedes and roast potatoes surrounded thick slices of snow-white pork, cut into sections. An enormous Yorkshire pudding rested in the centre of the table, next to a bowl of apple sauce and two gravy boats waited steaming and ready. But as far as George was concerned, the most noticeably pleasing feature of the whole meal was the largest, crispiest, golden brown, piece of crackling that rested across the top of his plate. Once this used to be his treat, his right; once, long ago and far away. It made him feel oddly special ensconced there with his lovely babies.

They talked of common interests and people they all knew. Kevin teased the girls about the young lads that hung around the street door. Min enquired after Josie and Archie and touched on Orla's health. Mary was fine with it and said how well she was doing. Alan insisted that Dad told everyone about the lions in Africa and how young tribesman had to make a kill with a spear before they could be accepted into manhood. George didn't want to cause any upsets and had tried to stay off the subject of his absent years, but the children wanted to hear about it all. Mary didn't seem to mind so he gave them a general outline, with Alan prompting if he left anything out, and correcting if a detail was slipped.

'If only he'd learn his school work this well,' George remarked lightly.

Mary's expression changed and she stood up to busy herself with the preparations of the custard. Twyford steered away and told an elephant joke, and when the apple pie was passed around the chill had dispersed and she seemed quite tranquil.

Kevin was happy and that made everyone at ease. He talked a lot, asking Mary and George their opinions, holding them together in conversation and then listening keenly, yet unable to contain a smile of amusement by their politeness to each other. It was an excellent repast, a heart-warming family moment and no money on earth can buy that. The men were full to bursting and the bed beckoned George, besides which, later on, the Shaw family were coming for tea to wish Kevin God's speed and a safe return.

The beer had loosened George somewhat and he felt he should thank Mary but couldn't steer his eloquence and found he was rambling all around the houses. He finally settled with, 'Thank you for a nice day, I enjoyed it very much,' and as he prepared to leave he barely heard the reply.

'I'm so glad.' She said. He turned to look at her, but she was facing away, washing the dishes which left him unsure whether or not she was being sarcastic. By the time he reached Min's house, he had decided she was, and chalked up another one pending repayment.

The woman rolled from the bed and went into the bathroom. "He's a strange one," she thought, not for the first time, then soaped herself all over and flannelled him from her body with the hot water. He paid well so she came when he called, but he never spoke. All through the coupling he would be distant, using her as an exercise to wear himself out then would gaze out of the window until she left, leaving him alone with his grimace. He had no pleasantries, no tenderness, but gave off an unnerving nastiness when he pummelled her body with his. She'd stopped being disgusted by the needs of men at the age of seventeen, since then only this man could make her feel shop-soiled and cheap. She dressed quickly, collected the notes he'd left by the door and closed it behind her.

Grogan lay his head on the pillow and focused somewhere near the stars. Unhappy with the treatment from his superiors, he assessed his position. He showed the correct respect, did their bidding and deliberately took on more and more responsibility. He could wait; he always did. Soon they would become more dependant on him and only then would they discover the full extent of his bill! His mind wandered back to the muddy trenches of the Somme, when Sergeant Major McShine had lain there dying from a hand grenade that joined him in the advanced trench he was sheltering in. The old bastard had crawled back to Grogan's pit for help with half of his lower body missing. Donald sat and smoked a cigarette watching the blood and life ooze from him, while the Sergeant Major fathomed out where the grenade had come from. McShine was fleeced, dumped and forgotten and Grogan was promoted. And so the war went on. He cared for no family or friends and firmly believed he was harder, because of no weaknesses, at least, none he would admit to. No scruples either; had killed easily and would no doubt kill again. He viewed his life proudly and scoffed at the ludicrous idea of working with Twyford. When ready, he would orchestrate that man's termination, and they would agree and charge him with the task. George would finally receive Donald's gift that the flare had failed to deliver those years ago. His memory traversed time to the days of Perth and Private Butler. He had despised the skinny runt. Until they had stopped him, the defiance Butler had shown against Grogan's heavy demands caused Donald to try and break his will, time after time, and all that happened was the man's antagonism grew stronger. It came to the point that, unless he was permanently taken care of, Grogan knew, one dark night, Butler would plant a knife in him. Consequently he had 'arranged' for the Private to have a very serious accident; unfortunately he only broke a leg instead of his neck. He recalled their counterstroke as if it were yesterday. Standing on that rock the following day, cursing this piss-poor troupe of green cockneys, when the least aggressive one looked in his eyes and pushed him out and away, off of that peak, to his death. He had meant for Grogan to die and his action was as easy as standing on a cockroach. It was pure chance that the others responded to training and secured his line halfway to hell. Donald met the reaper that day and feared to make that acquaintance again. "Bass, the mild one," he thought. Since then he lived by the rule, 'Trust no one!' They hung him there, longing to let him drop, demanding terms, and he soiled himself and agreed to everything, inwardly swearing revenge. That was when he really comprehended how dangerous they were as a pack. He backed off then but now they couldn't begin to imagine what he would produce. Wars bred deaths and Grogan manipulated any situation to climb higher. What did he care who was victorious providing he rose to the top. His deliberations gave him needed satisfaction but could only raise his humour to "testy".

Donald Grogan rented a Soho apartment in a block of twelve, whose entrance belied the size and security of it. Flat 3a, Elm Court, led through a plain brown door, out into an alleyway off of Dean Street. It was as if the block was built and then the seedy streets, like jungle creepers, had grown up around it, hiding it from view. He materialised among the raincoat-clad windowshoppers and caught a taxi to Canterbury mansions.

The Donna Laura was expecting him. 'Come in, Donald, can I offer you a drink?'

'A ginger ale please,' spoken with the respect due to a superior. He had been invited there for a discussion and they were alone. She enquired if everything was in place for Friday.

'Everything,' he assured her and waited for the reason of his summons to show itself. She spoke of an excellent future if all went as planned then wandered the room. Donald sat facing the front, aware of her movement behind him, feeling her eyes on his back. She came and seated herself opposite and absentmindedly played with the butt of her nine-tailed cat, fondling it was simply a habit and not necessarily done to excite him, nevertheless it did. Today, as all days when he needed to be in control, he employed the girl, whose name he didn't care to know, to immunise him against the heat that could take over his head and bake his brain then leave him desperate for the exquisite pain this woman inflicted so well. Even after his body's earlier sexual purging he felt a stirring but managed to smoothly curb it.

'You're not happy about enlisting Twyford. Why?' she asked.

Donald chose to be frank, 'I think once his usefulness is over, he should die and end the chain that could led back to us.'

'To you,' she corrected.

'I couldn't say it in front of the others but, in my opinion, he is not to be trusted.' said Grogan.

'And you are?' she queried with astonishment. 'I know you too well Donald. You don't really think it would be for our best interests, do you? I think you're perturbed that he might be better than you.'

'No!' argued Donald. 'That's not true. He's too mercenary, that's all, he'd sell us if he could. Believe me, I know him. The cautious thing would be to close the book.'

'If, and I only say if, I let you persuade me, who would do it?'

'I would,' he said too quickly.

With a facial expression that barely resembled a smile she threatened, 'Heed my words, Grogan; you will do nothing without my agreement. Twyford dies only when we say, and I shall supervise. I may let you hold him, I may let you watch, but he dies only on my order.'

Evil seeped from this woman and humbled Grogan… temporarily. 'With respect,' he asked, 'And his friends who have seen me?'

'You may have them when I decide the time is right.' The course was clearer and Donald was happy. The Donna Laura allowed him a few minutes to finish his drink then dismissed him. She wanted to be alone to plot Twyford's route to her and his ultimate penalty.

George awoke from a nightmare and sat bolt upright in bed. The madness of the dream was all mixed up but something terrible had frightened him, something insurmountable that left him useless. He shone his torch on the clock and discovered he had barely been in bed an hour and so laid back down and tried to sleep.

"Why are worries so big at night?" he wondered, then turned over and set himself to daydream of great moments and heroism: scoring winning goals, boxing and beating champions. Incredible things he wished may yet happen but still these dreams couldn't drop him that one note into sleep. He turned on his other side but that gave little assistance either then the fear for Kevin came in a rush. His heart thumped a faster beat, his breathing quickened and his forehead became cold and clammy. George appealed to a God that he had purposely ignored for years; a God who stood guard over others and with whom he had no right to speak. He prayed for an Angel to watch over his son and his family and offered his own life if Kevin could live. The effort left him fully awake and he mulled over the deal he had just struck. He had lived a full life. If good times were money he'd had thirty bob out of every pound, whereas Kevin still had last year's pocket money in his Dimple bottle. Yes, it was an excellent deal.

His son was to report to one of General Sir Bernard Paget's Battle schools which gave realistic combat training under live fire to the new recruits. Readying himself for the journey, Twyford browsed a book in the chair and at exactly four o'clock Kevin tapped on the window. It was teaming with rain and the only umbrella they could find was Min's who wouldn't be too pleased going to work without it. The brolly had been his father's and like all his old possessions was treasured by his mother. Once, while painting a bike frame George had accidentally given it a white stripe. Now when opened it resembles a question mark but keeps the rain off.

He took it anyway, looking on the bright side it might have stopped by the time she left the house.

It wasn't as cold as it had been and they settled down for a four hour car journey. George suggested that Kevin hopped in the back to grab some sleep and he would wake him an hour from the camp. Visibility was poor and the windscreen wipers worked overtime. Apart from army vehicles driving about the only civilian car they saw was a black Mariah, which pulled up next to them at a set of traffic lights in Fulham, and the two Bluebottles in the front scrutinised the shape of his nose. Rather than risk being pulled over he wound the window down and asked if he was on the right road for the A30. Police training came into force and they just glared at him.

'Look here,' he said, 'I'm conducting my son to an army camp in Devon. Now please, am I on the right road?' The aggression eased to scorn and they waved him on in front of them then drove right up his backside for two miles. He sped a little faster and they came even closer, faster still and they were almost on his rear seats. George waited for an approaching bend and stamped the brakes with his left foot then accelerated with his right. The police driver saw the brake lights flash on and hit the anchors. The Mariah's back wheels skidded to the left in the wet and he had to swing the steering hard left to right itself. George watched them slide in his rear-view mirror. The game stopped there and the Twyfords reached Taunton with no further problems. He woke Kevin and spent the last hour instructing him from whom and what to shield himself then, to say farewell, Twyford parked well away from the gates; they alighted the car and hugged each other. Kevin tilted his hat to the right for Dad's approval, smiled and swung his kit bag over his shoulder, then bowled through the gates with the utmost confidence. George took his handkerchief out as he watched him go and thought of the old W.W.1 song "Goodbye, goodbye, I wish you all a last goodbye". He blew his nose and sat for ten minutes before walking across to the three guards at the barrier. After explaining who he was, Twyford offered them a cigarette each. They all accepted but saved them for later. He gave them the packet (to start smoking again wouldn't bring Kevin back any sooner) and asked their opinion on how long the recruits would train before they go overseas. Fathers always ask the same question and it was kinder to lie. In three months they would be struggling through Italy with the 8th Army, so the guards informed George that training could last six to nine months. He guessed they were saying it for his benefit, but he could put his hand on his heart and relate to the family what he had been told. He wished them good luck and not in the mood to go racing around, drove back slower. It had stopped raining so Min wouldn't have to run up to the bus stop with a box on her head.

"See," he thought to himself, "it all works out in the end."

Feeling unusually low and needing to cheer himself up that afternoon George popped in to see Radna. She opened the door and gushed into his arms. Pleased and surprised by his visit, she had just returned from a shopping trip into the West End and had bought him a present. As he opened the wrapping it dawned on him that he had never even treated her to a box of chocolates. Her gift was a silver shaving set in a leather bag and was the sort of extravagance a man would never think of spending on himself. The shaving brush was pure badgers' hair and had a carved silver handle with his initials on it. The razor had a one handed swivel action and the shaving stick holder matched the brush. It was beautiful. Seeing how much he loved it, she produced another parcel that contained a handmade back scrubber. That, she informed him, was not leaving her flat and she was the only one who was allowed to use it on him. He thrilled at the suggestion and called for more hot water in number 6! Having never used "public" baths, Radna hadn't a clue what he was joking about but nevertheless went to prepare the bathtub and added oils while he stood and gazed. He never tired of watching steaming, hot water fall from brass taps at the twist of a wrist and indulged himself in the luxury of it all. She massaged his head with shampoo and he began to lose much of his malaise, his delicate parts were kneaded with perfumed soaps and a swelling made itself known, his back was scrubbed until it burned -kindling further stimulation -and then Radna took control. She slipped from her gown and descended on him. The bath was deep and easily big enough for two bodies to fit snugly together and the tingling heat of the water drove on their mounting excitement. They twisted and writhed rapturously until, with excellent timing, Radna faked an outstanding climax spurring George to succumb to a most pleasurable apex. He was spent; exhausted both mentally and physically and could barely raise the energy to dry himself. With a mixture of tenderness and vigour, she towelled him from tip to toe then lay his head on her breasts and let him sleep under crisp white sheets. Twyford was comatosed for a few hours and, when he awoke, had to drag himself from her embrace but promised that once this week was over his time would be her's and their life together would mean so much more.

Twyford drove home to Min's and straight away reported to his family. Mary looked drained to empty and his words did little to make her feel any better; she wanted no one to console her. People lose their sons in many different ways and accept it as a step in life, usually it's to a younger woman and he returns to see Mum when he can. This way the army was his wife and war was his new job, she would pray to God to make Kevin good at it. George prepared to leave and Alan asked to be taken up to bed for one of Dad's stories. Even at his age he had seen a weakness and pushed his luck, he looked at Mary and she nodded her consent. George swung him over his shoulder in a fireman's lift and carried him up the stairs.

When they were alone, Alan asked, 'Did they give him a gun?'

'Not yet,' said George.

'I'm gonna join up the first chance I get,' announced Alan with much thought. The adventure got longer and longer until

Mary called up a warning of lights out. They were both a little disappointed because neither found out the end. George kissed the girls and wished Mary goodnight.

"Taking Alan to bed was real progress," he thought and walked up the street, singing to himself "Long ago and far away".

He was bushed, his torch had been left in the car, the car had been left down the Square and the street lights were out -but the Queens was only five mins walk and seemed like a very sound idea. A couple of pints to unwind and then an early night. George felt pleasantly comfortable in the darkness and ambled along lost in his own thoughts. Out of nowhere, two large men gripped his arms from behind and thrust them up his back, a blow to the solar plexus forced him down and into the gutter. A car with no lights screeched to a halt next to him and the heavy door flew opened, smashing into his head. In seconds he was laid flat and searched, then rolled over, dragged to his feet and propelled into the back. His assailants sat either side and squashed him in with their bulk. The car sped off and George tried to take in what was happening. Another large raincoat drove the car and apart from a smaller fellow in the front, everyone else wore trilbies. It was like a gangster film. Twyford was frightened, these men were tough and knew what they were about. Each of his wrists was locked by a small truncheon twisted over the back of his hands and held fast. George could not see the driver and recognised none of the others. Clueless as to what was happening, he waited for someone to speak to learn what he could from an accent or a well-worded question. Meanwhile Hampstead rushed by, then Whitestone Ponds, past Jack Straw's Castle and finally the vehicle turned in through the gates of a large property that backed onto the Heath. He was manhandled roughly out of the car and saw that although the place seemed uninhabited it was also far enough from the road to be completely private.

Twyford was taken to a long room where a coal fire was trying, without much success, to warm it. Furnished with expensive hide armchairs, it also contained an old oak table, which could seat more than a dozen people, and a couple of standard-lamps that barely lit the room.

'We're going to have a chat, you and me,' said the apparent leader in an obvious Welsh accent. 'I hope there won't be any need for unnecessary violence.'

'So do I,' said George, sitting down and rubbing the bump on his head. He tried to understand what a Welshman had to do with him and why he should have gone to all this trouble.

Taffy spoke to the henchman that stood behind George, 'Wait outside would you and send Jurgen in.' Twyford looked swiftly around the room, the windows were shuttered and the door was the only way out. While he considered trying to run, the driver came in and removed his trilby. George recognised him immediately as the silent foreigner who had fought so well over the coal wharf. The man walked to a corner and sat quietly, listening to his master's voice. The Welshman spoke to him in German and, when he'd finished, explained to George, 'I asked him to be prepared to restrain you if you become aggressive.'

Twyford had understood all that was said and thought the pronunciation perfect.

'Look, I reckoned whatever your game was you'd made a big mistake, until he walked in. We've crossed swords before, me and him, now, what is this all about?'

The bantam Taffy sat on the table with his legs dangling and faced Twyford, 'I've been empowered to arrest you and hold you for treason and felony against the realm.'

'Treason!' yelled George in astonishment. 'You're fucking mad!'

The Welshman glanced in Jurgen's direction and reassured, continued, 'I'm sorry, boyo, but in my opinion you're guilty of giving aid and comfort to the King's enemies and of levying war against the government of Great Britain. Both charges carry life imprisonment except in wartime when it's the death penalty. I'm very sorry.'

George sat aghast and stared at the dishevelled, balding, little scruff. 'This is absurd. You're telling me because an oily, little runt like you makes up some ridiculous charge, you can have me shot?'

'Hung,' corrected Taff. 'I'm sorry but you got yourself in to it, you see.'

Twyford started to become frightened. "It is a bluff," he thought, "but what a bluff!" and tried to show a cool exterior. 'You know I haven't got any idea what you're talking about. Your threats haven't been wasted, but let's be serious now. What is this all about?'

The Welshman looked at him with tired eyes. 'You have committed acts of treason against the realm, in wartime, I'm sorry…'

George jumped at him and grabbed his throat with both hands. The Taffy's eyes bulged and his tongue protruded as George squeezed with all his might. A heartbeat later, Jurgen had his arm across Twyford's throat and choked him in a headlock. He pulled George back and away, but the Welshman's throat came too. The Kraut tightened his lock and George did the same. Jurgen shouted loudly in German, the door burst open and the big lumps crashed into the fray, knocking them all apart and in different directions. The three heavies then flattened Twyford while the Welshman wandered about, massaging his larynx. George was bodily lifted into an armchair and his limb movements suppressed. Oddly, he felt better for his outburst.

"Perhaps a finer idea might be to try a pinch more common-sense and contrition," he thought. 'Now it's my turn to be sorry,' said George with remorse. 'But I saw red at the slur you made, to suggest that I of all people was a traitor. For your information I won the military medal of honour in the Great War.'

The Welshman wasn't impressed, 'Scotland Yard have a file on you and there's no mention of that,' he said in disbelief, standing well away from him.

'You saucy bastard! Check with the war office, go on!' challenged George hotly. 'And while we're at it, let's see your authority.'

'I don't carry actual papers stating who I am. In the field we're safest not to.'

'Hah!' scoffed George. 'You could be fifth columnists for all I know. You want something from me, don't ya?' and testing the game, continued, 'Well, get someone in with real authority and we'll have that chat. Otherwise, fuck off back down the coalmine you crawled out of.'

Taffy finger-brushed his greasy, pencil moustache and thought about it then took a folded envelope from his wallet and handed it to Jurgen. He walked back to the safer side of the table while Twyford's arms were released and he was handed the correspondence. He opened it out and the words in the short missive stunned him. It read, "To whom it may concern, the bearer of this letter is known to me and acting on my behalf on business of a highly secretive nature. His work is of vital national importance and I charge you to assist him in every way possible and by all available means." It was followed by a telephone number for emergency use and signed Winston Churchill, Prime Minister of Great Britain.

George looked at the Welshman with genuine respect and handed it back. 'My sincerest apologies, had I seen that earlier all this antagonism would have been unnecessary. I will help you in anyway I can.' then sat up smartly and waited.

The Welshman began, 'My name is Rodney Blair and, before the war, I was a Professor of Economics at Oxford. I am now in charge of the Internal-External Security and protection of Sterling. Before I say anymore, tell me what you know of Operation Bernhard.' George had a dreadful idea of where this was leading but shook his head nonplussed. 'How long have you known Donald Grogan?'

Twyford counted the years briefly. 'About twenty five years, he was my Sergeant Major at the Somme. Up until three weeks ago, I hadn't seen him since the war.'

'Tell me, have you business dealings with him?'

George was in front of the conversation and he felt sick. He could not avoid the question, 'Yes,' he said, disgusted at his own stupidity. 'I'm buying forged notes from him and you're now informing me that he's working with the Nazis.'

Professor Blair said, 'I can see you've arrived.'

Twyford's mind was racing forward, telling himself his discoveries as each thought struck him and its immediate conclusion churned his stomach more. The machinery of his brain was overloaded and feverishly kicked odd words out loud, 'Wages. The market. Malla.' He screwed his eyes tight shut but still his wits were bombarded. 'My son's gone to fight the Germans and I'm helping them. We've got to get the notes back and destroy them. I've ruined everyone, we're all bankrupt. Karinna, the Township. Oh God!' Each notion galloping him further, unable to bridle the panic. 'Benny! I've got to stop it. No choice. All that work, what have I done? Bones. Oh no!' Then Grogan entered his mind and George poured all the blame and spite on Donald. The sheer malevolence that came over him stopped Twyford babbling and with the malice of forethought, swore inwardly to take the quisling's life and relish the act.

The Welshman examined him coldly and felt no pity. Everything that Twyford had valued had been destroyed. He'd been duped with the temptation of riches, the greed had blinded him.

Still now, George sat in shocked silence as wave after wave of reality swept over him. His life was finished, irreparable, and he had ruined all the people he loved. He had failed Old Cor Blimey and the Township, let down all the children, including his own, and probably removed their greatest chance of life. Once this got to court, the last and best that his own family might know of him was that he unwittingly betrayed England to her enemies. He would be found guilty and sentenced to death. George despaired at his own unquestionable destruction. He would have to do the decent thing and kill himself. Either way, all he could expect of this world was the shame of a traitor's grave.

Twyford couldn't rally himself. It was all over. Professor Blair spoke to him but his brain cut off the meaning of the words and refused to let them in. He looked at the insignificant little turd but couldn't rise enough hostility to bring himself round.

The Welshman motioned his men from the room and said quietly, 'We'll leave you with your meditations for a while.'

George closed his eyes. He was exhausted and wanted to sleep. 'Let it be forever,' he prayed, but the punishing trauma came at him with a fierceness. A hefty thwack of guilt struck him and jogged his eyes open. He could not accept it yet, wasn't allowed to! Attempted sleep would be disciplined by further jolts of conscience and self-reproach. With a haunted look on his face, he prowled the room and could only think of action. Face the inevitable. He had lost, but anything that could be salvaged was worth the effort, there would be time to wallow in self pity soon enough.

He banged on the door and tried the handle. They had locked him in, but his fists beat the wood louder until he heard Blair order the door to be opened.

'I need to continue,' said George, the cogs in his head clanging slowly into place.

'I think I've got the general picture. You have already bought and distributed the notes, have you?' asked Blair.

'Only half, the deal was in two parts. The next and final handover is to be this Friday. We can get them all.'

'No. You're not aware of all the facts yet. Let me tell you how this began. The underground that smuggled Jews out of Germany received information that something was happening in a munitions factory outside Dresden. Forged English notes were being printed there and were to be distributed throughout Britain to weaken the power of Sterling. The RAF razed the place to the ground and we thought that was the end of the problem. Then, six months ago, we heard that similar printing had started in Sachsenhausen Concentration

Camp. The place could not be bombed because it was full of prisoners. So the second choice was to get a man on the inside. This we did and he managed to keep us informed of the trials being carried out. A month later he reported that they were successfully printing good copies of English five pound notes. Sadly our man was caught and the information dried up but the camp was put under close observation twenty four hours a day. One night, a heavily guarded load left there and our people followed. It went through to a naval base in Holland. There, it was loaded onto a sub and we lost track of it. The next we knew was when the body of a black marketeer in Birmingham turned up with a mouthful of charred currency; garrotted. The police investigation uncovered a rumour of huge quantities of forged notes for sale and a name, Grogan. We were called in. Grogan's not a hard man to find, he led us to the Savoy and you.'

George nodded. If only they had come to him but, of course, they could not dare.

Blair continued, 'The Germans have given the project the name 'Bernhard' and occasionally we pick up radio messages regarding their operation here. We need to catch the complete network. Grogan is dangerous, but still only a messenger.'

'I can make a guess at one of his bosses,' said George. Blair's face showed keen interest. 'Joe Connaughty.'

'The American industrialist?' asked the Professor, quite taken aback.

'I thought you'd been following Grogan!' retorted George, incredulously.

'Not everywhere,' admitted Blair. 'There are places, like the Café Luxor, where we can't get in.'

'Looking at the state of you, I'm not surprised,' said George, but without the required amount of acerbity in his voice, the quip fell flat.

Rodney Blair ignored the remark and continued, 'Donald Grogan mixes with many people on the fringes of politics and it's impossible for us to keep all of them under observation.'

'How many men have you got?' asked George.

'What you see here, plus an elderly couple who have been watching you most of the time.'

'Oh yes,' said George, remembering Timmy on the bus.

'Now, let's go through this agreement you made to purchase the notes.'

Twyford was still full of remorse and wanted to confess everything but he was naturally a bender of truths and, as his story unfolded, he decided to alter the quantity purchased to four hundred thousand on the first deal. He reasoned to himself that he would try to regain the five hundred thousand and if he succeeded, and they gave him the opportunity, he would burn a hundred thousand with no harm done. But if he only got four hundred thousand back, then it would seem that he had recovered the full amount of his crime and it might just go slightly better for him. During his narration, it became clear that Blair was also unaware of the price per note, so that too was changed. He told them that the first purchase was made for four hundred thousand and cost five shillings each, i.e. twenty thousand pounds. The Professor was surprised how cheap they were, even when George explained about the recurring number problem.

'Where did you expect to spend it all?' he asked. 'It's an unimaginable task, surely.'

'Not if it's spread far and wide,' said George, and he described a more intricate weave of distribution than actually existed. He loaded it with complicated meeting points and payments, making it impossible for them to correct the predicament without allowing him a week's freedom.

For the next few days he still held the reins and would strive for any improvement. Sometimes in a fight, when completely outclassed and with no chance at all, a man accepts the inevitable hiding as long as he can land just one good punch, one blow by which to be remembered.

'You want the complete network?' said George. 'Then help me, advise me and let me do it for you.'

'Why should we trust you? You've left the country before, so don't tell me about your loved ones.'

'My son joined the army today because he wanted to be a hero like me. You'll do what you have to do but give me the opportunity to prove him right; I shan't be running anywhere. You know I'm your best chance to trap this filth. I ask only this – that you let me see them all swing before I take the drop'

He needed Twyford to want to do it yet Blair was still unsure. With the hangman's knot as his only reward assuredly George had nothing else to lose but this was not the type of man he understood. Blair knew that he, himself, was cornered and out of options. Fate had offered him one shot only with Twyford as the bullet, very reluctantly and against all his better judgement, he said, 'Tell me your proposals and I'll tell you mine.'

Part Two

...coming soon...

About the Author

St. Pancras born and bred, Alan Gooding was educated at Central Foundation Boys School in Shoreditch. His working life began as a fruit importer in Covent Garden and Spitalfields markets and still keeps his hand in.

Alan now lives in Hertfordshire with his wife and lists his hobbies as fitness training, skiing and savouring fine English ales in convivial company.

Available worldwide from Amazon

---

https://mtp.agency

https://facebook.com/mtp.agency

@mtp_agency